Judgment Day

David Witt

Fat Chance Publishing

JUDGMENT DAY. Copyright © 2019 by David Witt.

ISBN 978-1-7342023-0-4

FIRST EDITION

Cover Image from Freepik.com

Printed in the United States of America

To Karen, my lovely wife without who's unending support this novel would not have been possible. She has been a constant source of encouragement throughout our life journey together. I can't wait for our next adventure!

Special thanks to the Thursday writer's group who welcomed me with open arms and honest feedback. You offered me an education and a sense of community for which I am grateful.

It is also important that I thank Morgan Williams for his perspective and editing.

Judgment

Day

Chapter One

Saturday Noon New York

Larry Knewell was in a foul mood and he made sure that everyone on the busy Noon Day set knew it. Once again, he directed his wrath at Ken Garner, the producer of this hour of programming on the twenty-four-hour news network. "Tell me why I'm the back-up for Maria on a Saturday? I'm the weeknight prime-time host that drives the ratings around here. Having me on at noon on the weekend tarnishes my stature. It's like I'm slumming."

Ken had fielded some version of this question from Larry all morning after Maria Zaragoza had called in earlier to inform the network of the death of her mother. His job right now was to keep Larry somewhat calm. He knew that as soon as the lights brightened and the cameras rolled Larry would automatically transform into an award-winning charismatic host, just as he always did. Ken answered sarcastically. "Think of it as doing volunteer work for a charity. Play up your sacrifice to the audience to cover this hour while Maria is handling details of her mother's memorial service. You might even get a sympathy bump in your Q score."

The sarcasm went unnoticed as Larry only processed the blatant appeal to his ego, temporarily assuaging his ire as they neared the countdown to the start of the show. Ken thought to himself. *It's a slow news day. Just get through this hour and we'll get another host to fill in for this jerk tomorrow.* He clapped his hands together loudly and then addressed the talent and crew. "It's showtime everyone. Let's do this for Maria."

Larry shuffled his papers on the host desk one last time as Jared stepped in front of the camera to countdown the start of the show. "In five-four-three-two-one."

With that lead-in the cameras and set lighting suddenly went dark. Larry erupted, slamming his hand down hard on the desk. "Jesus Christ you morons! Can't you people on daytime do anything right!"

Chaos hit the set as everyone scrambled to find out what happened. Jared was the first to see the monitors showing the live feed from the network come to life with a strange face onscreen. "Hey, looks like we've been hacked!"

All heads swiveled to get a look at one of the seven monitors in the adjacent open newsroom that broadcast the live network feed. An unfamiliar, brightly lit porcelain-skinned face filled the screen. Larry took a close look at the hacker, admiring his onscreen image. In addition to the porcelain white skin, the younger man wore his pure white hair slicked back with just the right amount of product. His perfectly proportioned face was made dramatically more compelling with crystal blue eyes that seemed to glow from the inside out. His impeccably tailored lavender suit was complemented with a brilliant metallic purple tie and matching pocket square. After celebrating his fifty-fifth birthday last week, Larry was instantly envious of the intruder.

The hacker spoke strong, clear and confident. "Greetings to all of the people of Earth. Greetings to all of the peoples of the north, and to all of the peoples of the south. Greetings to all of the peoples of the east and to all of the peoples of the west. Greetings to the Jew and the Gentile, and to the Hindu and the Muslim. Greetings to the believers of all faiths both great and small, and to the atheist and the agnostic. Greetings to rulers and to those who are ruled. Greetings to all."

The unknown man paused for a moment as a voice from the control room shouted out new information. "It's not just us. Every network in the country is being hacked with the same feed."

As that information sunk in the unknown moderator continued. "I am Gabriel, messenger for the One Eternal God, Creator of the Heavens and Earth, Lord and Ruler of all. I stand before you today to announce that your Heavenly Father will be returning to Earth tomorrow."

He paused again as if letting his message sink in. Once more the voice from the control room shouted updated information. "This is world-wide! Every network in the world has been hacked."

Gabriel resumed. "Later today the Archangel Michael and his army will take control of the United Nations building in New York to prepare for the Holy of Holy's visit. At the appointed time tomorrow evening your Lord and Master will address political and spiritual leaders directly. Everyone else is invited to participate via television and social media. He will deliver a message of love and hope."

Gabriel paused again and turned toward another camera on the pure white set. "I am sure my appearance has caused confusion and fear in many. That's understandable, but that has not been my intent."

Now the camera pushed in, dramatically framing only his benevolently smiling face. "Please know this; God loves you and wants only the best for all. Be joyous of His return and thank you for your attention. Praise be to God."

With his message complete Gabriel bowed and the cameras cut to a choir of what seemed to be identical androgynous angels with baby-blue tinted skin, wearing billowing white robes. They began singing in the most perfect harmony imaginable in a language no one understood. All of the talent and crew on the set of Noon Today seemed frozen by the sight and song.

All except Larry Knewell. He was suddenly energized. "Come on everyone! This is the story of our lives! Careers will be made with how we cover this...this... event. Get me every religious, political, and military leader we've ever had on my show. I want them here in studio if they are in New York and on the phone if they're not. We're going to cover this thing non-stop and we're going to do it better than any other network. This is legacy stuff!"

As if on cue the choir finished their hymn and the hacked feed disconnected. Power was restored on set and Jared hustled back to his position as Larry pushed all of his previous preparation off of the host desk. He positively beamed as the countdown restarted. "In five-four-three-two-one."

Chapter Two

Saturday 1:00 P.M. New York

The CBN network feed of Larry Knewell holding court with Jacob Shadwell, director of World Evangelical Service was streaming on one of the ten muted monitors in the Situation Room at the White House. The talking heads had been parsing every word of the Gabriel video trying to discern whether this was indeed a message from God, or an elaborate hack by some unknown group. Ratings were going through the roof, just as Larry had predicted.

Everyone in the bunkered White House command center stood at attention as President Abigail Banister strode purposefully into the room. She gave a perfunctory "At Ease" as she made a beeline for Kalie Robinson, her National Security Advisor and Ferron George, her Secretary of Defense huddled around one end of the main conference table in the central area of the complex. She leaned in, resting her lanky frame with both hands on the table, her straight-legged pant suit giving her a praying mantis vibe. "What's the latest."

Barrel chested Ferron, dressed in his army uniform and the much taller Kalie, wearing a smart black suit, glanced at each other. Ferron spoke first. "We've had a couple of individuals taking credit for the hack, but their claims seem doubtful. Our thinking is they're just publicity seekers. Bottom line is that we're nowhere on identifying the culprits. We've reached out to our allies around the world and they're just as in the dark."

Kalie chimed in. "I've also reached out to my contacts in the tech word and had similar responses. They are very impressed by the ease at which these people pulled this off. Unprecedented seems to be the word of the day."

In frustration, President Banister stood and stomped her spiked Manolo Blahnik shoe so hard that it momentarily silenced everyone within earshot. She pointed to the TV monitor showing the CBN feed. "The whole world has an opinion on what's going on. We spend billions on security and surveillance every year, so stop telling me what we don't know. Tell me what we do know."

Kalie straightened even taller above her peers as she motioned toward an adjacent conference room. "Yes ma'am, follow me, please. We've prepared a briefing for you and key members of your cabinet."

As soon as everyone was seated, the first slide of the presentation appeared on the large monitor at the opposite end of the narrow side room. Kalie narrated. "Without warning, at noon eastern time, a simultaneous hack occurred impacting every network, independent television station, every radio station and every social media outlet broadcasting a live stream. This bar graph compares the number of targets of this attack compared to the cumulative number of attacks on any news media since we started compiling this kind of data."

The lines of President Banister's angular face hardened as she responded in shock. "I'm reading this right? This single attack was over a thousand times broader than all other attacks combined? Incredible."

Kalie's aqua blue eyes met the president's stare. "Yes ma'am, it certainly was." She turned back toward the screen and her shoulder length blond pony-tail flipped sharply. "This map shows the location of each known hack. Now, I'll overlay the internet connections that have identified any detected spread of corrupted code linking the attacks." When the slide advanced, no additional information was added to the displayed info.

Confused, President Banister asked, "What does that mean?"

Ferron clarified. "It means that this was thousands of simultaneous individual attacks, not one or two successful breaches which then spread around the globe. Once again, this was an extremely sophisticated operation."

Kalie nodded confirmation of the Ferron's assessment and then advanced to the next slide. "So far we've confirmed that the message was delivered flawlessly in sixty-seven languages with more reports filtering in from remote locations. Again, unprecedented in complexity and scale. The resources to pull something like this off..." Her voice drifted as she advanced to the next graphic.

A still frame of Gabriel filled the screen. "So far, we don't have any facial recognition matches to the man who calls himself Gabriel, messenger of God. Nor do we to any matches of the seemingly identical choir members shown later in the video." Kalie used a laser pointer to highlight her next comments. "His skin is obviously white, almost snow white, suggesting perhaps northern European origin. And, as of yet, we haven't been able to narrow down anything about his clothing either, suggesting hand tailoring. Vocal recognition has also been difficult due to the fact that he spoke so many languages fluently.

Kalie glanced around the long conference table taking the measure of each key attendee before moving on to the final set of slides. "Based upon what we currently know for sure, and I admit that's not a lot, we've come up with three broad conclusions about who... or what, is behind this event."

The slide revealing the first set of suspects appeared with a listing of ten known hacker groups. "We believe that the culprits, are on this list. We feel strongly that a previously unknown confederation of some combination of these computer hacker groups has banded together to pull off some sort of scam or act of digital terrorism. Their goal with this particular hack is unknown, but we've seen this kind of thing on a much smaller scale with groups like Anonymous or Lizard Squad. The consensus is that now that they've demonstrated their prowess, we'll receive some sort of blackmail request or other demand. A second possibility is that they want to totally disrupt our information-based society as we know it. Some kind of ultra-Luddite motive."

Kalie took a deep breath as her broad athletic shoulders reset under the stress of the moment. A chill ran up her spine as she delivered the blunt assessment of the situation. "As bad as this scenario is, it may be the best of the three. At least this is a threat with knowable enemies."

President Banister attempted to lighten the somber mood. "This reminds me of an old joke. It goes, 'So, Mrs. Lincoln, other than that, how did you like the play?'" An uncomfortable laughter filtered through the room acknowledging the deadly seriousness of the briefing. "Go ahead, Kalie, I'm not here to shoot the messenger."

A slight smile creased Kalie's burgundy blush lips as she advanced the presentation. "The second scenario is that this is first contact with an alien civilization." She paused again as an image of the famous bar scene from *Star Wars* filled the screen. "As far-fetched as this may seem, it does match a lot of what we know. A superior technological feat pulled off on a global scale that, at the moment, has stumped all of the best minds of our world. Perhaps they are using the God angle to lessen resistance or simply confuse us. It might have sounded crazy yesterday, but as we sit here now, does anyone think this isn't a possibility?"

The president spoke as mumbling among junior attendees seated around the edge of the room taking notes for their bosses became audible. "All right Kalie, I've been away from the church for a very long time, but I'm a preacher's kid, so I know where this is going. Go ahead and put it up there."

The next slide displayed an elderly, white bearded man, dressed in a flowing robe with a staff in hand, seated on a throne. "Lastly, we come to the God scenario. As a person who was also raised in church, I can tell you that this is perhaps the most ominous explanation. Christianity, and several other religions, believe that God will return to Earth and deliver his final Judgment. As I've understood it, most interpretations mean that this will be the end of the world. That's why the news media is calling this the Judgment Day event. This is the executive summary of what we know so far, Madam President. What questions or comments do you have before we discuss next actions?"

All eyes turned toward President Banister as she stood, her short, coal black hair glistening under the cool fluorescent lighting. She brushed her hand down her dark blue suit jacket smoothing a couple of wrinkles before addressing the room. "Two years ago, on a bitter cold January day, I was sworn in as President of the United States. I took an oath to preserve, protect and defend the Constitution of the United States."

She then turned first toward National Security Advisor, Retired General Kalie Robinson, then next to Secretary of Defense, General Ferron George as she now addressed them by their military rank. "Generals, upon your enlistment into military service, you both swore an oath to support and defend the Constitution of the United States against all enemies, foreign and domestic. None of us could have predicted that we would be facing this, but here we are, staring down a threat to our nation of unknown dimensions. I'm also keenly aware that each of us ended our oath by adding, 'So help me God.' This situation could put our resolve to the ultimate test, especially if this is God and he intends harm to the United States. I want all of you to know that as long as I am president I will fight until my last breath to live up to my sworn duty to defend this country. I know that I can count on each of you to do the same. With those vows as our foundation and guidance, what are our options?"

The president had made her point and sat down, signaling it was time to resume the briefing. On cue Kalie stood back up and picked up the slide advance device. "Thank you, Madam President." The next slide appeared with a first bullet point, *Communicate, Communicate, Communicate.* "It is vitally important that we do everything that we can to prevent panic in the streets. The last thing that we need is mass hysteria while we're dealing with this as of yet undefined threat. If people believe that the end is truly near who knows what might happen. We've put out a vague statement about getting to the bottom of this, but we're also suggesting, Madam President, that you go on national television and address the country."

President Banister quickly replied. "Already on it. My communication team is working on the outline of a speech which I'll read on air tonight. They're waiting on the recommendations that come out of this meeting to finalize everything."

Secretary of State Effie Louise used her ebony cane, which matched her dark skin, to slowly rise and speak up for the first time in her slow Louisiana drawl. "My phone has just been blowin' up. Some of our adversaries are even more spooked than our allies. China is freakin' out about how easily their internal controls were circumvented. This isn't just an American problem and it's an understatement to say that the rest of the world is clamoring for our leadership. I'll take the lead in coordinating with your coms team on some kind of statement that other countries can sign on to, demonstrating our leadership."

"Excellent, what's next Kalie."

The second bullet point materialized and Ferron stood to cover this recommendation, his medals shining on his snug fitting uniform, distracting from his considerable girth. *Deploy Armed Forces.* "Madam President, all service branches have been placed on high alert and I'm proposing that we activate all National Guard Units across the country immediately. We have contingency plans for events such as hurricanes or floods to protect key infrastructure sites like power plants, bridges, key government buildings, that sort of thing. We'll activate those plans. We have to keep our economy going until we know what comes next. Also, I recommend having continuous air cover and a couple of special forces teams join in the protection detail for the United Nations building in New York City. That Gabriel character specifically called out that location and we need to be ready...just in case."

Once again, the president affirmed the recommendation quickly. "Of course, Ferron. Make it happen. Next."

Kalie clicked the slide advance revealing the next bullet point, *Rapidly Expand Our Cyber Security.* "It's not a stretch to say that as good as we thought our current abilities were, we were exposed as completely unprepared for what happened today. I'm proposing an emergency declaration allowing us to tap into some of best resources of Silicon Valley and frankly, we don't have time to go through the usual government contracting processes. It's obvious that we need the best minds in the world working on this ASAP. If they can do this to our communications systems, what else could they do? Unfortunately, the answer is that in our interconnected world, they could do about anything. Again, with my history in tech, I am volunteering to take the lead on this initiative as soon as I get authorization."

The president turned to her left. "Hakeem, we need this ASAP; do you see any problem with that?"

Attorney General Hakeem Ali replied in his deep bass voice. "No, Madam President. Justice will have the authorization drafted and ready for approval by the end of the day."

The president nodded. "Kalie, start making calls immediately. We'll ask for forgiveness later if we get too far ahead of the paperwork. This is too important to wait." As adrenaline coursed through her body she pressed to move faster. "What else?"

One last time Kalie advanced the slide deck. *Become Experts in End Time Prophecies* appeared on the display. "If this really is God coming to Earth, then we're going to need someone with a lot more knowledge of end time prophecies than I possess." Kalie paused, not knowing how her next words would be received. She continued sheepishly. "Madam President, perhaps you know someone qualified?"

The president blushed then reverted again to humor as a defense. "Who knew that having the Dean of the School of Divinity at Harvard as an ex would ever come in so handy." Her next words revealed the sacrifice that making a call to Dr. Dallas Shendegar would require. "Things ended badly for us, as everyone who saw those campaign ads is aware. And I bet that he'll lord the fact that I need his help over me, but he'll do it." She sighed. "He's the best, and I'm guessing he'll remind us all of that fact... often. And unless he's changed, I'll never hear the end of it, but I'll make the call."

Kalie gave a knowing glance, understanding firsthand the tensions that come from dealing professionally with an ex. "Madam President, this is what we have now and I'm sure that facts on the ground will be changing rapidly. I suggest we get started on these action items and then update you again in a couple of hours."

The president stood and all in the room followed. "I believe that I have the best team ever assembled in the White House. I'm counting on all of you to prove me right. Now, let's go out and save the world."

Chapter Three

Saturday 7:00 A.M. Hawaii / 1:00 P.M. Washington D.C.

Sunlight pushing through the tiny slits of his closed bamboo window blinds and the near constant blinging of his phone interrupted Wade Jansky's dream. His sleeping mind had been replaying the perfect evening that he had just shared with his girlfriend, Quinn Kahale. Their relationship was still new, but things had been moving fast and the moonlit dinner on his back deck complemented with his home brew IPA beer and a little Maui Wowie had set the stage for an epic intimate evening. It was a perfect antidote for their seemingly stuck careers, his as a junior astronomer at the Keck Observatory and hers as an aspiring singer scraping by with bar gigs and a few thousand YouTube followers.

The blinging continued and groggily he mumbled to Qu as he reached for his phone. "Who the hell is up at this hour... on Saturday?"

Qu answered with closed eyes. "Just make it stop. Turn it off and come back to bed. My head is killing me." She then rolled away from the light and sound and pulled her pillow over her head, trying to block out the world.

With one eye mostly open and the other partially closed by sleep gunk, Wade tried to make sense of the flood of news updates as well as Instagram and text messages populating his screen. Unsuccessful, he sat up on the side of the bed, rubbed his eyes until both fully opened and took another stab at understanding what he was seeing. He scrolled through message after message trying to decipher the events that took place in the U.S. eastern time zone earlier today. He nudged the re-settled Qu. "Hey, wake up. This is serious."

Her answer was muffled under the satin cased pillow. "Uhhhg. Sweetie, even if it's another mass shooting, I can read about it later. Really, it's way too early."

"No, Qu. It's crazy...they say God is coming... like this week." He flicked through messages until he found a link to the Gabriel message. "Listen to this!" He placed his phone near her pillow covered head.

The playback began, "Greetings to all of the people of Earth. Greetings to all of the peoples of the north, and to all of the peoples of the south. Greetings to all of the peoples of the east and to all of the peoples of the west. Greetings to the Jew and the Gentile ..."

After a first muffled listen, she removed the pillow and fitfully opened her puffy eyes. "What the hell?" She slowly pushed back the sheet and joined Wade on his side of the bed. "That's wack... play it again."

Wade obliged and clicked the link to watch Gabriel one more time. "Apparently this went all over the world in like a hundred languages. Everyone is wigging."

A new, but familiar sound suddenly replaced Wade's now silenced phone. Last night his hobby telescope had set off an annoyingly loud sighting indicator, which he chose to ignore in pursuit of more sensually interesting opportunities. "There goes the alarm on my scope again. It's reminding me to check last night's results. I'll shut it off, then start a pot of coffee. No going back to sleep now."

After a trip to the bathroom and a rummage through Wade's closet to find one of his oversized shirts, Qu joined him in the sun-splashed living room. The smell of freshly brewed Kona coffee filled the open space and Qu poured a cup, flavoring it with organic French vanilla creamer. "What's happening now?"

Wade was sitting cross legged on the sofa in boxers and a tee, flipping through channels. "Let's check CBN." He chuckled. "If the world really is ending, I'm ditching work and going surfing."

Chapter Four

Saturday 2:00 P.M. New York

Larry Knewell took a gulp of an energy drink as he prepared to start hour three of hosting. While the military and political experts had been assigned to the hard news hosts, as the lead opinion talent, he had sole responsibility for the religious leaders. While this was not his preference, he was determined to prove to the network, and himself, that he was still the best and make his the most interesting segment of the day. Jared counted down the start to special coverage of what was now called the Judgment Day event. "In five-four-three-two-one."

Two hours ago, Larry couldn't stand being on weekend daytime duty. Now he practically shined. "Welcome to continuing coverage of Judgment Day. This hour I'm joined by a special group of panelists to discuss what is possibly the most important event in the history of the world. Mankind has had a deep yearning to understand our place in the universe, and if this is not some elaborate hoax, then we're about to discover some of those long-sought answers. Are we about to make our entrance into a galactic fraternity of planetary civilizations, or are we about to come face to face with God, creator of the universe? Is this a welcome visitor or are we about to face an event that will kill millions, or perhaps divide humanity into those that enter into eternal bliss and those that suffer eternal damnation? We'll touch on those and other profound questions during this segment."

The exaggerated gravitas of his delivery belied how much he savored his role in this monumental story. "Joining us again for this hour is Pastor Jacob Shadwell, director of World Evangelical Service. Thanks for sticking around for another segment." The pastor nodded as Larry continued the introductions. "Also joining us in studio is Rabbi Solomon Feldman of Temple Beth Israel, here in New York. Welcome Rabbi Feldman."

The rabbi answered politely with a slight bob clearly showing his black orthodox kippah head covering. "Thank you for the invitation at such an unsettled time."

Larry continued the introductions looking into camera two. "And, from our studios in San Francisco, we are joined by Guru Baba Mashni, self-proclaimed Guru of Silicon Valley. Welcome Guru Mashni."

The sanguine guru replied in a sing song voice. "It is my pleasure to be on your show once again."

Turning slightly, Larry looked into camera one again. "Lastly, joining us from our studios in Washington D.C. we welcome world-renowned physicist and self-described atheist, Dr. Son Young Kim. Welcome to the panel, Dr. Kim."

Dr. Kim smiled and swept a long unruly lock of silver-gray hair away from her face. "My pleasure, Larry."

Larry fell into his role as panel host as naturally as a cowboy swings his leg over a horse. "Earlier we discussed whether all of this is an elaborate hoax, or if this really is the announcement of the imminent arrival of God. The question for this segment focuses only on half of that question. What if it's true? What if God is coming to Earth tomorrow? Pastor Shadwell, we go to you first. If that's true, what would you tell our viewers?"

Camera two framed Pastor Shadwell, his conservatively cut silver hair parted perfectly on the right side. "Well Larry, thanks again for the opportunity to join this forum. I'm not totally convinced that this is the second coming. Many prophecies of the Bible, such as wars and rumors of wars are present today, but many others haven't yet been fulfilled, especially the arrival of the Antichrist. Having said that, if God is returning tomorrow, this will be a glorious day for Christians around the world. The Bible says in the Book of John, chapter fourteen, verse six that 'Jesus saith unto him, I am the way, the truth, and the life: no man cometh unto the Father, but by me.' That clearly means that Christians will be saved and the rest of the people of the world will face a terrifying prospect."

Simultaneously the other panelist began shouting over each other in objection. Larry fed off of the raw energy being generated, letting the uproar continue a few more seconds than his usual standard to milk the drama before adeptly taking back control. "Please, everyone, please! You'll each have your say. We'll go to Rabbi Feldman next, but first, I want to make sure I understood Pastor Shadwell correctly. It's your interpretation of the Bible that only Christians will be saved, and that all others will perish?"

"Yes, Larry. The scriptures are crystal clear about what will happen in the end times."

Rabbi Feldman began speaking forcefully over the pastor even before his last word escaped his lips. "The last thing that you can say, pastor, is that scripture is crystal clear on this subject, or many other subjects. Look, us Jews have splintered into Orthodox, Reformed and Conservative Judaism because we don't agree on a unified interpretation of the Torah and the Talmud. And talk about splintering, Christianity has Catholics and too many Protestant denominations to even count, all divided over biblical interpretation. I'm not going to claim that I'm speaking for all Jews, just my own humanly fallible understanding of my faith. I believe that God wants us to work to make our world better today. If he chooses to come again, perhaps now, or send a messiah as many Jews believe, I will welcome that day. I'll leave it up to you if you want to claim that you speak infallibly for all branches of Christianity."

Somewhat chastened, but still defiant Pastor Shadwell replied. "In Romans chapter three, verse twenty-three the Bible states, 'For all have sinned, and come short of the glory of God.' That definitely includes me, so, no rabbi, I don't claim infallibility; nor do I claim to speak for every Christian. Maybe I am wrong, but I'm not alone. Millions of other Christians believe the same as me."

Guru Baba Mashni had been twitching visibly, itching to join the debate. He jumped at his chance with the micro lull in the action. "You are both wrong. Mankind is living in the Kali Yuga, the last and most corrupt of the four epochs. Kalki, the tenth avatar of Vishnu, will arrive riding on a white horse tomorrow and begin cleansing the earth, ushering a new age of enlightenment. We will then achieve singularity, oneness with the universe."

"Thank you, Guru Mashni. So, you believe that this event signals the arrival of Vishnu? Many of our viewers may not have heard of Hindu end time predictions. Share with us the outline, the big picture so to speak of Hindu end time beliefs."

The guru gushed and his Indian accent brought his words to life in excited tones. "Yes, yes! It's quite fascinating, Larry. There have been three previous epochs or Yugas, each getting progressively more corrupt and immoral. This forth Yuga is the final and most corrupt yet. It will end with Kalki, the tenth avatar of Vishnu, destroying the demons and sinners on Earth leading to complete synergy, or oneness. The full cycle can then begin anew with rebirth. That is what I believe is happening."

Larry feigned genuine curiosity. "Very interesting, Guru Mashni, I look forward to learning more about Hindu beliefs. It's quite different from what we've just heard. But first, let's hear from our fourth panelist, Dr. Kim."

Larry smiled as he savored the fiery discussion between these fervent believers. He pointed toward the monitor with the feed from Washington D.C. "Dr. Kim, I'm tempted to describe your expression as a Mona Lisa smile. The question of the hour is, 'What if this is God?' You've heard these faith leaders. As a physicist and avowed atheist, what do you say?"

Once again, that untamed lock of silver-gray hair had slid down covering her right eye, and once again she swept it back behind her ear. In her flat academic affect, she answered. "Larry, let's consider the cold, hard, scientific facts. There has never, let me say that again, never, been a god seen on this planet verified in any scientific way. What is scientifically verified is that so-called god after so-called god has been abandoned or simply faded away. Think about the Greek god Zeus, or the Mayan god Hunab-Ku. Entire civilizations rose and fell fervently worshiping them, and where are those gods now? I'll tell you where they are. They live in Marvel Comic movies and on the pages of mythology textbooks. If this event isn't a hoax, then it's probable that this soon to arrive being is a representative of some advanced civilization making first contact. They may have harnessed some immense power or technology that makes them seem like a god to us, but no, they won't be a god, any more than Zeus or Hunab-Ku."

Larry leaned forward ready to challenge the conflicting panelists and drive a ratings bonanza when he paused, listening to Ken Garner's voice in his earpiece. Abruptly, his jaw tightened and his eyes narrowed. He squared to camera one. His buoyant host voice was replaced by a tone suitable for a serious journalist. "Panelists, it looks like we'll have to continue this discussion a little later. Right now, we're cutting away to Manuel Diaz with breaking news from the UN Headquarters here in New York. Manuel, what are you seeing?"

Chapter Five

Saturday 3:00 P.M. New York & Washington D.C.

The energy level in the Situation Room had ratcheted up by several multiples compared to earlier in the day. Video from F-22's on patrol over the UN Building in New York City were being streamed to monitors in the conference room. Secretary of Defense Ferron George pulled a handkerchief from his back pocket and dabbed beads of sweat on his broad forehead as he watched the Judgment Day event take an ominous turn.

The quick steps of President Banister's stiletto heels announced her return to the room. "Sounds like things are heating up. What's happening?"

Ferron shoved the hanky back into his rear pant pocket then pointed to the center monitor. "Operation Righteous Defender is now underway. Take a look at the images from one of our 22's. We've never seen a weather event like this."

Everyone in the room was processing the flickering images. President Banister spoke for most. "That's the blackest storm cloud that I've ever seen. And that lightning... it looks like it's aiming at our planes."

Ferron suppressed his urge to reach for his handkerchief again as he responded. "It's big and ugly and it's being shielded from our radar. We can't see anything beyond the outer edge. We've never seen radar jamming technology like this."

At that moment the plane initiating the video made a closer pass and was met by a near miss lightning bolt. "And every time we begin a run toward it, we get that reaction. Lightning flashing directly at our planes, but so far, it abruptly terminates mere inches from the aircraft. Seems to be warning shots across the bow, so to speak, and it all defies the laws of physics. I've ordered our pilots to get no closer than a hundred meters, for now."

Kalie rejoined the impromptu briefing. "As we suspected, this is not a natural weather event. Our weather operators report that the cloud is not moving in relation to surrounding air currents. On an otherwise sunny day it seems to have formed in just a few minutes ten miles off shore and then headed directly for Manhattan. I guess we can take the hacker theory off the board. This is either an invasion or God."

The president turned and snapped. "Ferron, until we make that call, consider the nation on war footing. It's been my experience that always being in a reactive mode gets you nowhere. Give me options."

The general took in a deep breath and then glanced at the hi-def image of the cloud on the monitor. "There's no bloodshed yet, so let's keep it that way. I recommend that we probe from a distance, see how it responds. I suggest that we fire a couple of AIM-120's at it, then see what happens. They would go straight through a normal cloud. If these do the same, then we'll detonate them over the Atlantic. If they impact a target, then we also learn something. Either way, it's low risk while the cloud is still over the ocean."

The frustration in her voice was palpable as the cloud continued on its path to New York City. "Do it now. It's time we go on offense."

"Yes, Madam President." Ferron was handed a phone handset and his chubby jowls danced as he gave orders. "We are green for two deliveries. I repeat, we are green for two deliveries." He handed the phone back to a colonel and all eyes locked onto the central monitor streaming video from an F22.

The pilot quickly maneuvered to an appropriate distance and position to send the missiles through the cloud. In flat monotone the pilot narrated. "Target lock acquired.... fox one, hot... fox two, hot."

A few seconds later he continued the launch sequence. "Fox one away...fox two away."

The missiles appeared on the monitor flying like supersonic darts fired from a cannon. They hurtled toward the cloud with blazing speed, one following the other until they pierced the outer edge of the menacing gloom. Instantly the glowing burners disappearing into the billowing blackness. The pilot continued. "Flying around to verify exit."

The G-force could almost be felt in the Situation Room as the pilot abruptly brought the F-22 sharply around the malevolent looking roiling ball of contained darkness. His voice returned on the speaker, this time with an edge. "The packages did not exit. I repeat, packages did not exit. No visual or audible impact, and no exit... They just disappeared."

The president's frustration boiled over. "That thing is headed toward the largest city in our country and it just swallowed two missiles! We spend more on defense than the next seven nations in the world combined. We need better options, and we need them now!"

Before he could answer, the colonel handling communications interrupted. "General, we have an update from New York. I'll put it on speaker."

The urgency of the voice of Major General Haas, ground commander of Operation Righteous Defender, demanded attention. "General George, the situation is rapidly evolving here in the city. That cloud has now entered Manhattan airspace and begun to lose altitude. We're calculating that it will be on the ground in less than ten minutes. Based on what happened with those missiles, I suggest that we evacuate all civilians in a five-block area as well as the remaining personnel in the UN complex. What are your orders, sir?"

Ferron glanced to his left. "Madam President, I also recommend that we get them out, but it's your call. What are your orders?"

She could feel their eyes staring at her, waiting for her direction. She put her hands on her narrow hips and seemed to look into the distance, all the way to New York City. The few seconds waiting for her answer felt like an hour. With resignation she answered with the wave of her hand. "Get them out. Get them all out."

Moments later she added, with quiet determination. "I want counter options on my desk within an hour. We're not going to submit to this kind of assault on our country, not without a fight."

Chapter Six

Saturday 11:45 A.M. Hawaii / 5:45 P.M. New York

As noon approached Qu had changed back into her clothes from last night. She hugged Wade around the waist tightly, then looked up, her golden amber eyes meeting his blue. "I don't know what's going on in the world today, but I do know that I enjoyed last night. I'd love to hang out with you here all weekend but I'm booked for two sets tonight at the *Riptide*. With all of this Judgment Day news, I bet the place will be packed. So, if you get bored, come and catch the late show." She squeezed a little tighter. "Maybe bring a toothbrush?"

He leaned down to meet her soft lips in a sweet goodbye kiss. He smiled mischievously. "I'll be there... unless the world ends."

Her small hands playfully pushed him away. "You jerk! Don't even joke about that. It's bad karma."

Wade laughed. "You know I'm just messin'. I'll be there."

He leaned down for one more kiss when the radio telescope alarm sounded again. She flinched. "Ugh!!! Shut that damned thing up!"

He settled for a quick peck on her bronze cheek. "I promise, I'll take care of it. I guess the universe is tired of being ignored."

Standing on his front porch he watched her get into her pink convertible Volkswagen Beetle. He waved goodbye as she backed out of the driveway, then turned back toward the computer interface of the telescope. "Now, what's so important, Mr. Scopie?"

Sitting down at his keyboard he deftly entered the commands for a twenty-four-hour summary. His eyes widened as he scanned the results. "What the hell?" He started at the top again and read more slowly, making sure that he wasn't mistaken. "This can't be right."

Grabbing his phone, he tapped Haskell's speed dial number. "Dr. Haskell, this is Wade. I'm going to need some time on Big Eye tonight."

The rebuff that he expected came swiftly. "You know that every second on our main scope is scheduled years in advance. Time is our most precious resource."

Wade pressed his boss. "Yeah, you've made that clear. But I think I've discovered something really important and we have to verify it as soon as possible. I think I've spotted a planet killer, and it's headed toward Earth."

For several seconds there was silence on the other end of the call. Haskell's usual haughty attitude was now very measured. "That's a very serious statement, Wade. What kind of proof do you have?"

Wade stood up from his computer at home and began to pace. "You know how I told you about my hobby scope here at home? Well, I set some funky search patterns, just for fun, and I found something. Something big. I think I found an asteroid coming from an almost empty quadrant of space, it's heading straight for us. I'm estimating ten kilometers, give or take. It's going to take Big Eye to confirm... or hopefully disprove my findings. Either way, we don't have time to wait."

Dr. Haskell's natural arrogance returned. "Hmm, Wade, that is interesting, but our work is much too important to interrupt based on something one step above a toy. Maybe we can refer it to the guys in Chile. I hear they're open to wasting time on half-baked theories."

The pacing continued as Wade urgently tried a new tack. "I just thought that someone of your stature would want to be part of possibly the biggest discovery ever in our field. You could become the most famous living astronomer in the world."

"My reputation in this field is secure, Wade. It's you who needs to consider if you have a future in astronomy."

The call had gone as he had expected, but not as he had hoped. Two years of suppressed emotion exploded. "Listen, you pompous ass! I've done your grunt work every day for two years without a single complaint, not one. This is for real and it can't wait. Damn it, life on this planet could be coming to an end, so I'm coming in tonight and confirming this, with or without your approval."

The dictatorial voice of his boss cut him off. "Now listen here, Wade Jansky. I run this observatory and I'm the one who decides where we look. If you don't like it, I suggest you find other employment... immediately."

Wade's previous explosion was simply a precursor. "Fuck you, old man! You're so damn stuck in your ways. The way that I see things you have two choices. You can try and stop me, and if you try, I'll kick your ass. Then I'll get the confirmation anyway. The second is that you can join me on what may be the most important discovery of our lives. It's your choice."

There was a long silence on Haskell's end. Finally, he responded. "Since you put it that way, bring your data and I'll meet you there tonight, but I want naming credit if this one in a million, junk science, off the wall sighting of yours pans out."

Wade shook his head in silent disbelief upon hearing the narcissistic offer. "You've got a lot of nerve, Dr. Haskell. It will be co-naming rights, and let's get one thing straight, my name's first. If we confirm, it'll be the Jansky-Haskell asteroid."

Chapter Seven

Saturday 6:00 P.M. New York

CBN's Manuel Diaz was on one of the monitors in the Situation Room reporting on the mystery cloud that now covered the UN building. The lengthening summer rays silhouetted him against the coal black background six blocks in the distance. The camera captured New York City and military tactical units moving like remote controlled toys in between him and the swirling darkness. Effie Louise leaned on her cane and spoke to no one in particular as she waited for the next briefing to begin. "Reminds me of nine-eleven. Images of clouds billowing in New York behind reporters who don't really know what's just happened."

Secretary of Homeland Security, Trusond Patel, entered the Situation Room with President Banister. She spoke, "Tru, tell everyone what you've just shared with me."

As Kalie and Ferron sat down, surrounded by the expanded number of junior staff members along the wall, Trusond stepped to the front while buttoning his dark brown suit jacket over this traditional button-down white shirt and red and blue striped tie. "Since that cloud appeared, we've received the first reports of citizens reacting. There has been looting in Miami, Kansas City and L.A. And we have reports of property crimes and violence, including arson. In addition, there are reports of bombings at three synagogues and ten mosques. No claims of responsibility, but there were spray painted crosses on at least some of the buildings. Suffice it to say, things are heating up. So far local authorities have things contained, but it feels like we're sitting on a powder keg."

The president addressed the room. "It's only been six hours since that Gabriel figure burst into our world and in that short time the threads that bind our society together are already beginning to fray. People are afraid and if we don't start providing them some kind of answers, some kind of example showing that we're getting a handle on this, who knows what we'll be dealing with by this time tomorrow. It's all of us around this table that shoulder the responsibility to come up with those answers, those examples. We have an alien force - maybe even God, who knows - parked smack in the middle of the largest city in our country. I get it, there's not a detailed contingency plan to deal with something like this, so it's up to us to build a plan on the fly."

She paused and made eye contact one by one around the table. "I know that you've been running at full speed without a break to even catch your breath since this thing started, and I'm sure you feel the enormity of the situation. Me too. But I want you to know that as stressed as you may feel, I believe with every fiber of my being that you are the best team in the world to handle it. I'm proud to have each of you here with me. Now, let's throw some ideas around and try to at least catch up with the news cycle once today. Ferron, you're up first."

Ferron stood as the room settled in for the start of the third emergency meeting of day. He seemed to wobble a bit, then steadied. "As you've seen on the monitors the cloud has now morphed into the shape of a giant column, the base of which now only covers the UN complex and not the original twenty blocks we were expecting. The towering column reaches from the ground upward, all the way to the edge of space. Think about that for a moment. We're talking about a swirling black spike extending sixty-two miles."

He paused and tugged briefly at his collar as if it suddenly felt too tight, before resuming. "Over eight million people can see it from their windows. Whoever's doing this is making another huge statement, this time without saying a word."

The general now wavered again and beads of sweat appeared on his forehead. Like earlier, he pulled his handkerchief from his back pocket and mopped his wide brow. "Sorry, it's getting a little warm in here with all of these people."

He continued. "Since it's now on the ground we have new options. I've been in contact with General Haas and we're recommending a two-pronged approach. Under the cover of darkness, we'll send a special forces team in through the sewer system to infiltrate the main UN building, get eyes on the inside. In addition, we've got a tank company at the ready. We'll probe the outer edge, out of sight of the media, and see what kind of resistance we face, see if we have better luck than with our aircraft. We need to find out which weapons systems might be effective against this thing."

Suddenly, the blood drained from Ferron's face and his hand clutched over his broad chest. He gasped and his knees buckled, sending him tumbling back in his chair. Kalie sprang to action, wrapping her strong arms around him, easing him to the floor. "Get the doctor! I think he's having a heart attack!"

The meeting room quickly transformed into a temporary emergency department as the president's personal physician took control of the EMT's administering first aid. Everyone cleared out while the medical team worked.

Kalie looked back toward the room that they had abandoned just moments before. She heard the doctor ordering the team. "Charging! ...Clear!" Then came the jarring sound of the defibrillator sending electrical voltage through Ferron's body. While not usually a woman of prayer, words suddenly came to mind. *Lord, he's a good man and we need him. Please spare his life. Please.*

For a second time she heard emergency commands. "Charging to three-hundred! ... Clear!" Electricity again discharged. She imagined Ferron's thick chest tensing while absorbing the shock. Turning away from the life and death drama, she wiped a tear from her cheek and joined the other members of the cabinet.

President Banister spoke to her team, now huddled together in the central space of the Situation Room complex. "While Ferron's well-being is on all of our minds, we need to take action in New York. I think that we should implement the military plan. Any objections?"

None were raised. Stepping in for Ferron, Kalie turned to the colonel who had been handling communication with New York. "Deliver the order to General Haas. We're a go with the plan. Is that clear?"

The long-limbed colonel saluted out of habit. "Yes ma'am." He spun on his heel to find secure communications out of the way of the medical team that was feverishly working to save the general's life.

Just then, Dr. Marcus Levy stepped out of the conference room where he had been attending to Ferron. He touched the president's elbow. "Madam President, a moment, please?"

They stepped a few feet away. "Ma'am, we're going to continue to work on him on the way to the hospital. So far, we haven't been able to restore a rhythm. We'll get him there fast to give him his best chance, but it doesn't look good. It may be that the damage to his heart was just too severe. I'm so very sorry to have to tell you this news."

She lowered her head for a moment. "Pass along my thanks to the EMT's. I know you are doing everything you can."

The doctor left her side, and after taking a few moments to recompose, she reconvened the team to deliver the news. "General Ferron George has served his country valiantly in war and in peace... and now it looks like he's in the fight of his life. Please keep him and his family in your thoughts and prayers.

Covered mouths and soft sobs answered her announcement as the gurney carrying his body rolled by with an EMT sitting astride his prone body, valiantly continuing CPR compressions. She continued. "They'll do everything they can to save him, but right now it's our duty to protect our country. I know that it will be difficult, but the country needs all of us on our game, and at our best."

One by one, each of her emotionally drained cabinet members reassured her of their readiness to serve. She shared both their readiness and their stunned sentiment. "Take a break, everybody. Step outside for a breath of fresh air, grab another cup of coffee, or whatever helps. Let's be back here in fifteen."

The group slowly dispersed. The president pulled Kalie aside. "Looks like Ferron will be out of commission for a while, or maybe worse. We'll need the Deputy Secretary here full time, immediately. Will that be a problem?"

Kalie craned her long neck toward the ceiling, then back down to the president. "No, ma'am. I'll be fine. Looks like we're both going to be spending some unexpected time with our exes."

Chapter Eight

Saturday 6:00 P.M. New York / 2:30 A.M. Sunday Tehran Iran

As his driver wheeled through the nearly empty streets of Tehran, President Hossien Namazi stared at his phone, replaying the Jabril video for the hundredth time. While he was undecided about the truthfulness of the broadcast, he was mesmerized by the voice. The flawless Persian spoken by the self-proclaimed messenger had caused him to at least consider its authenticity. He was sure that was why he was being summoned by Ayatollah Mohammad Ka'bi, the Supreme Leader, at this dark hour.

After a brief check, they were waved through the gates of the Office of the Supreme Leader by Islamic Revolutionary Guards, then escorted into the spartan residential section of the complex. At last he spied the traditionally garbed elderly leader in his receiving room, sitting in a rather non-descript arm-chair at a ninety-degree angle to an equally nondescript beige sofa. Both squared the corner of an unadorned sand colored rug.

As he had dozens of times before, he entered the room slowly, bowed, then addressed the Ayatollah. "As-Salam-u-Alaikum."

The greeting of peace was returned. "wa Alaikum Assalam wa Rahmatullah." With a gesture toward the sofa the religious leader bade him to sit.

An attendant brought a tea service, and after both men were served, the Ayatollah spoke bluntly. "Our internal communications controls were breached today, Hossien. Have you identified how this happened? More importantly, have you figured out how to prevent it from happening again?"

The president shifted on the sofa. "Supreme Leader, our engineers are working non-stop to identify the weaknesses in our systems, and so far, they haven't discovered exactly how this hack happened. It was a very sophisticated attack. We've also been in contact with our friends in Russia, who are just as concerned, and like us, they're searching for a solution. We will find a way to prevent this from occurring again. This is our highest priority."

No change registered on the Ayatollah's face as he replied. "Hmmm. As I suspected."

Seconds ticked by as the president waited respectfully for the Supreme Leader to continue. "Tell me, Hossien, do you believe that the man calling himself Jabril is truly the messenger of Allah? The same Jabril in the Quran?"

The president glanced briefly at a plainly framed photo of the late Ayatollah Khomeini, the lone decoration in the room, for inspiration. "Supreme Leader, I confess that I am intrigued and thrilled at the possibility that the time when Allah will punish sinners and bless the faithful is near. But so many signs and prophesies have not yet appeared. Most importantly, the hidden twelfth prophet, the Mahdi, has not made himself known. I beseech you for spiritual guidance."

Again, the Ayatollah sat thoughtfully in silence for a time, his robes rustling when he spoke. "As a young man I studied in Qom, sitting at the feet of some of the most brilliant minds of Islam. They taught, and I believed, that the day of Judgment was near, but in my heart, I did not think that I would live to see it. But prophetic events since then have gradually altered my belief. All Muslims took notice when Israel was re-established in 1948, taking sacred land in the process. Then, in the '67 six-day war, the Jews took even more land, leaving our Palestinian brothers nearly homeless. For me, that was when I knew for sure that my eyes would indeed see the day of Judgment. Now, with the events of this evening, I know that I will not only witness the day, but, if it be the will of Allah, I will play a role in hastening its arrival."

Hossien's dark eyes went round. "Supreme Leader, please, tell me of your vision!"

The glint in the old man's eyes hinted at his excitement but his voice remained serene. "Allah is signaling all by sending that cloud to New York, America's largest city. I will leave within the hour to be present at the UN, as a witness, when Allah delivers his Judgment against the infidel. Praise be to Allah that I will have lived to see the Great Satan's demise! Death to America!"

Excitement gripped the president. "Allahu Akbar!"

The corners of the old man's mouth turned up ever so slightly. "And you, Hossien, would you also like to play a part in hastening the Final Day?"

He could contain his growing excitement no more. Standing, he bowed again and implored the Ayatollah. "Yes, Supreme Leader! Yes! I await your command!"

The barely perceptible smile of the revered holy man widened a couple of notches on his wrinkled face. "Your faith will be rewarded, Hossien, your faith will be rewarded. This is what Allah requires of you. While I am away, as a witness, you must initiate Operation Zion Dagger."

The words hit Hossein like a mule kick to the chest. "You mean... you mean we're really going to do it? We're going to launch a ballistic missile toward Jerusalem?"

The Ayatollah nodded. "Not one missile, but a dozen. One for each of their tribes. The prophet, prayer and peace be upon him, has said, 'The Day of Resurrection will not arrive until the Muslims make war against the Jews and kill them, and until a Jew hiding behind a rock and tree, and the rock and tree will say: 'Oh Muslim, oh servant of Allah, there is a Jew behind me, come and kill him!' It is our sacred duty, brother Hossien, that we fulfill the prophet's words and hasten Judgment day."

Slowly Hossien sat back down on the sofa, cutting his eyes toward the old man. "Forgive me for my question, Supreme Leader, but are you sure it is Allah's will that we take that step? If we do this and judgment day doesn't come, then the other nations of the world will surely deliver their verdict on us. Their missiles will rain down on us over a hundred-fold. Our people will die by the millions and our lands will burn like Jaheem. Are you sure?"

He reached out and gently put his weathered hand on Hossien's knee. "My brother, this is why I am going to New York. I want to see Allah's Judgment with my own eyes. Only when I am sure it is Allah's will, shall we proceed. But we must be ready to act, if it is his will. Is your faith strong? Are you ready to prepare?"

Hossien's mouth set in a hard line. "My faith is strong. I am ready, Supreme Leader. I am ready."

Chapter Nine

Saturday 8:00 P.M. Washington D.C.

The hair and make-up artist put the final touches on President Banister. "There. That should do it. What do you think?"

The president took a sideways glance at the mirror. "It took a lot less make-up when I was twenty-five, before these crow's feet appeared, but not too shabby for fifty-six. Thanks Darla, you're truly a magician."

The president headed to the Oval Office where a camera and prompter were in place for her televised speech to the nation. The crew and set director seemed to move in both an air of professional energy and of a sense of an unknown, but foreboding future. Perhaps like after the attack on Pearl Harbor, or New York on September eleventh, except even more so. Those presidential addresses were big, but this was something different. It seemed much more profound. The director did a final round of readiness testing. "Camera, final check. Prompter, final check."

With both answering affirmatively she continued. "Lighting, sound, final checks." With both also confirming readiness she turned to the president. "We're ready when you are, ma'am."

The president finished a quick read-through of the paper copy of her short address, then removed her glasses and slid both the papers and glasses into the top drawer of Resolute, the presidential desk. Closing her eyes, she did something that she had not done formally in a long, long time. She said a quick silent prayer. *God, It's me, Abby. I know it's been a while, and I'm not sure if you'll even hear me anymore. But if my words are being heard, I would ask just one thing. Please give me strength to fulfill my oath to my country. I could really use a good old -fashioned blessing right about now. Amen.*

Opening her eyes, she turned to the director. "I'm ready. Let's make history."

Every network in the nation had given air time for the address and all went live simultaneously. "Good evening, my fellow Americans. Eight hours ago, our world changed. At this moment our scientists, our military, and yes, also our clergy, are engaged in determining exactly how our world changed. As I sit here tonight, I can't give you a definitive answer to that question, although I wish I could. What I can tell you for sure is that, as your president, I will represent the interests of our all citizens, whether Republican or Democrat, Christian or Muslim, Jew or Hindu, agnostic or atheist. I can also assure you that efforts are underway now to get to the bottom of today's events and chart a path forward to protect and preserve our nation... and our world. Rest tonight knowing that your elected officials are working tirelessly to get the answers that you want, and deserve."

She paused for a moment looking straight into the living rooms of the nation. "While your representatives are working for you, I have a request of each of you. Years ago, President Kennedy spoke to a different challenge, but I believe his words are also very apropos for today. He said, 'Ask not what your country can do for you—ask what you can do for your country.' I believe that he was asking each of us to do our best to make this country strong, by putting our community's needs ahead of our own needs, ahead of even our fears. Tonight, I'm asking every American to go out each day and continue to do what you've always done for your neighbors. If you are a pharmacist, go to work on Monday and keep our citizens healthy. Hair stylists, keep us fashionable and beautiful, and police officers protect and serve. What I'm saying is that until we figure this out, please watch out for one another in the best way you can, by making tomorrow as normal as possible. Panic will only weaken us."

Once again, she paused briefly to allow her words to sink in. "Throughout history our nation has defined our strength in different ways. We've defined it by our individual freedoms that are admired around the world. We've also defined our strength by our military power, power beyond any nation in history. While I'm proud to say that both of these definitions are true, I believe that something greater makes those strengths possible. I believe that American might is based on our values, our character, our hope of a better tomorrow. Tonight, I'm asking that each citizen be that beacon of hope to friends and strangers alike. I'm asking that the citizens of this country be an example to the world. An example of strength and of hope."

Taking a final breath, she closed her remarks. "Today has been a remarkable day, one like no other - ever. I want to assure you again that your government is committed to preserving and protecting you, the citizens of this great nation. As your president, I will do everything in my power to defend the United States of America to the best of my ability. May God bless each of you, and may God bless America."

Chapter Ten

Saturday 9:00 P.M. New York

Summer darkness fell on New York and the blackness of the cloud became nearly indistinguishable from the night sky. After hours of continuous coverage from the UN building and instant analysis of the President's address, the network switched to another segment with Larry Knewell. "Thanks, Manuel. We'll be back to you soon for an update."

Larry turned to camera two to reintroduce the panel. "I'm joined again by Pastor Jacob Shadwell and Rabbi Solomon Feldman here in studio. From San Francisco we're joined by Guru Baba Mashni, and from Washington D.C., Dr. Son Young Kim. Thank you all for being here with us again tonight."

In studio he looked straight into camera one. "Since we last spoke, we've had a significant new development. A massive cloud column has settled on the UN building just a few blocks from us. It's reported that the column stretches over sixty miles, all the way to the outer layers of the atmosphere. It's visible to millions of our viewers. We're definitely witnessing something big. Is this God? Is this first contact with aliens? Is this the end of the world? These are just a few of the profound questions that we will discuss on this Saturday Night Special Edition Coverage of Judgment Day."

Larry turned toward Pastor Shadwell. "Pastor, you've said that you believe this very well could be the arrival of God. Does the appearance of this cloud make you more or less certain of His arrival?"

Beaming, the pastor cheerfully replied. "Larry, prophecies are being fulfilled before our eyes. Chapter one verse seven of the Book of

Revelations says, 'Look, he is coming with the clouds, and every eye will see him, even those who pierced him.' When that cloud appeared, my heart filled with joy. Our Lord and Savior is coming and I rejoice! Christians around the world have been reaching out to me on Facebook and Instagram sharing how they are spending their time in prayer and fellowship before the rapture. It's an amazing time to be a Christian and I make a plea to anyone who is not saved. Please, get down on your knees, ask for forgiveness of your sins, and invite Jesus into your heart. You too can be saved and live forever in his arms."

Larry challenged him. "Pastor Shadwell, you make a compelling argument. Before we go to our other panelists, are you one-hundred percent sure of your interpretation of this event? Any room for alternative explanations?"

The pastor stood his ground again. "One hundred percent, Larry. One hundred percent."

Eyes twinkling, sure of more fireworks, Larry turned to Rabbi Feldman. "Rabbi, you've heard what the pastor has to say, that this event is the fulfillment of the Christian version of Judgment Day. What would you say to your congregation, and to America, this evening?"

Rabbi Feldman looked directly into camera two. "Larry, Christians have been both friends to Jews, and also our persecutors. Remember, Russian pogroms killed hundreds of thousands of Jews before Hitler's death camps killed millions more. They killed all of those God-fearing people with certainty that their interpretation of the Bible was correct. Forgive me if I question Pastor Shadwell's one hundred percent certainty today. We've seen his kind of religious zealotry before."

Pastor Shadwell erupted. "Who are you calling a zealot, you Christ killer!"

Larry forcefully restored order. "Whoa, Pastor Shadwell. Neither me nor this network will tolerate that kind of hate speech. I'm going to ask you to apologize to the rabbi and our viewers right now, or leave. What's it going to be?"

The visibly flustered pastor relented. "Rabbi, I'm apologize for my outburst. It's been a stressful day, and I went too far. The Jews were God's first chosen people, and Matthew, chapter seven, verse one says, 'Judge not, that ye be not judged.' Judgment is for God alone, not a mere man like me. I'm sorry."

Larry turned to the rabbi. "Please also accept my apology on behalf of the network as well."

The rabbi's haunting gray eyes burned with the memory of his ancestor's senseless deaths. "Unbridled words like those have consequences. People die. Just remember that, pastor. People die."

With potential FCC litigation avoided, Larry got the panel back on track. "I don't believe that you had finished your thought, Rabbi Feldman. Please continue."

Taking a cleansing breath, the rabbi spoke again, staring straight at the Christian leader instead of into the camera. "Pastor, I can quote scripture as well. On our exodus from Egypt it is written, 'And the LORD went before them by day in a pillar of a cloud, to lead them the way.' So, pastor, God led us Jews once before with a pillar of a cloud, the exact same kind of cloud that we witnessed today! If this is indeed God coming back to Earth, then this was a very clear sign to Jews like me that he will lead us to safety again." He added a jab. "Regardless of what others like you may say."

Ken Garner, the producer of the show, ordered camera one to cut to the pastor, stewing, yet holding his tongue. Larry grinned, relishing the moment. For a second his mind raced. *This is exactly what I needed! If the world doesn't end, I'll win another Emmy.* He snapped back into the moment and moved the discussion forward. "Guru

Mashni, we've had a cloud appear and engulf the UN. What do Hindu's have to say about clouds and end times?"

The upbeat holy man welcomed his opportunity. "It's great to be back on air with you tonight, Larry."

Speaking with active hands he continued. "You see, Hindu's believe in cycles. Birth, growth, decay, and renewal. This cycle obviously holds true for humans. We are born, grow old, decay and are then reborn. The same also holds true for our world and our universe. So, I also rejoice if this is the end of this Yuga. Renewal and goodness will surely follow."

Larry circled back. "What about the cloud? Does that fit with Hindu understanding of end times?"

Guru Baba Mashni chuckled. "Maybe a little bit, Larry. The Puranas say, 'And the clouds will pour rain unseasonably when the end of the Yuga approaches.' So, if this cloud eventually produces rain, then I guess we're three for three on cloud references tonight."

The optimistic view of the guru lightened the mood and Larry smiled. "Thank you Guru Mashni. Now let's go to Washington D.C. where we're rejoined by Dr. Son Young Kim. Dr. Kim, what do you, as a professed atheist, make of all this talk of Judgment day and clouds? Has your opinion changed since we last spoke a few hours ago?"

With a plain silver barrette now holding her independent lock of hair in place, she delivered her thesis in her usual monotone style. "Not really, Larry. Recall, I said that this could be first contact with an alien civilization that has technology we don't understand. Looking at the facts so far, that explanation holds up as well as any other on this panel. I just need more data to refine my hypothesis. Better data begets better science, and I bet we'll have more data soon. Then I'll do what any rational being does. As I get more facts, I'll adjust my opinion."

Larry folded his hands in front of him as he pressed. "I get that Dr. Kim. I'm just curious, do you see any case where you could be convinced that there is a God, and that he is visiting us now?"

Her hand moved to push back her habitually wild lock of hair even though it was now already held fast. "I'm a woman of science, Larry. I would need a lot more data than this to reach that conclusion, but I guess... I guess it's within the realm of possibility... but right now, no, I don't think that's the case."

Ken spoke in Larry's earpiece. "Wrap it up. We have developing news from the UN."

Sitting tall, Larry ended the segment. "Thanks to our panelists for sharing their expertise and opinions about today's event. It's a lot to take in. For now, we're sending coverage back to Manuel Diaz with breaking news at the UN. Join me again tomorrow morning when I'll be back in studio with continuing coverage of Judgment Day."

Chapter Eleven

Saturday 11:00 P.M. New York & Washington D.C.

Manuel Diaz was updating the CBN viewers on rumors of military action as the president and key cabinet members gathered once again in the side conference room in the White House basement complex. The president stood, her violet eyes looking subdued. "I have difficult, but not unexpected news to share. Our friend and colleague, Ferron George, passed away earlier today despite immediate and heroic efforts to save his life. It's awkward for me, and I'm sure for you, to be back in this room so soon."

A dark feeling of gloom filled the space, much like the black cloud in New York. Solemn expressions acknowledged her comment as she continued. "But, knowing Ferron as long as I have, I'm sure that he would encourage us to get on with our duties, especially on such a..." She paused searching for the right word to describe her feelings. "Such a fraught evening."

Glancing to her left she made eye contact with a new member at the table. "I think most of you know Deputy Secretary of Defense, Braxton Phillips. With Ferron's passing, he's now the acting Secretary. I've asked him to say a few words before we get a mission update from New York. Brax, the floor is yours."

General Braxton Phillips stood and his chiseled six-foot five frame towered over his seated peers. His confident smile and perfectly neutral mid-western accent contrasted to the Brooklyn born, and sometimes nervous, Ferron George. "It's an honor to be here serving as the Acting Secretary, but we all know that it's under the heaviest of circumstances. Ferron was both a friend and mentor to me, and I'll miss him dearly. He was a good man and a good soldier, and knowing him as I did, I'm in agreement with the president's assessment that he would want us to continue in our duties in such a pressing time."

Looking like a character from central casting with his broad shoulders and narrow waist fit in a tailored Air Force uniform, he glanced at the assembled cabinet members. "I know some of you better than others and look forward to working with each of you as we serve our country together."

His eyes locked with Kalie, his ex-wife, for just a second longer than the others. "Hopefully soon, it will be under better circumstances."

President Banister caught the glance between the two and thought to herself. *When they were together, they must have looked like Norse gods, a modern-day Odin and Frigg.*

The colonel in charge of communications spoke up. "Ma'am, I have General Haas ready to link in."

Her attention immediately turned to the monitor displaying the general. "It's about time. General Haas, hopefully you have some good news for us. What's the latest on Operation Righteous Defender?"

A concerned expression draped the general's face. "Madam President, at twenty-two hundred hours we initiated a two-pronged reconnaissance mission on that cloud. Seal Team Five entered the New York City sewer system five blocks from the main UN building. At the same time a tank company attempted to breach it's outer perimeter."

The president was impatient. "Yeah, we got that from the pre-mission briefing. What happened!"

The general pulled his shoulders back. "Madam President, first of all, I'm happy to report that there were no casualties on either team."

The president nodded approval while spinning her hand to suggest a speedier debrief. "Good news general, but what did we find out? How did it go? We're waiting."

The general cleared his throat then spoke in disbelief. "Quite frankly ma'am, I've never seen anything even close to what happened here tonight. The seal team went in fully prepared for anything. They wore full chemical warfare protection suits, masks, respirators... the whole shebang. And they carried our most advanced weaponry and communication devices. We lost all contact with them the moment they went under the outer edge of that cloud. Then twenty minutes later, the entire team came walking out of the cloud at ground level, completely naked. Not a stitch of clothing, no weapons, just buck naked and seemingly unharmed. And they were chanting, 'God is love.'"

"What?" The president asked incredulously. "How could that be? What did they say?"

Shaking his head from side to side the general answered. "It was dammed near unbelievable. These are some of the toughest and best trained soldiers in the world, and they strolled out of that cloud like they didn't have a care. They seem perfectly healthy too, but in their initial debrief they couldn't remember anything from the past twelve hours. Not a thing, not even what they ate for dinner. We're analyzing their blood and doing EEG's to determine how their memories were wiped, but so far we've got nothing."

With furrowed brow the president interrupted. "And the tank company, what happened to them? Tell me there's some kind of good news."

"Sorry, ma'am. That was just as bizarre. Once again, just like with the seal team, we lost all contact when they crossed the cloud barrier. These tanks were completely sealed and capable of withstanding nuclear radiation fallout for up to two hours. Like we saw with the seal team, the tanks came rolling out of the cloud back to the staging area. Take a look at these images!"

Still shots of the three tanks were projected onto the monitors. All had been painted like graffiti mural nature scenes. One looked like a mountain meadow, one a pristine lake, and the third a starry night.

The general continued. "When we got the crews out, they were in the same shape as the special forces guys. Naked and unable to remember anything. All instrument readings and visual recordings had also been wiped clean. Not a single clue about what happened in there."

Leaning back in her chair, the president flipped her pen toward the yellow legal pad on which she had been taking notes. The pen missed its mark and landed with a metallic thud before skidding across the conference table toward Kalie. Everyone waited for the president to speak as her pen was passed along around the conference table back to her. When Brax neatly placed the pen in the center of the pad, she leaned back in. "All right, General Haas. First, let's be grateful that your soldiers are all unharmed. I guess the good news is that whoever's inside that cloud doesn't mean us harm, at least not now."

She rubbed her eyes and then laughed softly. "And apparently they have a sense of humor. I mean, sending them out naked? Who does that?"

The general's shoulders dropped a bit. "Yes, Madam President, they do seem to have a sense of humor. In fact, there were even flowers stuck into the barrels of the tanks. I hope that's a sign of peace and not just their way of mocking us."

She picked up her pen again, and as is her habit, began tapping it slowly on the pad. After a few raps she opened the discussion. "All right, so far that cloud has eaten two missiles without so much as a burp, then turned some of our best soldiers and military equipment into peace propaganda pop art. Things are pretty tense around the country and I promised answers in my address tonight, promised that we would be getting a handle on this. We all know that this will get leaked. Pictures of naked soldiers and pretty tanks will not exactly inspire confidence."

The general lowered his head for a moment, then snapped back. "Madam President, we'll begin working on another plan, a different approach, immediately. We won't let you or our nation down."

"I know that I can count on you, General Haas. But in the meantime, how do we spin this so we don't look as clueless and helpless as we seem to be?"

Kalie volunteered. "At Space Rim, we had our share of embarrassing moments. Three years ago, we lost a communications satellite about thirty seconds into launch. Exploding rockets make terrific footage on the news channels and our stock price took a hit with each replay. My partners and I knew that we had to change the narrative quickly, so we publicized how much we had learned from the failure and pushed the story line that cutting-edge companies always have bumps along the road to true breakthroughs. In almost no time our share price rebounded. We did learn a lot from that loss and two months later we began a string of ten consecutive successful launches. Those who bought stock at our lowest point made a fortune."

Subtly, Brax leaned back. Once again, Kalie's brilliance was outshining him, but instead of bailing like last time, he seemed to decide to hitch a ride to the star. "Great idea, Kal. How about you and I work with General Haas and come up with our narrative of what's happened, before it gets written for us? Let's at least get ahead of the spin cycle."

Kalie shot him a hard glare at his use of her nickname in this ultimate power room. The kernels of his jealousy that ruined their marriage still seemed present five years later.

She answered coolly using his professional title. "Sure." "That's exactly what we should do, Secretary Phillips."

"Finally! If we can't beat this thing, let's at least win the spin. Good idea Kalie. You two circle back with General Haas and put together talking points that we can all use tomorrow. I think we should also announce Ferron's death at the same time. We'll offer our sincere condolences which should also humanize us, at least a little, demonstrate that the stress of this event affects us too."

The president now glanced around at her key cabinet members. "After tomorrow morning's briefing, I want you all out on the news shows selling our story. As they say, 'Fake it till you make it.'"

For the first time all day there were a few sincere smiles around the table and the president seized the moment to build her team's spirits. "I'm so proud of all of you. Nothing like this has ever happened to those that came before us in these seats. Today you showed that you're fighters, and that's why I chose each of you. You're the best. I'm going to be asking even more tomorrow, so other than Kalie and Braxton, everyone go home for a few hours to recharge. Let's be back here at six for the briefing and then we'll flood the morning shows. We already know tomorrow is going to be a hell of a day."

Chapter Twelve

Saturday Midnight Washington D.C.

Winding her way through the White House, President Banister finally made it to the master bedroom in the family quarters. She crept in hoping to avoid waking her spouse, but Jill's sweet voice pierced the silence. "Abby, I've been worried about you all day."

Abby smiled, clicking on a lamp, glad that Jill was not yet asleep. "Join me for a nightcap?"

The petite woman slipped out of bed and into a robe and fuzzy slippers. "I'll have whatever you're having, dear." She came over to Abby and wrapped her arms around her as if to share her energy and bolster her spouse. "I've been watching the news, I can't image what it's been like for you today. And I thought that your address to the nation was spot on. I doubt that anyone else noticed, but I sensed the burden that must be weighing on you."

Leaning down, Abby kissed the top of Jill's head. "I've had better days, that's for sure." She moved to the bar and poured a bourbon over rocks for Jill and made a double for herself. "I won't bore you with the details, but the situation is even worse than they're showing on TV. Worst of all, Ferron George died today. He had a heart attack right in the middle of a briefing. It was awful."

Jill looked up into Abby's glistening eyes, on the verge of tears. "Oh god, I'm so sorry. He was a big teddy bear of a man. I really liked him."

Abby wiped away the hint of moisture with the back of her hand and savored her first sip of the brown Kentucky liquor. "My address tonight wasn't the right time to announce it, we'll go public with it tomorrow morning. He was a good man and a trusted adviser. I miss him already."

With her arm draped over Jill's shoulder, the two walked toward the sofa and sat down together. Abby kicked off her high heels and let out a groan. "Aha." She put her feet up on the coffee table. "Tomorrow's going to be even more intense. On top of finding out if the world's going to end, Dallas will be coming here, to the White House." She laughed. "I'm not sure which I dread more, him or the end of the world."

Jill squeezed Abby's hand. "Why's he coming? He's been such a jerk to us for all these years."

Squeezing Jill's hand back she tried to reassure her. "We both know how he's treated us. What's it been? My god, it's thirty years now. Where did the time go?"

Her harsh words contrasted with her gentle voice. "If it had been forty years it would still be too soon for me. He's a spiteful man."

Abby sloshed her drink and the ice clinked reassuringly against the sides of the tumbler. She thought about Jill's assessment and took another long sip before answering. "I try to look at it from his point of view. He felt betrayed when I left him for you, and it hurt his career for a long time. Thank God attitudes have shifted since then. I think having a bisexual former spouse running for president actually helped him land his job at Harvard. I can hear him saying, 'God works in mysterious ways.'"

Jill snuggled closer. "I get that, but he didn't have to say such a mean thing during the campaign. Who does he think he is to say that marriage is only between a man and a woman? The other side made a commercial out of that comment and ran it over and over. Come on Abby, just call it like it is. He's a prejudiced asshole."

Abby took another long drink, contemplating her response. "You're right, of course, but I need him right now. While we disagree with him on his views on marriage, his knowledge on world religions is encyclopedic, and he specializes in apocalyptic prophesies. Plus, I won't have to worry about him holding back, he won't sugar coat anything. I can put up with him for a few days to get what I need."

Tenderly, Jill kissed Abby's slender hand. "Abigail Bannister, you're a better woman than me. Just one of the many reasons that I love you."

"Oh, Jill. We both know that's not true. I can be a pretty mean bitch, especially when we're apart for too long." Abby finished her drink and set the empty tumbler down with a clunk on the marble side table. "Now, sweetie, let's put thoughts of Dallas Shendegar out of our minds and get some sleep. At this age I need my beauty rest more than ever. I may be meeting God tomorrow and you know I'll want to look my best."

Chapter Thirteen

Saturday Midnight Washington D.C.

The small conference room within the Larger Situation Room complex had cleared out except for Kalie Robinson and her ex, Acting Secretary of Defense, Braxton Phillips. He leaned against the solid oval table. "Can you believe this? We both had a lot of ambition way back when we first got married, but I don't think either of us would have even dreamed that we'd be here, together in the White House Situation Room, advising the president. It's crazy. So, how've you been?"

Kalie closed the door with a slam and stayed several feet away with arms crossed. "Let's get something straight. On the job you will address me by my full name. Kalie. Not Kal. My title is also acceptable, National Security Advisor. Got that?"

Braxton raised his hands in defense. "Whoa. Where did that come from, Kal. I mean Kalie. Kal's what I always used to call you. What gives?"

Her eyes narrowed and her nostrils flared. "That's what you called me when we were married, before I caught you in bed with Vicky. We're not married anymore, hell, we're not even friends. We're peers in a workplace now, in the ultimate office job. So, don't glide in here and act like we're pals or something. I've worked hard to get here and I'm asking for proper respect. Is that clear?"

Frostily, he replied. "All clear, National Security Advisor Kalie Jean Robinson. Geez, I thought we were all past this after the divorce, but I guess not." He thought for a moment and then added, "Hey, the president called me Brax. Should I be offended?"

She shook her head and her pony tail slung from side to side. "Of course not, she's not our peer. She's the PRESIDENT. She can call any of us anything she wants."

Feeling better, after clearing the air, she pointed to an adjacent chair. "Glad that's out of the way. Now, let's get this done and get out of here. I've been at this all day and I could use a couple of hours of shut eye before it all cranks up again in the morning. Agreed?"

Chastened, he sat down. "Before we start, I meant what I said. You're right, this is a good idea. Spin this as a positive. It's really good, Kalie." He turned back toward the monitor where General Haas had last appeared. "Ready to get Haas back on the line and hash this out?"

The corners of her mouth lifted ever so slightly. "Absolutely, General Phillips."

Chapter Fourteen

Saturday 11:45 P.M. Hawaii / 5:45 A.M. Sunday Washington D.C.

For the past hour Wade and Dr. Robert Haskell had been loading celestial coordinates into the computers that drove both the optical and infrared telescopes high atop the dormant volcano. After spending thirty minutes of conflict free time with Haskell, Wade's defensiveness had melted considerably. "I appreciate you helping me do this; I wasn't sure if you would. My mind's been racing all afternoon and I really hope that my data is wrong, because if its right..." His voice trailed off without speaking the unthinkable.

Dr. Haskell had also mellowed since their phone call. "You were quite persuasive. I've been waiting on you to show some initiative, to demonstrate more than the ability to simply follow my orders. Plus, I think this is the first time that I've been challenged to a fist fight to get time on the scopes."

Blushing, Wade replied. "Yeah, about that. That's so not me. I haven't been in a fight since second grade. That stuff just fell out of my mouth. Sorry."

"Apology accepted. It's pretty funky hobby-quality data, but to tell you the truth, after seeing it, I would have been just as fired up, had I been in your shoes." Tapping in the final coordinates Haskell followed up. "So, how did the second-grade fight turn out?

"What, you mean with Jimmy Butler?"

"Yeah, what happened?"

Wade rubbed his chin and thought for a moment. "Well, he had a bloody nose and I had a busted lip. We both ended up in the principal's office with threats made about the potential black marks on our permanent records. Scared us stiff. Turns out you can disagree on whether Batman or Superman is stronger and still be friends. Life's funny. I could call him right now, if I needed him, and he would be on the next flight."

Haskell looked toward Wade across the console. "We're about set. Would you like to do the honors?"

With a smile that made him look even younger than his twenty-six years, Wade entered the final line of code, and with the flair of a maestro he pushed the enter key one last time. Nearly silent gears and hydraulics began moving the giant lens and antennas into place. "Here's to hoping I'm wrong. We'll know for sure pretty soon."

Haskell leaned back in his chair. "So, Wade, I'm curious. Where did you come up with these odd-ball coordinates? Why did you have your home scope looking at basically blank sections of sky?"

"Hmm, that's a good question, but it's kind of a long story."

"This is going to take a while, Wade. We've got time."

"Okay, but let me ask you something first. Did you grow up rich or poor?"

A quizzical look was Haskell's first response, then he rubbed his salt and pepper stubble of a beard for a moment. "I'm not sure how my upbringing matters, but I'll play along. I would say neither, my family was solidly middle class. My mother drove a minivan, like most of my friend's moms. We had plenty, but nothing extravagant."

Wade slowly spun his swivel desk chair around once, then stopped facing Haskell. "See, that's where you're wrong. When you're raised poor, like I was, people who had a car that didn't spend more time broken down than it did running, were all rich. I envied all of you suburban kids. I envied your clothes that didn't come from thrift stores. I envied your new bikes on Christmas instead of something from a fire department toy drive. See, I was raised poor, very poor."

"Sorry, Wade. I had no idea."

Wade spun his chair around once again like the kid he was just a few years ago. "My mom was a real piece of work. Even when we were at our most desperate, she always gave money to the church. Then, on top of that, she played the lottery every week. How could she do that when we had to go a food bank just to have enough to eat? She would say that as bad as things were, others had it worse and it was our duty to help when we could. As for the lottery, she said that the Bible said that God helps the helpless, and that usually described us. Like I said, she was a piece of work"

Leaning forward, Haskell checked a setting on the main scope. Satisfied, he commented. "Your mom sounds like a very caring lady. You were lucky in that regard."

The chair made another revolution. "That's easy to say now, but when I was in middle school being teased about my clothes and for sometimes living out of our car, it sure didn't feel that way. In fact, there were times when I hated her. No matter how much I complained about it, she kept playing her numbers and giving away money that we couldn't spare. Well, everything changed when I was a freshman in high school. Mom's numbers finally hit and we were instant millionaires. Life changed overnight. After she donated her ten percent tithe to the church, plus an extra five percent for good measure, I got a new bike for Christmas that year and a new car on my sixteenth birthday. She sent me to a private school to catch me up from my substandard education, then four years later I got into Cal Poly, then after that a master's at UC Berkley. I'm here today working on my PhD because my mom refused to give up on her numbers."

Haskell shook his head. "That's an amazing story, Wade, but I'm still not tracking. How does that get us here tonight?"

He spun around a fourth time. "Hang on a second, I'm getting there. You know how some people play their favorite numbers? Maybe they combine the birthdays of family members or some other kind of lucky numbers"

"Yeah, I know what you mean."

"Well, my mom took Bible verses and converted them into her lucky lottery numbers. Book, chapter and verse numbers became lotto gold. Luke six, thirty-eight talks about how you should give to receive. I memorized it, it goes 'Give, and it shall be given unto you; good measure, pressed down, and shaken together, and running over, shall men give into your bosom.' So, Luke converts to 0 and 3, because it's the third book of the New Testament. Chapter six became 6, and verse thirty-eight became, well, 3 and 8. One lucky September night, 0,3,6,3,8 were the winning Pick Five numbers. Crazy, huh? But that's what happened. We went from dirt poor to filthy rich overnight."

Wade spun around again before continuing his story. "These days I don't go to church, or anything like that, but back then, I was a dorky kid interested in astronomy being raised by a free-spirited religious mother. Looking back, it seems obvious that I would study Bible passages that mentioned comets. Now, as an adult I follow mom's example, I convert a few of the more interesting verses into celestial coordinates."

Realization dawned on Haskell. He was incredulous. "So, we're here tonight because you're playing biblical celestial lottery?"

One last spin around revealed a sheepish Wade. "Yep. That's why we're here. Matthew twenty-four, twenty-nine talks about stars falling from heaven, and Revelations chapter eight talks about a great mountain burning with fire in the sky, being sent to Earth. I figured, hey, if mom can hit the state lottery using that system, maybe it would work for me too. Why not? By the way, it's the Revelations coordinates that we just keyed in."

Haskell just shook his head in amusement. "Glad you didn't tell me that on the phone or we may have had that fist fight. Speaking of

God, what do you make of that Gabriel thing on TV? Think it's real?"

Wade ran his hand through his thick sun-bleached hair. "I watched it more than a few times this afternoon and I don't know what to think. In fact, I believe that I could convincingly argue both sides, but truth be told I've also wondered if this asteroid is connected. God, I hope I'm wrong."

The steady hum of computers and slowly turning gears driving the large telescope were interrupted by a binging indicator. They both spun back to the controls. Haskell spoke. "Looks like we got results faster than expected. Let's see if you're a winner."

Wade's hands began shaking as he pointed to a center monitor. "Please tell me that's not what I know it is."

"Holy shit, Wade. Your numbers hit... this is bad... this is really bad."

Denial was no longer an option and the full realization of what this discovery meant gripped Wade and he seemed to revert back to being a scared child. "We've got to tell everyone, right? We've got to let everyone know, don't we?"

Haskell tried to calm him. "Yes. But first, we need to reach out to other facilities around the world to begin the confirmation process. Think, Wade, think. There's still a slim chance that we could be wrong. There's protocol for this, and you've been trained on it."

"This is it, isn't it? This is the end." Wade fought back unexpected tears. "This can't be the end. I'm just getting my life together... there's a girl...I have plans..."

"Come on, Wade, get a grip. We're scientists, we've got a job to do, and fast." Haskell began pulling out his phone. "You start the emergency email notification process to China and Chile and I'll get a message to the president. She needs to know."

Even in his agitated state, Wade was dumbfounded and questioned Haskell as he wiped away the moisture from the corners of his eyes. "You have the president's number?"

He answered without looking up. "Of course not, but I do have it for the National Security Advisor. We met at a conference a few years ago."

"Cool. Did you date her or something?"

His cheeks flushed but Haskell didn't look up as he crafted a carefully worded text to Kalie. "That's a story for another time. You let me worry about this while you get those notifications sent. Okay?"

Wade regained his adult composure, "Uh, sure. No problem."

In a couple of minutes both men had sent their messages and sat back down in front of the controls, staring at the ominous data. Wade's phone text message alert sounded and he looked at his phone. "Oh shit. I'm supposed to meet Qu tonight. I totally forgot. I can't go now, there's too much going on here to leave."

Haskell patted him on his shoulder. "I'm not telling you what to do, Wade, but there may not be too many more nights left in our lives. How do you want to spend this one, hmm? I can handle everything here, if you want to go. Besides, you and I are going to be famous tomorrow. After all, we did discover the Jansky-Haskell asteroid, didn't we? Think hard about enjoying one last nearly normal evening before the circus comes to town."

Wade stared at his phone as he considered Haskell's words. He was torn between wanting to be with Qu and seeing this through the night. He turned to Haskell with an idea, this time asking with humble sincerity instead of challenging his boss to a fight. "Since this is all going down soon, could I bring Qu here tonight? She's special, and I'd like to share this moment with her."

Touched, Haskell answered wistfully. "Ah, young love. I remember it well. Why not, what's an unauthorized visitor going to matter now? Go ahead, bring her here. We could use a little Lady Luck."

Chapter Fifteen

Sunday 6:00 A.M. Washington D.C. & New York

Dawn was breaking as President Banister descended from the family quarters of the White House into the basement Situation Room. She entered the side conference room once again and even though she had not laid eyes on him in person for more than ten years, she immediately recognized the newest face at the increasingly crowded conference table. Her first thought was that like her, he had aged. He was three quarters of the way to being bald and his remaining hair was now more salt than pepper. His waistline was also a couple of inches thicker, but otherwise he looked the same.

She walked the short distance around the table to officially greet her ex with all of the power and authority in her voice that she could muster, to set the tone on her terms. "Dallas, I'm glad you could make it on such short notice. Welcome to the White House."

The balding bespectacled biblical academic stood and accepted her outstretched hand. "I'm glad that you called, honored to be here. I hope that I can add to your understanding of what's happening."

His diplomatic introduction was better than she expected *Maybe he has changed after all these years.* She returned a business-like smile and in her no-nonsense mode, she answered as she walked away addressing him, and the entire room. "I'm counting on it, Dallas, I'm counting on it. Please, have a seat everyone."

Returning to the head of the table she kicked off the meeting. "Good morning. I hope that you all got a few hours of sleep last night because it's going to be a long day."

She looked down the table toward her ex-spouse. "I've invited Dr. Dallas Shendegar to join us. He's the Dean of the School of Divinity at Harvard and I'm hoping that he can provide knowledge and insight on the God aspects of this event. Dallas, welcome to the team."

He gave a small wave to the cabinet members around the table as the president moved on to the first order of business. "Kalie and Braxton stayed late last night working with General Haas on some talking points that we can use with the media this morning. Please, share with us what you've come up with."

Kalie stood to speak as Braxton handed out written copies of what they were about to cover. "Before I start, the general wants it stated that he's working on another military option to present later today. Now, regarding these talking points, it's very important that we all stick to this script as closely as possible. We need to stay on message to reinforce that we know what we're doing, that we're getting a handle on this... event. Winging it in front of a national audience could really go wrong for both you and the administration. If everyone has a copy, let's review from the top."

A PowerPoint version of the memo now appeared on the center monitor. The laser pointer landed on the first point. *Announcement of Defense Secretary, General Ferron George's Passing.* "As discussed last night, we're leading with the announcement of the tragic passing of Secretary of Defense, General Ferron George. We're asking that everyone keep this simple and sincere. He was a great leader in both war and peace and he died briefing the president and her cabinet, apparently suffering a massive heart attack. Memorial and funeral arrangements have not yet been finalized." She paused and pointed to Braxton. "Also announce that Deputy Secretary Phillips is now the Acting Secretary. Keep your comments simple and direct. If you get any questions about the briefing he was providing, answer truthfully. 'That information is classified.' Any questions?"

There was initial silence and Kalie was poised to move to the next point when Dallas spoke. "I'm quite shocked to hear of the general's passing. It must have been difficult yesterday for everyone in the room. Learning of it now, I know that today will be a very tough day for his family. If time allows, Madam President, I would like to go to them as your representative, to express both yours, and the cabinet's, deepest condolences. I'll also make myself available for individual counseling for anyone here that could use a sympathetic shoulder."

She was both surprised and touched. "Yes, Dallas. Those would both be very appropriate. Check with Chief of Staff Cyrus to make arrangements. Thank you." She tapped her pen slowly on her blank notepad, keeping her eyes on the newest member of the team as Kalie prepared to continue the briefing. *Dallas Shendegar. have you really turned over a new leaf? Maybe the world really is coming to an end.*

Kalie moved the pointer under the words of the second bullet point. *We Have Made Contact.* "Now we get to the core of what we want to communicate. Keep in mind, we're spinning positive, true facts here. While we don't have many answers yet, we have sent two teams into that cloud and they have returned safely, clearly having been in contact with whoever, or whatever is inside. Questions?"

The tightly wound Secretary of Homeland Security, Trusond Patel, raised his hand as he spoke. "We're going to get bombarded with questions about the nature of our contact, who we communicated with, what was communicated... that sort of thing. How do we respond?"

"Same as with Ferron's announcement, 'that information is classified.' Remember, we're driving the narrative." A knowing smile crossed her silk-skinned face as she thought about the validity of the words that she had just spoken. "At least for now."

Grins and low giggles acknowledged the challenge that they faced. In the spirit of the teamwork involved in putting the communication points together, Kalie passed the laser pointer to Braxton. "Secretary Phillips will take over from here."

As she prepared to take her seat, she glanced at her phone which laid face up on the table, and noticed a new text. She spoke with an edge,

"Madam President, this is mission urgent. Please excuse me while I step outside."

Braxton stood as Kalie made her quick and mysterious exit. The next point rolled onto the monitor. *All Interactions Have Been Peaceful.* "This point is very important. As the president has so eloquently described, people are fearful of what all this means. They want to know, 'Is this God, the end of the world, an alien invasion?' Truth is we don't have any of those answers yet, but what we do know is that every interaction we have had so far has been peaceful. We sent two missiles, a seal team and a tank company against that cloud and all military personnel and equipment, other than the missiles, returned safely. Well, we think safely. We're still testing those two teams of soldiers for any lasting damage due to their short-term memory loss. And while we can't know what will happen today, it's important to lower the anxiety level as much as possible. So, please state clearly and forcefully that every encounter that we've had with the cloud has been peaceful. No fatalities and no known injuries." He smiled. "And before you ask, we provide no details about our naked soldiers or painted tanks. All questions get the standard 'That's classified', response.'"

As others laughed softly at the reference, Dallas was confused. "Naked soldiers, painted tanks? Apparently, I missed a lot yesterday. Could someone stay after the meeting and get me caught up? It will certainly be germane to understanding the religious connotations of this event."

"Of course, Dr. Shendegar. I'll personally bring you up to speed." After addressing the newcomer, Braxton was ready to advance to the next point when Kalie rushed back into the room.

"Sorry to interrupt, everyone, I just received news that changes everything." Her pupils flared as she turned her worried gaze toward the Abby. "Madam President, I just spoke with one of our astronomers at the Keck Observatory in Hawaii. They just spotted an asteroid, a big one, that's apparently on a collision course for Earth."

The president's jaw tightened and she forced her words. "Jesus Christ, can't we even catch a little break. Damn it, Kalie, I know this has to be bad, but tell me, on a scale of one to ten how bad is it?"

Kalie lowered her gaze and her broad shoulders sagged. "Ma'am, if this sighting is confirmed in the next hour or so, on a scale of one to ten, it's about a thousand. It's really bad."

A hush came over the entire room as Kalie's words fell hard. The president opened her mouth to speak when the colonel handling communications hesitantly broke in. "Madam President, I have General Haas ready to patch in from New York City. He says it's extremely urgent. Would you like me to put him onscreen?"

She flicked her fingers toward the monitor and spoke sarcastically. "Go ahead. Put him on. Let's see what good news the general has to add."

Dawn was breaking in New York City as General Haas appeared onscreen. "Good Morning, Madam President."

The president leaned forward, resting her elbows on the table, her sharp features amplifying the tension in her voice. "It's already been a pretty tough start to the day down here, general. I hope you're going to give us some good news, but I have a feeling you're not."

The general's haggard look and wrinkled uniform suggested that he had not slept much last night, but nonetheless, there was a lift in his voice. "Madam President, I can't speak for everyone, but I think a lot of people are going to be happy to see what daybreak has brought to New York City. Take a look."

The camera that had been focused on the general now turned toward the UN building. Gasps of amazement and wonder spread from one official seated around the conference table to the next as the camera panned across the UN complex. Her clenched jaw relaxed as she looked on in awe. "Wow. The cloud is gone... and that looks like a different building. What have they done to the UN?"

General Haas narrated as the streaming video switched to a camera drone that began to broadcast different aspects of the scene. "First of all, Madam President, while the cloud has disappeared, it's been replaced by what looks like delicate gold strands forming a fishnet design. The golden netting has taken the place of the outer edges of where the cloud column used to be. It's still a barrier, but now it's beautiful and shimmering in the morning sun. It's stunning to see in person."

The camera pushed in to take a closer look at the actual buildings as the general continued his commentary. "See the concrete parts of the structure that yesterday were a dull white? Well, overnight they've been covered in some kind of brilliant white glaze. We can't look at them here on the ground without sunglasses. It's amazing, but that's not even the biggest transformation. Take a look at the glass-clad main tower. Yesterday, the glass was tinted kind of a bluish green. Now, its covered in gold! The whole place is almost blinding it's so bright."

Dallas stared with mouth agape until words finally flowed reverently. "It looks like heaven."

Now the general directed the camera to pan up and the screen filled with movement. Circling inside the golden net cylinder that reached into space were... what? More expressions of amazement escaped unintentionally from the members of the cabinet. With awe, the president asked the obvious question. "What are they? What are we seeing?"

The general asked the drone operator to push in for a close up of one of the moving beings. "We've never seen anything like it. First of all, there are thousands of them, all the way up and down that cylinder. It's really hard to comprehend how many of them there are. They look like people, or at least human-like beings. They're wearing solid white form fitting uniforms, and what I can only sort of describe as silent, dazzling white, jet packs. Their heads are covered in gleaming white helmets with golden face shields. It's like they are on some kind of beautiful protective flying patrol of the site. Unbelievable."

Wonder transformed Dallas' face. "Then I saw another angel flying in midair, and he had the eternal gospel to proclaim to those who live on the earth—to every nation, tribe, language and people.' That's what the Bible says in Revelations. They don't look like the angels of the bible, but they're beautiful."

The cameras also caught another sight as they now panned to ground level. General Hass was quick to acknowledge it. "As you can see, Madam President, crowds are starting to assemble. Between the towering cloud last night and that golden fishnet tube sparkling in the morning sun, people are coming out in droves to see it for themselves. Working with city police, we've got it under control, but we're going to need reinforcements soon."

Braxton had remained standing and now answered the request. "General Haas, we'll work with the New York National Guard and redeploy more forces from upstate. I'll also ask for emergency authorization to make active duty personnel available for domestic deployment."

President Banister looked at her Attorney General. "Hakeem, make it happen."

Hakeem scribbled notes in his iPad as he answered. "Yes, ma'am. We'll have it ready for your signature in an hour."

Trusond Patel, Secretary of Homeland Security, piped in. "Madam Secretary, there's no good time to bring this up, but I need to brief you on other events from last night."

The pen of the president tapped a bit harder. "Thanks for the report, General Haas. Keep us updated if anything changes."

She turned towards the Secretary as General Haas' image faded. "Just rip the Band-Aid off, Tru. Get everything on the table. What happened last night?"

The thin secretary took his turn standing. "As I mentioned last night, Miami, Kansas City and L.A. had already experienced looting and violence. As the night progressed St. Louis and Milwaukee were added to the list. Reports are that there is a growing sense that the world is indeed ending. Ordinary citizens are following the examples of criminals who are using this as an excuse to steal things they've always wanted, and to settle old scores. National Guard troops are now deployed across the country to assist local police, but if these trends continue, they could be stretched thin in a day or two, maybe less. Also, we're seeing evidence of vigilantism. For instance, down in Colleyville Texas, just outside of Dallas, armed locals have started neighborhood watch patrols. Last night they killed seven and injured dozens in a firefight at a local strip mall."

A thin smile crossed the President's lips. "Hooray for the Second Amendment, I guess. I have a feeling it's only going to get worse when word of this asteroid hits the news."

Tru nodded, then added a final comment. "Madam President, I think that it's also time that we discussed emergency continuity of government plans in case public order devolves into total anarchy."

She felt the weight of the world on her shoulders as she considered her next words carefully. Remaining seated, she addressed the team. "I'm reminded of a quote from the writer Paulo Cuelho. 'Life has many ways of testing a person's will, either by having nothing happen at all or by having everything happen at once.' We're definitely in all at once territory this morning. You can't make this stuff up. It's already been a hell of a morning, after a hell of a day yesterday."

She paused and tapped her pen a few more time as she surveyed the team. "When something happens in life, it's never really just about what happens, it's about what we do about it, how do we handle it? For me, the answer is always to try to control what I can control."

She stopped, smiled wryly, then continued. "Some have called me tough, a task master, or a control freak as well as other more colorful descriptions. But I usually get results. That's not all that I am, but it's clearly part of my wiring. So, let's define some priorities for the day and accomplish as much as we can."

She began rapid fire delegation. "First, the asteroid. Kalie, with your experience at Space Rim you'll run point on how we deal with it. Whether it's God sent or a coincidence doesn't matter. We're going to do everything we can to destroy or divert or whatever we can to avoid ending up like the dinosaurs. Got it?"

She spoke firmly. "Yes ma'am. And by the way, the asteroid has a name. It called the Jansky – Haskell asteroid, after the two astronomers who discovered it."

"Good to know for my remarks to the nation later today." She paused for a few seconds, tapping them out with her pen on the yellow legal pad. "Jeez, I've been on TV more than any time since the campaign. Do you think it's too much to be on again today?"

An emboldened Dallas beat everyone else in speaking first. "Madam President, I know I'm just getting up to speed here, but I can tell you with certainty that when people are afraid, they want to hear from their leader. They want to know that you care and that you're doing your best for them. Leaders who hide are seen as cowards... and I can say definitively that if you are anything, you are not a coward. You're not interrupting their favorite show to talk about the economy or even war. You're discussing the very survival of the planet, and our species. I say talk to the people. You are their leader."

Kalie concurred. "Well said, Dr. Shendegar. These are extraordinary times and the usual rules are out the window. I agree, address the nation."

She glanced around the room and saw no disagreement. "All right then. I count on your honest counsel. Let's get back to it."

She turned to Braxton and resumed her rapid clip delegation. "Brax, I need you to be my voice with General Haas. He's a good soldier, but see that nothing big happens in New York City without going through you. Clear?"

A crisp, "Yes ma'am" returned.

Trusond was next in her line of sight. "Tru, you are the lead on starting continuity of government planning and in maintaining domestic order. Liaison with Brax as needed and work with Hakeem to get any other emergency authorizations you need. Do whatever you have to do, short of declaring martial law, to maintain order. If you think it's come to that, run your concerns by me. Got it?"

A smart, "Yes ma'am" answered her direction.

"Effie, ramp up communication with ambassadors from every country. Allies, adversaries, rich countries and poor, it doesn't matter. Like it or not this event is happening right here in the good old USA but it's going to affect every citizen of the planet. Be as transparent as possible, we're way past global politics as usual. Understand?"

Her velvety-smooth voice replied. "Yes ma'am. Every nation."

"Next is this God... or first alien contact? It's going to make a big difference in how we talk about this event and actions that we might consider. Dallas, you're lead on that. Lean on my chief of staff and anyone else you need for resources and help. We need to make a decision on who, or what we're dealing with as soon as possible."

The rapid-fire delegation now stopped, and for a moment as she pondered the implications of her next words. "Dallas, if this is God, and this is Judgment day, then we need to figure out how to guide the country until it happens, however it happens. I'm really counting on you."

His face beamed. "Madam President. I won't let you down. It's the assignment of a lifetime."

Even after his eloquent words just moments before, his newly evolved attitude still surprised her. The president now stood and rubbed her hands together slowly. Her exquisitely tailored purple pant suit set her violet eyes aglow. Her hands stopped their slow movement and she extended them toward her team. "The day before yesterday people might have referred to us as bureaucrats, elected officials, soldiers, statesmen or clergy. And they would have been right, we're all of those things. But today, we're also possibly the only people in the world that can save the planet from imminent destruction. One way or another, we're going to make history. We're each here on our own personal journey, but we can't do this alone. We need each other, we're a team. So, support each other, encourage each other and sacrifice for each other. I'm counting on you, and the world is counting on us. Go take care of business and report back here at eleven o'clock. I'll make my next address to the nation at noon, and as fast as events are moving, I'll need a progress update. Now, go out there and be what you really are: super heroes."

Chapter Sixteen

Sunday 9:00 A.M. New York

Manuel Diaz was wrapping up three hours of live coverage from New York City. The visual backdrop of the stunning transformation of the UN building as well as the sparkling golden net being patrolled by flying beings had been a ratings bonanza for his reporting. "Recapping our lead story, in the past twenty-one hours mankind has been witness to a dramatic new chapter of our history. Either God or an alien species has made contact with us, right here in New York. It's been amazing to witness and it will continue to unfold with the General Session scheduled at six o'clock this evening. Perhaps then we'll have a definitive answer to that big question. We'll take a break here and go back to the studio for continuing coverage of Judgment Day."

The live feed smoothly transitioned from the UN building to CBN headquarters a few blocks away. A refreshed Larry was eager to again be front and center in the developing story of a lifetime. Looking steely eyed into camera one he kicked off his segment. "Welcome back to continuing coverage of Judgment Day. Two days ago, we devoted three full hours to the budget fight on how to fund Social Security. It seemed pretty important at the time, didn't it? This morning, we're discussing different questions like, 'Are we alone in the universe?' And, 'Is God real'? What a difference a few hours make!"

Larry leaned forward toward the camera for emphasis. "As of yesterday, we found out that we will get answers to at least one of those questions, if not both. It started with the worldwide message from Gabriel, the self-described messenger of God. Yesterday we debated whether it was true, or all an elaborate hoax. A few hours later a giant cloud moved over the UN building just a few blocks away and we knew for sure that this event was not a computer hack. We witnessed the arrival of something supernatural, seemingly from beyond this planet, and perhaps something holy. Anonymous sources within President Banister's administration have spoken of a complete lack of effectiveness of our weapons against this force, possibly leaving us at the mercy of an extraterrestrial invasion. This morning we're witness to an out of this world transformation of the UN building and the spectacle of flying patrols protecting the site."

He paused dramatically, turning to camera two. "Yesterday all of this would have sounded preposterous, and yet today it's all very real. What does it all mean? To answer that question, our panel from yesterday returns. Once again, I'm joined by Pastor Jacob Shadwell and Rabbi Solomon Feldman here in studio. From San Francisco we're joined by Guru Baba Mashni, and from Washington D.C., Dr. Son Young Kim. Thank you all for being here with me again this morning."

All the guests gave their perfunctory acknowledgments while Larry set the parameters of their initial comments of the day. "A lot has happened since we were last together and I want to get your first impressions of the changes overnight at the UN. Specifically, has it changed your ideas on whether this is God, or not? Let's switch it up a bit and start in Washington DC. Dr. Kim, do the events of last night and this morning change your opinion?"

After being put on the hot seat yesterday, the renowned atheist seemed much more self-assured today. "Well, Larry. As I said, I will continually adjust my opinion as more data becomes available. Hearing the anonymous reports about our military and seeing the scene at the UN I'm more convinced than ever that we're experiencing first contact with an alien force."

Larry smiled, sure that this viewpoint would spur conflict with his other guests. "Tell us more, Dr. Kim. Why are you so sure?"

She answered confidently, with no concern over that once unruly lock of hair, now sprayed in place with a bit of curl. "Let's review the facts, Larry. First, we see beings flying with the aid of what are clearly machines. If they are angels, shouldn't they have had wings? Secondly, look at the UN building. It obviously had a makeover, but other than the extraordinary speed at which it was done, does it look like anything a qualified construction firm from Queens couldn't have accomplished? So yes, based on the evidence that I see, I still believe this is first contact with an alien civilization, not the arrival of a god."

Larry now looked into camera two and spoke to his guest in San Francisco. ""Thank you for starting our discussion, Dr. Kim. Guru Mashni, thanks for getting up early there on the west coast. You've seen the incredible images from New York. So, is this God, or Vishnu or something else?"

Guru Mashni had stepped up his television look by wearing a black kurta, a long-sleeved combination jacket and shirt, with delicate gold embroidery. The three gold buttons at the top of the garment brought the solid black Nehru collar together smartly. However, his buoyancy from yesterday had lessened. "Larry, thank you again for your gracious invitation to join the panel today. Looking at the images from New York, I am no longer as optimistic that this is indeed the end times foreseen in the Vedas. Kalki should appear on a white horse and amass an army to defeat all demons and sin. Singularity can then be achieved as this epoch ends. Flying machines are not mentioned at all in sacred Hindu writings. Those prophesies are many centuries old, so there could easily be things seen in the long-ago visions that were so fantastic to our ancient writers that they simply lacked the vocabulary to describe them accurately. Therefore, I reserve final judgment until we hear the address this evening from the UN."

Larry heard the guru's words and shift in mood from last night. "You seemed so positive and upbeat yesterday, Guru Mashni. Tell us more about your reticence today."

The guru shifted uncomfortably in his seat. "Things have happened so fast, Larry. It's not even twenty-four hours since we first saw the Gabriel video. None of what has happened matches sacred Hindu writings. Perhaps this is truly the end time, but if it is, then most of the texts that I've considered sacred for my entire life, for the entirety of my people's history, will be shown to be completely wrong. It's as if an ant has been challenged to eat an elephant in one bite."

A contemplative expression washed over Larry's face. "That's deep."

He then turned toward his in-studio guests. "Good morning Rabbi Feldman. Welcome back. Guru Mashni has expressed some profound unease over the most recent events and how they relate to his faith. How have these events impacted your thinking?"

Rabbi Feldman continued the guest's trend of more telegenic dress since yesterday. This morning he had a white prayer shawl with blue stripes draped over his shoulders in addition to his solid black kippah head covering. "Good morning, Larry. I appreciate Guru Mashni's struggles. I share many of the very same concerns about matching the words of the Torah and Talmud with what my eyes are seeing. One advantage that I have over the guru is that I live here in New York. From my living room window, I saw the cloud last night, and this morning I walked down to the UN and witnessed the gleaming transformation of the building, and those magnificent beings flying overhead. And I'll tell you, Larry, it's a glory to behold."

Larry interjected. "You're right, rabbi, I've been down there as well. As stunning as the broadcast images are, they can't full convey the overwhelming scene happening here in the city. It's almost too much for words, or pictures. Please, continue."

The rabbi nodded agreement with Larry's assessment. "While I share some of the Guru's concerns, the Jews have had a different historical experience. We've gone from God's chosen people with a homeland and a Holy Temple in our Holy City, to a people conquered multiple times and the complete loss of our lands. Now we have a homeland again, but over the ages Jews have been subjected to slavery, persecution and to being scattered across the face of the globe. Our faith has been tested over the eons, and many times we've considered new interpretations of our Holy Scriptures to match our situation. Seeing the majesty of what's happening here, I'm inclined to consider that even if this is not an exact match to our Holy Scriptures, perhaps it really is God. I, too, think we'll all know more later today."

"Hmm. Sounds like there is a consensus building among the faith leaders. After a night of reflection and the sights of flying machines at dawn, long held strict scriptural interpretations are being tested, or at least stretched. Pastor Shadwell, do you have similar concerns?"

The pastor sat with a dour expression, seemingly now uncomfortable in the spotlight. While the others panelist had freshened and tweaked their wardrobe in a camera-friendly manner, he had not. He had changed into a fresh shirt, but otherwise wore the same dark blue suit and red tie as yesterday. "Larry, this morning's developments have been a bridge too far for me and for millions of other Christians. We believe in the inerrancy of Scripture, that the word of God is inspired and infallible. What we all saw this morning in no way resembles the word of God surrounding end times. In fact, in Revelations, the book of the Bible devoted to end time prophecy, it is very clear that God's word on this subject is final. In chapter twenty-two, verses eighteen and nineteen we are told, 'For I testify unto every man that heareth the words of the prophecy of this book, If any man shall add unto these things, God shall add unto him the plagues that are written in this book: And if any man shall take away from the words of the book of this prophecy, God shall take away his part out of the book of life, and out of the holy city, and from the things which are written in this book.' I simply cannot believe that this is God."

Larry probed sharply. "So, Pastor Shadwell, are you leaving any room, any possibility of changing your mind based on what we hear from the address tonight, or you absolutely sure that this is not God?

I'm only asking for clarification because you seemed so certain that it was God just a few hours ago."

Pastor Shadwell sat silent for a few seconds with his eyes cast down. Finally, he spoke. "I think that it would be very hard for me or many other Christians to believe that this is really God, regardless of what is said or seen this evening. The only caveat I would offer are the words that I spoke yesterday. 'For all have sinned, and come short of the glory of God.' I am human and not infallible. That's what I believe."

Larry pushed for a definitive answer. "So, if I hear you correctly, there is still some small chance that you could be persuaded that this is God? Is that what you're saying?"

Pastor Shadwell's face pinched as he was forced to commit. "It's a very, very, small chance, but it's not zero. Is that clear enough for you, Mr. Knewell?"

A self-congratulatory smile creased Larry's face. "That's clear enough pastor, that's clear enough."

Chapter Seventeen

Sunday 10:00 A.M. New York / 3:00 P.M. Airspace Over North Pole

The specially fitted Air China Boeing 747-400 soared through the frigid arctic air above the North Pole. The knock on President Li Huang Zhou's office door was barely audible over the roar of the four engines. The sixty-year-old man sitting at the mahogany desk removed his glasses and rubbed his eyes. "Enter."

Wang Wie, his personal assistant, stepped into the well-appointed airborne office. "Mr. President, General Hu has urgent news and requests your presence in an emergency meeting."

The president rubbed his eyes again, then exhaled loudly. "What now? Have we been hacked again? Is another lunatic promoting a banned religion to our people?"

The deferential aid persisted. "Mr. President, he said it's very serious. A matter of gravest concern. What shall I tell him?"

The president picked up his glasses and slid them into place. "Tell him that I'll be there in a moment, but make it quick. I would like to have a couple hours of rest before we arrive."

The assistant made his exit as the president stood and stretched with arms above his head. He then stepped from behind his desk and made the short walk to the centralized meeting area. He first saw Xiu Ying, Minister of Science and Technology, the only woman in the trio of ministers accompanying him to New York. On the other side of the small dark wooden oval table sat Chen Yong, Minister of State Security. Lastly, he saw his old friend General Gao Hu, current Minister of National Defense.

All of them stood. General Hu greeted their leader. "President Zhou, I'm sorry to interrupt your preparations, but a matter of supreme urgency has been brought to our attention."

The concerned expression on the general's face was disconcerting to the president. He spoke as he joined the now seated group. "Tell me, old friend, what has happened, what is troubling you? Has that angel person inspired protests in our streets?"

"No, nothing like that, Mr. President. My concern is of a completely different nature. There is a newly discovered threat to our nation, and the world. I'm going to ask Minister Ying to explain, as it pertains to her field."

The turn to Minister Ying surprised Zhou. Dr. Xiu Ying was not only the sole woman invited on the mission, but also the youngest. Seeing these two older men defer to her raised the president's alertness to a new level. "Tell me, Minister Ying. What is the nature of the threat?"

The composed scientist sat with her back straight and shoulders square in her conservative black-skirted suit. "Mr. President, last evening our astronomers received an urgent message from American counterparts in Hawaii. They requested an emergency confirmation of a previously undetected asteroid."

She paused, measuring each word carefully. "Mr. President, it is my responsibility to report that our team has indeed confirmed the sighting."

General Hu and Minister Yong sat silently, waiting for either the president or Minister Ying to speak. The president broke the silence. "Xiu, tell me the meaning of this discovery. How does this threaten our people?"

Her hands balled into fists below the table. "Mr. President, on the current trajectory this asteroid will impact Earth in two weeks."

She hesitated before adding, "The size of the asteroid, Mr. President, is big enough to severely damage our planet, if not completely destroy all mankind." She bowed her head, seeming sorry to have had to be the one to deliver the somber news.

All eyes now turned to the stoic leader. He removed his glasses and placed them softly on the dark surface of the table. "I see."

Minor turbulence tipped the plane, creating a small wave in the crystal water pitcher resting at the center of the table. The president looked directly at each of his assembled ministers. "What contingency plans do we have to spare our nation from this catastrophe? Can we survive the impact, or are we already dead men?"

The older men looked intently at Xiu, hoping for good news, but with faces signaling no such belief. She hardly blinked as she delivered the verdict. "The international community has discussed this possibility for years, but the primary focus has been on early detection. With five, ten, or even twenty years advanced warning the hope was that, together, the nations of the world could muster a joint mission. Obviously, our hopes of early detection have fallen short. Having said that, I believe that there is still a chance, albeit quite small. It will require immediate action and an unprecedented level of openness with the Americans. It is a long shot, but we may be able to coordinate a response that could possibly save us all."

The president nodded. "General Hu, I have yet to hear from you on this matter. Tell me, what you think of this plan?"

The general stared hard at his old friend and his square face reddened as he answered. "The United States has been a bully for a long time, and now, finally, we have reached near parity with them. At this point, the Americans are in the dark about how strong we really are. Thirty minutes ago, I could not image a scenario where we would so willingly give away this hard-fought tactical advantage. Now, after hearing from Minister Ying, I can scarcely imagine we can do anything else."

The president turned his gaze toward Minister of State Security, Chen Yong. "Minister Yong, what is your counsel?"

The gaunt, sternly turned man replied is his usual snarling mode of speech. "I don't like this. I don't like this one bit. We've put up with their arrogance for so long, and now we're just going to lower our guard? It galls me to know that we must, but as my mother used to say, you don't have to give your neighbor a chicken if all they need is an egg. We'll do all that is required, but I'll make sure that they don't learn anything more than absolutely necessary. Should we succeed, China can come out of this crisis being seen as a full equal to the Americans."

"Hmm. Wise counsel, Minister Yong." The president leaned back a bit in his chair and folded his hands in front, looking like a professor about to quiz his students. "Tell me, ministers, do you think this has anything to do with that Gabriel video? That's why we're heading to New York, to witness this so-called god event this evening. And now we get this news. Are these things connected?"

Minister Yong sneered. "There is no god. I'm still not convinced that this isn't some elaborate ruse being orchestrated by the Americans. They're always using that kind of language, always talking about their god being on their side. I will not be surprised if we find that the Americans are behind this."

Xiu spoke up. "As a scientist, I can assure you that as much as we may want to blame the Americans, both the hack and that cloud are thousands of factors beyond even their most advanced technology. It's possible that those two things are connected, but I can say with certainty that the Americans are not behind it."

Again, the president prodded his friend and counselor. "General Hu, tell me your thoughts?"

The grizzled veteran tugged on his uniform to straighten wrinkles forming around his paunch. "In my village, the elders revered our ancestors. While I abandoned such things, as required when I joined the Party, I still remember those days. I remember candles lit and prayers to various spirits, asking for health, success and guidance, but never once did I ever hear an elder speak of some global apocalypse. Never once. And now, we hear this angel, on our airwaves, telling us that a god is coming? I say ignore him and focus on the asteroid. We know that's real. Everything else is just a sideshow to distract us for some unknown purpose. That's what I think."

The president nodded thoughtfully as he picked up his glasses and put them back on. With slumped shoulders he headed back to his private office, then turned to them once more. "Please reach out to President Banister. She and I must take action immediately if we are to survive... regardless of what we hear from this so-called god, there will be no rest for any of us until this is settled."

Chapter Eighteen

Sunday 10:30 A.M. New York / 4:00 P.M. Airspace Over North Atlantic Ocean

Passing through Norwegian airspace, the Ilyushin Il-96 aircraft carrying the Russian delegation continued over the North Atlantic toward New York City. The news of the coming asteroid and discussions of possible ways to prevent the demise of humanity had just concluded. Russian Minister of Defense Yevgeny Siminoff complained to the others seated around the small conference table in the plane's meeting area. "It's always Russia that has to clean up the West's messes. Was it not Russia that stopped Napoleon? And Russia that stopped Hitler? And now it will probably be up to Russia to stop this asteroid."

President Maxim Noskov joked, "So, Yevgeny, it's the west's fault that an asteroid is headed toward Earth?"

Even the perpetually grim Minister Siminoff smiled for a moment. "You know what I mean, Mr. President. The West treats us like a pariah until things go horribly wrong, then they beg us to help. We bail their asses out, and what does that get us, huh? More missiles pointed toward our cities? More sanctions on our economy? They are nothing but ingrates."

An aging Olga Kutrokov, Minister of Emergency Situations, nodded approvingly. "You are absolutely correct, Comrade Siminoff. They treat us like an outcast relative, but I see no other alternative but to bail them out again. Just as in those days of old, Mother Russia's survival is also in the balance."

Dressed in white robes and vestments with gold embroidery, Alexy III, Patriarch of the Russian Orthodox Church, brought final condemnation. "Western civilization has become godless, secular and radical. The moral vacuum created by their godless civilization is responsible for the rise of terrorist groups like the Islamic State. They are a hollow vessel, claiming God, but living only for their own vanity. It is the West that has brought God's Judgment. It is the West that has brought God's disfavor."

The president laughed and waved his arm back and forth. "All true, my friends, all true. The West does treat us badly, but as Olga has pointed out, our backs are against the wall. We must work with them to save ourselves. And to do that I'll have to put up with President Banister's mind-numbing optimism. That lesbo bitch truly drives me crazy."

He shook his head, then ran his hand over his bald pate as if to clear his mind. "Now, where was I? Oh, yes, the question that I have for you is, if we survive, how do we leave this crisis better than we enter? Some wily American once said, 'Never let a serious crisis go to waste.' We must take advantage of this difficult situation, correct?"

Olga smiled admiringly with her perfectly painted purple lips contrasting with her aged wrinkled face. "You are absolutely right Mr. President. We have more heavy lift rockets than the rest of the world combined. I can't imagine any scenario where they will not need our help. We should extract some kinds of concessions. It's only fair."

Yevgeny's mood continued to brighten and a smile actually creased his cue-ball head. "Well said, Olga, well said. If they desperately need our help, then we should be justly rewarded. I propose that we demand all nuclear weapons be removed from western Europe and all sanctions on our citizens and businesses be lifted. That would restore us to our station as the dominant power in both Europe and Asia."

President Noskov spread his arms wide. "Exactly, comrades, exactly. I agree with everything you propose, but think bigger. Much bigger. Think restoration of the empire!"

He paused and called to the attendant who dutifully stepped forward. "Tatyana, bring us vodka. We will be toasting." She turned and he slapped her across the backside, laughing loudly as she strutted away. "I like her spunk!"

The painfully pale woman with red rouged cheeks quickly returned with an ice-cold bottle of the finest Russian vodka. Filling a shot glass for each to the brim, she placed them at hand, then stepped a long stride away from the leader. President Noskov raised his glass. "Yevgeny, we will demand all that you have suggested, and more."

All eyes focused on him with glasses at the ready. "We are going to re-establish our historic place in the world. In addition to missile and sanctions removal, I am also going to demand the return of Ukraine, Estonia, Latvia and Lithuania. We will rebuild the empire! We have them over a barrel. How can the world say no?"

With a flourish he exclaimed, "K imperii!"

All raised their glasses. "To the empire!"

The Patriarch knocked back his shot and set his glass down loudly. "Talk of Empire is all well and good, we deserve our place in the world. But I remind you all of one immutable truth. If this is indeed God, then your plans amount to nothing more than sparks in a fire, a momentary flash. He alone rules the only eternal empire."

The president lowered his glass and cast a hard glance at the Patriarch. "Alexy, I would watch my mouth if I were you. Just remember, I alone rule Russia and I can shut down your church any time I please. You'll do as I say, or else. We're getting our land back, regardless of what we hear tonight. Do you understand?"

The old man sneered, seemingly unfazed by the threat. "You are cunning and powerful, Maxim, but God always has the last word."

His eyes sparked anger and his voice rose in a rapid crescendo. "Alexy!" He stopped mid-thought as his wondering eye caught another glimpse of the leggy attendant.

His expression softened as he considered other pursuits, for which he was also always ready. He began again, with the edge absent. "Alexy... I've decided that today I would rather drink than fight." He turned a leering gaze back toward the young woman. "Tatyana, another round."

He slowly looked her up and down, basking in the knowledge that the others were witnessing his appetites. "And please join us for a drink... so that I may get to know you better."

Chapter Nineteen

Sunday 11:00 A.M. Washington D.C.

Harried core cabinet members hurried into the main area of the Situation Room as the small conference room off to the side had become too crowded with the growing number of threats to the nation. President Banister was the last to arrive. She addressed her team immediately. "I'm sure it's been a busy few hours for each of you and I hope that you all got a lot accomplished. I'm addressing the nation in an hour, so let's get right to progress reports. Kalie, you start with updates on the asteroid. That seems to have moved ahead of the God thing in terms of urgency. Tell us some good news."

Kalie stood and a PowerPoint presentation loaded onto the large main screen. A computer-generated image of an asteroid hurtling through space filled the monitor. "The good news is that NASA and other branches of the government have thought about the possibility of this kind of event and real preliminary planning on how to deal with it has happened."

Her hands moved to her hips as she turned to face the President. "Unfortunately, that's where the good news ends. The first priority of their planning centered on early detection, preferably a twenty-year advanced notice. That ship has obviously sailed. The Chinese have confirmed our initial assessment that the extinction sized Jansky-Haskell object is a mere two weeks out."

Mumbling began among the people surrounding the core group seated at the conference table. The president spoke loudly. "All right everyone, we're on a tight schedule. Keep it down." She turned back toward her National Security Advisor. "What are our contingency plans?"

Kalie advanced the slide which featured drawings of futuristic looking spacecraft. "Several of these types of craft have been in the planning stages, but stalled due to lack of funding. Our only option on such short notice is to come up with new ways to utilize our existing tools and technologies."

She advanced the slide again, showing the still new Space Rim shuttle replacement vehicle. "Basically, what we need to do extremely quickly is re-purpose two spacecraft designed for near Earth operation into usable vehicles fit for a one-time deep space mission. Then we have to launch in about a week or so. We're working out exact timelines as we speak."

The next slide appeared, showing a CGI image of the crafts deploying small packages, one after the next. "We'll drop a picket line of remote detonation nuclear weapons in a line to try and push the asteroid onto a new trajectory that misses Earth, little by little as it flies by. That's much easier said than done, but our best option."

President Banister weighed in. "We have thousands of ICBM's. Why don't we just send them into space and blast this thing into oblivion?"

Mumbles of agreement followed her question. Kalie clicked to the next slide showing animated missiles flying from one point on the globe to another. "That was my first thought as well. As it turns out, those incredibly sophisticated weapons are designed to do one thing, and do it very well. They launch from land, sea or air, then go into space and return to specific coordinates on Earth, detonating at a specific altitude. Again, they do this very well, but you can't turn them into what we need, at least not quickly. First, there is the guidance system. It's all based on Earth coordinates, not flying thousands of miles in a straight line out of Earth's orbit using outer space coordinates. We could reprogram them, but it would take a lot of time we don't have. But the biggest challenge is the detonation mechanism. They're all designed to trigger the explosion at specific Earth altitudes to inflict maximum damage on our enemies. None of them have detonators designed to go off on impact or by remote control, and certainly not at specific outer space coordinates. Once again, developing and then installing that kind of detonator would take a lot of time. If we had three months... maybe, but we don't."

She paused a moment as she brought back the shuttle slide. "We have one option, and it's the longest of long shots."

The president tossed her pen onto her pad, landing it perfectly centered this time. "What are the odds we can pull this off in time?"

Kalie shrugged her broad shoulders. "The truth is, we've never tried anything like this, so any odds I give are just a spitball estimate. There are a lot of unknowns and a tremendous number of variables."

She glanced toward the ceiling, closing her eyes for a moment, seeming to calculate the odds. After a few seconds she hazarded a guess. "I'll say, realistically, two percent for full success. Maybe a ten percent chance of moving the object enough to avoid the total destruction of all life on Earth."

The blunt assessment sucked all of the extraneous side chatter out of the air. President Banister picked up her pen and once more began to tap. "Obviously, you'll get started right away on that option, but with those long odds I'd like some kind of fall back plan, even if it's not ideal. Put a small team to work on a skunkworks project to convert a few of those ICBM's as a last chance back-up. I don't like all of our eggs in one basket. Understood?"

"Yes, ma'am."

"We're all counting on you, Kalie." She turned her attention to the Acting Secretary of Defense. "Brax, give us an update on what's been happening in New York."

Braxton stood and the main screen switched from Kalie's presentation to a live feed from the UN site in New York City. The luminescent imagery from earlier in the day remained. "As you can see, not much has changed from this morning. The crowds of onlookers continue to swell, but with the transfer of National Guard units from upstate combined with NYC's finest, everything is peaceful and calm. We did spot some larger transport type vessels coming down the golden column, and it appears that the Gabriel being emerged from one, waved to the crowd and then went inside. It kind of looked like a Hollywood red carpet moment...without an actual red carpet... at least for now."

The inadvertent levity brought grins to several faces, including the president. She inquired, "No aggressive actions, expanding borders, nothing like that? Just a photo op for the tabloids?"

Braxton smiled, looking like a leading man in a Hollywood production. "I'm happy to say that at this moment there's not much happening up there, at least that we can see. I have discussed additional next steps we might take. After all, leaders from around the world are supposed to be entering that building later today and we currently have no way of guaranteeing their safety."

Banister stopped tapping her pen for a moment as she considered his comment. "We've been going a hundred miles per hour around here. I hadn't even stopped to consider that. What's the plan?"

The tall man sighed and rubbed the back of his neck. "It's a tough call, Madam President. Some of our most advanced weapons and best trained soldiers have been completely ineffective against these... beings. Here's what General Haas and I have come up with. First of all, we're going to be very up front with everyone who attends tonight's session. The United States can't guarantee their safety. Everyone who goes in, does so at their own risk."

"I'm sure that's not going to reassure anyone, including me. Beyond that warning, what security steps do you plan for us attendees?"

Braxton pointed to the screen. "Madam President, our plan has a couple of constraints that have limited our options. First, the invitation to the event specified that each nation would be allowed only four attendees. You and Effie plus two others."

Now Trusond interrupted. "Are we sure that the president should attend? I mean, I haven't heard your plan, but based on the ineffectiveness of our weapons so far, is there any way that we can guarantee her safety? Is it worth the risk of her assassination?"

This brought Dallas out of his chair. "She has to go. If this really is God, she can't be seen as snubbing an invitation from the Creator of the Universe! She would immediately lose the support of over seventy percent of the country."

Once again, Braxton pointed to the screen. "Ma'am, our plan is to send a body guard with you and the US contingent. He'll be one of our best men carrying a ceramic firearm and a variety of other natural composite weapons strategically hidden. We're hoping that these will get through any screening that they might employ. We'll keep working on additional ideas until it's time to enter, but in the end, it's your call whether you think attending is worth the risk."

Both he and Dallas sat down as the president pondered her response. In just a few seconds she answered firmly. "Dallas is right. As the president, I must step forward when my country needs me most, regardless of the risk. Now that that's settled, Tru, what's the update on continuity of government planning?"

Tru stood and spoke curtly. "For the record, ma'am, I ask that you reconsider attending. The country would immediately spiral into chaos should something happen, just when we need stabilizing measures most of all. It would make a bad situation worse."

She nodded. "Your objection is noted... but I'm still going. Proceed."

"Yes, ma'am. I understand. That makes my next set of recommendations even more urgent. I recommend that Vice President Puckett immediately go to the bunker facility at Mount Weather, in Virginia. I'd also recommend that Speaker Stemson be taken to the NORAD facility in Colorado. Should something happen to you, God forbid, they would be in different secure locations, maximizing the chances that one of your successors might survive whatever happens. Since many of us, as your cabinet members, are also in the line of succession, should the worst occur, Homeland is planning evacuations for us all. The same goes for members of Congress in subsequent waves, should circumstances warrant."

"Yes, make those arrangements." She looked around the room at her team. "It's not even twenty-four hours and we're planning for the very survival of our government. No wonder our people are freaking out."

Tru remained standing and now a slide for him filled the main screen. "That leads me to my next point."

Red dots were scattered across a map of the U.S. "These represent power plants where at least fifteen percent of employees called in sick or simply didn't show up for work today. So far it hasn't impacted power generation, but with the news of this asteroid and whatever comes out of this shindig at the UN tonight, this could go south very quickly. Just imagine the panic across the nation if our power grid fails. The rioting and looting we've seen so far would look like a kindergarten birthday party."

The strain on Tru's face stretched his lips thin. "Madam President, I'm readying a nationwide declaration of martial law for you to sign should that happen. I've already reached out to the Senate and the House and they are onboard."

"My God, Tru. I would be the first president since Lincoln to take that step. If we have to go there, we will, but before we do let's be damned sure that there are no other alternatives."

"Yes ma'am. I think we'll know if we must cross that line, just like Lincoln knew."

The president motioned to her right. "Effie, what's new at State?

Leaning all of her ample weight on her cane, Effie stood slowly. "Madam President, we've been in contact with every nation on the planet with news of the asteroid, as well as a high-level summary of what little we know about the identity of our guests. I did soften the details on the lack of effectiveness of our weapons. No need to advertise our true level of weakness at this time. It's no surprise that there were near universal offers of cooperation with whatever plan we try, especially from the Chinese." She softly laughed, "And Hell must be freezing over because we even got a joint statement from the Israelis and Palestinians. I guess news of impending doom can break down even that barrier."

"Good news, Effie. Based on Kalie's assessment we're likely to be calling in a few of those offers. Anything else?"

The Secretary of State had one last item for discussion. "We are allowed four attendees. You have already said that you and I will be attending. Sounds like we'll also have a body guard, so that makes three. I'm suggesting that UN Ambassador Thompson be our fourth. It is her beat, ma'am."

Banister rapped her pen on her pad as she considered the request. A few seconds later, she replied. "No... You and I are representing the U.S. What we need is a clear read on whether this is actually God... or something else. I want Dallas in there with us."

The soft-spoken Secretary of State shot a hard glance at Dallas. She seemed to think of objecting, but then her face softened. "Of course, ma'am. I understand."

Looking to the far end of the table, the president called on her ex-husband, now adviser. "Dallas. What's your opinion? Is this God or not?"

Dallas adjusted his glasses and stood. "Madam President, thank you for including me as one of the attendees for the event this evening. That request was going to be my first point this morning. I really need to see, hear and experience that event to provide a final answer. Having said that, here is my initial assessment."

"Most, but not all, religions have some sort of eschatology, meaning the study of end times. That includes all of the Abrahamic faiths:

Judaism, Christianity and Islam. Hinduism has its own version as did the ancient Mayans. Even zombie movies represent a new kind of eschatology."

"All right professor, we get it. There are a lot of theories out there about how everything could end. What about this one, the one happening right now on the ground in New York?"

The academic smiled sheepishly. "This whole thing has gotten me a bit carried away. I've studied it for my entire career, and now suddenly, here it is." He readjusted his glasses. "When I boil down everything that's happened in the last twenty-four hours, here's what I see. No end of the world scenario would check all the boxes of every religion. They all point the same way, but each have clearly defined steps and prescribed events leading up to the final destruction of the world. The question then becomes, does this event match enough of those varied predictions to validate that this is indeed God? With the discovery of that asteroid just hours after the Gabriel video went all over the world, I think that it does. I predict that many radical believers in each faith will reject that conclusion, insisting that their strict interpretation can be the only true version, but I think there is enough evidence here for most moderates in most faiths to say it's a very strong probability that this is God. I'll give you a firmer answer after the event tonight, but that's what I think right now."

The president stood, signaling that she was done with the meeting. "Thanks to all of you for the efforts that you have made during the past twenty-four hours. I value your counsel and know that I'll be asking even more of you in the coming days. Now get back out there and do your best for the American people. They need us now more than ever."

A jumble of "Yes ma'am" and "Yes, Madam President" filled the room. As everyone began to filter away, Dallas approached her. "May I have a word, Madam President?"

After his supportive stance since his arrival Abby had warmed, but she was still on guard. "Of course, Dallas. What's on your mind?"

He looked down, seemingly unsure of how to proceed. Gathering his nerve, he addressed her. "Uh, Madam President, I feel that I need to offer advice in an area that I am usually not qualified... but it's important."

She reached for his hand and felt his flinch at her touch. "Go ahead, Dallas. Say what you need to say."

"Uhm, women's fashion is clearly not my forte, but I think you should change clothes before you go on TV, and especially before tonight's event."

She laughed and did a slow twirl. "Don't you think I look nice today, Dallas?"

He stuttered. "Oh no...that's not it at all. I always think you look nice... wait..." Flustered, he started again. "What I mean is that everything you say and do from now on is going to be scrutinized for meaning and symbolism through this Judgment Day lens."

"Okay, Dallas. Just spit it out. What's wrong with my outfit?" She stood in a pose with arms outstretched.

He took a deep breath and his concerns spilled out. "Well, here's the thing. In the Book of Revelations there is a section about the 'Mother of Harlots.' She is evil and is a key indicator of end times. The author describes her as wearing scarlet and purple while being adorned with gold, precious stones and pearls."

He waved his arm slowly up and down highlighting her outfit. "Take a look in the mirror. To a certain segment of the population you look like a blinking neon light saying 'I'm the Harlot, and the end is here.' Combine that with your sexual orientation and ...." He didn't finish the sentence. "Let's just say I don't think that would be helpful to you, or the country."

Her face fell, softening her striking features. "Thank you, Dallas. Thank you for helping me avoid a self-inflicted setback. That would have gone terribly wrong and I wouldn't have even known why until it was too late."

She now looked at him with appreciation. "Any advice on what I should wear?"

His cheeks reddened as he answered. "Go with something white. A bride of Christ motif might not help, but it certainly won't do any damage."

Laughing, she put her hand to her head. "It's hard enough being a woman in this job, and now I have to consult the clergy for wardrobe advice!"

Chapter Twenty

Sunday Noon Washington D.C.

Darla put the final make-up touches on President Banister before her second television address in fifteen hours. "I like the summer white, very sophisticated for a noon appearance."

The president laughed. "Yes, Darla. I'm now getting divine guidance on my wardrobe choices. Who could have foreseen that?"

Darla forced a smile, apparently unsure what the president meant about divine guidance, then looked into the mirror, locking eyes with her sole client. "What do you think?"

Abby turned her head right, then left as she assessed her reflection, silently noting how well Darla had concealed the wrinkles that had become more prominent in the past year. "Fabulous as always Darla. You're really amazing."

She pulled the smock away in one swift motion, freeing the president. "Break a leg, ma'am."

President Banister smiled as she stood and out of habit smoothed the front of her embroidered white suit jacket. "Thanks, Darla. I'll take all the well wishes that I can get."

The stylist collected her brushes and make-up as Abby quickly made her way into the Oval Office, seating herself behind the Resolute desk. "How are we on time?"

The director glanced at the digital clock near her chair. "We're a few minutes after noon, but no need to rush. The network talking heads have plenty of material to fill the gap."

Getting comfortable behind the desk, the president repeated the same pre-address process that she had used last night. After rereading her paper copy of her prepared remarks, she again removed her glasses and placed them, along with the script, into the middle drawer of the iconic desk. Her first few sentences had loaded onto the teleprompter, awaiting her ready. Once again, she closed her eyes and prayed silently. *Lord, it's me again...Abby. Twice in two days.... how about that? It surprises me, too. I know that I have seriously questioned Your place in my life, and I know that You don't owe me anything. Maybe I don't even have a right to ask, but my people... Your people... are scared. I pray that You might bless my words, not for me but for them, and that they will be a comfort to the citizens of the United States. Thank You for hearing my plea and considering my sincere appeal. Amen.*

Opening her eyes, she looked again at the teleprompter and mouthed her first few words silently. She then turned to the director. "Ready when you are."

The director did her final check of camera, prompter, lighting and sound. "All right everyone, here we go in five-four-three-two-one."

Looking directly into the camera, the president began. "Good afternoon, my fellow Americans. Twenty-four hours ago, a series of events began to unfold that have changed how we see our place and future in this world, and indeed perhaps our place and future in the cosmic order of the universe. We all witnessed a global communication claiming that God was coming to Earth, specifically to New York City, and would be here today. Yesterday we also witnessed the arrival of a massive cloud, and today we have seen what can only be described as an otherworldly scene at the UN. We now know with certainty that we are not alone in the universe. Those events alone would mark this weekend as the most momentous in human history, but more news has arrived today that competes with those headlines."

She paused for a moment, adding drama and tension. "As most of you have probably heard, this morning we learned new, and equally compelling news. Astronomers at the Keck Observatory in Hawaii identified a previously unknown object heading toward Earth. The Jansky-Haskell asteroid is expected to reach our planet in two weeks with the potential to destroy most of the life on our planet."

Letting that news sink in, the president took in a deep breath before continuing. "I come before you today to tell you about this administration's plans and commitment to you, the citizens of this great country. First of all, I want to acknowledge the prospect, perhaps even the probability that these two events are connected. While there is not complete agreement among religious leaders, biblical scholars with whom we have consulted believe that there is a good chance that this is God arriving on Earth and that the asteroid is related to his arrival. The event at the UN this evening will surely shed more light on this possibility."

Once again, she paused, the weight of her words stealing her breath. Summoning all of her reserve strength, her shoulders pushed back and she continued with steely eyed determination. "Even with these events happening in the space of just one day, I want you to know that your government is responding, not standing idly by, waiting. This evening I will be leading the American contingent to the UN event to ascertain first hand, the nature and intentions of our other worldly visitors. The outcome of that meeting will clarify the scope and direction of our next steps. Preliminary plans are being discussed now on our national response, and I ask your patience and understanding as we finalize our actions."

Leaning forward with resolve, her violet eyes narrowed, and she only exaggerated a little. "I can also report that NASA has planned for the possibility of an asteroid like this threatening Earth, and that there are strategies to prevent the most devastating effects. I want to be clear, there is a plan to save our planet and our scientists are confident that we can achieve success. The plan will require utilizing new technologies and unprecedented global cooperation. With that said, this administration is ready and committed to doing everything we can do to provide for your safety, and when accomplished, has the promise of uniting the planet in a way never before seen in the history of mankind."

After laying out the situation and the administration's overall position, the president relaxed a bit. Now it was time to again ask for a commitment. "The truth is that this is a very scary time. There is a possibility that these will be the last two weeks of our existence. We have solid plans to prevent that outcome, but it could happen. What I am asking now is, how do you want to spend those next two weeks? For many the initial reaction will be to resign themselves to their fate and turn inward, or to your social or religious communities. I understand that reaction, it's perfectly normal. It promises comfort in the most trying of times."

A reassuring smile softened her visage. "But I ask, do you want to spend these last two weeks in New York City, or Miami, or New Orleans without electricity for air-conditioning or lights? Do you want to spend these next two weeks in Cincinnati, or Denver or Seattle without food on grocery shelves? I don't think that you want that for yourself or for your family, so I am asking each of you again, as I did last night, please continue to go to your jobs. If you want to spend time in worship or community, please do so, but balance it with your responsibilities to your family, to your greater community, to your nation."

She turned her head slightly and her short black hair caught a glint of light, or perhaps it was one of the many recently emerging silver hairs. "I close with this. In Luke, the Bible says 'Do unto others as you would have them do unto you.' I used to think of this golden rule as something to guide me in individual relationships. I treat you well, because that's how I want to be treated. But in today's situation, I think of it in greater terms. Let's say that your child needs emergency surgery, you want the hospital to be open, doctors and nurses ready to swing into action. And what about the next accident on the freeway? We need the ambulance and EMTs, but we also need the tow truck and driver to haul away the wreckage. In today's interconnected world, everyone counts on everyone else to keep the whole enterprise running. I'm not asking anyone to forsake their faith, or to ignore these monumental events. I'm simply asking everyone to consider their responsibility to be there for their neighbors."

She paused one last time. "Finally, I want to again acknowledge that this is a time like none other in human history. In these difficult days, I ask that each of you shine, show your best to others. Live like heroes in your neighborhood. And above all, may God bless each of you, and may God bless America."

Chapter Twenty-One

Sunday 7:00 A.M. Hawaii / 1:00 P.M. Washington D.C.

Shortly before dawn, security notified Dr. Haskell and Wade of a gathering pack of TV and print journalists forming at the main gate of the Keck Observatory. Wade peeked out of one of the office windows, then turned back toward Qu. "I'm so glad that you're here. I wouldn't want to face them alone."

Dr. Haskell joked. "Hey, I'm not exactly chopped liver. I'll be there with you. I wouldn't miss it for the world."

Qu blushed. "I don't have any business going out there with you two. I'm just here for emotional support. And besides, I'm still in my show outfit. Neon spandex is not exactly morning wear for most people."

Wade laughed. "You look great to me, and besides, you nailed it, I'm happy because you are here for support." He then put his arm around the petite woman. "And if I had thought about it for just a minute, I would have named the asteroid after you."

She sounded aghast. "Thank God you didn't! I don't want to be like women named Katrina, always associated with a killer hurricane. Thanks for the thought, really, but no thanks."

He laughed then tapped Haskell on the shoulder. "I'm ready when you are. I could use some sleep and that won't happen until we get past them."

Haskell nodded and took a first step toward the door. "I'm going to speak first. After all, I do represent the entire facility."

"I'm all for that. In fact, I hope that I don't have to say a word."

Together, the trio advanced down the driveway, then through the gate. Boom microphones swooped down toward them and cameras competed for best angles. Questions from the crowd of journalists drowned each other out, until Dr. Haskell took control. "Thank you all for being here this morning. I have prepared a few remarks and then we'll take some questions."

The din from the assembled scrum of reporters subsided as the senior scientist stepped forward. "Good morning. My name is Dr. Robert Haskell, lead astronomer here at the Keck Observatory. Last night this facility identified an asteroid which had not previously been observed. Fellow astronomers in both China and Chile have since confirmed that the asteroid is on course to impact Earth in fourteen days. This discovery was led by fellow astronomer, Wade Jansky. He's one of our promising young scientists who has been researching an area of space which previously had shown very little activity. It's because of his curiosity and insistence that we're all here today. Now, we'll take a few questions."

Once again, questions rushed toward them like an ocean wave crashing on a white sand beach. Haskell pointed to the female reporter with the loudest voice. "You, there in the front.

She held a microphone close as she spoke. "Melissa Starkly for NNC. This is for Dr. Jansky. Why did you decide to look in that part of space?"

Shyly, Wade stepped forward. "Uh, just to set the record straight, I'm still working on my doctorate. So just call me Wade, okay? Sooo... the short answer to that question is that my mother inspired me to use Bible verses and convert them into outer space coordinates. I took a verse and plugged it into my home telescope and eventually got a suspicious reading."

Wade's cheeks flushed as he continued the sanitized version of the story. "Dr. Haskell supported my strong hunch, and together we were able to confirm the asteroid."

He stepped back in line with Dr. Haskell and Qu as more questions were shouted. Haskell identified the next questioner. "You, with the CBN hat."

"Alvin Hayes reporting for CBN. Wade, now that we've heard how you got your coordinates, do you think that your discovery is associated with the Judgment Day event in New York City? Is this how God is going to destroy the world?"

Exasperated, Wade flung his arms out. "Come on. How the hell should I know? We're astronomers, doing science. Sure, I played around with some funky algorithms on my spare time and got a lucky hit. But how would that make me qualified to make that kind of link? I'm just glad we found it and at least have a chance to do something about it. That's all."

More questions were flung like mud toward them. Dr. Haskell again took control. "One final question, this time from a local reporter. In the back, with KHNL. What's your question?"

"Alani Kalami reporting. This question is for both of you. What do you think the odds are that we'll be able to destroy or alter the course of the asteroid?"

Wade quickly looked toward Dr. Haskell, hoping he would take this one.

Dr. Haskell lowered his head, seeming tempted to dismiss the question, but after a few seconds he looked up and locked eyes with the reporter. "Let me be clear, that question is outside of my specialty, so the answer that I give is purely speculative. I don't know what plans NASA and other agencies around the world have prepared for an event like this. What I do know is that this has never been attempted, so I'm guessing that the odds would be tough, but not impossible. Anything to add, Wade?"

Flustered, Wade stepped forward. "No... I mean, I' don't have anything other than what Dr. Haskell just said."

The cameras were all focused on him when inspiration hit. Knowing full well the likelihood that this might be the last two weeks of the world, he threw caution and academic decorum to the wind. His face brightened and he reached back for Qu's hand, pulling her up beside. "I do have one other thing to add. This is my special friend, Quinn Kahale and she's one of the best rising singers in the world. And just like I discovered the Jansky-Haskell asteroid, you should discover her on YouTube or catch a live set tonight at the Riptide. You're going to love her music, like I do."

A shocked Qu blushed and held tightly to Wade's hand. Then she waved to the cameras before looking up into Wade's ocean blue eyes. She mouthed silently, "You sure know how to rock a girl's world."

Chapter Twenty-Two

Sunday 4:00 P.M. New York

Air Force One taxied to a stop on a secure section of JFK airport tarmac. President Banister caught a glimpse out her window of the Air China jet already parked in the adjoining space. "Invite the Chinese over and let me know as soon as the Russians arrive."

As if on cue, the Russian plane appeared, taxiing toward the other two parked flying presidential offices. She stood from her plush cabin seat and headed toward the large conference table in the mid-section of the aircraft. Stopping at the next row, she offered a hand to Secretary of State, Effie Louise. "Looks like the gang's all here. How much vodka do you think Noskov drank on the trip over?"

Effie accepted the assist in standing and then began her cane-aided stroll through the plane. "Mmm, Mmm, that man sure loves his booze." She laughed loudly, "He kissed my cheeks at that Vienna meeting and I swear it burned my skin."

Dallas had taken the seat to the left of the head of the table and Effie moved to the right. Their assigned Secret Service Agent had discreetly found a seat near the front where he could surveil the entire meeting area. Soon, both foreign delegations arrived and began mingling around the table.

As predicted, Maxim Noskov gave sloppy welcome kisses on the cheeks of all the dignitaries. He even planted a wet one right on Dallas' lips, causing the tightly wound religious scholar to blush brightly. Abby smiled at the same sex introduction from the tipsy Russian and its impact on her ex. It seemed the appropriate time to call the meeting to order. "Distinguished leaders and guests, welcome to New York. I wish we were meeting under more joyful circumstances. Please, everyone, take a seat."

The delegations self-sorted with the Chinese on the right and Russians on the left and Abby got down to business. "Yesterday, everyone's day was interrupted by the simultaneous global announcement of the imminent arrival of what may be God."

General Hu gave an audible, snarling, "Harrumph."

Abby avoided making eye contact with the gruff general and continued opening remarks. "As we all learned this morning, a potentially devastating asteroid was discovered on a direct path toward our planet. While each of our governments and citizens may have differing thoughts on the validity and meaning of the God question, there can be no doubt that we must work together if we are going to have any hope of saving our world from that massive inbound object."

President Noskov leaned over to his Minister of Defense and whispered, louder than he probably realized. "Here come the unicorns and rainbows."

The comment reached Abby's ears, but she ignored it. "I've asked all of you here today so that we can hopefully pledge mutual assistance to each other in an all-out effort to avoid the potential of destruction of most life on our world. The future of mankind depends on our powerful nations working together. The United States is prepared to coordinate a joint effort, but it will take significant contributions of ideas and resources from all of us to even give us a chance of success. I'll pause here and ask that President Zhou and President Noskov add their introductory comments."

President Zhou remained seated as he removed his glasses and placed them perfectly square on the leather portfolio binder that he had brought onboard. He looked first at Abby, then toward Maxim. "Madam President, Mr. President. China stands ready to work together to defend our planet from this natural disaster. When our Chang'e 4 robotic lander touched down on the dark side of the moon in 2019, we clearly demonstrated our advanced space capabilities. While certain cutting-edge technological achievements may remain off limits, China can be counted on as an equal partner in this effort.

We could scarcely care whether this is a god or not, but we are deeply committed to saving our one-sixth of the population living on Earth today."

The Chinese response was exactly as Abby had expected and she smiled approvingly. "The United States is pleased to be joined by The Peoples Republic of China as an equal partner in this vital endeavor."

She shot a spiked look toward the Russian leader. "President Noskov, we look forward to hearing your comments regarding this serious situation."

The bald world leader stood and spoke in a voice too loud for an enclosed room of this size, His comments aimed at Abby. "The world might end and this is one time that you are not trying to blame Russia." His words slurred a little as he continued. "I guess we can call that some progress, eh Madam President?"

He glanced at his Chinese counterpart. "Unlike you, comrade, Russia does not feel like an equal partner. Time after time Russia has been singled out for sanctions and we continue to have missiles directed towards us."

He again directed his gaze toward President Banister. "If Russia is to join in some kind of joint effort to perhaps short circuit God's will, or the will of some alien, then changes must be made to our future relationship. Do you understand, Madam President?"

The hairs on the back of Abby's neck stood. As she feared, she was getting the drunken version of Maxim Noskov. Worst of all, it was the belligerent drunken version. "I hardly think this is the time for negotiation, Mr. President. We have one world, Maxim, and if we don't work together, there will be no future relationship. For that matter, perhaps no future at all. We could really use your help, and you have my commitment to work together to relieve sanctions as soon as this is over. But we only have two weeks to take action or it won't matter. I ask again that you join us to save the planet."

Noskov's face reddened and he roared. "That's exactly the kind of drivel I expect to hear from Americans, especially from a dyke bitch like you. You in the West always treat us like shit and then come crawling back when you're in trouble. That's what will happen this time as well. When you realize how much you will need our heavy lift capacity you'll be groveling on your knees. Then you'll gladly trade sanctions relief and territory for our help. Mark my words, you'll see."

President Zhou sat back and clasped his hands, resting them on his portfolio binder, seeming to prepare for the fireworks to follow.

Abby stood and faced the heavy breathing Slav. "How dare you talk to me like that, Maxim! You don't have to like me or how I live my life, but you damned well better respect me! You think these sanctions bite? Just wait and see what the full wrath of the United States feels like should we make it out of this jam. And then you go and try to use this disaster as blackmail leverage? What a jackass! If you don't want to be part of the solution, then please leave... now. The era of stone age dictators is over. Take your Neanderthal brain and go back to your frozen homeland."

The Russian remained standing and spoke to his delegation. "See, arrogance and insults, as usual. It's us against the rest of the world, like always. If this is God, He may condemn them to hell tonight because of their sins. We're leaving this den of vipers. Wait and see, they'll come crawling back, just like always."

The Russian delegation stood and followed their hot-headed leader off of the plane, leaving the American and Chinese teams bewildered. Abby sat as she spoke to her remaining counterpart. "That could have gone better."

President Zhou allowed a small smile. "Let's see how this evening goes. Perhaps a talk from his god and a sober tomorrow might yet change his mind. If not, then China and America will work together. Our advanced capabilities can achieve success. Then we will become the only two superpowers of this world and Russia will be stuck with HIM as their leader."

With her pulse rate returning to near normal, Abby responded, "I hope that you're right, Mr. President. And I also hope that karma bites him in the ass."

Chapter Twenty-Three

Sunday 6:00 P.M. New York

A throng of paparazzi snapped pictures from a secure distance as each four-person national delegation walked through the main entrance to the UN. Inside, identical androgynous purple beings, dressed in matching white-tie tuxes, greeted each group with a visual scan. Their eyes started at the top of each guest's head and continued without blinking until their gaze reached the floor. Since no traditional security devices were to be seen, Abby assumed that this was their way of checking for weapons and since their Secret Service Agent wasn't stopped, then either they missed his carbon-based arms, or more likely they considered them as one would a child's pop gun, amusing but useless.

After the presumed search, each nation's attendees were escorted to their individual country desk by a different tuxedo clad being. The president commented on their escort's look. "Their lavender skin tone might take some getting used to, but I just love that bob. The curl in front gives it style and sass. Maybe I'll try it."

Only Effie commented as both the Secret Service Agent and Dallas looked forward stiffly. "It's too short for my taste, ma'am, but I can see it on you. I'll bet that cut will be on the next cover of *Vogue*. It's just darling."

The agent walked ahead of the group and gasped as he entered the General Assembly Hall. He regained his composure quickly, but as Dallas caught first sight of the inside of the great hall, a gasp wasn't sufficient. "Hallelujah! Praise be to God!"

Following closely, Effie was nearly speechless and grabbed the president's arm to stabilize herself. "Ma'am, they're flying!"

Abby steadied her friend and counselor. "Magnificent!"

Outside, the alien beings flew with what seemed to be ultra-high-tech jet packs, but inside was a different story. Here they witnessed what looked like the angels described in the Bible, human-like beings with wings protruding from their shoulders. And they flew effortlessly, sometimes flapping their wings to gain speed or altitude and sometimes gliding around the stage, with an occasional foray through the large hall, above the invited attendees.

Turning her head as she walked, the president attempted to take everything in when something new caught her eye at center stage. "What do you think is behind the curtain?"

Dallas stopped in his tracks. "Good Lord! Could it be?" Shocked, his voice now trembled and rose and for the first time he slipped, calling her by her name instead of the more respectful ma'am, or Madam President. "Abby, it might be the Ark of the Covenant!"

Their escort continued leading them to their assigned desk halfway back from the stage. They followed with eyes dancing from one incredible sight to the next. Once seated, they had time to soak in the entire panorama and inspect the obscured object on stage. Dallas could barely make out what appeared to be a raised platform supporting a large box. What looked like poles for carrying the object remained attached and seemed to stick out on each end. "This is amazing! I never dreamed that I would ever see angels on Earth... much less the Ark of the Covenant! It's supposed to have been lost to history, or in heaven, and yet here it is, apparently. Wow, I can't believe my eyes!"

Abby nudged him. "It's been a while since I've studied the Bible, or watched *Indiana Jones* for that matter. How about a refresher?"

His academic side quickly overcame his excitement at witnessing this spectacle first hand. "Sure, of course. In the Old Testament, the Ark of the Covenant represented God living among his people. It's a wooden box covered in gold. Inside are supposed to be the two original stone ten commandment tablets. Some accounts say that there is also a golden jar of manna and Aaron's staff from their exodus from Egypt. And see the outlines of two the angel like beings on the lid? They're called cherubim. God is said to appear, or be seated above them whenever he wishes to speak to either the high priests or directly to his people. Everything is supposed to be covered or veiled because for human eyes to look directly upon it is said to invite immediate death. It's also mentioned briefly in the Book of Revelations, so it all fits. Amazing!"

Effie leaned in. "So, I take it that you're leaning even stronger toward the God theory, that this is the real deal?"

"Absolutely. Having it all happen here at the UN, in New York doesn't exactly mesh with how the Bible foretold, but yes. I'm definitely leaning even more that way." Even in his excitement he hedged. "I still reserve my final Judgment until after we see what happens next."

Taking her eyes away from the flying angels and possible Ark of the Covenant for just a moment, the president glanced around at the audience and pointed several rows ahead. "Look, Pope Urban is here. Can't wait to hear what he has to say about all of this. And over there, Maxim Noskov's sitting as straight as a board. It's either the fear of God, or he's sobered up. Hopefully that's a good sign."

Without warning, massive elevators on each side of the Ark of the Covenant began lifting a choir, the one last seen on the Gabriel video yesterday. They again wore billowing white robes which dramatically highlighted their baby blue skin. Dallas spoke reverently as they sang. "I've been to a lot of worship services, but I've never experienced anything like this. I can't understand a word, but I feel so warm inside. Incredible..."

The wings of the angels now synchronized to the beat of the music making it a hypnotic sensory experience. As the song progressed, not even a whisper could be heard among the illustrious attendees. All seemed captivated.

When the song ended, Gabriel walked to center stage in front of the columned veil. "Welcome distinguished leaders, guests, and viewers world-wide. I am Gabriel, messenger for the One Eternal God, Creator of the Heavens and Earth, Lord and Ruler of all. Tonight, you will hear directly from the great I Am, speaking to the hearts and minds of His creation on this world. And as you will hear, his love is infinite. Now let us worship in song once more before his message."

With that pronouncement, the choir began again with another distinctly different, but equally mesmerizing hymn, and once again the audience remained transfixed, as if under a spell. When the music finished, the house lights went dim, almost obscuring the Ark of the Covenant through the veil.

A few seconds later a bluish white orb began to glow above the ancient relic until the entire auditorium was engulfed in a sea of all-consuming light. A single whispered syllable escaped Abby's lips as she raised her hand to partially shade her eyes. "Wow."

Her eyes quickly adjusted as a deep authoritative voice filled the large auditorium from corner to corner, and everywhere in between. The spoken words arrived with such force that she felt physically pushed back in her seat. "Greetings, My children of Earth. I have been called by many names since your species became the dominant life force on this world. I am called Yahweh, Vishnu, God and Allah, to name just a few. I claim these names and all others. In addition, many holy men and women inspired by Me have also walked among you. Abraham, Moses, Jesus, Mary, Muhammad, Buddha, Confucius and Joan of Arc all trod this Earth representing some of the best examples of holiness that mankind could offer. In all of them and many, many more I am well pleased. In fact, one of them sits beside me in heaven. In their words and deeds, they demonstrated that this species could rise above its self-destructive and outright hostile tendencies towards one another, and even unto the planet itself. And throughout your history, tens of millions of your brothers and sisters have practiced kindness and grace toward their fellow man. Their examples have been an inspiration to many, and their spirit and works have been noted."

The disembodied voice paused for a moment, and Abby sensed a change in tone immediately as the address resumed. "Yet, dear children, despite these Godly teachings and physical examples of holiness, mankind has continued its ever-increasing spiral of warfare. You have exhibited a consistent refusal to work together to care for the common good of one another. It has been far more common to see armies clash, with both claiming that I am on their side, than see armies allied to feed the hungry and clothe the poor. My children, it did not have to be this way."

Abby realized that she had not even blinked since the voice began speaking and she took a moment during this small stoppage to force herself to do so. He continued. "Therefore, it is with a loving, yet heavy heart, that I make my physical reappearance on this planet. As your scientists have confirmed, an object that has been in existence for millions of years is heading for Earth. With a word, or a thought, I could redirect or destroy it."

Again, He paused before continuing with pain seeming to infuse His next comment. "But based on your species words and actions, as well as your inclinations for continued self-harm, I have elected to allow the object to continue on its path, just as I allowed a similar object to continue on its path millions of years ago."

She could feel her heart in her throat and a burning tear winding its way down her cheek as He continued. "My children, I will not forsake you at that hour. I will be right here, ready to receive your souls into my very being, just as I have received your ancestors. You will finally be able to exist in the never-ending peace and love of your Creator. All people are my people, and all will experience oneness with me. As a sign of My love for all, I will be moving My temporary encampment to cities around the world so that many may witness their Creator's presence firsthand."

A wave of different emotions rushed over her like a tsunami churning everything in its path. Deep feelings of acceptance, acceptance of her, and of everyone by this being claiming to be God. Feelings of hope, hope in an eternal life. And the warm embrace of love, a perfect love.

Yet these feelings wrestled with equally powerful conflicting emotions. Feelings of rejection of continued life for mankind as a species. Feelings of depression at realizing that she and everyone else could have done more for their fellow man and perhaps entirely avoided this fate. And a searing loneliness at realizing the God that so many prayed to for help would turn his back on efforts to save this world that He claimed to have created.

She gasped for breath, understanding that He had made it clear that He loved them, yet equally clear they would be on their own should they chose to try to deflect or destroy the asteroid. The conflicting reactions triggered a torrent of tears that now ran freely down her face. Despite the sobs she remained transfixed, unable to avert her gaze as the disembodied voice continued. "Fear not, my children, I will wrap you in my arms and you will know complete fulfillment and bliss in Me. Until that moment arrives, care for one another in love and experience a small measure of peace here on Earth."

The brilliant light increased in intensity even more until it felt as if it were shining through her body. His voice now shook the foundations of the building. "Please, My children, understand that love conquers all... and that I love each of you... in this moment... and for eternity."

Slowly the glow above The Ark of the Covenant began to fade and the choir began singing again. The crescendo and nadir of the encounter with God, or whatever being this was, left Abby physically and emotionally drained. Glancing toward Effie, Dallas, and the Secret Service Agent, she sensed the same as they all sat in muted silence. When the angels finished their second song, Gabriel reappeared onstage. "His Holiness has expressed his love for each and every one of you here tonight, and to all viewing around the world. And, as you've just heard, we'll be traveling around the world to demonstrate His love for all peoples. Tomorrow, we'll be moving to Moscow and after that, Beijing. I'll be posting future stops soon. As the choir prepares to sing one last song, I send God's blessings. All shall soon be one."

Chapter Twenty – Four

Sunday 8:30 P.M. New York

The hard news anchors of CBN had spent most of the day talking about the discovery of the Jansky-Haskell asteroid, and the past couple of hours dissecting what happened at the UN. Now it was the turn of the opinion side of the network to earn their advertising dollars. Larry fidgeted like a horse in the starting gate, anxious to get back on air during this historic time. Finally, the countdown finished and his show was again front and center in American homes. His pent-up energy nearly overpowered his opening words. "Welcome back to coverage of Judgment Day!"

Settling a bit, he launched into his opening monologue. "This morning we were weighing the existential question of the existence of God. Was this his return to Earth, or an alien first contact? Was this the beginning of the end of the world? It was all very esoteric, with opinions divided across the board."

He turned toward camera two. "Now, less than twelve hours later, we have new facts and entirely new questions. The phrase 'Jansky-Haskell asteroid' has entered our vocabulary, signifying impending doom. The world has heard, and seen a declaration of both love and condemnation from what may very well be God. Positions are being taken on many sides by faith leaders, and by every man, woman and child in the world. To help us make sense of it all we welcome back our panelist, representing a diverse cross section of opinion."

Larry turned first to his guests on set. "Once again, I'm joined by Pastor Jacob Shadwell and Rabbi Solomon Feldman here in studio. Gentlemen, it's been quite a day, hasn't it?

Rabbi Feldman spoke first, again sporting his beautiful prayer shawl. "It's been an emotional day for me. I hope my words can convey the range of thoughts and feelings that I've experienced. It's a truly remarkable time."

Pastor Shadwell was terser in his opening remarks. "Remarkable? That's the word that you use to describe the arrival of the Antichrist?"

Larry flinched at the controversial statement, then immediately understood that it could be the line that would catapult the show to new ratings highs. He bought himself time to frame it for maximum effect. "Those are strong words, pastor. Hold that thought and I'll come back to you after we welcome all of tonight's panelists."

He now turned again toward camera one. "From San Francisco we're joined by Guru Baba Mashni. Welcome, Guru Mashni, to Judgment Day coverage. I look forward to hearing your thoughts on today's events."

Tonight, the effervescent Hindu teacher wore an almost glowing golden threaded Kurta, with onyx buttons going halfway down his chest. "Once again, it is my pleasure to be your guest at such an auspicious time."

Smiling now, Larry continued the intros. "Glad to have you, Guru Mashni." He now turned to camera two to welcome the final panelist. "And from Washington DC, we welcome Dr. Son Young Kim. Thank you for joining us again tonight, Dr. Kim."

The staid academic had again stepped up her TV image. Gone was the gray cardigan sweater from the previous appearances. Tonight her updated hair style from the previous broadcast complemented a slimming burgundy colored suit over a crisp white blouse. "Always my pleasure, Larry. And thanks for including me in such a diverse panel of experts."

With introductions complete, Larry quickly turned to his reliable bomb thrower. "Pastor Shadwell, you used the term 'Antichrist' in your introduction. That's a very loaded word. Would you care to explain?"

Larry sat back, knowing that the ratings meter would crank even higher as soon as the pastor opened his mouth.

Pastor Shadwell raised his index finger and repeatedly jabbed it toward the camera as he spoke as he spoke. "That's right, Larry. Like I said earlier today, I believe that the inerrancy of God's word. To me and millions of other Christians, what we heard from the UN tonight was in some ways inspirational, but was in no way consistent with God's holy word. Plain and simple, it was heresy. Therefore, if what we heard was heresy, how does God's word explain it?"

He held a worn black King James version Bible aloft in his right hand as he continued. "In the Book of First John, chapter two, verse eighteen, it is made clear. 'Little children, it is the last time: and as ye have heard that Antichrist shall come.' With that so-called god speech tonight, we have confirmation of God's word. The Antichrist is trying to confuse and deceive God's people, just as foretold. Praise be to the one true God!"

Larry strained to contain his excitement at the fiery start to the segment. "That's a stance that I'm sure will be controversial, pastor. I mean, that voice spoke of Jesus, and becoming one with our Creator. That sounds an awful lot like my admittedly limited understanding of Christian views. How do words like that make this the Antichrist?"

"Come on Larry! Open your eyes, and your heart. As I have said before, Christianity teaches that the only way to salvation is through acceptance of Jesus Christ as Lord and Savior. Christ's sacrifice brought grace to those who accept him as their Lord. All others will perish in Hell. That's the foundation of our faith! And speaking of Hell, I didn't hear a word about that, did you? All I heard was some new-age mumbo jumbo. And that's exactly what the Antichrist would say to confuse and lead Christians astray. It's apostasy for any Christian to believe what we heard tonight!"

Larry probed, "Do you think that you speak for all, or even the majority of Christians?"

His sour mood turned even more dour. "Unfortunately, I don't think so. The Bible is such a source of truth. Second Thessalonians chapter two, verses three and four say 'Let no man deceive you by any means: for that day shall not come, except there come a falling away first, and that man of sin be revealed, the son of perdition. Who opposeth and exalteth himself above all that is called God, or that is worshiped; so that he as God sitteth in the temple of God, shewing himself that he is God.' Larry, it's as plain as the nose on my face. The Antichrist is here and is pretending to be God, just as the Bible predicted, and millions of Christians will believe the lie. Only the faithful remnant will truly be saved."

Larry feigned disbelief, but was really happy that the outspoken pastor set the tone. "That was truly unexpected, pastor. Let's see how our other panelists received the message. Let's go next to the other side of the spectrum. Dr. Kim, as the self-described atheist on the panel, what did you think of the message? Do you think this is God?"

Dr. Kim was her consistently dry self. "It was quite the show, wasn't it? We finally saw what looked like angels and heard some terrific music. If I had ever heard of a church or religious group that believed in evolution and spoke so persuasively against war and for taking care of our fellow man, then I might not be an atheist today. But none of that really matters does it? A killer asteroid is heading this way, and that so-called god, the one who speaks of peace and love, says we're on our own. He says he created this world and now he's just going to let it be destroyed? What kind of just god does that? So, while I have different reasons for my beliefs, I'm with Pastor Shadwell, this isn't god."

Larry pushed. "So, if this isn't god, then why would an alien civilization even bother to show up now, just as we might all be wiped from the face of our planet?"

She threw her hands in the air. "I have no idea, Larry. I've been trying to figure that one out. All I know is that a just god wouldn't destroy his creation, would he? So, if it isn't god, then it's something else. I just need more data to say exactly what that might be."

"So, we have two of our panel in the 'No' camp. Let's go to the west coast. Guru Mashni, you saw the same broadcast as Pastor Shadwell and Dr. Kim. When we last spoke, you had doubts. Where do you stand on the question today? Is this God or not?"

Joy infused his words. "It was the most glorious thing that I have ever seen! I only wish that I could have witnessed it with my own eyes. Vishnu speaking directly to me... to everyone on the planet. How can this be anything except the greatest moment... ever! It was almost complete nirvana."

Larry smiled broadly. "I can feel your happiness from three thousand miles away. Let me ask, why are you so confident, and why did you use the name Vishnu instead of God?"

Guru Baba Mashni radiated positivity. "Let's take the easy part first. I say Vishnu, because during the telecast He said that was one of His names. I choose to use that name today because it is of my culture, and according to His own words, any of His names are correct. In regards to why I am so confident, I remind our viewers that Hindu end time beliefs points toward ultimate singularity, the state in which all are one. To be clear, the Puranas foresaw nothing like what we all witness tonight, but the overarching message rings true. The end of this Yuga is nearly here and we will all become one in Vishnu. After that, a new cycle should begin."

"Very interesting, Guru Mashni. And the asteroid? Does that fit with Hindu prophesy?"

The Hindu leader basked in the question. "I'm happy to say that it does. The Puranas say 'In the year named 'Subhakriti' in the month of November a 'Dhumaketu', that's a comet in English, would be sighted in the southern region, due to which innumerable lives would be destroyed.' While it's not November, the words recorded thousands of years ago are about to be fulfilled."

"The score now stands at two against this being God, and one saying, yes." The host grinned, silently reveling in the panel discord. He next turned to his other in-studio guest. "Rabbi Feldman, where do you come down on this ultimate question. Is this God or not?"

The Jewish leader sat in silence for a few moments before answering. "This has not been an easy decision for me, Larry. And I want to be very clear, I'm in no way speaking for all Jews, I'm only speaking for myself. In fact, I'm sure that other Jews will feel completely justified in taking the opposite view."

Once again, Larry feigned compassion. "I understand, rabbi. Today's events are causing the same kinds of discussions and divisions across the globe. But for you, in this moment, what do you believe?"

A deep breath momentarily expanded the gorgeous prayer shawl draped over his shoulders. "Part of my decision, I'm sure, is influenced by seeing the cloud and the transformation of the UN building with my own eyes. Those signs are impossible to discount or deny. They are beautiful and clearly not of this world."

He paused as the importance of the decision weighed on him. "On the other hand, many of the words from tonight were foreign to me. They were not in alignment with Torah or the Talmud. They make me ask myself, 'How can this be God?' It is not an easy decision for me, not easy at all."

His personal decision-making process played out live. "And yet... and yet that message of love. I can't get it out of my mind. The message of God calling all of his children home to his bosom rings so clear to my soul. He loves us, and wants all of us to reside with him, forever. As I understand our teachings, this is the ultimate message of God to his creation. So, even though the end of the world is not happening in any way like I expected, I do believe that this is God calling us home."

"And the comet. Does the Torah or Talmud speak to that?"

"As with so many other things connected with these events, there are matches, near matches and complete misses with our Holy Scriptures. The prophet Joel said 'Alas for that day! For the day of the Lord is near; it will come like destruction from the Almighty.' Could that be a description of Jansky-Haskell? Maybe? I don't know."

Again, Larry went to his scoreboard analogy. "Our panel of religious experts are split. Two say no, this is not God, and two say, yes, it is God."

He was about to go back to each panelist again for expanded comments when Ken Garner spoke into his earpiece. The skillful host adeptly changed course. "Thanks again for the analysis from our distinguished panel. I understand that there is breaking news outside the UN building. For now, we'll be going to Carmen Candiotti with live coverage of an announcement from Pope Urban the Ninth. Please join me back here tomorrow for continuing coverage of Judgment Day."

Chapter Twenty-Five

Sunday 9:00 P.M. Washington D.C.

Abby and the presidential entourage that had traveled to New York went straight to the Situation Room upon arrival at the White House. Chief of Staff Cliff Cyrus brought a copy of the statement that the communications team had put together after the God speech. "This is the final version based on what we discussed, ma'am. We've added your comments about another address to the nation tomorrow evening."

"Thanks, Cliff. I would like to speak to the country tonight, but there's still so much up in the air that it might do more harm than good. This lets everyone know that their government is at work, and hopefully we'll have more details tomorrow. Get it out."

Cliff stepped away and Abby now faced her full cabinet for the first time since the crisis began. "Hello everyone. Welcome to the Sunday night emergency meeting to discuss the end of the world."

A mixture of wry smiles and looks of sheer terror reflected back at her introduction. "While each department of the government is equal, in this time of national emergency I've kept a tight circle to respond as fast as possible under rapidly changing circumstances. Now that we've heard the pronouncement from the UN this evening, we're clearly transitioning into a new phase of the crisis. I want to keep that tight circle for daily reporting, but we're going to need everyone working together to keep our country functioning, and give us the best shot at avoiding planetary destruction."

She looked over at her Secretary of Commerce, Sandra Eccles. "Sandy, I won't need a daily briefing on banking deregulation, but if our monetary system becomes stressed, I'm going to need you working hand in hand with Tru over in Homeland. Got it?"

"Yes ma'am. Absolutely."

She pointed to Rick Davis. "Same for Veterans Affairs. If we need an emergency call up, you're to work with Brax over at Defense."

He answered as quickly as Sandy. "Yes, ma'am. Of course."

She sat down with a tired sigh. "All right then, let's do an update and debrief since our get together this morning, get everyone up to speed. Dallas, you start. Did we all just experience God?"

Dallas sat tall, relishing his role. "The short answer is that it depends on who you ask. The pope has just come out on the yes side. He forcefully declared on behalf of the one point two billion Catholics in the world that what we all saw and heard was God. On the other hand, Ayatollah Mohammad Ka'bi has declared that Shia Muslims do not accept that what we all witnessed is Allah. I'll have more complete numbers tomorrow, but rough estimates tonight are that sixty percent believe it is God, and forty percent don't."

She pressed, "And you, Dallas, you had a front row seat. What do you think?"

He answered without hesitation. "What I saw is nothing like I ever imagined, and it doesn't resemble the prophesies of any of the major religions, so I understand why many people are skeptical. But for me, the power and clarity of the message of love was undeniably holy. I was moved to the core in a deeply spiritual way, and for that reason alone, I believe with all my heart that I saw God tonight."

She waved across the table. "Anyone else like to share their thoughts or views on the subject?"

After a few seconds of silence, Tru spoke up. "I have never spoken of my faith at work before. For me, it's a private matter. But with all that has happened since yesterday, it suddenly seems very appropriate. I'm a Hindu, and as Dallas has described, what I saw on TV tonight was nothing like the Puranas describe. Yet, I too felt the same truth. It was a powerful message."

"Thank you for sharing your thoughts on what transpired tonight. Would anyone else like to share their views?"

Rick Davis cleared his throat before speaking. "Madam President, I certainly respect Tru's views as well as all others who believe we witnessed god tonight, but I disagree. I don't know who, or what that being is, but more importantly, I don't think it matters at all whether Tru is right or I'm right. The cold hard facts are that if we are to save this planet it's up to us, as humans, to do it. That being said he could save our planet, but won't, and I for one don't want to just throw up my hands and resign myself to oblivion without at least trying to save this world. We have to try, don't we?"

Abby tapped her pen on the ever-present pad. "That's putting a fine point on where we stand. Any other comments before we move on?"

From the end of the table, Secretary of Labor, Rebecca Moreno, spoke up. "Madam President, I have a different viewpoint, and I hope that's okay."

Abby responded emphatically. "Of course that's okay. This is not a black and white thing. Go ahead, Becky."

The red headed labor leader spoke timidly. "At thirteen years old I was baptized as a born-again believer in the church where my father still serves as the pastor. In the years since then my walk with my Lord and Savior has only become closer. And throughout my life I have had a premonition that I would live to see the rapture, that I would live to see the end of the world. I'm not expecting anyone to understand that, only accept that this has been a part of who I am for as long as I can remember."

Abby spoke sympathetically. "Our constitution guarantees that your faith and your beliefs are your business, Becky, and even if it didn't,

I would still expect everyone on this team to respect each other's personal religious convictions. Speak freely."

Her head had lowered as the president spoke, and now rose, locking eyes with Abby's. After a halting start her resolve firmed. "Madam President, tonight I believe with all my heart that I heard my God speaking directly to me with a very clear message. And while it's not happening the way that I envisioned, I have prepared for this moment my entire life."

She wiped at the moist corner of her eye and continued. "Ma'am, it has been the professional pinnacle of my career to serve my country as part of your cabinet. And I believe that you have been the best president to serve our nation in my lifetime."

Her upper lip quivered. "But I ultimately serve a higher power, and tonight I believe that He has commanded his followers to devote our remaining time on this Earth to serving others. And while one can argue that this job is all about service to the American people, I feel led to submit my resignation and devote my remaining time on Earth in a more hands on role in my community. As my God has said, we need to feed and clothe the poor, and that's what I plan to do. I feel terrible about leaving now, with all this going on, but like I said, I answer to a higher authority. I hope that you understand."

Abby sat in silence for a moment, torn between wanting to argue the point about the best way to serve her fellow humans, but knowing in her heart that anything less than total support for this tough decision made by Becky would be a betrayal of her own code on how to respect and treat others. "Our founding fathers made the First Amendment to the Constitution a declaration of the freedom of religion. They said that Congress shall make no law respecting an establishment of religion, or prohibiting the free exercise thereof. Who am I to disagree with that? I'll certainly miss you as part of the team, but it would be wrong of you to serve in ways that violate your core beliefs, and wrong of me to expect that you would." She looked with compassion on Becky. "And, if we are successful in finding a way out of this alive, I would hope that you would consider rejoining the team."

Becky looked at her quizzically. "Respectfully, ma'am, I...I really don't think that can happen. God Almighty has spoken. Maybe you didn't understand. This world as we know it is going to cease to exist and we'll all be swept up in His embrace in two weeks."

A tough smile met the comment. "I'm a fighter and I've overcame some pretty long odds in my life. So, as long as I'm president, we won't quit. We'll put our heads together as a team and use our God given abilities to fight for our survival. Besides, I was there, in the room while He was speaking, and He did say to take care of one another. But I didn't hear a word about not trying to save our world. I do respect your beliefs." Abby's tone now sharpened. "And I ask you to respect our choice to fight."

Becky quickly gathered her things from the table as the others looked on. She walked away, then stopped at the door and turned, now speaking with a quiver in her voice. "I love you all, and I'll pray for you."

Abby purposely waited several seconds after Becky's departure before continuing. "If anyone else feels the same way and would like to leave, now is the time. This is going to be a hell of a challenge, and I want a fully committed, all-volunteer team."

She paused again and Tru spoke up quickly. "I'm in, ma'am, one-hundred percent onboard."

One by one all of the other cabinet members made similar pledges of full support. After hearing each of them, the chill of Becky's public profession had been completely turned around. A new sense of camaraderie infused the room.

Abby smiled broadly. "All right then, we've got a planet to save. And if we want to save it, we're going to have to do it ourselves.

Let's get to it. Kalie, what's the latest on our plan to change that rock's course?"

Kalie sprung from her seat and once again the screen at the end of the table lit with a PowerPoint presentation. A new verve fueled her words. "As I indicated earlier, this won't be easy, but it is possible. First of all, we don't have a spacecraft designed for this mission. No one in the world does. The closest we have is from my former employer, Space Rim."

On the screen a craft vaguely resembling the old decommissioned first-generation space shuttle appeared. "It's a smaller vessel than the old shuttles, and that's a wonderful thing if your trying to reduce weight for near Earth missions. That's not so great if you want to use it for our needs... and that's the good news."

Another slide rolled up. "Here's a picture of one of the two certified craft, docked at the space station. Unfortunately, that's as far as either has ever traveled. We're going to need to get as far into space as possible to meet and then attempt to divert the asteroid. To do that, we're going to need to add extra fuel capacity, and that's going to take away cargo space that we need for the nuclear devices. Assuming we get those fuel cells installed and weapons loaded by next Sunday at the latest, we'll be launching without any testing at the higher cargo and fuel weight. I know from my own experience at Space Rim that will be extremely dangerous. One wrong equation in the programming and everything goes boom."

Slide three now populated the screen and it showed smiling Space Rim crew members. "If we manage to do the modifications, and the craft and crew survive the launch, this will be a one-way trip. There's not enough storage capacity to take fuel for a return. None of the crew will survive. This is a suicide mission to save the planet."

The last slide replaced the smiling faces with a digital image of the asteroid sent from the Keck Observatory telescope. "If all of that works perfectly, I'm still not sure if we will be able to deliver enough firepower to do the job on this monster. My two percent estimate this morning may have been optimistic."

The somber assessment weighed on the faces of the cabinet. The president had questions. "Thanks for the update. This is THE priority for everyone here and I expect every department to lend assistance in any way needed. Keep pushing, and get it done at any cost. By the way, have we heard anything from our Chinese friends? Have they offered anything that is new, or different?"

"At this time, we've just started the conversation. I think they are in the same place as us, scrambling to figure out what assets they have to meet this challenge. A generic offer of help has been made and I have a call set for tomorrow morning with Dr. Ying, their Minister of Science and Technology. I'll know more then."

"I hope they have a surprise for us. This morning I said I wanted another option, a Plan B, some way to reprogram at least some of our ICBM's. What's the update on that?"

Braxton now stood. "While Kalie was working on getting the shuttle plan operational, I took the lead on how to re-purpose at least a few of our ICBM's. Kalie laid out the technical challenges necessary to make that happen this morning. Designing, manufacturing and then mounting the new detonation system is in itself a significant obstacle. The good news is that I've been contacted by a small Israeli company working on something similar for a project that is so black box that we didn't even know of its existence until today. It's still a long shot, but the odds are not as long as they were earlier."

Abby smiled. "Finally, some good news!"

Braxton resumed. "On the issue of reprogramming the guidance system for outer space control, we're at a crossroads. There is no way possible for government programmers working twenty-four hours a day to get this done. There are just not enough hours in the day using the number of qualified personnel on the payroll."

Braxton paused and spoke before advancing the PowerPoint presentation with a slide from yesterday's first presentation. "Remember yesterday, just after the Gabriel video? It feels like a long time ago, but it's only been about thirty-four hours. I wasn't here then, but I've been informed that at that moment in time, our number one assumption was that a hacker, or group of hackers was responsible. In thinking about our programming problem, perhaps these groups could be our salvation."

Trusond nearly jumped from his seat. "Whoa! You're not considering giving those guys access to our nuclear stockpile? Can't we tap into universities and private industry? I mean, who knows what groups like that might do if they get in!"

Braxton turned calmly. "Tru, these aren't normal times, are they? We have some very hard choices to make, and we need to make them tonight... tomorrow morning at the latest. We have to do a massive amount of coding. We're going to draft every university and private industry programmer we can, but it will take some time to get them up to speed and working together as a team. These guys are already networked, and that's a huge advantage when we only have a few days to get this done. Using every programmer that we can find, we have a chance... a small chance, to get some of those rockets reprogrammed. Without them, Plan B doesn't happen, period. I get it. If we do this, we'll have a cyber-security nightmare to clean up later. But if we don't?" He shrugged his shoulders. "If we don't, maybe everyone on the planet dies. Those are the cards we've been dealt. I'm open to any other suggestions... from anyone. But we need to make our decision quickly. Every hour counts."

With that he and Kalie both sat down. No one said a word as President Banister tapped her pen on her pad, weighing the stark choice that had just been floated. After almost a dozen raps on the pad she addressed the room. "Time is not on our side, so we'll make that decision before we leave this table. But first, I want to get the full lay of the land. Effie, what's the latest on the diplomatic front?"

The Secretary of State looked visibly tired and stayed seated as she responded. "Leaders from every corner of the globe have been putting out statements on whether they believed this was God, or something else. Civil leaders are roughly in line with the report from Dallas on religious leader responses, roughly sixty percent yes, twenty percent say no, and twenty percent undecided." She laughed softly. "Leave it to politicians to be undecided, even at a time like this."

She resumed, "For the most part, everyone wants to know what we're going to do? Can we stop this... can they help... that sort of thing. It's times like these that remind of us all that the U.S. really is the most powerful country on the planet."

Abby nodded. "With great power there must also come great responsibility. That's in the Bible, right Dallas?"

Dallas grinned. "Almost. The Bible says 'From everyone who has been given much, much will be demanded; and from the one who has been entrusted with much, much more will be asked.' The quote you used is actually from Spider-man."

Everyone around the table either snickered or laughed outright, including Abby. "God, it sure feels good to laugh a little. Thanks for the moment, Dallas. Tru, you get to follow that. What's the word from Homeland Security?"

Trusond Patel rose, not smiling even a little. "I can't top that, so I won't even try. Ma'am, things have gotten worse since last night. The message from God was watched by almost every household in the country and large portions of society now believe that the end is imminent, leading many more to either check-out and wait for the end, or take the law into their own hands. Police are doing their best, but they are rapidly being outnumbered by armed civilians. We're talking a nation-wide run on grocery stores. Those that had money went out and tried to do two weeks' worth of shopping to get them through until the end. Those that didn't stole what they needed, daring anyone to stop them. Worse still, we're getting early reports that power generation is slipping by the hour. I think it's time for you to sign a national declaration of martial law."

The president sighed. "I really don't want to go there yet. I've asked our people to continue to show up for work and specifically to help us keep the power on. Let's wait until tomorrow. If things go downhill even more, it will be a monumental but easy decision. I guess that brings us to continuity of government. What's the latest?"

"Well ma'am, there has been progress on that front. Vice President Puckett and Speaker Stemson have both been relocated to their respective secure bunkers. In addition, we've notified all of the cabinet members, as well as all senators and representatives, of their assignment to three potential waves of evacuations to secure facilities. We're ready, but we'll wait as long as possible to actually begin those actions. There is a high possibility that taking even the first batch of our highest-ranking officials to protected locations would trigger more panic. It still seems surreal that we're even talking about this sort of thing."

"Thanks for the update, Tru. It's surreal for all of us. And speaking of surreal, any last thoughts or comments on bringing those hacker groups into our midst, before I make my decision?"

Trusond cleared his throat. "Madam President, I would have considered it an act of treason had you suggested this forty-eight hours ago, but, as has been noted, a lot has happened since then. Now, as I listen to these presentations, and reflect on our current dire situation, I think that it would be treason not to at least try. It's not an ideal choice. Hell, it's an awful choice. But when the alternative is considered, I think it's our only choice."

Around the table heads nodded in silent agreement. The president waited for a full thirty seconds to be sure that no one else stepped forward to object. "Make the outreach, Braxton. Let's see if their desire for survival is stronger than their desire for anarchy."

Chapter Twenty-Six

Sunday 11:00 P.M. Washington D.C.

Abby walked through the dimly lit corridor of the residential wing of the White House until reaching the family quarters. She exchanged pleasantries with the Secret Service Agent outside the door to the living room. "Goodnight, Sam. I really appreciate you watching out for my Jill. She means the world to me."

"Yes, ma'am. My pleasure. I'm here to protect and serve."

She wearily patted the attentive agent's arm. "That's what we're all trying to do, Sam. That's what we're all trying to do."

She quietly entered the family quarters unsure whether Jill was awake or not. The glow of the TV gave her the answer. "Hey, sweetie. How was your day?"

Jill sat cross-legged on the couch in a pink short, silky, sheer nightgown with a bowl of popcorn nestled on her lap. Her concerned eyes locked with Abby's. "Oh, honey. You must be exhausted. I'm worn out just trying to keep up with what's happening on TV. I can't imagine your day." She patted the couch. "Come, sit."

Abby spied the wine glass on the end table. "Any pinot grigio left? It goes better with popcorn than bourbon."

Jill popped up from the couch, slid on her fluffy matching house shoes and headed to the refrigerator, quickly returning with a half full bottle. "All for you, my dear. Now come over, have some popcorn and pinot, and decompress."

Hand in hand they headed to the couch. Abby sat and let out a gentle groan as the overstuffed cushions enveloped her. "Ahhh. This feels good, but I'm not sure if I'll be able to get back up. Even my bones feel tired."

Laughing, Jill handed her a glass filled to the rim. "Lucky for you, we can always call Sam in and pull your ass up, if it comes to that."

"Just another perk of being president, I guess, but it sure doesn't make up for the day I've had. On the plus side, no one died in front of me today, so that's a win."

Jill snuggled close and gently poked Abby's ribs. "That wicked sense of humor is going to get you in trouble someday, Abigail Banister."

"It's kept you laughing all these years, hasn't it? Think how boring your life would be without me."

Jill turned serious. "Don't even talk about life without you. I don't think I could handle it."

Abby pulled her close. "Where did that come from?"

"On the news they talked about the vice president and speaker being evacuated and they speculated about you. They said you might be going next."

She leaned down and kissed her softly. "I'm not going anywhere, at least not yet. And even if I do have to leave, you'll be right by my side. We're a package deal. Nothing, and no one, is going to separate us."

"I'm scared, Abby. That asteroid's coming, and maybe God. It's all just so unbelievable." Jill took her wife's hand in hers. "Speaking of God, that was the most powerful thing I've ever seen on TV. What was it like seeing it live?"

Abby took a long sip. "As powerful as it must have been on TV, I bet that it was at least a hundred times more in person. We've been away from organized religion for a long time, so I wasn't quite sure what to expect. But even Dallas, who lives this stuff, was blown away. The angels and the choir were spectacular, but the message was so much more so. It penetrated my very being. It's hard to describe, but I just knew in the deepest part of my soul that He was God, and He was speaking truth, directly to me. It was amazing. I wish that you could have been there."

"Me too, just so that I could be with you. That's really all that I want." Tears welled and her eyes glistened. "I hope that they can keep that rock from killing us all, but if they can't, promise me that we'll be together when the end comes. Abby, promise me."

A few hours ago, she was defiantly kicking rude Russians off Air Force One. Now, this hard-shelled woman let her tears fall. "I love you Jill Sommers, and the thought of facing the end without you rips my heart. I'll do my best to save us all, but if I can't then we'll face it together, hand in hand. I promise."

Jill buried herself in Abby's embrace as sobs wracked her frame. "Hold me close tonight, like when we were young. If this is our last two weeks, I want to make every minute count."

Abby pulled her wife even closer. She ran her fingers through Jill's soft, lush honey tinted tresses. Her heart pounded in her ears as the pent-up emotions from the day sought a physical release. Ancient animal instincts surged forward through the emotional opening and without thinking, her lips searched their match. The soft beginning of the ensuing kiss progressed quickly with mutually aggressive tongues pushing and mingling, their tears adding primal salty taste. Abby reached with her right hand and caressed Jill's breast through the silky gown and a soft pleasured moan echoed from mouth to mouth.

Abby pulled back slightly, ending the kiss. Her teary eyes glistened as she looked deeply into Jill's own shimmering crystal blues. The exhaustion of the day fell away as desire pumped through her veins. She gently caressed Jill's cheek and her voice lowered to its sexiest register. "I'll never let you go, my little minx, never." She winked at her lover, like she used to do when their love was new. "Let's move this to the bedroom and pretend we're twenty-five again."

Chapter Twenty-Seven

Monday 7:00 A.M. Washington D.C. / Thirteen Days to Impact

Abby waltzed into the Situation Room in a great mood in her blue over blue skirted suit. She hoped the same would be true for her team. The scowl on Trusond Patel's face quickly brought her back to hard cold reality. It was obvious that none of her inner cabinet members were as refreshed as she. "Looks like the past forty-eight hours haven't just been just a bad dream, eh?"

The attempt at humor fell terribly flat on her weary appointees. Tru spoke first. "No ma'am, and it's only gotten worse since last night."

The weight that had momentarily been lifted crashed back on her shoulders. "That sounds ominous. You have the floor. What's going on?"

A map of France filled the screen behind Tru as he stood. His laser pointer went to a location in the northwest corner of the European nation, near the English Channel. "The nuclear power plant in Penly is on the verge of a meltdown. They hope to contain it, but that's far from certain. This is exactly the kind of event that concerns me most."

Memories of a pleasant evening evaporated like a mirage and her no-nonsense demeanor returned, cladding her like a protective suit of armor. "How did it happen, and what does it mean for us?"

"They are not sure if it was an accident or sabotage. They were operating with only seventy percent staffing when it happened and a valve that should have been closed was left open. That single error started the cascade and they've been on the edge of catastrophe ever since. Precautionary evacuations have begun and panic is right around the corner. And while a meltdown would be a disaster, the contagion of absenteeism could shut down the continent's power grid. We simply can't let that happen. Madam President, I'm asking you to declare martial law now."

The brusque request set her aback. "Okay... Tru, how did things go last night, here, in the U.S.? Did we have any close calls?"

The dark circles under his eyes were deeper than usual, contrasting with his dark tan skin. He snapped. "Yes, Madam President, we did. The Watts Bar nuclear plant in Tennessee had an incident similar to the one in France, but luckily, we caught the problem sooner. Ten more minutes and we would be dealing with the exact same disaster as across the pond. Seems a mega-church in the area held an outdoor revival service and a lot of the employees at the facility skipped work to attend. This contagion is real, ma'am, and it's getting worse. We must take action...today... or else..."

All other cabinet members sat quietly, glancing from Tru to the president, and back. She replied calmly. "This is exactly why you're the man I want at Homeland. Your zeal to protect our nation is being tested, and it will be tested even more in the coming days. I value your counsel and expertise. Tell me more about how things went elsewhere last night. Any rioting or looting? Were there religious mobs torching churches or mosques as we've seen in the past few nights?"

His already tense posture stiffened to extreme and his forehead furrowed. "All of the above, Madam President. What started as a calm night after the UN God address quickly turned ugly. Milwaukee is in flames. A hundred and thirty confirmed dead, including twenty police. It started as looting with armed store owners and police fiercely fighting back. Molotov cocktails were thrown which started a few small fires. High winds then spread the flames from building to building until it began incinerating entire city blocks. Its only forty percent contained at this time. Oakland and Boston had similar, but smaller outbreaks, and a host of other cities like Louisville and New Orleans were right behind them. It was a rough night."

For the first time today, she began tapping her pen on her notepad. "I see. And religious incidents?"

Tru sighed. "Mostly scattered broken windows and hate language like 'Jews Killed Jesus' and 'The Only Good Muslim is a Dead Muslim' spray painted across the denominational spectrum of buildings. We did have one major violent occurrence." He paused and put up a slide showing yellow police tape around a house of worship. A hand went to his eyes, wiping away moisture from the corners as he advanced the slide filled with small individual photos of men, women and children killed in the attack. "An armed gunman entered a synagogue in Minneapolis and killed thirty-five... fifteen were children."

He wiped his eyes again and now spoke quietly. "The suspect has been identified as a well-known Neo-Nazi, who is still at large. He posted a tweet that he was linked to some group called God's Infantry. We need this declaration, ma'am, before things really get out of control."

Gasps, and sobs from a couple of the junior members on the second row behind the cabinet members followed Tru's update. All eyes went toward Abby as she silently processed his words. "You've made a compelling case, Tru. It was a bad night. But let's hear from the others before I make that decision."

Tru's shoulders sagged and his head lowered as he took his seat. "Yes ma'am."

Abby turned toward Brax. "What's the update from Defense? Any good news?"

Brax's uniform appeared slightly wrinkled indicating that he had spent the night in the Situation Room. "Definite change from last night, ma'am. Everything has returned to normal in New York. The golden column, patrolling angels, they're all gone. Disappeared all at once around midnight. Almost simultaneously a black cloud appeared over Red Square and St. Basil's Cathedral just after dawn.

They've evacuated the area, just like we did, except it's right next to the Kremlin. Looks like good old Maxim Noskov is going to have a front row cloud view for a few days."

A smile crept across the president's face. "Serves that prick right. He was such a jerk when he was here. Let's see how he likes being powerless while a self-proclaimed deity plunks down in his country's biggest city. I suspect he won't think it's so funny, will he? Thanks for some good news this morning. What about the hackers, how's that going?"

"Surprisingly well. It took a little convincing to get them to believe that our offer wasn't a trap, but after that, they were all in. I don't know if it's a shock, but as a whole, they're not a big god believing group. They seem very motivated to find a way to avoid getting extinguished by this asteroid. I'm not minimizing the risk of a security nightmare, but all in all we've taken a good first step. I'll have more specifics at our next briefing."

The pen tapped three more times as the president turned toward her National Security Advisor. "You're up Kalie. How's it going on the shuttle front?"

She remained seated with hands folded on the table. "The good news is that one shuttle is home in Arizona for refitting and the other is almost on the way. On the other hand, the engineering for the refit is already way behind our aggressive schedule. If it's all right with you ma'am, I'm going to get out there today and put some more urgency into the process. You have my word we'll get it done."

"Go out there and kick some ass, Kalie. They'll listen to you. By the way, anything from the Chinese yet?"

Kalie smirked. "I'll be talking with them in a couple of hours, but surprisingly, as you just suggested, I did get an unexpected call from Russia this morning. Seems having a black cloud over your capital opens hearts and minds to cooperation. No specific offer yet, but suddenly they seem to be open to working with us."

"Karma really is a bitch. I wish I could see the look on old Maxim's face this morning!" Abby's smile broadened as she turned toward Effie. "What else is happening on the international front?"

The seasoned diplomat shared the president's humor at the change in Russian attitude. "Well ma'am, it's a real mixed bag out there today. The Arab world is very unsettled. I mean even a lot more than usual. Somewhat surprisingly, most of the Sunni Muslim nations are on the side that this is God, which is in alignment with the official state opinion of Israel. The Shia are diametrically opposed. The Ayatollah is radically vocal in his opinion. He's even making veiled threats about hastening the quote "real" arrival of God. We're trying to decipher what that means in terms of what he might do. We've had some cable intercepts sent over from the C.I.A. and it's concerning."

Every cabinet member perked up at her words as she continued. "There's a chance that they may be trying to start World War Three. We're monitoring the situation carefully."

Dallas piped in. "Effie, I may be able to shed some more light on why they might be thinking that way. Let's get together after the meeting, if that works for you."

She nodded to him. "As far as the rest of the world, everything is at the extremes. There are peaceful demonstrations along the south side of the Korean DMZ with talks on opening the gates for family reconciliations. Then over in Kashmir, Hindu and Muslim radicals are sending suicide bombers into each other's neighborhoods. India and Pakistan are both threatening nuclear escalation. So, while everyone is offering to helping us if we need anything, we've got a world teetering on the edge."

The president acknowledged the sentiment. "Our fast-paced world seems to have gone into overdrive, every action amplified."

"Yes ma'am. Everyone is hyped up about something."

The president now pointed to her ex. "We've heard religion mentioned in several updates already, Dallas. How are things playing out across America after the big event last night?"

"As I mentioned last evening, there seems to be a roughly sixty-forty split on believing if this was God or not. Those numbers seem to be holding up today. What's becoming clearer is how those decisions are impacting actions by associations, congregations and individuals. Somewhat surprising to me is that both the believers and non-believers are adopting some of the same tactics. Tru referenced a mega church holding a revival last night. Events like that are being held all over the nation, by all sides. The desire for community and reinforcement of belief is strong whether the church or believer thought this was God or not. People want to come together in stressful times. This feeds into what worries Tru. If a majority of people from both sides believe that it's more important to be with their tribe, so to speak, than going to work, we've got a real problem."

More tapping of the pen accompanied the religious overview. "How do you see this unfolding in the next few days?"

Dallas rubbed his stubbled chin. "We're in uncharted waters, Madam President, but my reading is that this trend is only going to accelerate as we get closer to the end date. Media coverage fanning fear and loss of hope will be the accelerants. It's only going to get worse."

Once again there was silence around the table. Abby sat in concentration, weighing her options. "Thank you, Dallas, and to everyone for your assessments and updates. Tru, you've made a compelling case for declaring martial law. It can certainly be justified, hell, its more than justified, but I'm going to let this play out some more before I take that step. I want to see how the day goes, then address the nation again tonight before we go there. I believe in our people. Besides, once we ring that bell, it can't be un-rung. Let's try a little faith first."

Tru grudgingly accepted her verdict, but with a warning. "I say this with the utmost respect, ma'am, but delaying is a mistake. When it becomes clear that faith isn't enough, it may already be too late."

Chapter Twenty-Eight

Monday 4:30 P.M. Tehran / 8:00 A.M. Washington D.C.

Thirteen Days to Impact

A nervous President Hossien Namazi called the special session of the Iranian cabinet to order. He nervously rubbed his hands as Supreme Leader Ayatollah Mohammad Ka'bi took a seat at the other end of the oval shaped table. In a halting voice, Namazi started the meeting. "Welcome home, Supreme Leader. It is a rare opportunity to have you join us. We implore you to share your insights into the events that you witnessed in New York."

The soft, assured words of the holy man contrasted with the harsh, bright lighting of the room. "Praise be to Allah for this day." He bowed, then continued. "The Quran and Hadiths are extremely clear. Before the Mahdi can be revealed, a war between faithful Muslims and the Al-Masih ad-Dajja must occur."

All those gathered sat in attentive silence as their state and spiritual leader paused once more. When he spoke again, it was now in a fiery authoritative tone. "I have traveled to the arrogant city of tall buildings, and there I witnessed evil. Behind a curtain I heard the voice prophesied for centuries. I heard the voice of the Al-Masih ad-Dajja."

Hossien grasped the significance of the old man's words. "You're saying it was not Allah, but the Deceiver? How can that be? I heard the voice describe himself as Allah, and he called Muhammad a holy man. Isn't that what Allah himself would say?"

No one else at the table dared speak, or look directly at the Ayatollah. Returning to his mellifluous voice he replied. "Dear Hossien, one must consider what was not said, as well as what was.

Not a single mention of the Mahdi? Would Allah not include that, especially in the land of the infidels? Your words answer those questions. What we all heard was not Allah, but the Deceiver, just as prophesied."

Swallowing hard, Hossien continued. "And our Sunni brothers who have said that they heard Allah? Are they also infidels?"

The Ayatollah waved his hand dismissively. "Our Sunni brothers... The ancients have said 'Although Allah, the Exalted, has not created a creature worse than a dog, yet a Sunni is worse than even a dog.' Look at what they've already done! Egypt has made peace with Israel! How can that be holy? Allah will slaughter them before he finally destroys the infidels. Some will change their ways and see the truth, but most will not. But be not deceived, their apostasy will not taint our fidelity."

The president sat stunned. With a dry mouth, he spoke again. "What then would you have us do, Supreme Leader?"

With a grandfatherly smile, the old man replied with words spoken as softly as a spring rain. "Hossien, Allah has chosen us for this day as surely as Muhammad was chosen as his last prophet. Immediately prepare twelve of our secret nuclear missiles to be targeted on Jerusalem. They are to be at the ready upon my word. At the appointed time, you and I will be the vessels chosen by Allah to at last reveal the hidden Mahdi."

Hossien felt his chest tighten as he chose his words carefully. "Your words are my command, Supreme Leader. The weapons will be at the ready." He drew a breath, trying to summon even one extra ounce of courage. "I ask a question... as one not as learned as you, Imam. Does the Quran or the Hadiths leave any room for alternative interpretations of these events? Any other possible actions or outcomes which will keep us within His will?"

Clasping his hands in front, the spiritual leader sighed. "Allah understands your hesitancy, Hossien. It is a natural human emotion. Recall the story of Ibrahim when he saw a vision of himself offering his son Ishmael as a sacrifice. Imagine his burden of taking his own son's life to be obedient. It must have been an overwhelming weight to bear."

He smoothed his beard and continued. "Then, surely with sorrow, he shares the vision that he has had with Ishmael. How hard must that have been, Hossien? Can you even imagine his pain, his hesitancy?"

Looking down at the table, Hossien answered quietly. "No. I cannot, Imam."

"And yet, Ishmael hearing his father's words, agreed to fulfill the command of Allah in the vision. He was willing to give himself as a sacrifice to be obedient to the will of Allah. Can you even imagine the faith of that boy?"

Again, Hossien answered in the negative. "No. I cannot."

The bare beige walls offered no relief as the Supreme Leader closed his case. "Hossien, that is the faith of our people. Their faith is your faith. Even your very blood, coursing through your body, gives you the same willpower to make the hard choices, to remain in His will, just as both Ibrahim and Ishmael chose. Will you, too, be obedient, Hossien?"

In his silence with his head remaining bowed, Hossien became aware of his heart beating. Hearing the rhythmic thumping a calm descended upon him. As he raised his head, a serene gaze met the old man's eyes. "Yes, Imam. I will be obedient to the will of Allah."

A self-satisfied smile returned from the leader. "Good, Hossien. Good."

With calmness, Hossien added, "And as with Ibrahim and Ishmael, Allah may yet rejoice in our obedience and instead provide a greater sacrifice instead of tens of millions of souls."

Chapter Twenty-Nine

Monday 10:00 A.M. New York City / Thirteen Days to Impact

The ten o'clock hour approached. Ken Garner clapped his hands together. "Be sharp, everyone. We're in a ratings war."

Last touch-ups of makeup were applied to Larry and final mic adjustments were quickly made. Even though it had been less than forty-eight hours since the initial Gabriel video, a new normal was being established. New guests were becoming regulars. God had spoken and the cloud and heavenly hosts had left New York. That's not to say that all was well in the world. Reporters covered riveting stories of cities being rocked by violence. News of religious attacks shocked audiences. Nations threatened each other with war. No, these were not normal times, but humans are remarkably adaptable, including the crew and commentators on CBN.

Larry Knewell sat at the head of this new calm. In the hours since the Gabriel video changed everything, he had become the most watched person on television. Perhaps it was his focus on the big questions. Was this God, or not? If this was God, whose God? Questions like that filled his time slots. Other shows covered story lines like the search for the Minneapolis synagogue killer. Those stories might soon appear on his show, too, but for now he was riding the ratings wave of the grand questions that seemed to represent the heart of this event. At the appointed time, Jared stepped in front of the camera to count down the start of today's morning edition of the show. "In five-four-three-two-one."

The ratings success had reassured him that he was still king of the airwaves and an air of supreme confidence radiated from the host as the adrenaline-fueled first hours of the crisis were now supplanted with a growing sense of understanding of the key story-lines. "Welcome to Monday morning special edition coverage of Judgment

Day. Today the sun rose in the east and the forecast is for a hot day here in New York. An example of a perfectly normal celestial event on this planet. We don't really think about the significance of this daily occurrence. After all, it's happened every single day for billions of years, and besides, there's nothing that we could do about it, even if we wanted to. In thirteen days, something is going to change. Either we won't survive the impact of Jansky-Haskell and no one will be around to witness sunrise on our barren world, or we'll have successfully changed a celestial event by diverting the asteroid."

He paused and shifted his gaze to camera two. Today his pace was more controlled, his tone more commanding, no longer on edge as events seemed to change the narrative hourly. "This morning we'll explore the question of mankind's rightful actions and options as we confront this new reality. It has already been established that the effort to save the planet is a long shot, so for me, it boils down to one question. If we can divert the asteroid, should we? After all, most people believe that God has spoken and declared that this is the end. He's going to allow the destruction of Earth and welcome all people into eternal bliss. Is it ethical, or even possible to successfully fight against God's will?"

A relaxed, almost sincere smile crossed his face as he turned to welcome the returning panelists. "Joining us here in studio once again are Pastor Jacob Shadwell, Director of World Evangelical Service and Rabbi Solomon Feldman of Temple Beth Israel. Welcome again, to the both of you." With both acknowledging their introduction Larry transitioned and once again introduced his two remote guests, Guru Baba Mashni and Dr. Son Young Kim.

With the panel set, Larry began the discussion. "Today we'll start with Dr. Kim. Let's get your thoughts on the question of the day. Is it ethical, or even possible to successfully fight against God's will?"

It was now completely obvious that Dr. Kim was receiving professional advice on dressing for television. The frumpy gray cardigan from Saturday was ancient history. Today's look was a flattering black blazer with curve cut lapels. The jacket covered a sheer, skin toned camisole that dipped just enough to show a pinch of cleavage. And the unruly lock of hair that seemed to have a will of its own two days ago, was now trimmed and part of a new, perky, asymmetrical cut. Her monotone voice, however remained as flat as a vinyl record. "Larry, that's one of the benefits of being an atheist. I only deal in science, not mystical verbal misdirection, so this is a very easy one for me. I don't believe that being we saw in New York is god, and besides, even if he was, he said that we're on our own. Let me be clear. I want to live a long and happy life, and for that to happen, we not only have to try and divert that asteroid, we have to be successful. I'm cheering for the president and all of the people trying to make it happen. I wish them all the luck in the world and I couldn't care less about the supposed will of god. The odds may be against us, but we'll save ourselves, or die trying."

"So, it's all black and white? Just mankind alone in the cosmos? No room for gray... or god?"

She gave a half smile. "There are no unicorns either, Larry. It really is just us against a cold, uncaring universe. Well, us and any other life forms, like the ones that seem to be visiting our world right now."

The host feigned a shiver. "That's a rather bleak assessment of our current situation... and life in general. Any room for hope in your world view?"

"Well, of course there's room for hope. Think about the advances that we've made in medicine. A diagnosis of HIV-AIDS was once a death sentence. Now it's managed with long term maintenance drugs. In that way, it's now a lot like diabetes, or high blood pressure. The patients and scientists back in the Eighties and Nineties had hope, and science answered those hopes, not some mystical being who hasn't been seen in thousands of years. That's the kind of hope that I have, hope that the scientists and engineers working together on this situation can pull off a remarkable feat... and I believe they can."

"That's a very straight-forward view, Dr. Kim. Let's turn to Guru Baba Mashni in San Francisco and see if his answer is as clear cut. Guru Mashni, if Vishnu has ordained that our time on Earth is over, is it right that we should try and circumvent his will by changing the course of that rock?"

Today the bubbly Hindu teacher had reversed his kurta color scheme from yesterday. Instead of a flashy golden garment with black buttons he wore an equally stylish black vestment with solid gold buttons. "As always, Larry, I'm pleased to be your guest. Your question is a good one, but the answer is not as simple as Dr. Kim would suggest. You see, there is a tension in Hinduism between fate and free will. Karma implies that we eventually get the fate that we deserve, so it can be seen as predetermined. But there is also an acknowledgment that the decisions that we make on a daily basis can change how we begin our next incarnation, as we strive to achieve nirvana. That's the tension for an individual, but the question that you ask is about our entire species. Are we all bound by our fate, or is free will still an option for humanity as a whole? That's a tough question."

Larry laughed softly. "Yes, Guru Mashni. That's why we have you as a guest, to share your insights into these pressing issues. Where do you come down on this question?"

The guru maintained his serene visage in the face of Larry's pressure. "I will first say that I do not speak for all Hindu believers across the world. We are a very large community with many diverse interpretations. Having said that, I personally believe that our Creator is in charge, but he gives us the individual free will to live our lives, and inherit the consequences. With that as my basis, I say that Vishnu already knows if we will be successful, but gives us the choice to try and save the planet. I personally am preparing to enter into his synchronicity, but if others wish to try to prevent this, they will ultimately succeed or fail based on the will of Vishnu. That is what I believe."

Eyes narrowed, Larry challenged. "With all due respect, Guru Mashni, it sounds like you're trying to have it both ways. If I heard you correctly it sounds like you're saying whatever God wants to happen, will happen, and that we're free to try to change that, but it won't really matter. It sounds to me like your version of free will is an illusion. It's like me watching some sci-fi movie of my future life. I may see myself acting like I have free will, but my fate is already decided, my movie's script is already written, even if I don't know the ending. Is that how it works?"

The smile had been replaced by a scrunched up, exasperated visage. "Kind of, but not really... I mean... like I said, it's complicated. I'll just say that two things can be true at once. Vishnu can be all knowing about the future, but at the same time, we do have our own agency. We do have free will."

Larry picked up the notes on his desk and brought them down on their edge, straightening the small stack. He spoke with more than a touch of sarcasm. "Ah, the mysteries of religion."

In the control room Ken Garner directed camera one to shift to Rabbi Feldman as Larry now brought him into the conversation. "Rabbi Feldman, we've been presented with two very different views on our question of the day. To Dr. Kim, it's just a matter of math and our ability to execute a very difficult plan. Guru Mashni however, insists that we do have free will to try and stop this asteroid, but at the same time, what ultimately happens will be the will of Vishnu, or God. It seems we won't know until the asteroid gets here, but it's all going to be according to His plan. How does all this square with Judaism? I ask you the same question that I asked them. If it has been divinely ordained that our time on Earth is over, is it right that we should try and circumvent his will by changing the course of that rock?"

The rabbi sported a new black kippah, this one with small white embroidered Stars of David around the outer edge. Otherwise his dress of dark suit and white prayer shawl with blue stripes draping his shoulders remained the same from yesterday. "This has been a really interesting learning experience for me, as well as hopefully for our audience. While I knew of the main constructs of Hinduism, I was unaware of their teachings on free will. Seems we have a lot more in common than I suspected."

"Please, rabbi. Tell us more."

"Well, it seems Judaism has struggled to square the opposing ideas of free will and predeterminism in much the same way as Guru Mashni explained. For example, Jews were given the Torah with a set of rules to follow, like the Ten Commandments. If there was no free will, why would God give us these rules? But at the same time, we have examples in the Torah such as God telling Abraham that his descendants would fall into slavery in a foreign land, only to be set free later, to return with great wealth. That promise occurred centuries before the actual event. It seems those humans that made choices in the intervening time thought they were acting with free will. But were they, or were they simply acting out a plan already determined by God?"

Larry thought for a moment. "Perhaps they were making their own choices, but God simply knew what they were going to do. Could that be the answer?"

"I wish it was that easy, but there are also plenty of examples in the Torah where God directly intervened in the affairs of man. On our exodus from Egypt, it is written that God repeatedly hardened the heart of Pharaoh so that he would not initially release the Israelites. Did the Pharaoh have free will in those examples, or was God exercising his right to divine providence? We have ended up in the same place as the Hindu thinkers, and arrived at the same answer. Most Jews believe that it is true that we humans have free will, but at the same time it is also true that our Creator can exercise divine providence as he wishes."

Larry gave a singled disappointed head shake. "Once again, religion provides a muddled response."

Rabbi Feldman objected strongly. "That's not fair, Larry! Just because it's not black and white, like our atheist friend presents, doesn't make our understanding wrong. We believe that human understanding is limited, but that our God knows all. Just because we can't verbalize His truth easily, doesn't make us wrong. In the end, we know that our God is sovereign, and that's what really matters."

As with the guru, Larry pressed, but this time with stronger emphasis. "So, rabbi, should we even bother to try to divert this rock, or should we simply throw up our hands in acceptance and wait for our extinction? This isn't some theology class where we can debate and then go have a beer. There are life or death decisions to be made immediately, on a global scale. What do you personally think we should do, and will it even matter?"

The spiritual leader folded his hands and brought them to his chest. "I am a humble and fallible man, as are we all. Here's what I believe."

He looked upward, as if silently petitioning for divine guidance before continuing. "I believe that each person should follow their own heart in accordance with their faith. I believe that God made man, and part of his design included imbuing us with a strong survival instinct, so therefore I believe that we are made by God to fight for our existence until our last breath. Until that time comes, I will counsel my congregation to do all that we can to somehow prevent our destruction. I will also tell them not to be afraid. Not to be afraid if our efforts succeed, or if they fail, because everything is already in God's hands. Is that clear enough, Larry?"

"I ask the hard questions because these are extraordinary times, rabbi, and people are looking to us for answers. Thank you for sharing your thoughts and advice based on your faith... but much remains cloudy."

Ken directed Camera Two to push in on Pastor Shadwell as Larry readied his transition. The faith leader's newly pressed suit and bold print tie signaled a return to his high energy norm. The fiery religious man fidgeted in his seat, seemingly anxious to comment. Larry noticed the movements and smiled, confident that the Christian representative would add to the tension that had already built. "Pastor Shadwell. You've publicly stated that you don't believe that this is god, but instead that it's actually the Antichrist. Is that still your position this morning?"

"Absolutely, Larry. Absolutely. That's why I'm so confident in saying that not only do we have the moral obligation to divert this heavenly object, I can say with complete certainty that we'll be successful."

Larry cocked his head. "You're going to need to explain that. How can you be so confident that we can change the course of the object in time?"

He spread his arms wide for emphasis. "It's simple. I believe in the inerrancy of Scripture, that the Bible is inspired and infallible. The Bible tells us exactly how the world will end, and this is not what is written. That means that this will NOT be the end! Plain and simple. And if this is not the end, then either our human efforts will be successful, or the one true God will step in and change the path himself."

A slow nod proceeded Larry's words. "I think I understand your logic. Since this version isn't in the Bible, then it's not going to happen, period, full stop, end of discussion. Wow, that's a lot of faith in the inerrancy and infallibility of the Bible. Any doubt, even just a tiny sliver?"

His eyes blazed with the intensity of the sun as he answered assuredly. "No doubt whatsoever, Larry, not even a sliver."

A soft laugh escaped from Larry's lips. "So, you're recommending everyone go to work and do everything they can to help the cause, right?"

"One hundred percent. I implore everyone to keep doing their jobs. We need everybody doing all they can to fuel this effort that God is surely blessing. That's what I'm asking of my flock and what all real Christians should do."

The hair on the back of Larry's neck tingled as he sensed another ratings spike. "Speaking of all Christians, I understand that the Pope has made it clear that he, and therefore all Catholic Christians, believe that this is God. Is the Pope wrong?"

The pastor's cheeks flushed immediately and he answered incredulously. "The pope? You mean mister infallible? Christians have been disputing his authority since Martin Luther penned his Ninety-Five Thesis in 1517. One man, one entirely fallible man speaking for all of Christianity? Show me where that's at in the Bible. I can tell you where it's at, it's not there. That whole structure was bought and paid for by selling forgiveness of sin, they called them indulgences. Is that in the Bible? No, it's not! Christ would be ashamed. Yet pope after pope blessed the practice for centuries, so pardon me if I think their whole structure is an abomination."

Conflicts drive ratings, and on the inside Larry reveled. But sensitive to the millions of Catholic viewers who had just been insulted, Larry masked his pleasure with fake disdain. "Pastor Shadwell, aren't you doing the same thing by claiming to speak for Christ himself? Doesn't that make you a hypocrite?"

The hot-tempered evangelical took a half step back. "Let me clarify, Larry. I have nothing but love for individual Catholics. In fact, in my family I have aunts and uncles and cousins who are believing Catholics. They are good Christian people, but there are some fierce doctrine differences within our faith, similar to those mentioned by Rabbi Feldman and Guru Mashni within their faiths. Sometimes I get a little fired up when talking about them. I disagree with many things about the Catholic Church, but I think that discussion would be best handled at another time."

Larry was set to explore that subject, but Ken was in his earpiece. "We've got video of violent clashes in Russia. Wrap it up, we've got to get in on the air before the Wolf network does."

Chapter Thirty

Monday Moscow 6:30 P.M. / New York City 10:30 A.M. / Thirteen Days to Impact

Katya Popov stood with her CBN mic in hand as the cameraman framed the massive God cloud far in the background. Between them and the cloud a violent clash between protesters was taking place. From New York, lead news anchor Sterling Roosevelt spoke. "Katya, what's happening in Moscow?"

After a couple of seconds of delay the former model turned reporter replied. "Sterling, as you can see, the God cloud arrived here in Moscow earlier today. As in New York, we're seeing the black version now and, if the pattern holds from earlier, there are expectations of the golden net version tomorrow."

"We see, Katya. What's happening with the demonstrators in the square? Who are they and what are they protesting?"

She briefly looked backwards and as she returned her gaze forward, the camera pushed in for a close-up of her high cheek boned, instantly recognizable face. "This all began as soon as the UN meeting ended in New York last night. In an interview with a Russian network, President Noskov said that what he witnessed was not God, but some alien invader who would next be heading here, to Moscow. He vowed to do all he could to prevent that from happening. Obviously, he wasn't successful. Meanwhile, on another network, Alexy the third, Patriarch of the Russian Orthodox Church, was equally adamant in proclaiming that what he saw with his own eyes was indeed God, and that He would be welcomed here. Supporters of each leader have filled Red Square. Police kept them apart for most of the day, but vodka fueled anger unleashed violence.

Shouts and insults turned into fist fights and stabbings as the day progressed."

Sterling interrupted. "Our viewers here in America are seeing footage that your crew shot earlier. It looks violent, but unorganized. What's happening now, and what are they chanting?"

Thick brown lashes batted over her sparkling gray-green eyes. "Just as we went on air, regular units of the army arrived on the scene. They brought a new level of intensity to Red Square as they broke up the opposing mobs. The alien invasion protesters are chanting something that roughly translates 'Resist the invasion' while the pro-God side answers, 'God rules all, resistance is useless.'"

"Interesting. So, Katya, I guess the armed forces are entering on the side of the president's protesters, is that right?"

"Yes, Sterling. There are also rumors that an arrest warrant has been issued for the patriarch. At this point, the president remains firmly in control of all the institutions of power."

Just then a wisp of smoke entered the frame and Katya coughed. "They're firing tear gas, Sterling. We have to go!"

The images from the live stream began to bounce and jostle as the CBN crew began sprinting away from the deteriorating situation. Sterling spoke to the fleeing crew. "Yes, go. Get to safety! We'll check back with you when you're in a secure location."

The feed from Moscow went black and Sterling intoned prophetically to his American viewers. "We wish them Godspeed as they make their getaway. Somehow I don't think this is the last time that we'll be reporting on scenes like this."

Chapter Thirty-One

Monday Penly France 6:00 P.M. / New York City 12:00 P.M. / Thirteen Days to Impact

Gaspard Marchand held the portable radiation detector near his face as he looked into the CBN camera on the outskirts of Penly, France. When he heard the New York based host introduce him in his earpiece he spoke in perfect but thickly accented English. "As you can see, Sterling, I'm a safe distance from the reactor."

Sterling spoke with urgency. "We're thankful for that, Gaspard. It sounds like it's been a terrible day there. What's the latest?"

The youthful reporter briefly glanced back and pointed to a column of steam rising above the facility in the distance. "It's awful. The plant has suffered a total meltdown and they have been forced to release contaminated material into the atmosphere. As of yet, there's no estimate as to when the event can be contained. This is an environmental disaster. I'm standing upwind of the facility, so I'm in no immediate danger at the moment. However, I'll have to be brief because the government is increasing the five-mile evacuation zone to twenty miles. That order goes into effect in just a few minutes."

Sterling leaned forward. "Have there been casualties?"

Gaspard affirmed. "Nine from the initial accident, and dozens more plant employees were exposed to at least some radiation, six of them are in critical condition in hospital."

A quick glance at his computer cued the next question. "We only have to think back to Chernobyl to understand how bad this is. Other than this national nightmare, how are things in the rest of the country?

"Not well, Sterling. The immediate area remains in the dark. Électricité de France, the main supplier of power in the country has managed the grid well enough to keep the lights on in Paris, but most of the rest of the nation is without power."

Sterling sighed. "Sounds pretty tough, how is the government reacting?"

An alarm could be heard in the distance. "I'm going to have to make these my final comments, Sterling. The twenty-mile evacuation notice has been given. The government has issued a martial law decree. Employees whose jobs have been deemed critical must report to work, or face immediate arrest. They are then being transported to their place of employment and are being forcibly held there until everything ends, or we divert the asteroid. It's a severe response, but I understand. Just look at what happened here."

Again, Sterling speculated on the future. "I agree, Gaspard. I bet we'll soon see similar responses here, and around the globe."

Chapter Thirty-Two

Monday 3:00 P.M. Arizona / 6:00 P.M. Washington D.C. / Thirteen Days to Impact

Minority partner and Space Rim facility manager, Nick Ravel guided Kalie along the floor of the hanger being utilized as the designated shuttle refit area. They climbed a ladder to a platform above the open cargo bay of the first shuttle, named *Nina*. Nick pointed down and spoke over the intermittent noise. "Our first priority is to strip as much volume and weight as we can in order to add additional fuel cells and still have room for the warheads. As you can see, we're making progress."

What Kalie saw was a shuttle bay barely transformed. Her words were sharp and pointed. "What part of extinction do you not understand! Damn it, Nick, I know that you're working quicker than ever, but we've got to move a lot faster, ten times faster."

Nick recoiled, then pushed back. "You know the safety rules, Kalie. We're not trying to refit a Winnebago; this thing has to survive a launch. Remember three years ago, when we lost that satellite rocket? You saw the fireball. Another explosion ten seconds after lift-off won't do us any good."

Kalie's eyes bore into him and her face reddened. "Yes, I saw the damned explosion, Nick. It almost cost us the company, but the stakes are so much higher now. Obviously, safety matters, but everyone dies if we don't move faster. We've got to change the mindset here, starting with you. That bucket of bolts launches successfully on Thursday, Friday at the latest. That's the bottom line. I don't care what kind of corners you have to cut or how much it costs." Her voice now rose to full shouting level. "Nothing else matters, do you understand?"

Everyone within earshot stopped working and turned to see the chastened facility manager being dressed down.

His voice lowered to a near whisper. "Yes, Kalie. I understand."

Their eyes remained locked as the adrenaline coursing through her body slowly ebbed. The blood faded from her cheeks and her voice returned to near normal speaking level. "Good. I'm glad we're clear on that." She glanced toward the office area. "I'll be setting up shop here until lift-off. Do you have an open space that I can commandeer?"

"We'll find something, I'll have Cathy help you get settled." Nick looked down at the shuttle. "We accomplished a lot when you were here, didn't we?"

Kalie touched her former business partner's elbow. "We sure did, Nick. I was straight out the Air Force, Miles was straight off Wall Street and you were straight out of NASA. We thought that there was nothing we couldn't do together. We made a good team, didn't we?" She glanced around, searching. "By the way, where's Miles, anyway?"

Nick laughed. "You know Miles, the thrill seeker. He's on an expedition to the South Pole. It's taking him a few days to get back on such short notice."

Her mouth curved into a smile as an image of her and Miles summiting Mt. Everest together two years ago came to mind. "A thrill-seeking money-man. They broke the mold after him, that's for sure."

Nick turned serious. "He still talks about you, now and again, you know. Whatever happen to you two, anyway?"

The strong woman that had just run over him, now blushed and averted her gaze. "He is exactly as he seems, a smart, rich, fun guy. The kind that every girl dreams about. Let's just say it's complicated, that sometimes things just don't work out."

An internal panel inside the shuttle bay finally released from its mooring, coming down in a bang. Nick shouted down to the crew. "Great job, guys. Only eleven more to go. Now that you've got the hang of it, get the next one down in half the time. Think you can do it?"

The foreman shouted back. "Sure thing, boss. Sure thing."

Nick turned his attention back to Kalie. "Now, where were we?"

The moment had passed and her steel demeanor returned. "Nice job raising the expectation with them. I need you to set up a short meeting with every crew before their next shift. They need to hear their marching orders from both of us. We push them to their limit twenty-four hours a day and this ship launches by the end of the week. Time's not on our side."

Chapter Thirty-Three

Monday 7:00 P.M. Washington D.C. / Thirteen Days to Impact

Outside the White House opposing groups gathered in Washington's oppressive July heat. They marched, waved signs and tried to shout over each other. The thousand or so people in each side were separated by heavily armed riot police. A contingent of soldiers were positioned just outside of the city on high alert, ready to respond on a moment's notice.

Looking out over the masses through a window in the family quarters, the president stood with an arm draped over Jill's shoulders. Chants of "Respect God's Will" slightly outdid equally fervent shouts of "Save Our World." An idle thought formed and spilled from her mouth. "As crazy as it was with President Spade, he never had to deal with anything like this. Kind of makes me jealous."

The remark prompted an involuntary snort from Jill. "True, but I wouldn't advise you to include that comment in your address tonight. Even as badly as his term ended, he still has loads of supporters. You've got enough to worry about without kicking that hornet's nest."

Abby pulled her close and kissed the top of her petite wife's head. "Don't worry, sweetie. I reserve those snide remarks just for you." She squeezed Jill for a moment. "In fact, I'd rather just stay here with you and make snide remarks about other people that I don't care for, but that's not an option. I need to head to the evening briefing, then prep for that address."

Jill's arm went around Abby's waist returning the hug. "I'll be waiting."

Abby embraced her again before they parted, then began making her way to the Situation Room. While the weather outside was hot and bright, even as evening approached, the windowless basement Situation Room existed in perpetual cool florescent lighting and the glow from huge monitors and dozens of computer screens. Everyone stood as Abby strode in, her silvery-gray chiffon tunic fluttering in her brisk pace. A perfunctory, "As you were" set the room back to work. Her cabinet awaited at the main conference table, now surrounded by two rings of aides and assorted peripheral staff.

"Good evening everyone, let's get right to it." She spoke even before taking her seat. "Tru, you're up first. What's the state of the homeland?"

Compared to this morning, Tru appeared even more spun up. "The good news for today is that none of our nuclear power plants are experiencing a meltdown." He let that statement breathe before continuing. "Unfortunately, several plants have gone offline around the nation as staffing shortages rose again. This is our biggest problem and we're heading the wrong way fast."

Abby rubbed her chin as she absorbed the bad news. "What else is going on out there today, any good news?"

Tru sighed as a slide appeared on the big screen. "Two new developments are now beginning to compete for attention." He pointed. "This is a picture from outside the White House an hour ago. Competing protests like this are popping up all over the place, in big cities and small towns alike. Social media is being used to coordinate both sides in new ways. There's no single leader yet, just kind of free-flowing digital word of mouth about where and when to gather. These protesters don't represent the majority of people, just the most extreme on each end of the spectrum. The groups that believe this is God are rallying around the general idea that we shouldn't be trying to thwart God's will by trying to block the asteroid. Their placards and banners say things like "Respect God's Will" and "Resistance is Useless." The other side spouts slogans like

"Save Our World" and "Resist the Invasion." Mostly the protests have been peaceful, but in Birmingham the alien invasion side hurled Molotov cocktails and fired weapons against their philosophical foes. A firefight broke out between both heavily armed groups and ninety were killed. I expect these kinds of demonstrations will only grow, especially as we share details and progress reports on our efforts to divert the asteroid. A new wrinkle is that we're also beginning to hear more reports of radicalized militia's, like that God's Infantry group, led by a religious fundamentalist named Carson Appleton. It's the same group referenced by the Minneapolis synagogue killer. They are starting to talk about taking an armed stance. It's just talk now, but who knows what they might do?"

The tapping of the pen on the pad commenced and her brow furrowed. "That sounds ominous and I really hadn't anticipated updates possibly causing problems. I'll need to think about that." She thought for a moment, then glanced at him again. "You said two developments were of concern. What's the second?"

A picture of an empty grocery store filled the screen. "We touched on this yesterday, but it's now a full-blown emergency. This is becoming a common sight all around the world, including here in the states. Most stores are completely out of food. Even if all of the workers were to continue to show up, it's doubtful that the shops can keep up with demand much longer. And the more that the media reports on the behavior, the faster it spreads. Churches, synagogues and mosques around the nation are running food banks based on the words spoken by the being they believe is God, but they too are beginning to run low on even the basics. But empty shelves aren't the real problem, it's what happens when those that get less begin to get hungry. Combine that with the fact that we have more civilian firearms in the U.S. than we have people and you begin to understand my concern. A hungry mother or father with a gun might do anything to feed their starving children."

Abby looked up at the ceiling for a few seconds, then back down, glancing slowly around at the table. "It's just two and a half days since the Gabriel video, only twenty-four hours since God's announcement. The veneer of civilization really is thinner than an egg shell and apparently even easier to crack. Any other issues, Tru?"

"Unfortunately, there are a multitude, like another mosque burning and a rise in vigilantism in all kinds of forms, but these are the top of the heap, at least for the moment."

"All right, I'll add a few words in my address tonight, hopefully at least slow the deterioration." She looked toward a smaller monitor to the right of the main one. "How about we get an update on our shuttles from Kalie. Can you hear us okay there in the desert?"

Kalie had remotely joined the meeting from Space Rim headquarters. "I can hear see and hear everyone just fine, ma'am, and things are picking up here."

The corners of her mouth lifted slightly, finally something to smile about. "Please tell us some good news."

Kalie looked directly into the camera with a glass wall behind her. The backdrop showed a crew in white coveralls at work. "We've simplified things with two crews working twelve-hour shifts. Coordinating with the facilities chief we've had meetings with them at the most recent shift change. I think I've got the mindset adjusted down here and the pace of activity has picked up substantially. We're going to be ready to launch even if I have to light the fuse with a match."

The president leaned forward excitedly. "Great news, Kalie. And how about the second shuttle. Has it arrived yet?"

Kalie hesitated. "Uh, about that. Seems there was a group of protesters that made their way onto the tarmac and delayed the takeoff of the jet scheduled to ferry the shuttle. It's delayed three hours. That doesn't sound like a lot, but we need every minute we can get. I'll have a plan in place to make up the time as soon as it arrives."

"Let me guess. It was a pro-God group."

"Yes ma'am. And like Tru mentioned, they were chanting, 'Respect God's Will' over and over. They were peaceful, but they linked arms, sat down and surrounded the jet. Security forces had to drag them away. I'm asking for increased security here in the desert as soon as possible."

Abby sighed again. "At least they were peaceful." Then she turned toward Braxton. "Make sure she gets everything she needs."

He promptly replied, "Yes, ma'am. I'm on it. It will be the most secure facility on the planet."

Looking back at the monitor, she wrapped up Kalie's debrief. "Good work out there, Kalie. You know how much the world is counting on you."

"We won't let you down, ma'am. I promise."

Moving on, the president turned back to her Acting Secretary of Defense. "Brax, what's the latest on our hacker team and getting some ICBM's ready for peaceful use?"

Tru was seated next to Braxton, and his near perpetual worried look contrasted with the general's easy smile. "The good news is that we let those guys, and they are mostly young men, into our systems and they haven't sabotaged anything... yet... that we know of. In fact, working together they've made a lot more progress than I expected. I think we'll have the guidance problem solved in plenty of time."

A wave of relief washed over Abby's face. "That's really good news, Brax. Really good news."

"I agree ma'am. But before Tru mentions it, I will. We've made a deal with the devil. If we do survive this asteroid, we'll be living in a completely changed, and more dangerous world. We've opened up our most sensitive nuclear secrets to some pretty nefarious dudes. Who knows what they might do?"

"Let's focus on saving the world from one disaster at a time. I would be thrilled if in two weeks we get to face that challenge."

Tru tilted his head and a half smile accompanied his sarcastic response. "I can't wait."

He wasn't trying to be funny, but the remark triggered the president and several cabinet members to chuckle. Abby answered, "God bless you, Tru. You are the perfect choice for Homeland."

He blushed at his unexpected recognition. "I try, ma'am."

"All right, Brax, where are we with the efforts to install new detonation systems on those warheads. It won't do us a damned bit of good to get them in space and have them just sit there."

Now it was time for Braxton to frown. "We're not quite as far along with that half of the equation. We did get the detonator plans from the Israeli's and it looks like they will work, if we can get them built and installed. That's where we've run into problems. We did emergency contracting with a preferred supplier, but half of their workers didn't show for their shifts today."

Abby leaned forward, closed her eyes and gently rubbed her forehead. "This problem is going to affect everything we try to do, isn't it?" It really wasn't a question that she expected someone to answer, just an acknowledgment of how people were responding to the news of the potential end of the world.

After a few moments of silence, Brax spoke up. "We're using local police to round up enough of the employees to get an assembly line moving."

Raising her head, Abby asked, "Is that legal?"

Braxton's smile returned. "I figured that I would ask for forgiveness later rather than permission now. After all, we're trying to save the world from extinction."

Tru piped in, "A declaration of martial law would certainly cover it. Just saying."

Abby shot him a knowing look. "Let's save that discussion for the end, okay?"

Tru held his hand up in mock surrender.

Abby continued the debrief. "All right, Effie, how's the world spinning today?"

It was Effie's turn to utilize the large central monitor. The slide showed steam rising above a nuclear reactor site. "As you've all heard, the nuclear power plant in Penly France had a meltdown today. Contamination from the site is drifting over France and big parts of the continent. For future discussion, ma'am, their president has declared martial law as a result of the disaster."

Abby nodded, having been briefed on it earlier. Effie glanced at the president as the next slide loaded, showing clashing protesters being shot with rubber bullets fired through clouds of tear gas. "And in Russia, your best friend, President Noskov, is struggling to contain growing civil discord. The pro-God versus alien invasion clash has grown exponentially, with Maxim resorting to jailing the head of their Orthodox Church. He thought that would calm things, but it did exactly the opposite, and it's all happening right there in front of God in his cloud."

Dallas spoke in disgust. "No wonder He's willing to let that asteroid kill us all."

The president sighed, "Just another dark chapter in our story. I like to think that we've had more good ones than bad, but when I see things like this, I'm not so sure."

Effie agreed. "You got that right, ma'am, but there may be bigger problems brewing."

The president's frown deepened. "That's been the trend for the past two days, Effie. What's the next shoe about to fall?"

The next slide advanced, showing a satellite photo of white circles in a desert environment. "This is a field of suspected underground missile silos located in in Iran. Human intelligence is reporting an unusually high level of activity at this, and other sites around the country. The Ayatollah has come out strongly saying this being is their prophesied Deceiver and in talking with Dallas, we think we have an idea what they might be up to, and it's not good."

Her hand motioned to speed it up. "Spill it, Effie. What flavor of crazy are they brewing?"

"Well, ma'am, Dallas tells me that since they believe that this is not God, they need to do something to speed the arrival of the quote, *"real"* God. We don't know for sure, but we think that they may be planning to nuke somebody, and that somebody is probably Israel. Fits with their fundamentalist view that Israel must be destroyed before the hidden Imam reveals himself, ushering in God's triumphant return."

Her high cheek bones reddened and an exasperated Abby vented. "It's not enough that the potential end of the world is imminent, they want to start World War Three just so that it can end their way? Like Dallas said, God was right last night, we do keep coming up with new ways to be cruel to each other."

Eyes watched and waited, calculating whether she was finished. She wasn't. "Well, screw them. It's one thing for God to wipe us out, but it's not okay for them to do it. Besides, I don't want to find a way to save the world only to inherit a nuclear scorched planet. Give me options ASAP, understand?"

"Yes ma'am. I'll work with Braxton to have a plan on your desk by noon tomorrow."

Slowly, the color in her face began to return to normal as everyone waited silently. "Any more good news, Effie, or are we ready to move on?"

Her sing-song delivery belied the darkness of her words. "That's the worst of it for now, ma'am, but tomorrow's another day."

A single "Ha" escaped Abby's lips as she turned to the newly recruited religious expert. "Anything to add on the God front that hasn't already been covered?"

Dallas leaned forward, clasped his hands, then placed both elbows on the table. "I think everyone has been very clear on how His arrival is impacting almost all parts of our world. What I can add this evening is more clarity around my comments this morning. I've been in contact with key faith leaders across the country on both sides of the God, alien invasion divide. Like Tru mentioned, seems there are radicalized factions on the God side that are preparing to go beyond protests like we're seeing here and like the ones that Kalie mentioned. Word is they are actively arming themselves, becoming vigilante groups dedicated to stopping any efforts to deflect the asteroid... by any means necessary. They see themselves as God's soldiers and will gladly die in His service. I can almost assure you that it's going to get violent. Combine that with the challenges that we've already talked about, like food shortages, concerns about power grid failures, etcetera, we could be looking at a completely unpredictable situation. Things are going to go south fast. I just can't say exactly how."

A pall fell over the room, and again all eyes turned to the president. "I guess that leads us to talking about the imposition of martial law.

In a few sentences, I want each of you to make your best case for or against imposing it now. Tru, you start."

The thin Homeland leader stood and buttoned the top button of his dark brown suit jacket. "I think you know where I stand ma'am. We need to keep the country functioning if we're going to survive these next two weeks. Declaring martial law gives us the tools we need. We risk things getting so out of hand that we won't be able to restore order if we wait. I see no reason to delay the inevitable." With that, he unbuttoned his jacket and sat back down."

She looked at the monitor. "Kalie, where do you stand."

A loud exhale preceded her comments. "Wow, here we are. I'm looking at what we have to accomplish just to give us a chance at diverting that rock. The smallest delays will quickly add up, giving us no chance for survival. On that basis alone, I'm with Tru. If not now, when?"

Abby nodded, then pointed to Braxton. "What do you say?

Taking Tru's lead, he stood as well. "Madam President, I fully understand the magnitude of ordering martial law across the entire country, it's been over a hundred and fifty years since a president took this step, but Lincoln did it to save the nation. We're facing an even bigger threat, so even though it's a big decision, I'm with Tru and Kalie. We don't have any other option."

She pointed to Effie as Braxton sat. "And you. Effie, where do you stand?"

Effie leaned on her cane to stand. "Ma'am, other nations have already taken this step, so you won't be the first, and the rest of the world is counting on us. As I see it, there are no do overs on this one. I counsel erring on the side of being proactive rather than waiting for things to get worse. I'm a yes as well."

Lastly, she turned to Dallas. "So, religious expert. What would Jesus do?"

He caught the humor of the 1990's Christian bracelet fad. "WWJD, that's a good one. While I'm not qualified to answer whether you should do it, I can say that you're on solid biblical ground if you choose to go that route. Romans thirteen is clear, 'Let everyone be subject to the governing authorities, for there is no authority except that which God has established. The authorities that exist have been established by God. Consequently, whoever rebels against the authority is rebelling against what God has instituted, and those who do so will bring judgment on themselves.' Several other religions have similar sentiments, so if you think this is a just course of action, you have biblical cover."

She opened the floor to the other cabinet members in attendance. "Any other thoughts on the subject? Anyone?"

Attorney General Hakeem Ali was the only one who spoke. "Madam President, I thought we might end up here tonight. I've got a final draft ready for your review. All we need is your signature."

Her gaze made its way around the table, searching for any signs of disagreement and finding none. "So, its unanimous." She paused for a few seconds. "I came to this briefing believing that we weren't at the point of a declaration, that we had more time. But the threats discussed and the advice given has been illuminating. As Effie made clear, we get one shot at this - no do overs."

She took a deep breath. "And while I believe in the character of the American people, their optimism and desire to do the right thing, they elected me to be their leader. I've fought my entire career to protect individual rights, but no one could have foreseen what's happening now. And the American people chose me to make the hard choices in the toughest times. It pains me to see our country, our world in this state, but based on these conditions, I now concur with your advice. It's time. I'll announce it tonight in my address to the nation."

She stood, signaling the end of the meeting. "Seems we're making history on a daily basis around here."

Chapter Thirty-Four

Tuesday 5:00 P.M. Moscow / 9:00 A.M. Washington D.C. / Twelve Days to Impact

Katya Popov stood in front of a window with a view of the golden strand version of the cloud reaching from Red Square to the edge of space. White-clad patrols flew inside in apparent protection of the site, just as they had in the United States. Sterling Roosevelt checked in with the CBN Moscow correspondent. "Katya, What's the latest from Moscow?"

"As expected, we're seeing the golden net version of the cloud today. It's the same pattern that you witnessed in New York."

"Looks like St. Basil's Cathedral has a new luster, just like we saw with the UN building."

The attractive reporter turned for a moment and admired the beautiful structure that gleamed in the late afternoon sun. "Absolutely, Sterling, it's a stunning sight. We were on Red Square this morning to witness sunrise, and it was almost a religious experience." Her perky disposition faded as she continued. "Unfortunately, government troops swept in and expelled everyone. That's one of the reasons that we're here, a few blocks away."

Worried tones tinted Sterling's voice. "We've heard of increasing clashes. What's happening on the streets?"

As if on cue, an explosion and subsequent ball of fire could be seen out of the window framing the journalist. She flinched, then moved away from the glass. A quiver registered in her voice as she answered. "Yesterday we reported on street clashes between God protesters and alien invasion protesters. That has given way to confrontations between different factions of the military. Most remain loyal to the president, but several units have rebelled in support of the patriarch, who remains jailed. Fists and Molotov cocktails have been replaced with mortars and bombs. It's real war zone now."

"I see, Katya. And it appears that this is going down within blocks of the glittering cloud. What's the official word from the Kremlin?"

Katya calmed her jitters. "President Noskov has sworn swift retribution for the rebels. No quarter will be given and no prisoners will be taken. It's the death penalty for all who disobey."

Another explosion could be heard in the distance and again Katya flinched. Sensing the impending end of the interview, Sterling asked his last question. "Speaking of swift responses, President Noskov swore that he would resist the cloud's arrival in your country. Were there any attempts to make good on that promise, or was it all just hot air?"

Katya's eyes darted from side to side before focusing on the camera. "Nothing has been officially reported from the Kremlin, but eye witnesses report that a fighter jet attempted to pierce that cloud in what was described as a kamikaze attack. The rumor is that the plane disappeared and that the pilot walked out of the bottom of the cloud an hour later. It's said he was completely nude, if you can believe that."

Another blast could be heard and the window from where Katya had begun her report, shattered. She screamed as shards of glass fell around her feet. Her chin trembled and with a 'deer in the headlights' expression she nervously signed off. "We've got to move to safety, Sterling. We'll contact you when we can."

As the feed from Moscow went dark, Sterling looked directly into camera one. "For those who question President Banister's declaration of martial law, I give this situation as evidence of the wisdom of that decision. God help us if anything like that happens here."

Chapter Thirty-Five

Tuesday Noon New York City / Twelve Days to Impact

Coverage of the declaration of martial law in the U.S. and the widening civil war in Russia dominated the news on cable outlets, led by CBN. The news division had featured journalists, like Katya Popov and current administration officials including Homeland head Trusond Patel, all morning. In addition to those events, new voices were gaining exposure on the airwaves. Scoring a major scoop, Larry persuaded one of these new voices to join the panel today. Carson Appleton, a charismatic leader of the fringe religious group called God's Infantry, had advocated armed resistance to the declaration of martial law on a Facebook video, which had gone viral. Previously unaffiliated individuals and groups around the country were swearing allegiance and support.

Larry was excited and glanced at his notes as makeup was applied right up until the last seconds before show time. He thought, *I've still got it,* as Jared began the countdown. "In five-four-three-two-one."

"Welcome, America, to this noon edition of Judgment Day. There is an old saying that 'desperate times require desperate measures.' I'll posit there has never been a more desperate time than mankind is facing now. We have seen times of war, of famine, of plague, and yet none of those desperate times threatened to erase humanity."

For dramatic effect, Ken directed him to pivot his gaze to camera two. "Last night President Banister suspended the Constitution and declared martial law with all civilian authority now under the direct command of our military, using this reasoning as the basic defense of her action. In response, Carson Appleton, the leader of a group called God's Infantry, went on online and argued that Americans should take up arms against what he called an immoral and illegal act."

Larry sat just a bit taller as he paused for a moment. "In today's special edition coverage, we're joined by Mr. Appleton as we discuss the moral questions around the president's decision and his call for armed rebellion. Before we begin our discussion, let's take a look at a clip from that his post."

On screen the handsome, blond haired man appearing to be in his mid-forties and dressed in cammo, began speaking. "America was founded by patriots fighting tyranny. Our God-fearing founders refused to live under a corrupt government that used the military to enforce their edicts. Back then our forefathers were concerned about being taxed without representation by that royal brute, King George the Third, and they took up arms."

Carson's videographer pushed in for a close-up. The group's distinctive white shield shaped insignia, a red crucifix overlaying crossed rifles, loomed large. Carson continued, "Today, God-fearing Americans are facing a new and even more tyrannical leader. This nation's sexually depraved excuse for a president, Abigail Banister, has ordered the armed forces of our great country to put down any resistance to her blasphemous goal of defying the will of God. The will that was proclaimed right here in America!"

He glared angrily as he continued. "Just like our brave founders, we say no to tyranny. Today we say no to this evil woman defying God's will. And just as they did, we are taking up arms, and we ask true believers around the country to join us in our righteous fight again this Jezebel!"

Ken Garner stopped the clip, and once again, Larry sat front and center. He feigned a frown, sensing what this historic opportunity could do for his career. Quickly, he introduced his returning panelists before sharing a split screen with Carson Appleton. "Those are strong words, Mr. Appleton. Words that might get you arrested, or even killed."

Carson was wearing his same garb from yesterday, but today a cache of weapons formed his backdrop. "Yes, they are. First, I want to say thank you for this opportunity to share my views with you, your panelists, and with America. I don't take this stand lightly, but I know this is what God demands of his servants."

Larry grinned wryly. "It sounds as if you are definitely in the God camp. Right?"

The brash, self-declared American guerrilla responded immediately. "Without a doubt. I mean come on, look at what He's already done. He's demonstrated His power; no nation can stand against Him. Look, He has inspired the people of Russia to rise up against their wicked ruler. That can happen here too, when His people band together."

Larry lit the fuse for conflict with his regular panelists. "There are going to be others who might deeply disagree with your interpretation of events. What do you say to them, and our viewers who disagree with you?"

Carson shrugged. "Come on Larry, just look around with an open mind. A Holy God has spoken and done mighty works. All He asks is that we accept His gracious offer of eternal peace. The Bible says, 'Do you have eyes but fail to see, and ears but fail to hear?' It's not that hard. It's right in front of us. A Holy God is telling us what to do, and a blasphemous sexual deviant is defying His word. Who should Christians believe?"

Larry questioned him further. "And the resistance stance, are you serious about open and armed rebellion against the United States government?"

Carson gave a half smile and spoke without emotion. "Operational planning is already well underway against this illegal regime. The world will soon see the wrath of God wrought against this illegitimate government."

Masking his glee, Larry turned to Pastor Jacob Shadwell who once again joined in studio. "Pastor Shadwell, here is a fellow Christian who takes a diametrically opposed view as you. You've said this being is not God, and that the president should do all that she could to deflect or destroy the incoming asteroid. How do you respond to Mr. Appleton and those who agree with him?"

Today, Pastor Shadwell wore a traditional gray suit with lapels too wide to be contemporary and too narrow to be retro. He would have looked at home in any community bank in America. While his attire was subdued, his temper wasn't. "Larry, scripture is crystal clear on this subject. First of all, this is NOT God! He has been perfectly clear on how our time on Earth will end, and this is not the way that He promised!"

The preacher's face reddened as he continued. "Secondly, I suggest that Christians read First Peter, chapter two, verse thirteen. It says, 'Submit yourselves to every ordinance of man for the Lord's sake: whether it be to the king, as supreme. or unto governors.' I suggest that Mr. Appleton take a closer look at his Bible, and that all Christians should obey this order and support the president!"

Larry sensed an opportunity to spark the firebrand. "So, you're saying the Bible instructs Christians to obey civil authority, no matter what? How about situations like slavery, here in America. The Confederacy used Bible verses they said condoned the practice. Should Lincoln have just accepted that, leaving millions enslaved?"

The pastor squirmed. "Well, uh, that was truly evil. And, uh, the Bible does speak of how that should be addressed." He paused, mind racing to find an appropriate scripture. His face lit like a neon sign as he landed on a biblical passage. "In the Book of Jeremiah, we're told of prophets who spoke, but not by His direction. 'Therefore thus saith the Lord concerning the prophets that prophesy in my name, and I sent them not, yet they say, Sword and famine shall not be in this land; By sword and famine shall those prophets be consumed.' I believe that this verse would justify Christians taking up arms against a truly evil government. And that's what happened in our

Civil War. But to be clear, I don't believe what President Banister ordered was evil. In fact, I believe it was God sent, since I don't believe that being masquerading as God is God. We must support her so that God's real plan can be fulfilled."

Larry gave half a laugh. "Pastor Shadwell, I do believe that you could take a Bible and argue with yourself. I would love to hear more, but first let's check in with our other panelists. Guru Mashni, where does Hinduism come down on the question of obeying the government, or armed revolt?"

The guru's teal blue kurta with gold neckline embroidery shimmered under the remote studio lights, but his usual effervescent mood was absent. "Larry, I have to say that I am appalled by this man's call for violence. Mahatma Gandhi demonstrated that peaceful resistance is the just way to reject bad government. Blood in the streets is not the answer."

"What he advocates is quite shocking, Guru Mashni, and I understand your distaste. Both Mr. Appleton and Pastor Shadwell have quoted scripture to defend their position. What do Hindu sacred writings have to say on the subject of rebellion?"

A slight shoulder shift set waves of light rippling down his garment. "That's a tough question. You see, in ancient India, the religious rulers were also the civil rulers, so there was no tension between the two. And Dharma was the basis for the legal system. It's based on natural laws in which specific rules are derived from an ideal, moral, and eternal order of the universe. Although I believe it is the right way for a legal system to operate, it is wide open to interpretation, especially in a modern, connected world. A case like this would be very problematic."

Larry's forehead creased and his nose crinkled. "So how would you ultimately sort out it out, the declaration and the subsequent call for rebellion?"

He looked heavenward for a moment before answering. "I can assure you, Larry, that my interpretation could surely be challenged by others, but for me, ultimately, I believe that this being is Vishnu, and what we do won't really matter. His will is going to ultimately prevail. Therefore, I would counsel obedience to the president's order. Why fight against the inevitable?"

Larry replied sarcastically. "So, we're back to the belief that everything is preordained, that we don't really have free will. Isn't that a cop out?"

Guru Mashni's cheeks reddened. "Life is not black and white. There's a lot of gray, that's just the way it is."

Turing to his other studio panelist, Larry questioned. "Rabbi, what do you think of this martial law versus revolt situation, and do you have a way out of this free will quandary?"

Rabbi Feldman substituted a white kippah with small blue embroidered stars of David around the outer edge, thus matching his beautiful prayer shawl. "I'm amazed at how many similarities there are between Judaism and Hinduism when you get down to core beliefs. The Talmud says 'Thus saith the Lord the King of Israel, and his redeemer the Lord of hosts; I am the first, and I am the last.' That tells me that God created the world and he will be the one who decides its end. Mr. Appleton, God did not need your help to create the world, and he most certainly does not need your help now. Set your ego aside and rejoice in his Holiness, don't descend into hatred."

Larry's forehead creased in frustration. "Rabbi Feldman, Guru Mashni and Pastor Shadwell all quote scriptures urging obedience to the president's order based on the belief that God's plan will be fulfilled, regardless of what we do, while Mr. Appleton urges armed revolt using the Bible to say that Gods plan can only be fulfilled with armed resistance."

He took a cleansing breath, then introduced Dr. Kim. "As our resident atheist, what would you say to our viewers and to your fellow panelists? "

Dr. Kim switched out her stylish black blazer over the pretty camisole for a fuchsia pink dress with plunging neckline, contrasting her look as well as her views. "No wonder we've had so many religious based wars. They all pick and choose what they want out of their supposed holy works to justify whatever they want to do anyway. Guru Mashni said that this is not black and white. I say that he's wrong. The choice is clear. Do nothing and be obliterated or at least try to save ourselves, as the president advocates. That's black or white."

"What do you say about the view that we should accept this is the will of God, and just wait for the end?"

Her eyes burned with anger. "That's suicide. Which of these fine gentlemen's' religions advocate that? It's in our DNA to fight for our survival, not beg for our death!"

Larry smiled. "You make a compelling and straightforward argument, Dr. Kim. Let's check back in with our newest panelist and see if any of these arguments has changed his mind. Mr. Appleton, has anything you've heard altered your thinking?"

His eyes were dull as if his soul had departed and when he spoke a chill reached through the airwaves from his remote location. "Nothing has changed. With God on our side we can't be stopped. Soon enough you'll see, everyone will see." With that he severed his link to CBN and this screen went blank.

A worried expression washed over Larry's face. "I don't think we've seen the last of Mr. Appleton."

Chapter Thirty-Six

Tuesday 4:00 P.M. Hawaii / 10:00 P.M. New York City / Twelve Days to Impact

Qu watched Wade paddle close to shore before standing and carrying his board up the sandy Ke'ei Beach where she waited on a blanket. She smiled, "Looks like some good waves today."

Her warm smile melted him as he tried to ignore the young marine standing guard about ten yards away.

Wade picked up his towel and dried his muscular body. "Yeah, I had some long rides."

Qu waved to their escort, "And you had an audience. I guess you'll be on the pro circuit soon."

"Ha-ha." Wade looked over at the guard and waved as well. "It's only been a few hours since Homeland put us under protective custody, and it already feels really creepy. I mean, would somebody really want to hurt the Keck faculty? I'm just glad that we could talk him into letting us do this. Seems like a pretty cool guy."

She looked up as he grabbed a beer from the small cooler, then sat down next to her. "Pretty cool... except for that machine gun."

He couldn't keep the smile from his face. "Well, other than that it's a beautiful day... if you don't count that killer asteroid that we're tracking."

A short laugh escaped her lips. "You had to bring it up, didn't you? You're here in paradise with a hot girl in a bikini, and you're thinking about a rock?" She leaned toward him and kissed his cheek.

This is how it had gone since the discovery. Craving to be near each other as often as possible, while coping with the first-hand knowledge of exactly how many hours might remain. Wade took a long drink from the bottle of Mexican beer. He set the bottle down and looked deeply into her eyes. "I only wish that I had met you sooner." He leaned closer and kissed her soft lips gently. "You are perfect in every way, and I love you."

Her dark eyes lit like twin stars at the unexpected first use of the L word. She searched his face trying to see if he was serious, or still just joking around. Seeing only sincerity, she pressed her lips against his in a long luscious kiss, then gazed into his eyes as their bodies separated. Her heart pounded and her mind raced at light speed as she considered whether Wade was just another guy, or something more.

The next day she would tell her best friend that subconsciously the gravity of the impending arrival of that asteroid focused her mind like a laser as her reply gave voice to a crystallized realization. "I love you too."

Chapter Thirty-Seven

Wednesday 6:00 A.M. Washington D.C. / 3:00 A.M. Phoenix / Eleven Days to Impact

A soft summer rain fell on the capital city as the now regular morning briefing was about to start. The number of government functionaries surrounding the cabinet members seated at the long conference table had continued to expand in opposite direction of the countdown clock now installed in the secure facility. The constant metered race to zero added a visual component to the sense of urgency in the room and across the world.

The president carried a cup of coffee to her seat at the head of the table and a hush fell over the room as if some unseen verbal dimmer switch had been turned down. She glanced at the countdown clock and dispensed with formalities. "Eleven days, five hours, fifty-nine minutes and fifty-nine seconds." She scanned the faces around the table, her usual sparkling violet-blue eyes seemed hard this morning, like frozen amethyst stones. "We've got a lot to do, so let's get right to it. Effie, I saw some disturbing headlines on the TV while I dressed this morning. Give us the latest."

"Madam President, bad things are happening around the globe. For starters, the Russian government has fallen. Although the coup isn't complete, Alexy the Third has been freed from prison and has been installed as the new leader by pro-God elements of the armed forces. It's rumored that President Noskov fled Moscow and was killed in an airstrike at a military base on the outskirts of the city. While our intelligence hasn't confirmed this, that's the chatter that we're intercepting."

The president shot a quick glance toward Tru, thankful for his insistence at declaring martial law here. "I remember wishing that karma would bite him in the ass, but I didn't want this. That means we'll get no help from their new government to try and stop this asteroid, right?"

"That's right, ma'am. They killed thousands of their own people, believing that they were doing God's will. We'll get no help from them."

The first taps of pen to pad began. "Is that the worst, or are we just getting started?"

Effie's forehead creased. "That depends. The cloud has now landed in Tiananmen Square and we have no idea how that's going to play, but the bigger news is that Gabriel has announced the next stops on the cloud tour. What's going to happen when they go to Najaf, in Iran, Delhi, Rome, and Mecca, with a final stop in Jerusalem, just in time for the asteroid's arrival."

"Holy moly." Dallas' words escaped his mouth before he could stop them. "Excuse me, everyone. It's that she just named the most important cities for both branches of Islam, for, Hinduism, for Catholicism, and for Judaism. Covering the UN building is one thing, but what's going to happen when that cloud takes over the most sacred sites of the largest religions in the world?" He rubbed his balding dome, trying to wrap his mind around the potentially volatile possibilities. "Wow."

Effie confirmed his concern in her soft Southern drawl. "Uh huh. That's right Dallas. And let me give everyone an example. Intelligence has now confirmed that Iran is readying missiles for a nuclear strike on Jerusalem. How will this cloud landing on their holiest site three days from now affect their already twisted logic?"

Looking toward the president, Effie continued, "And on top of that, Madam President, Israel knows of Tehran's plans and is preparing a preemptive strike of their own."

The air conditioning suddenly seemed too cool as a shiver ran down Abby's spine and goosebumps brought the fine hairs on her arms to attention. "What a world we live in."

She took a sip of coffee and swallowed hard. "And as bad as that war would be, we still have this bigger problem. Brax, you work with Effie on options to try and stop them from mutually destroying each other, but I don't want that planning to slow down our efforts to stop that rock. That's the real game ender. Got it?"

They answered in unison. "Yes ma'am."

She tapped her pen again, then used it to point to Braxton. "Speaking of that rock, what's the latest?"

Braxton gave half a smile. "We're definitely making progress, ma'am. We're beginning the process of loading the first batch of warheads onto a transport plane to take them to Space Rim. I'm headed to Amarillo to personally accompany them from the Pantex plant to Kalie."

"That is good news. Are they ready for launch?"

His smile widened. "Almost, ma'am. We've overcome the initial delays and the first of the new detonators are almost finished. They're being shipped from Michigan as we speak. Hopefully, installation will go smoothly tonight and we'll be able to load them the moment the first shuttle is ready."

Abby released a sigh of relief. "Some good news for a change. Kalie, can you keep that trend going?"

Her remote feed from the Arizona desert filled the large monitor. A swarm of night shift workers could be seen moving in the background. "Good news here as well. We've found a good rhythm between the design team and production. I think we'll be able to launch on Friday, and work has started on the second shuttle. With all that we've learned on this first one, we will be able to turn it around even faster." She smiled. "We're shooting for the second launch on Saturday, that is if Braxton can deliver the second batch of warheads on time."

Braxton laughed. "Don't worry about me, Kal, I'll hold up my end. You just worry about yours."

This time she not only let the use of her nickname slide, but beamed as she replied. "We'll be ready, Brax. You just get yourself and those nukes here soon."

Even in this high stress environment, Abby noticed the warmth between them. *Huh, maybe their spark wasn't totally snuffed out. Good for them.* The corners of her mouth turned upward just a bit as she shifted to the next cabinet member. "Tru, we've had a couple of good news reports. Can you keep it going?"

The dark circles under his eyes had deepened. "I can at least start with some good news. Seems martial law has had a positive impact on internal security. Looting has been reduced almost in half, and other than Milwaukee, we're not seeing nearly the same level of rioting and fires."

"That's certainly good news, Tru. What's bothering you?"

He sighed, apparently sorry to be the bearer of bad news yet again. "Our first concern had been the random violence as well as the shutdown of basic services, like electricity. While those risks are not gone, they have certainly declined. What's taking their place is organized and armed resistance. That God's Infantry group is a prime example."

Dallas chimed in. "I've watched their videos and read up on their ideology. They were fringe and pretty much ignored until this God event happened. Now their militant advocacy of armed disobedience to any civilian rule they feel contradicts God's will suddenly seems like a real option for those that believe we should not be trying to stop this asteroid."

Tru pointed toward Dallas. "Exactly, and they're not just a lot of talk either. We have an undercover operative in the group and arms of all size are flooding in. They have some real firepower at their disposal. They can't replicate what happened in Russia, but they can raise a lot of hell."

The report earned a couple of taps of the president's pen. "Use whatever means necessary to neutralize their threat. I hate to say this, but we'll apologize for trampling their first amendment rights when this is over. What good are constitutional rights if there aren't any people left to protect?"

Tru shook his head in agreement. "Exactly, Madam President. I'm on it."

She now turned to Dallas. "We've already talked a lot about God this morning. Anything else we should know today?"

He raised his eyebrows momentarily before he spoke. "Effie already broached what I feel could be the most important subject discussed today. I'm going to put together a document forecasting how each religion might react when that cloud arrives in their holy city. It won't be definitive, but I'll get it to everyone ASAP to provide at least a best guess as we prepare our potential responses. Things could get messy fast."

A short laugh came from Abby. "Ha, as if they weren't already?"

Dallas blushed. "Yes ma'am, I should have said messy-er."

Abby stood, signaling the end of the meeting. "I would like to say that things can't get worse." She paused for a few seconds. "But we all know they will."

Chapter Thirty-Eight

Wednesday 3:00 P.M. Outside of Amarillo Texas / Eleven Days to Impact

Twelve hours ago, Chad Bostrom recorded his goodbye video, ready to be uploaded as soon as his mission was completed. Now he lay alone under camouflage netting outside of the Pantex plant near Amarillo. He had remained almost completely still for the past ten hours under the blazing Texas sun passing the time in prayer and wiping sweat from his brow as he awaited final instructions from his leader. He startled when his phone vibrated. "Good afternoon, General Appleton."

Carson answered from the safety of his hidden bunker nestled in the Black Hill mountains of South Dakota. "Chad, how are you holding up? Are you ready?"

Chad's prone lanky frame stiffened, as if he was standing at attention in the presence of his commanding officer. "I'm fine sir, ready to go."

A knowing smile slowly crept across Carson's face. "And did you take the Valium on schedule?"

"Yes sir, two hours ago. Just checked and my resting heart rate was fifty-eight beats per minute."

This news widened the smile. "You're a good soldier, Chad. Make that a great soldier. Oh, and your farewell video was excellent. You're giving closure to your family and friends and I really liked the end, giving all of the glory to God. You're a righteous patriot and a friend. I'm proud to serve with you."

A slight quiver accompanied Chad's response. "I feel the same way about you, sir. You're doing God's work and I'm ready to do my duty."

Carson exhaled. "My friend, the appointed time is here. Any last words?"

There was a moment of silence from Texas followed by a succinct reply. "Only that I'll see you in God's embrace soon, sir."

"Amen, my brother, amen. I'll see you on the other side."

"Yes sir." With the personal talk over, it was time to complete his mission. He immediately set up the tripod for his phone and began video streaming his final preparations back to Carson's base.

He heard the approaching roar of the jet carrying the first batch of nuclear warheads to Phoenix as it lifted off. He slung the camouflage netting away and swung the Stinger surface to air missile launcher to his shoulder and activated the controls, making sure that he was in frame for the video. It would have been nice to have a spotter, but after serving two tours overseas, he felt more than confident that this would be an easy shot.

He placed his left hand under the tube mechanism, angling it skyward, his finger on the trigger. He spotted the still low flying cargo jet approaching, then looked through the sighting scope, aligning the cross hairs. As soon as he achieved a lock, his finger squeezed the trigger. The missile fired from the launcher and sped to Mach Two in a matter of seconds. Moments later a fireball exploded over the scrub grass plain.

He looked directly into the phone's camera that had captured everything. "We did it! Direct hit! Take that you harlot! No one can stand against the will of my God!"

In the next second a drone locked onto his position and a violent flash was the last thing transmitted to the God's Infantry base. Carson winced, then coolly spoke to his lieutenant. "Upload this footage and his farewell message to the internet as soon as possible.

The world should know that Chad was a hero... and that he's our first martyr."

Chapter Thirty-Nine

Wednesday 4:30 Washington D.C. / 1:30 P.M. Phoenix / Eleven Days to Impact

The phone rang in the residential section of White House just a few minutes after Abby had arrived. She hoped for a few minutes of down time and a very late lunch with Jill before the evening briefing. She let it ring as she swallowed a bite of her ham sandwich, washing it down with water on the fourth ring. "Hello?"

Trusond's agitated voice replied from the Situation Room. "Madam President, we need you here immediately. There's been an incident."

Her muscles tensed involuntarily. "What's wrong Tru? How bad is it?"

He raised a worried hand to his head. "Ma'am, there's really no good way to tell you this." His mind raced, searching for the right words. "Ma'am, there's been an incident."

"Yes, Tru, you told me that. What happened?"

Embarrassed, he started again. "The plane carrying the first batch of warheads had gone down. There were no survivors."

"What? How could that happen? Our plans..." Then it hit her. "Brax was on that plane, wasn't he?"

"Yes, ma'am, he was."

Stunned, she glanced at Jill as she replied. "Oh my God, I'll be right down."

As she hung up the phone, Jill rushed and wrapped her arms around her wife. "What happened, dear?"

In disbelief Abby's words tumbled out. "Somethings happened in Texas. They tell me that Braxton is dead... and I'm sure that's not the worst of it." She squeezed Jill tight and a tear ran down her cheek. "I'm sorry, sweetie, but I have to go."

Abby wiped the tear away. "I've got to pull myself together. They can't see me like this." She pulled a tissue from a box on the sofa table and dabbed, trying not to smear her make-up. "I'll be back as soon as I can, sweetie."

She leaned down and gave a goodbye peck on Jill's tear stained cheek, then quickly made her way downstairs. The swift walk did her good as she made a determined entrance into the Situation room. "I want answers, now! What the hell happened?"

Tru had regrouped and stood as video from the scene was steamed to the center monitor. "Ma'am, I'm sorry to report that just after takeoff, a lone attacker launched a surface to air missile that was a direct hit on our transport plane. All aboard were killed and radioactive material from the unarmed warheads has contaminated the ground and is being blown across west Texas, toward Oklahoma."

Abby remained standing at the head of the table. "Do we know who did this?"

Tru pointed to the technician running the video. A new stream began and Tru introduced the content. "This was loaded onto the web almost immediately after the attack by that terrorist group, God's Infantry."

The video showed a man aiming, then launching the missile and the fireball at impact. After his celebration and immediate execution, his farewell video began to roll next. Tru let it go a few seconds, then asked for it to pause. "We've had these video's taken down, but it seems that Carson Appleton is making good on his armed insurrection threat."

The president slammed her hand down hard on the table. Her voice blazed with anger and the veins on her neck bulged like those of a weight lifter in the gym. "I want his head on a pike by this time tomorrow! Does everyone understand?"

Startled by the outburst, background noise hushed into library silence. Tru answered for all. "Yes ma'am. He's a dead man."

Her anger began to subside and she slowly sat down. "This sure screws the hell out of our plans. I know it's early, but what's our back up?"

The Homeland Secretary followed her lead and took his seat as well. "We already had a second shipment scheduled, so I'll work with..." His word trailed off as he realized what he was about to say. "I'll work with appropriate Defense personnel to speed that process up as fast as possible. I'll have a firm timetable to you, ASAP."

Abby caught the slip and it turned her stomach, but she pressed ahead. "We'll mourn Braxton in due time, but right now we're literally between a rock and a hard place. Get Joint Chiefs Chairman Hagans up to speed. I trust him and I want him to be the next man up whether that's the chain of command or not. Got it?"

"Yes ma'am. I'll work with Cliff and get him here in time for the next briefing. I'll also work with the communications team to get an appropriate message to the news media, if you would like."

Her thin lips pressed tightly for a few seconds. "Damn it! I'd rather keep this quiet for a while but I'm sure a few million people saw those videos before we yanked them. So, yes, Tru, and thanks."

Her mind skipped ahead like a pebble across water. "Get Kalie on the screen, I need to talk to her."

The technician handling the video scramble to make the arrangements.

With a slight lull in the action, Effie jumped into the conversation. "Madam President, while we are all shocked and saddened by today's events, I do have some good news to offer. I've been in contact with the Chinese and learned some very interesting information."

Abby turned toward her. "We could all use a dose of that, Effie. What's up with President Zhou?"

"Well, for one thing he's been freaking out behind the scenes after what happened in Russia while the cloud was there, but it's been a lot calmer in Beijing. He's making good on his pledge to add as many ICBM's to our joint defense as we can supply detonators and guidance system upgrades for. Lucky for him, most Chinese citizens are reacting like this is a mobile art installation, taking selfies and things like that, but I think the fear did push him to let us in on a little secret."

"This sounds interesting, Effie. Do tell, what have they've been hiding?"

Effie looked conspiratorially over her glasses and grinned like the proverbial Cheshire cat. "Seems they've been working on a space-based laser that's way more advanced than we imagined, and they think they can use it to help. It wouldn't be able to destroy the entire asteroid, but if it were to break into smaller pieces from our combined nuclear shield, they might be able to zap at least some of them into even smaller pieces. It's not a complete game changer, but it's something."

The president was about to answer when the technician interrupted. "Madam President, I have your National Security Advisor onscreen."

Abby gave a thumbs up to Effie as she turned toward Kalie. Puffy eyes and red cheeks peered back. "Oh, Kalie, we're all so sorry for your loss. I speak for all when I say that we wish we were there to wrap our arms around you."

Kalie wiped away a tear with the back of her hand. "I'll be fine ma'am. I mean we've not been close for a while. It's just the shock."

From off screen someone handed her a tissue. "Besides, I'm more upset about what this does to our schedule. We don't have time for these kinds of delays."

"You're right, of course, but this is the hand we have to play now. You just get both of those shuttles ready and we'll get those warheads to you as soon as we can. Tru is working on that as we speak."

She pulled her shoulders back and her voice lowered. "We'll be ready here, ma'am. You can count on us. I won't let those bastards stop us, no matter what it takes."

Chapter Forty

Thursday Noon Washington D.C. / Ten Days to Impact

With the fast pace of the news cycle and the sheer amount of moving parts in the plan to save the world, news of domestic terrorism resulting in Braxton's sudden death had already receded from the foremost concern. At the early morning briefing Kalie reported that the second shipment of warheads had arrived and new detonators were being installed. The Chairman of the Joint Chiefs of Staff, Declan Hagans, had been brought up to speed and reported that the hacker group was now ahead of schedule and were bringing the Chinese up to speed on implementation for their ICBM's. The main sore point from the morning had been that Carson Appleton was proving harder to apprehend than anticipated. That fact made it topic number one for the noon briefing.

The president's tone was blunt as she addressed Tru. "Tell me that we've made progress on catching or killing that son of a bitch."

Tru sat square shouldered but his face was down fallen. "Progress, yes, but he's still in the wind. We raided his bunker in South Dakota, but he was already gone. We've identified how he's communicating with his followers and that should help us track him down. We'll have him soon."

The answer didn't seem to satisfy her. "Sooner than later." It was a statement not a question.

He looked her straight on and replied, "Yes ma'am. Very soon."

Abby next turned toward the center monitor with Kalie joining remotely. "How are things going in the desert this morning."

In the brief seconds of her time delayed answer, sirens filled the gap, startling everyone around the table in the Situation Room. Tru stood and shouted. "We're under attack! Get the president out of here!"

In the fury of moving bodies, Secret Service Agents rushed forward from their positions around the room. One on each side, they took her by the elbows, gently but firmly, speeding her rise from her seat and then immediately spiriting her to a door on the left side of the meeting space.

She spoke insistently. "You've got to get Jill. I'm not leaving until she's with me."

Allan, the agent she knew best, answered in clipped bursts. "Yes ma'am. We're getting you to safety first. David is right outside of her door. He knows the drill. You'll be together soon. This way ma'am."

A muffled quick succession of explosions followed her from the basement Situation Room into a tunnel leading to a secret underground complex. Allan stopped. "We'll wait here until we know more about what's going on outside."

The noise from two more explosions filtered through the reinforced concrete walls of the bunker and other members of her cabinet now joined her. Abby was impatient. "What's happening out there, and get Jill down here NOW!"

Tru came to her side. "Madam President, the White House is under attack. The early report is a combined drone and mortar assault. Counter measures are being deployed as we speak. I'll have a better picture of what's going on in a few minutes."

From an adjoining tunnel Agent David McGanz emerged cradling Jill. Blood dripped from a gash across her forehead. "Don't worry ma'am., it's not as bad as it looks." He pressed a handkerchief firmly on the wound and sat her down on a narrow bench against the wall. Paramedics rushed to attend to her wound.

Abby was by her wife's side in an instant. "Oh sweetie, are you okay?"

Jill managed a weak smile, then winced as sterile gloved medics cleaned the wound and applied surgical tape, mostly stopping the bleeding. "I'm okay. I tripped and fell when I heard the first explosion." A peep of a laugh followed. "The coffee table is definitely harder than my head."

Abby leaned in close and hugged her, whispering in her ear. "Oh God, Jill. I'm so glad that you're safe. I'll get the assholes who did this to you." She stood, now tenderly holding Jill's hand while addressing the paramedics. "You guys take good care of her, she means the world to me."

They answered affirmatively in unison as Abby looked down looked into Jill's eyes and squeezed her hand. "Now that you're safe, I need to step over there for a few minutes. We won't be out of sight. I promise."

On her walk to her team she noticed Jill's blood on her white silk blouse and the thought of losing her wife fueled anger at the perpetrators of this deed. She lit into her cabinet. "I'm a whole new level of pissed. No one hurts my wife and gets away with it. What the hell is going on out there?"

Again, Tru provided the update. "Information is still coming in, but from what I can tell, a coordinated attack was launched from several locations. Our anti-drone and air defense systems reacted and stopped most of the incoming fire, but there have been collateral casualties, especially among the demonstrators who were protesting in the street. Sounds like we've neutralized most of the attackers but not without suffering some damage to parts of the White House."

Abby sighed in disgust. "We're going to see uploaded videos of this attack in a matter of minutes, aren't we? This is the work of Carson Appleton, isn't it?"

Tru met her gaze head on, feeling the pressure, but bound by his responsibility. "We won't know for a few more minutes, but I'm guessing yes. It's right up his alley. He can't stop us by himself, so he's trying to build support through terrorism."

As she listened her anger burned. "This is national security ...and now it's also personal. Enough of this shit, do you all understand?"

Affirming nods and mingled "Yes ma'am's" answered, then Tru steered the conversation to a new subject. "Madam President, it's my duty to advise you that we need to implement continuity of government plans fully. We need all members of Congress as well as you and the cabinet in secure locations. We'll get this guy, but who knows how many plots are already in motion? We have to do it."

Abby glanced over at Jill, now sporting a large white bandage on her forehead above her left eye. As the paramedics repacked their bags, Jill caught her gaze, smiled weakly and raised her hand in a small wave. Abby returned the wave and smile, then turned back to her cabinet assembled in front of her. "As much as I hate to take this step, it's for the best. If we stay it just put's a target on our backs and endangers civilians as well. Make it happen."

A wave of relief swept across Tru's face. "Thank you, ma'am. It's the right decision. Now Effie for sure must be in a different location as she would be fourth in line should something..." He stopped. "well, you know."

"You don't have to sugar coat it Tru, we all know what's at stake."

He nodded, then continued. "The good news is that Dallas isn't in government, so he could be at your location if you like.

"Yes, that would be helpful."

Tru continued in all seriousness. "And, Madam President, I would also like to be at your location. Homeland Security is number fifteen in the succession line. If it gets all the way to me, I don't think it will matter."

The president found this funny, and laughed. "I get what you're saying, Tru. But don't sell yourself short. As head of Homeland you are very important. I think it would be a good idea to be at separate locations, just in case."

He blushed as he now saw the humor. "Yes ma'am."

With the seriousness of their discussion, no one had noticed that it had become quiet, as explosions had ceased. Allan stepped forward. "Madam President, we've been given the all clear."

Relief registered as her tense shoulders fell just a bit. "All right everyone, follow Tru's directions. Stay in touch today as new information becomes available. I would like to have everyone at your assigned location and ready for a virtual meeting in the morning." She took half a step, then added one final thought. "Oh, and let's be clear. I want Carson Appleton in chains or dead by sundown."

Chapter Forty-One

Friday 9:00 A.M. Tehran / 12:30 A.M. Washington D.C. / Nine Days to Impact

An unsettled mood emanated from the Iranian cabinet as President Hossien Namazi called this second special session of the Iranian cabinet to order. He stared down to the opposite end of the oval table and once again saw Supreme Leader Ayatollah Mohammad Ka'bi. He dispensed with formalities and first addressed Amir Zarif, Minister of Defense. "The cloud of the Deceiver has left China and is now here. What is the latest news?"

As the only member wearing a military uniform, Zarif stood out. "Unlike in Russia and China where the cloud settled in their capital cities, in our nation it has settled in Najaf, completely engulfing the Imam Ali Mosque."

His statement provoked grumbling among the other attendees and he allowed a few moments of low murmurs before he continued. "By choosing a location over one thousand kilometers from our capital and instead selecting our most holy site, I believe that the Deceiver is making a bold and public statement. He mocks us."

The president leaned forward. "And how are our people reacting, seeing this black cloud take over the mosque?"

Amir stammered. "Uh, it has been a tumultuous scene, but it is now mostly under control. As people thronged to see the sight, our initial police presence was over whelmed. Thousands broke through the barricades and ran into the cloud shouting 'Death to the Deceiver'. Reinforcements arrived and order was restored... that is until those thousands exited the cloud, walking back completely naked, shouting 'Allahu Akbar'. They have been detained and have no memory of the encounter, yet they continually chant, 'Allahu Akbar' again and again. This has stirred dissent among the masses as some now believe that this is indeed Allah, despite our official statements to the contrary. Fights within the crowd are now common."

Hossien thanked Amir for the update then locked eyes with the Ayatollah, dreading the words that he expected to hear, but feeling as powerless as an ant on a train track to stop the oncoming express. "Supreme Leader, you have heard the news from Najaf. What counsel do you wish to provide regarding this matter?"

The elderly spiritual leader stroked his beard and his dark eyes sparkled. "Blessed is the truth of the Quran. The Al-Masih ad-Dajjal is as cunning as promised. He is confusing the faithful and it is our duty to reveal his true nature and bring about the war between the Muslim and the Jew. Only then will the Mahdi reappear and bring about Allah's perfect will. It is time for us to act."

The president braced himself with a deep breath, dreading what he felt compelled to say next. He forced the words though his lips while trying to appear sincere. "I understand, Supreme Leader. Preparations have been made. The missiles are ready."

The Imam continued to slowly stroke his beard as he unblinkingly stared at the president, the corners of his mouth subtly lifting. "Tomorrow the cloud will transform into its golden net form, making it ripe for ridicule. A noon launch will demonstrate that unlike those Sunni dogs, true Islam will not bow down to this false god. Allahu Akbar!"

A muscle in Hossien's jaw involuntarily twitch before he regained his composure. He forced a fake smile. "As you have spoken, Supreme Leader, so shall it be done. Allahu Akbar."

Chapter Forty-Two

Friday 9:00 A.M. Camp David, Raven Rock & Mount Weather / 8:00 A.M. Offutt Air Force Base Nebraska / 6:00 A.M Phoenix / Nine Days to Impact

The large screen in the presidential bunker located under Camp David glowed empty until one by one the video feeds from remote locations across the country populated individual squares with familiar faces. She and Dallas watched as Acting Secretary of Defense, Declan Hagans, joined from the nearby bunker at Raven Rock Mountain with four other cabinet members. Tru and four other cabinet members, as well as Vice President Puckett, linked in from the bunker at Mount Weather in Virginia, while Effie and four others followed next from their location in the bunker under Offutt Air Force base in Nebraska. Last to be added to her screen was Kalie from Space Rim headquarters in Arizona.

After technicians finished their checks the president called the virtual meeting to order. "I trust that everyone can see and hear me okay?"

Everyone answered at once resulting in a garble of "Yes ma'am's."

The cacophony of voices raised a smile on the president. "This is going to take some getting used to. I'm sure that we'll get good at it just in time to go back to D.C." Her optimism was contagious, even across the miles that separated them.

She continued, "We'll run this as close to how we would if we were in the same room. Let's start with Homeland. Any good news to share?"

Tru almost smiled. "Some, ma'am. An hour ago, a special forces team cornered components of Carson Appleton's leadership group in a Klan compound outside of Dawson Springs, Kentucky. After a brief but intense firefight, twenty-eight of his supporters were killed." His near smile faded as he continued. "Unfortunately, Carson Appleton was not among the dead and we suffered three casualties as well."

"Damn it, I want this guy to pay for what he has done. Spare no expense in his capture or death, understand?"

"Yes, ma'am. I understand."

She tapped her pen as she curbed her ire. "I'm sorry for our loss of life. Please send my condolences to the families and let them know that their loved ones died heroes."

"Yes ma'am. I'll make those calls as soon as possible."

She sighed. "Anything else from Homeland?"

Tru soldiered on. "While the take down this morning degraded Appleton's operation, he still has many followers who remain capable of continuing his quest. They remain dangerous. And we continue to have major concerns about workers in key industries not showing up for work, as well as what's becoming routine clashes between local militias and armed thugs."

Abby saw his strain and offered support. "Your team did good work today. Twenty-eight fewer domestic terrorists helps our cause." She paused as another topic now came to mind. "Oh, Tru, how is our continuity of government relocation playing across the country?"

"I don't have a complete picture yet, but it seems to be dividing along two thoughts. First, people seem to understand that the attack on the White House put civilians at risk more than us, so they seem to understand the logic. But on the other hand, many also view it as putting our needs first and wonder why they shouldn't do the same.

That could show up in ways like people not showing for work in crucial positions... or worse."

"I see. What can I do to minimize those reactions?"

"Your statement last night was a good first step. I think we need to wait until we have a better idea of how this is going to play out before take our next step. Lord knows we already have enough on our plate for today."

"Agreed." Sitting with Dallas in the quiet underground room, she pointed to the next face on her screen, just to the right of Tru. "All right, Declan, what's the latest from Defense?"

The war wizened Acting Secretary exuded calm competence. "Ma'am, I'm happy to report that all remote detonators have been installed on warheads in Arizona and have been loaded into the shuttle bay. It's now up to Kalie and her crew."

The president gave two quick raps of her pen on her pad. "That's fantastic news! And how about the ICBM's? What's their status?"

One of the medals on his uniform caught the light and a twinkle beamed to all of the call participants. "We have good news there as well. Those hackers have really stepped up to the plate. Programming of the guidance systems is almost complete on our missiles, and they are rapidly getting the Chinese up to speed. The new detonators are taking some time to install, but if things continue at this pace, we'll be able to launch the first batch by Tuesday."

The steady rap, rap, rap of the president's pen resumed. "That's good news, general, but it seems to be cutting things mighty close. Any way we can get it done by Monday?"

Declan's jaw set firm. "We'll do everything that we can to speed things up, ma'am."

She nodded, "I know that you are all doing your best. With that said, let's go to the desert next. What's the latest at Space Rim?"

Kalie's eyes were puffy and she wore glasses today instead of contacts. "We've been working non-stop ma'am, and we also have good news to report. All of the warheads have been secured in the shuttle bay and the vessel is now on the launch pad. Fueling operations have just commenced. We're working on an expedited schedule, and should be able to launch this afternoon, around 3:00, local time."

Spontaneous cheers and hand claps streamed across the virtual meeting. Abby's face lit up like a billboard in Times Square. "That's fantastic news, Kalie! I knew that you were the right woman for this job. This truly is good news."

Kalie adjusted her glasses as uncertainty clouded her face. "We've put all we had into this, and I'm proud of the team."

Abby interjected. "I sense a 'but' coming."

Now a small smile forced its way onto her face. "You would make a good poker player ma'am. I just need to remind everyone that with our need to get this shuttle launched immediately, we haven't had any time for testing. We've changed the total weight and its distribution in the craft significantly. Every space launch carries risk, and this one even more so. Just say a prayer for us this afternoon."

The rapping resumed. "We will, Kalie. We will. Let us know if you need anything else. All right, let's shift gears and go to State. Effie, what's the good news outside of the U.S.?"

The fluorescent lighting from the Nebraska bunker gave her dark skin an ethereal sheen, but her silky toned voice centered her comments firmly to Earth. "Ma'am, there's an old movie from the sixties called *It's a Mad, Mad, Mad, Mad, World*. I think that pretty well sums up what I have to report this morning."

"Hmm. I don't like the sound of that."

"Yes ma'am, I can assure you that I feel the same way. While we've been focused on saving the world, the God versus alien invasion debate has played out in some dangerous ways. Let's talk Russia first. The pro-God forces are now firmly in control, and assets tell us that they are debating whether to launch a preemptive strike against us to stop our efforts. They haven't taken firm steps to begin the process because one side of the new government believes that it won't matter, that God has spoken and His will be done, while the other side wants to take no chances that we might be successful. And that's not the worst."

The hair on Abby's arms stood at attention. "Okay, Effie. If you're trying to scare me, it's working. I'm guessing it's the Iranians who are raising the crazy bar, right?"

Effie's slow, deep laugh rolled gently across the virtual meeting screens. "Bingo, you are absolutely correct. A new source has contacted us and spilled the beans on their plans. Seems the Ayatollah has ordered the launch of twelve nuclear missiles against Israel... tomorrow."

A single word slipped out of Abby's mouth. "Shit." All of the cabinet waited as her pen sharply struck the legal pad. "You said a new source, right? Can we be sure, can we trust them?"

Effie sat up straight. "We can absolutely trust them, ma'am. It's their president."

The revelation landed like a rock thrown into a pond, spurning ripples of thought. Abby spoke first. "Why... why would he do this? What's his motive?"

"He says that he wants to save his nation from the inevitable retaliation." She paused for a moment before adding, "And he says that he disagrees with the Ayatollah. He believes that this is God and that based on His words of peace on Saturday, he could not be part of killing millions."

Abby tossed her pen, landing it square on the pad. "Wow. This is playing out in unexpected ways. I admire the courage of his convictions, 'cause he's a dead man if this is ever found out. What are our options? Anyone?"

Declan answered first, "Ma'am, I think this lands on my plate. We've done a lot of war planning against possible Iranian moves just like this. There are a couple of ways to approach the situation. Traditionally we would publicly threaten them with massive retaliation, but I don't think that will work this time because they believe that this is a matter of obeying Allah's will. I think the Ayatollah would go ahead and gladly see the entire population of his nation become martyrs rather than be unfaithful."

Dallas interjected. "You are absolutely correct, general. That's exactly how they would react."

He resumed laying out the options. "The second option is a preemptive strike against them, just wipe out their capability. Unfortunately, that would also come at a huge cost of innocent lives. And even if we don't do it, the Israeli's would just go ahead anyway. That leads us to option three. It's risky, but if it works, it could prevent any loss of lives."

Abby picked up her pen. "Don't keep us waiting, Declan. Spit it out."

He took a deep breath, then leaned in. "I wasn't here when we invited those hackers to the party, but they've been surprisingly effective. As you know, Madam President, we've conducted cyber warfare against the Iranians before, with some success I might add. But their defensive software has gotten much better. Now that many of those computer nerds have finished their part in reprogramming guidance systems for our ICBM's, we could turn them loose on the Iranians."

Her eyes squinted, questioning his plan. "That sounds great, unless I'm missing something? What are the risks?"

He tilted his head. "Well ma'am. If all goes right it would be a spectacular covert success. But it could all go sideways in so many ways. Maybe they get it done halfway, and six missiles head toward Israel instead of twelve. Then we just hope that their anti-missile defenses work? At best that spreads highly radioactive debris across the entire region. Or maybe a rogue element of hackers intentionally sabotages our efforts from the inside, after all, less than a week ago we would never have trusted them. Do we really trust them now?"

"Hmm, all good points. But we don't have time to debate the pros and cons, do we." She tapped her pen three more times. "I'm going with my gut here, Declan. Get the hackers on the case. Their will to survive has driven them to do the right thing so far. Let's hope that continues." She paused in thought, then added words she never hoped to say. "Declan, let's be ready with a plan B, just in case." She paused again. "Let's hope it doesn't come to this, but if it does, be prepared to wipe them out if the hackers fail."

The usually reluctant warrior dutifully replied. "Yes, ma'am. I understand and agree. These aren't normal times."

The president turned to Dallas, sitting beside her. "Any last words, Dallas? Any predictions for the next few days?"

He scooted forward in his seat, "Only that this God versus alien invasion debate is only going to spread like an infectious virus. And like flu season, there is going to be a death toll. The only question is how high is the final body count."

Chapter Forty-Three

Friday 3:00 P.M. Phoenix / 6:00 P.M. Camp David, Raven Rock, Mount Weather

& New York / Nine Days to Impact

Tension filled the control room at the Space Rim launchpad. Kalie paced behind the back row of technicians who monitored everything from the pulse rate of the commander to the dust content of the air outside. She was always anxious at launches and while she had never smoked, she understood why it was allowed in the control room during the old Apollo days. Anything to take the edge off.

Two hours ago, she had personally spoken with Commander Rick Ebocs and First Office Michael Jones prior to their final pre-launch routine. She had done this dozens of times during her time at Space Rim, but this time was different. These men knew that this was a one-way trip, that even if everything went right, they would die in space, and yet they were remarkably upbeat. Nick declared, "Two men's lives in exchange for the world's survival. Who wouldn't take that deal?"

The cold, hard math was undeniable, but the words still turned her stomach. Her throat tightened as she pushed down her mounting emotions. "I wish I could take one of your seats."

Outside, the mood was considerably lighter. CBN's Manuel Diaz had flown in to lead the onsite reporting, with the space shuttle *Nina* and her two attached rockets serving as his backdrop in the distance. Perspiration beaded on his forehead even as he stood in the shade of a well branded CBN canopy. "It's a hot day in the desert and with launch scheduled for less than three minutes from now, emotions are running high here in the public viewing area. Let's meet two of those that are enduring the heat to witness this historic event."

The camera pulled out, bringing a smiling middle-aged couple into frame. "This is Brad and Becky Podlaski, who drove in from Los Angeles. Why did you travel all this way to be here today?"

Becky looked on with an exaggerated, first time on TV smile, as her easy-going husband spoke. "Manuel, there has never been a day like this... ever. We're big supporters of the president and we're super happy that she's fighting to save us all. I believe that her plan is going to work, and I want to be able to someday tell my grand-children that I was here, that I witnessed this event. I'm super stoked."

"I see." Manuel replied, "And speaking of the president, what do you think of her decision to leave the White House and go to a secure location?"

Brad swiped his forehead, but not before a bead of sweat rolled down into his eyes. "To tell you the truth, I hate to see her leave, she's such an inspiration. But I understand. Twelve people died outside the White House yesterday. Why risk anymore innocent lives when it can be avoided. Hopefully, she'll be back there soon, and this nightmare will end."

"And you, Mrs. Podlaski, what would you like to add?"

He moved the hand-held microphone over to the stage-struck woman. She giggled nervously, then her voice cracked as she replied. "Well, Manuel, I want to show my support for the brave astronauts who are making this sacrifice for all of us. They're heroes, and my thoughts and prayers go with them."

Manuel now turned to his left and the camera followed, leaving Brad and Becky behind. A pre-selected solitary man now came into frame. "Joining me now is Jeff Hastings, from nearby Tucson Arizona. Jeff, you've made the short trip here to stand outside in blazing heat. What's your motivation to be here today?"

Jeff, dressed in surplus desert camo pants and a sweat dappled sand colored tee-shirt spoke forcefully. "I'm here with hundreds of other like-minded Americans protesting peacefully to make our voices heard. This administration's efforts to defy God's explicit will is an abomination, and we want to make that clear to all of the world."

"I see. And what do you think of the president's decision to leave Washington?"

His brows drew together and his eyes narrowed. "In addition to being a sinner, she's now also shown herself to be a coward. I'm ashamed that she's the president of this great nation."

Manuel squared to the camera as it pushed in, leaving only him in frame. "There you have it, America. Two diametrically opposed views about our president and this launch that's about to take place."

As if on cue, sound-waves carried the roar of the booster engines across the sand to the assembled mass of expectant humanity. Billowing white smoke filled the launch area as the shuttle strained to break clear of the clamps that secured it to Earth. The large countdown clock finally reached zero and the clamps released, freeing the beautiful, powerfully complex machine from this world. Manuel turned to witness. "There she goes, America. The hopes of our planet riding with her. God bless those brave men, and Godspeed. Let's listen in for a moment on the communication to the shuttle as we watch her soar."

Back inside the control room Kalie had continued to pace, also listening to the communication between the crew and control team. Martin Barnett filled the spacecraft communicator chair today, officially designated as CAPCOM. "Clear of tower, over."

Commander Rick Ebocs replied, "Roger, roll initiated."

Calmly, Martin continued with the prescribed sequence. "Good roll program confirmed. *Nina* heading down range."

Ten seconds later, an equally cool Rick noted the next set of launch communications. "Throttling down to ninety-four percent. Three engines running normally. Three good fuel cells. Three good APU's."

"Roger, *Nina.* Your readings confirmed."

Another ten seconds passed as Commander Ebocs' voice remained business-like as he spoke the first words not on the normal script. "Phoenix, we're getting some extra vibration up here. Seems to be coming from starboard aft."

A chill ran down Kalie's spine, understanding the possible significance of those words. Her fear subsided a couple of notches as Martin replied. "We copy, Nina. Sensors confirm. Readings remain in normal range."

Rick returned to script. "Velocity, twenty-three hundred feet per second. Altitude, five point three nautical miles. Downrange distance, four nautical miles."

"Roger, *Nina.* Go to throttle up."

Commander Rick Ebocs spoke the words that he had said on five previous missions and hundreds of times in the simulator. "Roger, Phoenix. Throttling up."

Kalie's eyes widened and her hands went to her cheeks as a fireball filled the large monitors of the control room. "Oh... my... God."

Twin columns of white exhaust spiraled away from what had been the shuttle as the external boosters were blasted away from the destroyed craft. All of the ground-based flight crew frantically tapped computer keys, hoping what they had just witnessed wasn't real. Seconds passed until Martin finally spoke... to no one... and to everyone. "Flight control working the situation. Obviously, a major malfunction."

Chapter Forty-Four

Saturday 2:30 P.M. Najaf Iran / 6:00 A.M. Washington D.C. / Eight Days to Impact

A parade review stand had been erected directly in front of the now glimmering cloud engulfing the Imam Ali Mosque. The original purpose had been to provide a physical platform on which Supreme Leader Ayatollah Mohammad Ka'bi would confront the Deceiver, face to face, after the Iranian ICBM's rained nuclear destruction on Israel. That purpose could not be fulfilled as the missiles failed to launch, but a public display had been promised, and one would be given. Huge crowds had already gathered to see the cloud, now in its golden net state, and the promise of this spectacle multiplied the numbers. Flying patrols inside the net looked down on the scene as chants of "Death to America" and "Death to the Deceiver" competed with fervent cries of "Allahu Akbar."

The Supreme Leader, flanked by his cabinet and senior armed forces leaders, stepped to the microphone and delivered his standard greeting before getting to the business of the day. "In the name of Allah, the Beneficent, the Merciful. All praise is due to Allah, the Lord of the Worlds; peace and greetings are our Master and Prophet, Muhammad, and upon his immaculate and infallible household, especially the one remaining with Allah on Earth."

As the loud speakers blasted his voice to the throng, an immense roar responded, as all believers could agree with this sentiment. After the cheering subsided, he continued. "Today we witness an abomination, an ugly evil among us, engulfing our most holy shrine."

This statement riled the masses as many cheered the Ayatollah, while others considered the thousands who had entered the cloud and returned singing Allah's praises. In addition, seeing the remarkable gleaming changes to the mosque with their own eyes, as well as the brilliant white patrols inside the glistening golden net, substantial numbers had decided that this was far from ugly, and a new chant began. Calls of "Open Your Eyes, Open Your Eyes," began competing for the attention of the millions.

The Ayatollah ignored the change, plowing ahead as the elite soldiers protecting the stand lowered their guns to firing position. He looked down from his perch and stretched his hand toward President Hossien Namazi, now on his knees with hands bound behind his back. "Before us is a traitor to our nation, and to Islam itself."

Boos and derisive cries were now sprinkled in with the cacophony of competing views. He continued as the spectacle was shown on huge screens. "This devil in our midst chose to give his allegiance to both America and the Deceiver, above his own people, and even above Allah."

He pointed to the cloud, then continued. "He single-handedly gave unfettered access to our nation's most sensitive and important secrets which thwarted our attempt to rain down destruction on the Jew today and hasten the return of the Mahdi. At this moment, we should be celebrating triumphantly and mocking this so-called god, but instead we're here to render judgment on this traitor."

This added confusion to the percolating hoard, many just now learning of the Ayatollah's secret plan. He continued with anger tinting his words. "While I know that Allah will provide another path for his imminent return, it is now time to smite this snake in front of his false god."

A dozen Imams, dressed in ceremonial garb, stepped forward and one by one picked up two fist sized stones from a cone shaped pile. Some juggled the stones slightly, measuring their heft as they circled the bound and gagged president. The decibel level of the crowd now increased exponentially. Scattered gunfire now joined the mounting chaos. Many officials on the raised stage exchanged nervous glances and eyed the exit stairway.

The Supreme Leader continued on, impervious to the growing unpredictability of the mob. His voice rose with the final verdict. "In submission to the ultimate will of Allah, I condemn this betrayer to death by stoning. Death to America, death to the Deceiver, and death to Hossien Namazi."

As if a match struck and landed in a deep pool of gasoline, the crowd erupted in unfocused violence, rushing the raised platform. The protective guard unleashed nonstop automatic sprays of bullets as the cabinet members and other officials charged the stairwell, trampling over each other as they tried to escape the hoard. Soon the protective gunfire ceased as supplies of ammo were exhausted confronting an unending wave of humanity that swarmed over them like a thundering herd of wildebeests.

Next, the platform began to shake and as if waking from a trance, the Ayatollah only now understood the rage that he had summoned. The platform tipped swiftly, crushing several of the functionaries. The Supreme Leader was catapulted into an angry group who began attacking him with bare hands, seeking to tear him limb from limb. Rivulets of red began to run between the stones of the ancient square as competing groups turned on each other, fighting as if possessed, intensifying the blood fever.

The madness raged on and some angrily rushed inside the golden cloud, where they were met with rays of light fired from guardian weapons. When hit by the neon blue beams, they stopped in their tracks. The stunned protesters stood still for a moment, as if transformed into mannequins, before disrobing. One by one they turned back toward their rampaging countrymen and began singing as part of a clothes free choir. In perfect harmony they sang, "Allah is great, Allah is good, Allah loves all" over and over again. The heavenly guardians then resumed their patrol in their never-ending orbit around the Imam Ali Mosque.

Chapter Forty-Five

Saturday 8:00 A.M. Washington D.C. / 5:00 A.M. Phoenix / Eight Days to Impact

A somber mood hung over the just convened virtual cabinet meeting like pungent smoke downwind of a forest fire. Yesterday afternoon's shuttle explosion over the Arizona desert coming on the heels of the dispersal of the government into secure bunkers had cast a pall over the prospects for the plan to save the world. Last night President Banister had once again gone before the nation in a televised address pleading for everyone to have faith that the plan could still succeed despite the setbacks, and support the country by going about life as normally as possible.

She called the meeting to order with Dallas again sitting by her side in the Camp David facility. "I want to thank you for the dedication, optimism and hard work that all of you have shown throughout this ordeal, especially in the most recent few hours. We're faced with an immense challenge of immeasurable proportions and you are handling it with dignity and a never-say-die attitude. That means the world to me, and it will prove to be the deciding factor if there is a way to save our planet. With that as our ultimate goal, let's go around the horn and see where we stand. Kalie, let's start with you. Yesterday was a hard day for everyone, and I know it was especially hard for you. Where are we now?"

The dark half-moons under her reddened eyes spoke volumes before she even opened her mouth. "We lost two good men yesterday. They knew that they wouldn't survive this mission, and they volunteered nonetheless, but they shouldn't have gone out like that."

Abby spoke words of comfort. "I know that you were close to them. We're all so very sorry for the tragic loss. It must have been hard enough to say goodbye to them in the first place, but to see it end like it did..." Her voice trailed off in sadness.

Kalie lowered her head for a moment, determined not to shed another tear. When she faced the camera again, a new determination had transformed her gaze. "Nothing we can do about that now. What's done is done." She briefly turned and pointed through the glass wall behind her, showing the virtual attendees that technicians were hard at work on the second shuttle. Facing the camera again, she explained. "We've redoubled our efforts to overhaul the *Pinta*, and with yesterday's failure, the crews are even more determined to get her ready for a launch tomorrow."

The president grasped at the slightest ray of hope. "That's really good news, Kalie. Have you isolated what went wrong with the *Nina*? Can we be sure that it won't happen again?"

Kalie looked like a battle-hardened soldier down to her last clip of ammo. "We think so. We believe there was a mistaken calculation of weight distribution combined with a failed sensor that doomed the *Nina*. We're going with that as the solution, because if we don't launch tomorrow, it won't matter. The third shipment of warheads arrived last night, and they'll be loaded later today. Madam President, there will be a launch tomorrow, regardless of the risks."

"You're in all of our thoughts and prayers, Kalie. I know that you're doing your best, and that's all that I can ask." Turning her gaze to a different section of her monitor, Abby switched topics. "Effie, I hear that a lot has gone on in the rest of the world since yesterday. Bring us up to speed."

From her secure location in Nebraska, Effie gave a half-smile. "It's been a tumultuous few hours, that's for sure. General Hagans can share more about how the Iranian missiles were stopped, I'll deal with the aftermath. In case you haven't seen the news in the last few minutes, here's a look at the bloodbath in Iran."

A short clip rolled as Effie narrated. "The unpredictable impact of having the cloud visit a nation continues. As you can see, the Ayatollah was railing against both the cloud and his disgraced president when things spun out of control. Watch as he orders the stoning of the man who gave our hackers access to their nuclear weapons."

The bloody scene was reminiscent of a B-grade slasher movie. Guns fired and knives flashed as one of the fanatics grabbed the Supreme Leader by his turbaned head, exposing his neck. In one swift swing the holy man's head was decapitated and the crazed attacker held his trophy high, blood oozing down his arm. As the short clip ended, she summed up the aftermath. "The Iranian government has fallen and most of the likely candidates who would seize control were also killed. A charismatic colonel in the Quds Force is claiming power, but it's unclear if the nation will follow him. It will be a mess to deal with if the world survives, but at least it seems this nuclear threat against Israel has been eliminated."

The extreme nature of the clip shook everyone and Abby's dark humor bent couldn't be restrained. "I guess the Ayatollah should have had a continuity of government plan, huh Tru?"

The gallows humor had the intended effect as low laughter followed her sarcastic comment. Tru was quick to reply. "Sometimes the cautious do inherit the world, ma'am."

She laughed. "You're our designated worrier, Tru, and we love you for it." With the mood lightened, at least a little Abby continued. "We'll be back to you in a few minutes, but first I want to hear from General Hagans. Declan, very good job stopping those missiles. Tell us all about it, and what else is going on out there."

The seasoned soldier deflected the praise. "Just doing our job, ma'am. All the credit goes to the hackers and to the late president of Iran. He understood the risks when he helped us and he did it to save millions of lives. I think he'll be remembered as a hero. And those hackers, they're something else. God help us if we survive this."

"We've had that conversation a few times. We've made our deal with the devil and we'll happily live with the consequences, if we get through the next eight days alive. How about our ICBM's? Are we still on track?"

Declan replied sharply. "Yes ma'am. I'm happy to report that progress continues to accelerate. You wanted us to push for a Monday first batch launch and it's looking more and more that we might make that stretch goal."

She let out a sigh of relief. "Thank you for your leadership, Declan. This could be the difference."

Again, he deflected the praise. "I'm just building on what Braxton started. He built the structure, and the teams have been working around the clock. They should get all the credit."

"You're a good man, Declan. The country is lucky to have you." She now glanced to the next face on the monitor. "All right, let's check back in with our resident worrier. What's the mood over at Homeland?"

Tru smiled at the good-natured kidding, then immediately reverted back to character. "Unsettled is the word of the day, ma'am. The loss of the *Nina* combined with our activation of continuity of government plans has had a measurable impact. Beginning last night, we saw a ten-point jump in absenteeism at key installations, like power plants. And that's with martial law in place. More and more people think that this is the end and they don't want to spend their final days at work. Our troops will do what they can, but I believe the situation is only going to worsen, especially if the next shuttle launch fails."

"Hmm. This has been a major concern since the beginning. Would another address to the nature help?"

Tru took a few seconds, seeming to search for just the right words. "Ma'am, the way you have shot straight with the American people is the major reason that we're in better shape than nations like Russia and Iran." He pressed his lips together, then gave his blunt assessment. "To tell you the truth, ma'am, nothing short of that shuttle going into space tomorrow is going to make a bit of difference at this point. If that doesn't happen, the best we'll be able to do is try to manage the decline, minimize the chaos."

There was no pithy retort from the president this time. "Thank you for the unvarnished appraisal, Tru. We all know the stakes, and the odds. I can't blame anyone for wanting to be with their friends and family at a time like this. Let's all keep Kalie and her team in our prayers and send them all the good vibes that we can. She's the best, and I have full confidence in her."

Kalie piped back in. "I won't let you down, ma'am."

The president looked at her through the lens, wishing she could give her a big hug. "I know you won't, Kalie. I know you won't."

Others chimed in their support, then, after a minute or so Abby turned to Dallas. "Any final words on from our God corner?"

His head cocked slightly. "I've reached out to contacts around the country, from as many faiths and sects as possible. What I'm hearing aligns with what Tru is saying. The mainstream American is either going to work or staying home and embracing their family and friends. However, because of Carson Appleton there remains a virulent strand of fundamentalism that is intent on trying to stop us from saving the world."

Tru concurred. "We're seeing the same kind of indicators on fringe group chat rooms, but we haven't been able to identify any specific threats." He chuckled, "This is another thing that keeps the worrier up at night,"

Abby smiled, appreciative of his attempt to lighten a dark topic. "That's a good way to wrap things up this morning. We need the worriers and the warriors to pull this off. And a little luck wouldn't hurt either."

Chapter Forty-Six

Saturday Noon Phoenix / 3:00 P.M. Washington D.C. / Eight Days to Impact

Commander Corey Blevins and First Officer Isabella Rojas exited the shuttle simulator, completing their final run through in advance of their Sunday launch. Kalie had observed the flawless practice and now they walked together silently to the debrief room. An air of apprehension surrounded the trio as Kalie finally spoke. "Everything depends on our success."

After the explosion of the *Nina* yesterday, the determination remained but the enthusiasm level had slipped. "Great job in there. I'm fairly confident that we figured out what went wrong yesterday, and have fixes in place. This has to work."

Corey acknowledged her sentiment. "It's a shame about Rick and Michael. They were good men, heroes. We should be celebrating their accomplishment today instead of mourning their loss. We'll make sure their sacrifice was not in vain."

Kalie touched his elbow before the two crew members walked into the debrief room. "You two are making the ultimate sacrifice to save us all. I can't thank you enough. I just wish that I could change places with you."

Corey stood straight and looked her in the eye. "I'm doing this for everyone, but more importantly, I'm doing this for my family. I want my children to have an opportunity to grow up and have lives of their own."

His words pierced her to the core. "Three boys and two girls, right?"

He smiled broadly. "Yes ma'am. They're the light of my life. I would do anything for them."

She squeezed his elbow in support. "I know you would, commander. I know you would." She glanced down at her watch. "If you'll excuse me, I have a meeting with the payload specialists. We're not going to send you guys up with an empty bay."

As she stepped away, Corey felt his silenced phone buzz in his pocket, pulled it out, then glanced at Isabella. "Give me a sec, I need to take this."

"Sure, I'll be right inside."

He put the phone to his ear, then spoke in hushed tones. "Missy, this better be important."

Expecting to hear the voice of his wife, he was shocked when a male replied. "Yes, Commander Blevins, this is very important."

"Who is this." He demanded, "What are you doing with my wife's phone."

The deep voice on the other end of the call taunted. "We had to get your attention, Corey. Do I have your attention?"

Desperation crept into his voice. "Yes... yes. What do you want? How did you get this phone? Where's my wife?"

The anonymous man laughed before answering. "One thing at time, Corey. Now, are you listening carefully?"

"Yes! What's going on?"

"All right, now that I have your attention, listen carefully. We have your wife and children. Do you understand?"

"What? What are you talking about? They're at her mother's house."

The voice on the other end laughed again. "Well, that's where they were. Now they're with us, and we brought along the mother to complete the set. Would you like to speak to your wife?"

Corey's mind raced and his voice trembled. "Yes! Put her on!"

Speaking between retching sobs Missy's voice reached his ear. "Corey! Is that you! They have guns."

He felt a pit form in his stomach. "Have they hurt you... or the kids? Tell me that you're all right!"

Missy sniffed, then answered. "So far they haven't hurt us. They took us in a van, and now we're all tied to chairs in some abandoned building. I'm scared."

"Thank God you're safe."

The male voice replied. "Oh, they're safe for now, Corey. How long they stay that way depends on you. Do you understand?"

Confused, he immediately replied. "Yes... no... wait, what do you want from me? Money?"

Once again, the voice laughed, this time louder. "We don't want your money, Corey. We want you."

"I don't understand? Me? What are you talking about?"

"There's no way that shuttle lifts off without you. So, if you want your pretty wife and beautiful children to live to see tomorrow, all you have to do is join us here."

The pit in Corey's stomach expanded to the size of a beach-ball as realization of what they wanted set in. "You're one of them, aren't you? You want us all to die."

"You're looking at it all wrong, Corey. We have a higher calling. We want us all to live in eternal bliss with the one true God. What could be more glorious? So, Corey, you need to decide. Shall we start killing the Blevins family now, or will you join us here and save them all? I need an answer."

His training kicked in and he rapidly sorted through possible solutions. The voice again demanded an answer. "Corey, we're going to start with the youngest first. That's Lilly, right?"

Like a slot machine locking in three cherry's he arrived at a decision. "Yes. I'll come. Don't hurt them."

Corey could hear the satisfaction in the man's voice. "You've made a wise decision, Corey. Get in your car immediately and head south from the site. We'll call with directions as you drive. And remember, we'll have eyes on you the entire way, so don't try anything stupid or we start shooting. Understand?"

"Yes. Please don't hurt them. I'm on my way."

One last instruction was given. "Be on the road in five minutes, or else."

The phone went dead in Corey's hand. He tried to pull himself together, then stuck his head in the debrief room. "Isabella, can I have a word, out here."

Isabella joined him in the hall and immediately sensed something amiss. "What's wrong?"

His hand wiped across his mouth. "Terrorists have my family, Izzy. They're going to kill them unless I leave right now."

"What?" Her eyes blinked repeatedly as she processed what he was saying. "What do you mean?"

He grabbed her arms just below her shoulders and stared hard. "They want to stop this launch and they're going to kill my family if I don't leave here right now."

"You can't. They can't."

He squeezed her arms tight. "Listen, Kalie said she wished she could help, so now's her chance. She can take my place and I can save my family. We can do both."

Izabella broke free, pushing his hands away. "You can't do this, Corey. The whole world is literally depending on us. You can't leave!"

"The world is depending on this mission, not me. You've heard her talk about all the time that she's spent in the simulator. This flight can still go, and I can save my family. I'm leaving now, Izzy. I'm begging you, please give me a ten-minute head start before you let the cat out of the bag. I have to do this."

He wrapped her in a quick hug, then turned and headed for the exit, leaving her standing in the hallway, stunned. After a few seconds she made her decision, summoning her most calm persona, she opened the door of the debrief room. "I need a short break. Be ready when I get back."

Chapter Forty-Seven

Saturday 6:00 P.M. Hawaii / Midnight Washington D.C. / Eight Days to Impact

Wade and Qu sat on high stools at a table at the already half-full *Riptide*. In two hours, she would be doing her first set of the night in front of a packed house, which MTV would broadcast live. The plug that Wade had given during that press conference at the observatory had accelerated her career. The imminent arrival of the asteroid had brought a sense of acceleration to everything and seeing her go from a singer struggling to make ends meet, to the next big thing in less than a week was a prime example. Wade washed down his burger and fries with the last drink of his Hawaiian craft beer while Qu picked at her salad, nervously sipping water.

After the waitress cleared the table and Wade ordered another beer, he reached for her hands. They were as cold as ice. "Nervous?"

Her mouth twitched. "Can you tell? Jeez, so much is riding on this... and I don't want to screw up on national television."

"Oh Qu, you're a star ready to go super nova. I've known that since the first time I saw you. You're going to rock the world."

That made her laugh. "Yeah. I'm going to go down in the record books all right. Going from a nobody to a somebody in less than a week, just in time for the apocalypse to end it all. It would make a terrific *Lifetime* movie."

It was his turn to laugh. "A Grammy and an Emmy. Surely, we can sign you to a major motion picture and pen a Broadway play to complete the sweep. Add that Oscar and Tony that you would win and I would be dating an EGOT!"

She sighed. "All the what ifs..."

"Come on now. It could still all happen, have a little faith."

She glanced up at the TV above the bar. "You mean after those terrorists kill the next shuttle commander and his entire family? Let's be real."

Wade kept smiling as he gazed at her lovingly. "They say they have a backup plan, and I believe them. And even if it does all end next weekend, we would still have each other for the rest of our lives, however short."

She met his gaze. "Aww, Wade, that's the sweetest thing anyone has ever said to me. Have you always been such a romantic?"

His goofy grin became a more sincere smile. "Kinda, yeah. I saw how rough things were for my mom and I promised myself that when I found the right woman, I would treat her like a queen. I've always wanted a forever love."

Her eyes moistened. "You sure know what a girl wants to hear, I'll give you that. Who wouldn't want that kind of love?"

He released her now warm hands and reached into his pocket, fishing out a diamond engagement ring. Kneeling, he looked up at her dark sparkling eyes. "Qu, you are the most amazing woman that I have ever met, and when I'm with you I feel complete. I hope you feel the same way about me. I know this is moving fast, but it's a crazy world right now, so I figured there's no time to wait. Qu Kahale, would you like to be together for the rest of our lives, whether that's a week, or a year, or a hundred years? Would you make me the happiest man in the world tonight?"

Her hands shook and her mind raced. "Oh Wade...what are you doing?" Her bottom lip quivered. "It's so sudden." She looked down at him with a lopsided grin. "This can't be happening, can it? I mean, come on."

"Qu, haven't you always wanted a beach wedding? All of your friends and family celebrating your happiness? If not now, when?"

She was a ball of jangled nerves, yet couldn't move. "I've never felt this way about anyone, ever. But wow, would we be crazy?"

He looked up with a glint in his eye. "Has there ever been a better time to be crazy?"

Her face flushed as emotions surged. She stretched her jittery hand toward the ring. "Let's be crazy together, for however long that is. I love you, Wade Jansky."

Chapter Forty-Eight

Sunday 9:00 A.M. Washington D.C. / 6:00 A.M. Phoenix / Seven Days to Impact

Looking back, the dark mood from yesterday's virtual cabinet meeting now seemed like an absolutely sunny day. The violent murder of Shuttle Commander Corey Blevins and his entire family by religious fundamentalists was not only a blow to the plan, but just plain stomach turning. Carson Appleton's terrorists had made their point, even as it cost them their own lives. Their propaganda spread faster, even as sites like Facebook pulled down pages exalting them as the latest martyrs for the cause.

Everyone was feeling the stress as President Banister started the meeting. "In 1940, things looked very bad for the British. The French army had fallen and Germany was threatening invasion of their island nation. In that moment Winston Churchill spoke words that I think are very appropriate for us as we find our backs against the wall. He said, 'Let us therefore brace ourselves to our duties, and so bear ourselves that, if the British Empire and its Commonwealth last for a thousand years, men will still say, "This was their finest hour."'

She looked directly into the camera, willing her determination to each member of her team. "Today, it's not just the British Empire and Commonwealth that will look back with admiration, it's the entire world. All of you are braced for duty, and willing to go to any sacrifice to save our planet... none more so than our own National Security Advisor, Kalie Robinson."

Abby paused, collecting her thoughts before she began paying a living tribute to a soldier who was about to embark on a suicide mission to potentially save them all. "Due to the murder of

Commander Corey Blevins, our very own Kalie has stepped up to serve as commander of the second shuttle, launching later today. It's a tremendous validation not only of her extraordinary dedication to the nation, but to the incredible arsenal of skills that she has brought to her role. She has not only spearheaded the shuttle project, but will now climb into the *Pinta* and complete the mission. There is not enough gratitude in the world to thank you for your service and your sacrifice."

Kalie had sat stone faced through the president's praise, her Sphinx like visage remaining fixed. "I'm doing what I was put on this Earth to do. While I didn't know it at the time, every experience that I've ever had in my entire life, has been leading to this moment. Seeing the way that it's all played out, I'm at peace."

Her face now transformed, becoming totally self-assured. "In fact, I'm more than at peace, I'm excited. It's a powerful feeling when you know with one-hundred percent certainty that you are exactly where God wants you to be."

The president smiled. "You are an inspiration to me, to this administration, and to the world. You're a real hero."

The iron-willed woman blushed. "I'm just doing what needs to be done, that's all."

"Kalie, we thank you for your service and for what your sacrifice will mean, for everyone. Words will never be able to fully express the depth of our gratitude."

She bowed her head slightly, accepting the praise. "Thank you, ma'am."

Abby blinked a couple of times, hoping to keep the moisture in her eyes from collecting into a tear, then cleared her throat. "Okay then, let's move on to other pressing business." Without stopping she quickly dabbed the corner of her right eye with the back of her hand. "Tru, tell us where we are on getting the full story of those terrorists who killed the Blevins family."

Tru's eyes also glistened following the touching tribute from the president. "First of all, Kalie, I want to add my thanks for what you are doing. You are an inspiration."

The wave of gratitude seemed to grate against her personal sense of duty, so she simply said, "Thank you."

After a slight bow of his head he began. "Tragically, a previously unknown group calling themselves 'Divine Justice' linked with Carson Appleton and used Commander Blevins' family to lure him into a death trap. From the info that's been gathered, we know that there was never any intention of sparing any of their lives. They became cold blooded murders whose sole purpose was to prevent the shuttle launch and to sow seeds of despair across the world."

"They just want us to simply accept that this asteroid is God's will, and we should all just wait for the world to end?"

Tilting his head, Tru continued. "Sort of. They are aligned with his theology, but they are much less sophisticated. Until last Sunday, these were just four seemingly normal guys who attended the same church. They fell for the lure of eternal bliss for all and self-radicalized. Then they connected with Appleton, and a week later this is how it ended. That's what makes this kind of threat so hard to prevent. We're using the declaration of martial law powers to step up surveillance by tech companies like Google and Facebook trying to identify threats like this sooner, but it's like looking for a needle in a stack of needles. I'm hoping that these kinds of threats will subside after we get the shuttle launched."

Abby was back in driver mode. "Good. And what's the update on keeping the country running. How did things go last night?"

Tru glanced at his notes. "As predicted, we're slipping. Last night the power went out in New Orleans and Birmingham. Civil and military authorities did their best, but they're also seeing defections. Over two hundred people were killed between the two cities, and we're holding on by a thread in dozens of other places. We really need that shuttle to launch to give people some hope."

The president continued, hoping to speak success into being. "All right then, Tru, we'll have good news by the end of the day." She looked at the next screen. "Effie, you're up next. What else is going on in the world today?"

Effie's brow furrowed and her face hardened. "Ma'am, as you know, things have been unstable in Russia since the fall of President Noskov. Alexy III has been installed as the figurehead leader, while radical factions have been fighting behind the scenes to actually rule. A winner has emerged who wants to wait for the apocalypse, while the losing faction has taken over control of one of their nuclear missile facilities. We've just learned that they might try to launch a missile toward Arizona to stop Kalie's launch. I shared this info with General Hagans just prior to this call."

Urgency commanded Abby's voice. "What's the plan, Declan. Can we stop it?"

The general was blunt. "We don't have time to turn the hackers loose on them, so we'll be at the mercy of the GMD systems we've been developing. It's probably fifty – fifty if we can shoot it down. We'll see if all those years of investment pay off. And I'll also contacted the Chinese. They are totally on our side on this, and who knows, they might have capabilities that we don't know about. It can't hurt."

"Son of a bitch. Seems like two steps forward and one back." Her voice hardened as she continued. "Declan, make contingency plans for a preemptive strike. I don't want to do it, but that shuttle has to launch today. Starting World War Three is still preferable to having the whole planet wiped out. Understand?"

"Yes ma'am. I'll be in close contact all day."

The president looked back to Effie's screen and her sarcasm returned. "Any other good news out in the world?"

In fact, Effie did have good news. "The cloud has moved from Iran's chaos to a warm welcome in India. It has landed on the historic parliament building in New Delhi and celebrations are happening there and across the country. It looks like a second Holi festival. You know, the one where all those colors are thrown on everyone in the crowds. It's so different than what happened in Iran."

The thought of all those happy people dancing while being pelted with splashes of vibrant colors brought a crinkled smile. "Good for them, maybe we can show God there is hope for us yet."

"Agreed, ma'am. Sure beats the massacre from yesterday."

She glanced at Dallas. "Anything to add?"

Dallas kept his comments short. "Just that we should expect more of the unexpected. As our possible expiration date nears, ordinary people are going to continue to check out and focus on family and faith while the fanatics from all faiths and sects are going to become increasingly dangerous. I predict that we're going to have a hell of a week."

Chapter Forty-Nine

Sunday Noon Washington D.C. / 9:00 A.M. Phoenix / Seven Days to Impact

Chief of Staff Cliff Cyrus ran at a full sprint toward the president seated in the common dining area of the Camp David Bunker. "Madam President, you're needed in the communications room immediately. It's urgent."

She pushed away from the table and spoke with her mouth half full of salad. "What the hell's going on now?"

"It's the Russians, ma'am. They're launching."

They sprinted with her high heels clicking down the barren concrete hallways. In moments they were looking in on General Hagan's as he coordinated the response. A rush of adrenaline gave her words extra urgency as she asked again. "Declan, what the hell is going on?"

His eyes were fixed on a feed from Ft. Greely Alaska as he answered. "That rogue Russian faction has launched three ICBM's. Our intercepts are blasting off as we speak. We'll try to destroy them at their apex in space. It's the first live use ever. God, let's hope they work."

Her screens now split three ways with one showing Declan, one showing the Ft. Greely Alaska control room, and one showing the rockets blasting out of their underground silos. "Damn it, Declan, we were just talking fifteen minutes ago. You said they weren't ready to launch, that we had more time to consider a preemptive strike. What happened?"

The general kept his eyes on his screens, avoiding direct eye contact with her. "I don't know, ma'am. We'll figure that out later. What we need to do now is take these bad boys down before they reenter the atmosphere on a direct course for Phoenix. Then we'll decide what we do about those bastards. First things first."

Rockets screamed skyward and blips on radar screens commanded everyone's attention. Command room technicians calmly relayed speed and altitude readings of both the Russian missiles and the U.S. countermeasures. The president listened in to the chatter silently, knowing that the very survival of mankind hung in the balance. The monotone readings built over the minutes to a finale. "We have locks on all three targets. Countdown to intercept in five-four-three-two-one."

Seconds seemed like hours as readings bounced from satellites to Earthbound receivers. Were they successful? Was Phoenix about to be destroyed? Her heart raced in anticipation of the answer. Suddenly, wild cheering erupted in the control room as back slaps and high fives dominated the scene. "Did we do it, Declan? Did it work?"

At last the weathered warrior allowed himself a smile as he looked directly at his president. "Yes ma'am! We did it! All that money on R&D was worth it. The system worked exactly as planned."

She raised a fist and pumped it excitedly. "Hell yes! We're still in the game. We still have a chance. That's damned good news, Declan. Damned good news!"

While not as exuberant, he seemed just pleased. "Yes ma'am, yes ma'am, yes ma'am. Whew, that was close. I couldn't be prouder of those men and women." His allotted time for happiness now reached its endpoint. "Ma'am, as pleased as I am at this moment, we must decide now how we're going to address this blatant move."

"Jeez, Declan. We just shot down three nuclear missiles heading for the U.S. and we don't even get a full minute to celebrate." She laughed. "We're not getting paid enough, are we?"

He laughed softly, seeming to appreciating her attempt to lighten the gravity of the decision that they were about to make. "No ma'am, we're not. But we didn't sign up for this gig to get rich, did we?"

She smiled wistfully. "No, that's not why we're here. But I didn't think we were signing up for all of this either." She sighed, contemplating her choices. "Okay Declan, Let's roll through our options."

The momentary high had completely evaporated in the intensity of their next decision. His brow furrowed as he outlined potential responses. "The most direct approach is to respond in kind, send three of our missiles to destroy that site. It would eliminate any future attempts to stop the shuttle launch and send a clear message to anyone else with bad intentions."

"Yeah. It's proportional and easy to explain. You try to hit us, we hit back. And the downside?"

"Well, we could be starting World War Three. And, the Russians can rightfully claim that they didn't do this, that we're punishing them for the acts of rebels, that we didn't give them a chance to clean up their own mess. That's usually a good argument, but right now I'm not sure if the faction nominally in charge has the resources to take care of this situation. And if they can't, another attack could come before we get the shuttle into space. Can we take that risk?"

"That's the question isn't it."

Declan outlined the next possibility. "Option two has the biggest downside and the biggest upside. We can publicly threaten to destroy the site if another launch happens and hope that assured destruction restrains them. The downside is they choose the martyr path and launch anyway. We're back to hoping our defensive systems work and then retaliating anyway. The upside is that we could avoid killing a few million people and potentially starting World War Three."

"And option three?"

"Take the high road. Ignore the attack and focus all energy on the shuttle launch. After launch, we let the world know what they did and hope that global condemnation follows. It might strengthen the hand of those that want peace over there and enhance our reputation. That we're strong enough to turn the other cheek so to speak."

She pondered her next words, knowing that history would judge her, that is if humanity survived to write this history. "Doing nothing is off the table, the stakes are just too high. And at the same time, I want to thread the needle on our response. Respect Russia, but definitively end this threat. We have to get the shuttle up today."

"Okay, so how do you want to proceed?"

Her violet eyes grew hard. "Tell the Russians that they have one hour to wipe that site off the map or we'll do it for them. And make sure they know that this is not a negotiation or a threat, this is a promise."

He answered with a swift, "Yes ma'am."

She leaned in. "God might stop us, a launch failure might stop us, but I'll be damned if a bunch of rogue Russians are going to stop us."

Chapter Fifty

Sunday 6:00 P.M. Washington D.C. / 3:00 P.M. Phoenix / Seven Days to Impact

President Banister spoke privately with Kalie one last time before she boarded the *Pinta*. While Kalie was at peace with the mission, Abby was heartbroken. Kalie was only a few years younger than her, but Abby sometimes felt like she was the daughter that she never had. Seeing her climb into that shuttle reminded her of the sacrifice that Abraham was asked to make with Isaac. The biblical story had never felt so real, especially as she was almost certain that if this was truly God, he would not step in and save the sacrificial offering this time.

With weariness in her voice she addressed the members of her cabinet dispersed across the continent. "This is it everyone, this is for all the marbles. They're hoping that the right fixes were made to achieve a successful launch, but they're working past all safety measures. Kalie is sitting on top of more than a million pounds of explosive propellant. May God be with her."

A smattering of "Amen" and "Yes ma'am's" followed her declaration. She spoke again as she turned to her left. "While we are not all agreed if this is really God or not, I've asked Dallas to say a few words in prayer. I figure it certainly can't hurt."

He bowed his head. "Dear Heavenly Father, thank you for the blessings that You have bestowed on all of mankind. Among those blessings is a spirit of insatiable curiosity and a zest for life. Today we come in reverent respect to ask You to bless this launch and protect the lives on board. Their mission is to prolong the blessings that You've so freely given to us, Your creation. We ask for success in their endeavor so that we may continue the path of discovery and abundant life that You have wanted for us since from the beginning. We pray that with the success of this mission we can become more perfect in our pursuit of Your will, in spite of our human weaknesses. Thank You for hearing our sincere pleas as we ask these blessings in Your name. Amen."

As preparations for final countdown continued, Abby filled the time with current business. "Declan, please send my personal thanks to Alexey for taking care of those Russian rebels. We simply couldn't risk having them destroy our best chance of survival."

Declan grinned. "He didn't want to do it, but we made a strong case that his regime might be short lived if we had to take care of his mess. Seems his survival instinct is also very much intact."

Abby smiled. "Could help us reset our relationship if we make it through this. It's going to be a new world and we'll need all of the allies that we can get."

As the countdown passed the one-minute mark she glanced at feed from Mt. Weather. "Tru, what's the latest from Homeland?"

He looked as anxious as a cat in a dog park. "It could be better, ma'am, that's for sure. Eighteen percent of the country is now without power. With a successful launch I'm hoping that it doesn't drop too much more, but if not..." His voice trailed off, not wanting to speak an evil into existence.

White billowing smoke began filling the live stream from Phoenix. Abby tensed. "It's game time."

For the second time the large countdown clock reached zero and the clamps released, freeing what could very well be mankind's last hope for survival. Inside the control room Martin Barnett again filled the CAPCOM chair and once again spoke his first choreographed words of this launch. "Clear of tower, over."

The last dance began.

First time Commander Kalie Robinson replied, "Roger, roll initiated."

Calmly, Martin continued with the prescribed sequence. "Good roll program confirmed. *Pinta* heading down range."

Ten seconds later, Kalie confidently relayed the next set of launch communications. "Throttling down to ninety-four percent. Three engines running normally. Three good fuel cells. Three good APU's."

"Roger, *Pinta*. Your readings confirmed."

Seconds passed nervously for the president and the nation as the launch sequence continued. Kalie's voice soothed them all. "Phoenix, First Officer Rojas and I report a smooth ride. Repeat, smooth ride."

Martin's tenor remained unchanged. "We copy, *Pinta*. Sensors confirm. Readings remain in normal range."

On board, Kalie glanced to her first officer who continued the task of guiding what amounted to an enormous, continuous explosion to lift the shuttle past the bounds of Earth, proud that two women were in command. The sequence continued. "Velocity, twenty-three hundred feet per second. Altitude, five point three nautical miles. Downrange distance, four nautical miles."

Without even a hint of nerves Martin repeated what had been his final words to the previous shuttle. "Roger, *Pinta*. Go to throttle up."

Onboard, Kalie caught a glimpse of Isabella making the sign of the cross as she prepared to accelerate. She smiled, hoping to feel increased G-forces press against her and not instantaneous nothingness. Her hand moved as she spoke. "Roger, Phoenix. Throttling up."

The pressure on the two crew members pushed them back in their seats even more as their speed increased. Spontaneous cheers came from the president's virtual call as well as from spectators around the globe. Martin, however, remained as cool as a mountain stream. "Vector looking good, *Pinta*."

Smiling from ear to ear, Kalie tried, unsuccessfully, to match his calm. "Roger that, Phoenix. The view is great from up here!"

The president fought back tears of happiness as she mumbled to herself. "You go girl. You go!"

Back in Phoenix, Martin continued the sequence. *"Pinta* now at sixteen miles altitude, already seventeen miles downrange. Standing by for solid rocket booster separation. Booster officer confirms staging. Guidance now converging, the main engine steering the shuttle on a pinpoint path to its destination. Two minutes, twenty seconds into the flight, *Pinta* already traveling 3,200 miles an hour, thirty-five miles in altitude, fifty miles downrange. The propulsion officer reports the orbital maneuvering system engines have ignited, *Pinta* kicking on its afterburners for 1:23 for the phase of powered flight."

Kalie now stated the obvious. *"Pinta*, negative return."

At this altitude there was no turning back under any circumstances.

Martin confirmed. "Negative return."

More technical jargon flew back and forth from the control room to the *Pinta* as their speed reached seventeen thousand miles per hour. Martin spoke again. "Now standing by for external tank separation."

Inside the shuttle Kalie prepared for the loud boom when the external tank jettisoned away from the shuttle. "Initiating external tank separation." She flipped three switches in the correct sequence and the explosion pushed the large central tank away from the craft. She now spoke like an excited child on Christmas morning. "Separation complete. Smooth sailing on the *Pinta*."

A mini celebration erupted in the control room. While danger is never completely absent in space travel, the most difficult part of the launch sequence was now behind them. Martin finally allowed a little emotion to seep into his voice. "All readings normal, *Pinta*. Godspeed to you on this mission. Thank you for your sacrifice and bravery. We're all counting on you."

Even with more steps remaining in the launch sequence and a lot of work ahead of them, Kalie and Isabella allowed themselves a moment of self-congratulation as they looked into the starry blackness of space in front of them. And even though this was a one-way mission, adrenaline pumped through their veins and they were happy. Kalie looked to her left. "We did it, girl!"

Isabella raised a nearly weightless fist in the cockpit. "Hell yes, we did it!"

Chapter Fifty-One

Monday 6:00 A.M. Camp David / Six Days to Impact

With the shuttle safely launched and ready to begin deploying armed nuclear explosives along the path of the oncoming asteroid, there was a sense of relief among the president and her staff. While huge challenges still lay ahead, it was the first real opportunity to catch their breath in the past nine days. Abby decided to start the day outside of the bunker to try and uncover answers to a question that had been on her mind since Dallas walked into the White House last Sunday.

She greeted him as he joined her at a table on a screened and covered porch overlooking the immaculately tended compound. "Thanks for joining me, Dallas. Finally, a chance to just talk, with no life or death decision hanging in the balance. What do you think of the place?"

A staff member silently offered coffee, which Dallas gladly accepted. "It's beautiful up here in the mountains. One of those kinds of places that I've heard about but never expected to see. And the history, wow, don't even get me started."

She smiled. "I know what you mean, I always feel like a visitor. It's a place that truly belongs to the people."

A Secret Service Agent with an automatic weapon passed a few yards away as a reminder that this tranquil morning was anything but a normal breakfast. A platter of assorted fruit and pastries soon arrived and both selected a sampling to break their fast. After a few bites Abby delicately broached the reason for her invitation. "Dallas, I appreciate the counsel that you have so freely given during these trying times. It's been very insightful and helpful."

He blushed. "My pleasure, Madam President. I felt it a duty and an honor to serve when asked."

She advanced her agenda slowly. "And the nation is better off today because of your service."

She took a sip of the now cooled coffee. "I have to say, Dallas, I have been a bit surprised by your apparent change in regards to me. I mean, it's a pleasant surprise, no doubt, but a real surprise none the less. If you don't mind me asking, what's different now?"

It was Dallas' turn to sip coffee as he collected his thoughts. "Do you remember the Bible story of Moses wandering in the wilderness for forty years?"

She took a bite of cantaloupe and quickly chewed, swallowing before answering. "I vaguely remember, but I'm fuzzy on the details. Refresh my memory."

"Okay, well after Moses parted the Red Sea and escaped Egypt, the Israelites had the chance to move very quickly into a new land promised by God."

"I'm starting to remember. Please, go on."

"All right, so Moses sends twelve spies to do a reconnaissance of the land and the defenses of the current occupants. Well, ten of them returned and said that the land was indeed fertile, but the inhabitants had strong fortifications and they didn't think that the Jews had enough power to conquer them. Only two, Joshua and Caleb, said that not only did the land flow with milk and honey, but they also reminded everyone that God had already promised this to them. God almighty would provide the power. All they had to do was have faith and believe."

Dormant memories from childhood Sunday School came flooding back. "Now I remember. God punished them for the sin of doubting him and he made them wander through the desert for forty years.

Joshua and Caleb were the only men of that generation who were allowed to enter the promised land all those years later. Right?"

His chubby cheeks began to redden. "That's the long and short of the story. Those that lacked faith and vision were made to wander."

Abby tensed. "And you feel like I made you wander in the wilderness?"

His hands raised quickly. "No, no, no. Not at all. I'm the one who made me wander for far too long. I was the one who doubted God's plan. Don't you see?"

Her posture relaxed. "Maybe it's the stress we've all been under lately, or maybe I've just been out of church too long. How about walking me through it?"

He rested his hands on the table and reset. "See, way back when we were newlyweds, I thought I had everything figured out. God seemed to bless every move of my young life, especially that opportunity to spend a semester at the Vatican after we were married. I went and that's when you met Jill and ... well we know what happened next."

Abby answered defensively. "Yes, for the first time in my life I was honest about who I really was, and I fell in love."

His cheeks reddened to a deeper shade. "Yes, of course. I see that now, but back then I questioned God for the first time in my life. I mean, I seriously questioned him. My doubt condemned me to wander my own wilderness until I understood that just because my life with you didn't turn out the way I expected, it didn't mean that it wasn't God's plan. It wasn't quite forty years, but it was a long time."

Emotions seemed to wash across his face and she could tell that this was not an easy conversation for him. Yet she needed to know more, so she did what she always did, she kept asking questions. "So how did you get from there to here? That must have been some journey."

He placed his fork on his plate. "You know those five stages of grief?"

"Yeah, I think we've all lived through those at some time or another."

"Well, I spent a really long time in Denial and Anger. For years I thought this was a passing phase for you, that I couldn't have missed all those signs about your sexuality, that you would snap out of it and come back to me. Then I would hear about some great new thing that you were doing, like going to law school, then being the youngest attorney to argue a case before the Supreme Court. Denial was no longer an option, so I transitioned to Anger."

She touched his hand. "I'm sorry that you were mad at me. I hated that you were hurt."

He pulled his hand away, seemingly ashamed. "That's how I felt, I didn't say it made sense. And I was only kind of mad at you, I was mostly mad at God. How could he do this to me? Bring a woman like you into my life, into marriage, only to lose you to... a woman. Let's just say I felt betrayed by you both for a long time."

She spoke softly. "That it must have been difficult, especially in your field. I'm guessing more than a few people passed some harsh judgment."

A weak grin met that comment. "To say the least, and it didn't help my job prospects either. The unspoken truth was they all thought I was a fool for not seeing what was right in front of me"

"That wasn't fair. I mean I wasn't even able to accept my own truth until I met Jill. How were you supposed to know?"

He now smiled wistfully. "Well it all worked out for both of us, didn't it? I moved through Bargaining and Depression fairly quickly and finally achieved Acceptance. That's when I met Maggie. Together we charted a new path for us and our growing family. I studied and taught in some really out of the way places, learning more about some very obscure religions. It rounded my resume in a way that few others could match. The Harvard job opened when you were a candidate for president, and that probably put me over the top. I think that it was all part of God's plan to put us where he wanted us, and in his timing."

Abby suppressed a laugh as this was exactly what she had told Jill about him getting that position. "I can see how you could feel that way, but that brings two other questions to mind. First, do you think God, if this is God, put us in this position so we can succeed in avoiding mankind's demise?"

"Well I certainly hope so, and it would make sense but as I just told you, I was mistaken about God's will back when we were married. I've learned to live in the moment and let Him show me his path in His timing. And your other question?"

"It was about that commercial that ran during the campaign. Why did you say that mean thing about Jill and I?"

"You mean the 'In God's eyes marriage is between a man and a woman' comment?"

"Exactly. That one really hurt."

He lowered his head. "They took a comment from years ago and edited it. What I actually said was that *I used to believe that* in God's eyes marriage is between a man and a woman.' I had just started at Harvard and I just wanted all this to go away. My life was finally back on track and I just wanted do my job. I thought that anything I said would be used by one side or the other and make things worse, so I just stayed quiet. It wasn't my finest hour and I know it must have hurt you and Jill. I feel awful about it." Now he reached for her hand. "I'm sorry."

Reflexively, her humor returned to form. "Oh Dallas, I'm way past that now, but watch out for Jill, she's not as enlightened about forgiveness. There might even be a voodoo doll with your likeness somewhere in the White House."

He laughed. "I always loved your sense of humor. And thanks for the heads up. I've studied Haitian hexes, so I'll practice my apology before I see her."

Chapter Fifty-Two

Monday Noon Deep Space & Camp David / 9:00 A.M. Phoenix / Midnight Beijing / Six Days to Impact

The *Pinta* had traveled nearly 360,000 miles in the eighteen hours since launch with Kalie and Isabella marking all kinds of "firsts" along the way. The most important milestone was that they were now farther from Earth than any human, ever, exceeding the former mark set by the astronauts of Apollo 13 in 1970. In fact, they were now over 100,000 miles further and counting, meaning that had reached the first point of deployment. Back home, their mission was the talk of the planet and in the past twenty-four hours hospitals reported a global surge in baby girls named Kalie and Isabella. While they were becoming celebrities on Earth, they were preparing for the dangerous mission of placing nuclear explosives in a picket line to attempt to alter the path of the Jansky-Haskell asteroid.

Isabell suited up to enter the now open payload bay while Kalie would operate the robotic arm inside the craft for final placement of each package. Kalie helped secure the last fitting on Isabella's suit. "Remember, our goal is clean deliveries. Better to miss a mark by a thousand miles than to have a catastrophic error, understand."

Isabella clapped her gloved hands together. "Mission first. I know the stakes. Help me get into the airlock."

The process of deployment was straightforward, but not without risks. Isabella would be in the open payload bay freeing each device from its mooring, allowing Kalie to operate the robotic arm from the aft flight deck control station. Working together they would lift each device and place it in its strategic alignment.

With one screen showing the open bay and another attached to the end of the robotic arm, Kalie had a clear view of the environment. She spoke into her headset. "Good feed, Izzy. All set on this end."

The fully suited first officer gave a thumbs up before using a large but weightless wrench to free the first weapon. "Number one set for deployment."

While Kalie watched the screens aboard the *Pinta*, back on Earth the scene was broadcast to the world. The president and cabinet each tuned in from their secure locations as almost every global citizen who still had working electricity sat glued to their sets. The mechanical "fingers" at the end of the boom gently squeezed the freed device. "Package one secured. Commencing deployment."

As the tense operation to save the world played out in space, Manuel Diaz reported breathlessly from Phoenix, where a huge crowd had gathered to watch the feed from space on giant screens. "Mankind's hope rests with the teamwork of Commander Kalie Robinson and First Officer Isabella Rojas, the two brave women who are sacrificing their lives in an attempt to save ours."

Kalie extended the mechanical arm to its full length. "Package one set for deployment in three-two-one." She gave a gentle push and released the grip of the controller resulting in the shuttle slowly separating from the liberated, fully armed device. Relief tinged happiness added a bounce to her words. "One down, ninety-nine to go."

The president high fived everyone near her. "She said two percent chance a week ago and now she's making it happen!"

In the desert, cheers erupted. Manuel surveyed the situation for his viewers. "You can feel the energy. After a week of despair, finally a ray of hope. This longest of long shots might actually work."

Nearly one million Chinese gathered in Tiananmen Square at midnight local time to watch the spectacle. They too cheered as President Zhou stood in a review stand applauding the effort. He spoke encouragingly to General Hu, the Minister of National Defense. "Old friend, we may yet survive this curse."

Hu's religious hostility resurfaced. "Just as I suspected. Those who believe in so called gods are fools. We can only trust in science."

Zhou cautioned. "Let us hope that is the case, let us hope. And if we are wrong, we will know soon enough."

Back on the *Pinta* Kalie had secured packet two and was extending the boom when something happened. "Shit!"

Her expletive traveled at the speed of light from her position 100,000 miles past the moon's orbit to antennas around the globe. The feed to the rest of the world was on a ten second delay, giving Martin time to pull the plug on the broadcast. He replied to the *Pinta*. "Received your latest transmission. Can you detail the nature of your problem?"

Kalie was working the manipulator control stick furiously. "Phoenix, something's wrong with the arm. Its fully extended with package two and seems to be frozen. I'm working the problem, but would appreciate any help that I can get."

"Affirmative, *Pinta*. We're on it. Follow protocol on your end as we work it down here."

"Roger that, Phoenix."

Kalie spoke to her partner in the open bay. "Izzy, I can't see anything on the exterior cameras. Can you get eyeballs on the boom?"

"I can't see anything from here. I'll take a look from the end of my rope." She bent slightly, then jumped, slowly lifting herself weightlessly up, past the top of the cargo bay, stopping with a tug at the end of the attached tether. "I need a better angle. Give me a sec."

Kalie stopped rotating the manipulator controller, not wanting it to suddenly break free and hit her space walking crew member. "Getting antsy down here. See anything?"

Izzy craned her neck, extending her view to the fullest extent while remaining attached to the shuttle. Still unable to see any problem, she activated a suit thruster for less than a second to rotate into a better position. She spoke despondently. "Okay, I see what's going on."

"Now would be a good time to share! Come on Izzy, what's wrong."

Isabella cursed beneath her breath. "Fuck." She started again, this time in full situation mode. "Commander, we have a damaged boom. Looks like it was struck by some sort of space debris, square on the final extension joint. I see hydraulic fluid spraying everywhere, which probably triggered the complete arm shutdown. Not good."

While the rest of the world was removed from the live feed, the president and her cabinet were still receiving the broadcast. Abby moved her hand toward her mouth, but resisted an urge to chew a nail. She spoke to her scattered team. "God almighty! Why does everything have to be so damned hard! And just when things were looking up..."

Back onboard the *Pinta*, Kalie spoke to control. "You copy that, Phoenix? I think I know what you're going to say, and I don't think I'm going to like it."

"We copy, *Pinta*. Give us a minute to work it down here. Hold tight."

Back onboard the conversation continued. "Come back in, Izzy, we both know how this is going to go."

She cursed as she worked her way back. "Damn it. Of course we can't do the toughest job in space the easy way. That's not the way the universe works. We'll have to.... ooff"

A sound, like a blind-sided football player having the wind knocked out of them, echoed in Kalie's ear. Alarms began sounding at the control station.

Kalie spoke in a rapid clip. "Talk to me Izzy. What's going on out there?" She spoke louder still. "Talk to me, girl!"

Izzy's faint voice replied. "Can't breathe... I'm hit... Leaking."

Fearing the worst, that a pebble sized chunk of rock had hit Isabella at the speed of a bullet, just as had probably struck the boom, Kalie switched camera views, desperate to see what was happening outside of the cargo bay. Finally, a partial view showing Izzy flailing like a rag doll at the end of a length of yarn, hands trying to close a blood-stained gash on the side of her suit. "Hold on! I'm coming!"

Kalie raced to the rack holding her space suit and frantically began gearing up. Martin's voice came over the intercom, this time full of emotion. "The mission first, commander! The mission first! If we lose you, everyone dies."

Isabella's whisper sounded in Kalie's earpiece. "Listen to them, Kalie." Her gasps grew weaker. "It's too late for me..." She groaned, pain infusing each word. "It's up to you... save... save... save the world."

Chapter Fifty-Three

Tuesday 6:30 A.M. Rome / 12:30 A.M. Camp David / Five Days to Impact

Dawn broke over Italy, and as proclaimed by Gabriel, the black version of the cloud had relocated from New Delhi to the Vatican. St. Peter's Cathedral was shrouded by the swirling darkness, the cathedral's spectacular structure sure to emerge tomorrow as a gleaming enhanced version of itself. The familiar pattern was now fixed, from the United Nations building, to the Kremlin, to Tiananmen Square, to the Imam Ali Mosque, and most recently to the Indian Parliament building. Important and symbolic structures transformed by the being professing himself as the one true God. And while the reception had varied from place to place, a statement was always made, without a word being spoken. Knowing what to expect, the crowd here far exceeded any of the prior stops.

Pope Urban the Ninth stood on scaffolding facing the huge crowd with several cardinals seated on each side. The cloud behind serving as a historic backdrop. God had come back to Earth and He was making His home in Rome for two days on His global tour.

The mood was triumphant as Urban addressed the faithful. "On Sunday, April first, 2018, Pope Francis delivered the Urbi et Orbi blessing at the end of the Easter Sunday Mass, right here in St. Peter's Square. His words on that day ring true again. Let us remember."

The crowd cheered at the mention of the former pontiff's name and the current pope welcomed their response with raised arms. When they calmed, he continued. "He said 'Our God is a God of surprises. At the beginning of the story of salvation, it was full of surprises, with God telling Abraham 'Leave your land and go'. It's one surprise after the other. God does not know how to announce something to us without surprising us. The surprise is what stirs the heart, that touches you precisely there, where you're not expecting it. To say it with the language of young people, the surprise is a 'low blow,' because you're not expecting it. He goes and stirs you."

The crowd roared louder still as three thousand meters away, Luca Ricci adjusted the cross-hairs on his Schmidt and Bender rifle scope, listening to the pope's speech through his earbuds. "You want to talk about something unexpected, huh? Well, so do I."

He grinned at the opportunity at humor as he again checked minimal wind readings on the mostly calm morning. This would surpass his longest shot since killing a Taliban bomb maker from twenty-eight hundred meters back in 2016. He snuggled the fiberglass stock of the rifle close to his chin, the mid-section resting on a small bipod stand. "I think your apostate head will be surprised when this round blows it off of your shoulders."

The pope turned his attention to the cloud pillar which reached all the way to space. "Our God continues to surprise us! He surprises the entire world with his words of peace and comfort as he dwells among us on our last days on Earth."

Luca listened to his own heartbeat in his ears, calming himself as his mind centered on words from the Book of Romans in the Bible. *Vengeance is mine; I will repay, saith the Lord.* He whispered to himself to fortify his will. "Use me Lord, for I am your servant. Just as I destroyed the apostate in Afghanistan, I will destroy this believer in false gods before he leads your flock astray."

Raising his arms again, the pope exhorted the faithful. "Lift your hands in praise of the Creator, the Maker of the Universe!"

Luca squeezed the trigger of his specialized weapon. Nano seconds later, bits of brains and bone splattered the cardinals nearest the pope as the bullet hit its mark.

It took a second for the realization to set in and for true pandemonium to begin. Security personnel rushed forward covering the holy man, not yet fully comprehending the full extent of his massive injury. Cardinals scrambled toward their injured leader even as armed protectors tried to pull them away, toward cover. The crowd screamed and ran, not knowing if more terror would rain down on them.

Luca quickly disassembled his rifle, packing each section into the weapon's custom fitted carrier camouflaged as a ragged guitar case. Satisfied with his dedicated service, he began to softly sing an old American Christian children's song." I may never march in the infantry, Ride in the cavalry, Shoot the artillery. I may never shoot for the enemy, But I'm in the Lord's army!"

Chapter Fifty-Four

Tuesday 9:00 A.M. New York / 6:00 A.M. San Francisco / Five Days to Impact

It had been over a week since CBN featured Larry Knewell and his panel. Hard news stories like the explosion of the first shuttle and the events in Iran were driving ratings, pushing his opinion segments to the background. With so many acts of violent regime change in relation to the cloud visiting cities around the world, however, the head honchos of the network relented to his badgering to get back on air. He could barely contain himself as the show went live. "Welcome back to Judgment Day!"

Larry beamed as he squared to the camera. "It's great to be on air, speaking to our faithful audience to address the most momentous event of our age. In the time since this panel was last together, we've seen the overthrow of both the Russian and Iranian governments as well as the assassination of Pope Urban the Ninth earlier today. In addition, we've seen domestic terrorists shoot down a shipment of nuclear material bound for our shuttle effort as well as our first shuttle disaster since *Columbia*. All efforts to successfully deploy the nuclear picket line have seemed cursed, including the death of First Officer Isabella Rojas. It almost seems if a divine hand is trying to cause chaos and prevent us from saving ourselves."

After his summary of events since their last show, he turned to camera two and framed their question for discussion today. "When we last spoke with our panelists the discussion center on whether we had free will to determine our own fate, or whether it was all predetermined by God. That seemed a very theoretical debate at that time, but now, faced with the litany of events that seem to be working against the efforts to stop this extinction event, I will ask our esteemed group to weigh in on whether God IS actually putting his hand on the scale to decide our fate. Let's reintroduce our guests this morning."

Larry turned to his in-studio guests first. "Here in New York I'm again joined by Pastor Jacob Shadwell and Rabbi Solomon Feldman."

Pastor Shadwell's face glowed with the intensity of a small sun. "Can't wait to get started, Larry."

Rabbi Solomon seemed to revert to his even-tempered form. "Always a pleasure to join you and this panel."

Larry now glanced at two screens bringing his remote guests into the conversation. "From San Francisco we're joined by Guru Baba Mashni, and from Washington D.C., Dr. Son Young Kim. Thank you two for being with us again today."

Dr. Kim hadn't gained an ounce of personality in the week away and replied in her usual monotone voice. "Thank you, Larry. Thrilled to be here." Even the word 'thrilled', was delivered as flat as a pancake.

Lastly, the usually bubbly guru answered in his bouncy voice. "I'm honored to be included among this prestigious group."

With the panel re-introduced to America, Larry teed up the topic. "At the top of the segment I detailed some of the big events that have shaken our world in the last seven days, events that seem to hinder our worlds efforts to prevent our own destruction. What I'm asking each of you is whether you think God is causing these events to bring about his ultimate plan to destroy this world. Let's go to Dr. Kim first. What do you have to say about this? Is God hindering our efforts?"

Although her monotone delivery stayed the same, she had taken her furthest step yet into contemporary fashion with a lock of her gray hair now dyed a fluorescent pink. "Larry, I could go on and on listing the reasons for each of these events. Things like the sheer magnitude of difficulty in transforming a shuttle and then launching it in one week, without the benefit of any testing. Or I could talk about the historical instability of Mid-East repressive regimes. Both of these are proximate explanations of recent events, but let me get to the root of my answer. Listen to me everyone. There... is... no... god. Now repeat. There... is... no... god. When you accept that fact then you will see clearly that we're attempting things that have never been done before, and of course there are going to be setbacks along the way. But look at what we've already accomplished. Commander Robinson is out in space deploying nuclear charges as we speak, even if she's having to do it the hard way. And we're supposed to be launching those missiles later today. Mankind is using our finest science to give us our best possibility to succeed while that alien being masquerading as god hides in his cloud, not lifting a finger to help."

The corners of Larry's lips rose, overcoming his desire to look impartial. This was exactly the kind of started he wanted for this segment. "So, there is no God? Millions of people would fiercely disagree with you, Dr. Kim. And as evidence, they would say just open your eyes. He and His angels are right there in front of you, defying the laws of physics on a daily basis. What do you say to that?"

She threw up her hands. "Just because an illusionist does a trick that seems impossible to explain doesn't mean that there's real magic in the world, does it? I'm not saying that this being isn't powerful or smart, just that they're not god."

Shifting to the first of his in-studio guests, Larry brought Rabbi Solomon into the debate. "Rabbi, it's been a week since you were here. Time for observation, reflection and prayer. As you sit here today, do you believe that God is actively intervening in the affairs of man?"

The Jewish leader who had previously raised the bar on telegenic wardrobe finery had changed his approach. Today he was dressed all in black, setting a somber tone. He sighed. "The truth is that I don't think it really matters. As Dr. Kim mentioned, we're facing tremendous technical challenges to even try to save this world. I believe that God has spoken and this world will end. I don't think He has to intervene to make that happen. I think He was just stating a fact based on his ability to see into the future. These things are happening because we are a simple and sinful people. Just look at Russia and Iran. Brother killing brother, like we did in our own Civil War. He didn't need to lift a finger to cause us to fail. We're fully capable of doing that all on our own."

Larry shook his head to the side. "Wow, that's a pretty pessimistic view of mankind, don't you think? I mean, to Dr. Kim's point, we have managed to overcome some long odds already. But you think it's already game, set and match? It's all over?"

The rabbi looked him squarely in the eye. "I'm not saying that in a bad way. I mean, after all, we've been promised paradise in communion with the Creator of the Universe. That's a pretty great way to go out, right? I'm just saying that God promised an end to this world eons ago and now it's coming to pass. Maybe not exactly as I expected, but it's happening nonetheless. And He's not causing it, He's just here to save our souls when it does."

The cable host feigned a chill. "Still, rabbi, that's a harsh assessment. We'll now turn west, to Guru Baba Mashni for his perspective. Guru, is God, or Vishnu as you call Him, intervening in our affairs to cause us to fail in our attempts to save our world? Is your assessment as tough as Rabbi Feldman's?"

The guru's attire of a lemon-yellow silk kurta seemed to forecast an optimistic response. "As always, Larry, I always appreciate your gracious invitation to join you on this panel. To answer your question, I fully believe that Vishnu can, and has, intervened in the affairs of man throughout history. Having said that, my viewpoint is much the same as Rabbi Feldman. There is ample evidence of both the challenge of somehow stopping that asteroid as well as the history of man behaving very badly toward our brothers and sisters. As philosophy teaches, the simplest explanation is usually the best."

"So, even if Vishnu is not intervening, do you think that our world as we know it will end in five days?"

The guru smiled broadly. "I am ready for synchronicity and I am excited for synchronicity." The holy man brought his hands together in front of his chest. "And yes, Larry, I do believe it will happen next Sunday."

Larry rubbed his chin. "Let me see. So far no one believes that God is intervening in our affairs to stymie our efforts to avoid the collision. With that said, we have one panelist who believes that we can avoid that fate while two others think it will happen. Last to weigh in on the question is Pastor Shadwell." The host turned and addressed the firebrand. "You've heard the others, pastor. Where do you land on this question? Is God intervening to ensure our demise?"

With the enthusiasm of a carnival barker, the pastor nearly sprang out of his chair. "Praise be the Lord, Larry. Praise be the Lord. It might surprise you, but I agree with the atheist on the panel more than these other two supposed godly men."

Again, Larry was forced to rein in the fundamentalist preacher. "As I told you before, Pastor Shadwell, degrading other religions will not be tolerated on this network, so either apologize now or leave the show."

With a knowing grin, the pastor apologized... sort of. "I'm sorry if anyone was offended by my words." Barely taking a breath, he relaunched his diatribe. "But the one true God has spelled out His plan of salvation through His son, Jesus Christ. And how the world will end is laid out clearly in the Book of Revelations. What's happening now is not God's plan, plain and simple."

A drop of spittle flew through the air as he spun himself up. "Since last week I've been leading the efforts of prayer warriors to the one true God, not this faker hiding in his cloud. We've been praying day and night that our God will bless the efforts of everyone involved in the fight to save this world, and I believe that it's working. I mean, just look at the odds that we've already overcome. That lunatic Carson Appleton conspired to shoot down that plane full of nuclear weapons bound for Phoenix. Did that stop us, I ask? No, it did not, and I believe that's because God is on our side, helping us along, guiding the hands and feet of those on the front lines of this fight. And for that reason, I know that we'll be successful in the efforts to shunt that big rock aside. The one true God is guiding our hands!" He paused, then raised his index finger. "And nothing is too big for our God!"

Larry's eyes twinkled. The pastor never failed to deliver the fire and the emotion. "Wow, Pastor Shadwell. That's quite the argument. You're saying that God is intervening, it's just that the one calling himself God here on Earth now is not your God. He's some kind of... how did you phrase it... a faker? Did I get that right?"

"Absolutely, Larry. Despite the long odds, rest assured that the efforts to save this sinful world will succeed. Someday we'll be judged by God, but it won't be Sunday."

News of the impending ICBM launches was coming in Ken spoke in Larry's ear, asking him to wrap the segment. While he usually let his guests have the last word, Larry decided to add his own take. "For more than a week our world has witnessed real extraterrestrial events of astounding proportions. A credible claim has been made that God is here, with us. Looming annihilation is eminent, with only a long shot chance of survival. Our panelists have done their best to help us understand these events and what they mean, and I am appreciative of their insights. And yet, even with our potential end at hand, they have not been able to reach a consensus on what it all means. I wonder... does that say more about God ... or about us?"

Chapter Fifty-Five

Tuesday 10:00 A.M. New York / 9:00 A.M. Minot North Dakota / Five Days to Impact

Manuel Diaz was again at the forefront of CBN remote coverage of key Judgment Day events. The Air Force had allowed selected members of the media onto the highly secure Minot Air Force Base in North Dakota and he had set up shop with his back to the open prairie hiding the buried silos containing some of Americas most destructive weapons. Manuel spoke with as much gravitas as he could muster. "In the darkest days of the Cold War, hundreds of missiles were encased in hardened crypts, on constant alert, always ready to defend our nation from foreign enemies. They waited silently, ready to unleash destruction on those who would do us harm. Today we hope to see these weapons of devastating power rise from the depths of American soil on a mission, not of destruction, but of salvation. Thankfully this back-up plan was put into place, because after the first shuttle explosion they have become critical to the mission. Should they succeed, they will not obliterate an enemy city, but move a big rock, and in doing so, save us all."

While America, and indeed the world, watched cable news coverage, the president and her cabinet listened in on the secure communication from the base. She spoke reverently while they waited. "If these missiles launch, we owe a debt of gratitude to Braxton, may he rest in peace. He was the one who found those Israeli's working on a detonator that we could use, and he's the one who pushed us to use the hackers to reprogram the guidance system. I wish he was here to see the fruit of his efforts."

Kalie joined the remote call from space, her voice stoic. "He was a good soldier doing his duty. We all miss him."

No one dared add a comment, instead listening quietly as the countdown continued. Finally, Declan spoke. "All systems go, ma'am. This is it."

An anonymous female voice continued the counted down that had begun with 'item 1' and had continued counting through the pre-launch checklist. "This is project command. Item 128, missile suspension release. Item 129 missile closure open."

A blast of orange flames erupted from silos across the wide-open field as the launch commenced. "Item 130, first stage ignition to missiles."

The missiles blasted from the fertile South Dakota soil. The President clasped her hands, speaking softly over Item 131. "God help us all."

With the missiles quickly rising into the morning sky the voice continued. "Item 132, TMO roll maneuver complete."

The Acting Secretary of Defense now piped in. "Madam President, looks like complete launch success. All birds on their way."

Cheers erupted across the video conference call as the image of one hundred individual tongues of hot exhaust pushed their cargo toward space. Abby's voice quivered with excitement. "Great job. Declan. Great job. I guess now we wait?"

The smiling warrior replied. "Yes ma'am. We'll know fairly soon if they are all headed to the correct space coordinates. So far everything's looking good."

Relief gave birth to hope as she addressed her team. "All right then, we're in business. While we wait for the next update, let's hear from everyone on what else is happening. Let's go to Kalie first. Looks like you've got help on the way."

The dark circles under her eyes couldn't dim her temporary enthusiasm. "Thank God. Best news I've heard in a while."

The president broached the delicate subject of First Officer Rojas' death. "We're all so sorry that in addition to sacrificing everything, you're having to do it all alone. How are you?"

Stone faced, with no more tears to cry, Kalie answered plainly. "Thanks for asking, ma'am. Please let Izzy's parents know that she died quickly, she didn't suffer long."

"Don't worry, we'll take care of everything here. You've got more than enough to do out there."

Kalie added, "And let them know that I set her free. She's officially the first burial in space of a non-cremated human."

The macabre discussion sickened Abby. Acid rose in her throat and she swallowed hard to keep it down. She coughed, took a sip of water, and in a gravelly voice continue, changing the subject. "So, how's the backup plan working out?"

Weariness tinged Kalie's reply. "The exoskeleton suit gives me the power to manually shove the packets out of the cargo bay, but it's not easy. I'm working on thirty-six straight hours without sleep, but only eighteen more devices to deploy."

Sympathy coated Abby's words like honey. "We are forever in your debt, Kalie. Please take care of yourself."

A wry smile looked back. "An old friend once told me that we can all sleep when we're dead. I'll have them all positioned by dinner tonight. Then I will rest."

"God bless you, Kalie. You're in all of our prayers."

"That means a lot, ma'am."

Abby now turned to Trusond, "That's the update from space, how are things here on the ground?"

The Homeland Security Advisor looked as haggard as his counterpart aboard the shuttle. "Ma'am, America, and in fact most of the world, is going dark. On Sunday, eighteen percent of the nation had lost power due to workers simply not showing up to work. This morning that number stands at thirty percent. In addition to Birmingham and New Orleans major metro areas like Baltimore, Chicago and Denver are experiencing blackouts. Having said that, we're in a lot better shape than a lot of other places. Half of the EU is out as is most of the middle east, with the exception of Israel. They're too afraid of their neighbors to let their guard down."

"Damn it, Tru. I was hoping for better news. Do you think these ICBM launches will help stem the tide?"

His posture stiffened, seeming resolved to match the standard for personal responsibility set by Kalie. "Perhaps they will slow the rate ma'am, plus I'm working on a plan to deputize some of the more responsible militias to aid in our efforts. It's risky, but we're running out of options."

She leaned in, toward her camera, willing her support toward her loyal deputy. "I trust you, Tru, and I know that there's no one else I'd rather have working this problem. Let me know if there's anything that I can do to help."

"Yes ma'am. Speaking of help, it might be a good idea to plan another address to the nation after we're sure that these missiles reach their destinations."

"We're thinking the same way. I think I'll wait until the Chinese launch tomorrow. We'll have all of our planet's defenses on the way then."

Tru spoke plainly. "I'll leave the timing up to you ma'am, but the longer you wait, the fewer people will see the address. The math is clear, if we continue on this trend, more than half of the nation will be without power by this time tomorrow."

"Damn it, Tru. I don't like your math."

The worn-out adviser cracked a weary smile. "I don't either ma'am. I guess it's the new math they're teaching the kids now."

Her smile was instantaneous. "Yeah, we'll go with that. It's just new math." Abby now turned her attention to other pressing issues. "Effie, what's new at State?"

Effie looked into her camera from her secure location in Nebraska. She cocked her head to the side, knowing that she would be delivering challenging news. "Well ma'am, like everyone is saying, the world is an unsettled place. Tru mentioned how large swaths of the planet are effectively going back to the stone age with no electricity. That's true, except all of the guns still work just fine. Russia and Iran are a mess, and most of Africa is without power. Age old grudges are being rekindled. There is a race war in South Africa with staggering casualty numbers on both sides. That conflict alone is going to make the '94 Rwanda Genocide look like a family feud. If we do survive, we'll be inheriting a much more dangerous world."

Abby looked at her squarely as one side of her mouth twitched twice, not wanting to appear insensitive, yet clearly prioritizing her efforts. "You paint a grim picture, Effie, truly tragic. Any other time, we would be leading the world response, but we can't worry about it, at least not yet. We'll start picking up the pieces on Monday, if we make it. Otherwise, it won't matter. What will matter is China. What's happening there?"

Effie's eyes caught the fluorescent lighting in her secure room. "Well, there's good news on that subject. According to their minister of state security, they are on schedule to launch fifty of their own ICBM's tomorrow. They've really stepped up as a world power and if we do survive this, we'll be recalculating the balance between us and them. But like you said, all of that can wait until Monday."

"And their power grid, how's it holding up?"

Although seated, Effie leaned on her cane. "They're at nearly one-hundred percent. This is one time where banning most religions for decades is paying off. There's no split there, everyone's on the side of wanting these missions to succeed."

The president looked to her left to Dallas who had sat quietly so far. "Speaking of religion, any updates or advice?"

Out of habit Dallas moved to push his glasses up, even though they had not yet slid down his nose. "The fault lines are pretty well set. There remains a risk from lone wolf extremists and small groups following Carson Appleton, but of more importance, a big portion of the population has simply checked out, devoting their time to worship or family. Most people are just waiting to see if the world will really end, with God saving our souls in one last hurrah for mankind. I guess we'll all know in five days, right?"

Declan Hagans broke in with an update. "Fortunately, I have news that might help answer that question. All missiles have cleared Earth's bonds and are on course to their assigned locations."

Abby smiled amusingly. "Don't count mankind out yet. We've still got a few cards to play."

Chapter Fifty-Six

Tuesday 10:00 P.M. Outside of Hominy Oklahoma / Five Days to Impact

On the banks of the Arkansas river the gas-powered generator hummed at the edge of the encampment, providing power to this tiny darkened section of the country. Without any light pollution for hundreds of miles, the stars shone bright and seemed closer than anyone gathered around the campfire could remember. On the run and running out of places to hide, Carson Appleton had taken refuge with this motley crew of sympathizers. He held a tin cup aloft in a toast. "To the return of our God and to the fulfillment of His plan."

Mumbles of agreement echoed his sentiment as the eleven other camo-clad men and their girlfriends or wives concurred. In unison, they downed good American whisky in a single satisfying communal gulp. Seth Gruber, leader of this band of protesters, stood and poked the fire, sending sparks floating upward and outward, carried by the draft until their light faded. "You really think that 'Saber Rattler' guy can do what he says?"

Carson held the glass whisky bottle by the elongated neck and poured another drink before passing it around the circle again. "I saw what he can do when we were stationed in Kandahar. He managed to steal money from Mexican drug lords while we were living in that shit-hole. Kept us in whores and hooch the whole time we were there. He's got the skills. I know he can do it. I mean, he's one of the ones that helped reprogram those missiles that launched today, and I know for certain that he hates the government. The real question is, will he do it, and that's where we have to take him at his word."

The bottle reached Seth and he tipped it into his cup, listening to the glug-glug delivery of fresh liquor. Finishing his pour, he passed it along. "We've had to put up with that perverted dyke for two long years and haven't been able to do a damned thing about it. Now, with God's help, we can take her out. We'll be doing our small part in His master plan to deliver us into His arms. I wish I could see her face when she and that faggot wife of hers get what's coming to them."

Sliding a bit lower in his folding camp chair, Carson agreed. "Yeah, and even if that bunker of hers is strong enough to withstand a direct strike, the radiation will be so high that she won't be able to come out until we're all whisked away in the rapture."

"For sure, and it will knock out all communications as well, so even if she lives, she can't lead that misguided attempt to stand in God's way. The effort will fall apart without that Jezebel cheerleader. My God, I hope your Saber Rattler doesn't lose his nerve."

Carson slurred his words as the conversation and his drinking continued. "Or get found out. I mean, he's not the only hacker they invited in. One of them others could be on the lookout for something like this. I mean, knowing their reputation, that's what I'd do if I were in charge."

Seth took another gulp. "Carson, I don't think they are as smart as you. Guess we'll know for sure by this time tomorrow night."

After a long sip, Carson laughed. "Might have to get the news from short wave radio at the rate things are going. Even those assholes on CBN will be off the air by then."

Stumbling, Seth spilled his remaining whisky as he nearly fell into his new girlfriend's lap. "Hey beautiful, let's take this party to our tent."

She pushed him back up and laughed. "You're drunk off your ass, mother fucker. Bet you ain't even got any party left in them pants."

He grabbed her roughly by the back of the neck and slung her forcefully to the ground. He loomed over her, his free hand clenched into a fist. The laughter around the campfire evaporated as all eyes turned toward the volatile situation. The adrenaline pumping through his body negated much of the outward effects of the alcohol and his slurred speech improved. Cold and menacing words punched her hard. "Listen bitch, you ever question my manhood again somethin' bad's liable to happen to you, understand?"

She turned toward him as she slowly made her way onto her knees, her voice quivering as she looked up, seeing the fire reflect in his dark eyes. "Hey baby, you know I'm just messin'."

Looking down he saw her trembling smile and he brushed her damp cheek with the back of his hand before making a vow. "We only got five nights left, baby. I'm gonna' do things to you that you ain't ever imagined. Me and you gonna' squeeze in enough agony and ecstasy to last through eternity, you hear?"

Her eyes widened, taking in a dark side of a man she had just recently met. Trembling lips whispered fearfully. "Yeah, baby. Anything you want."

Seth's anger subsided with her submission and he looked heavenward, shouting at the top of his lungs. "God bless the end of the world!"

Chapter Fifty-Seven

Wednesday 10:00 A.M. Camp David / 10:00 P.M. Beijing / Four Days to Impact

President Banister entered the compact studio in the Camp David bunker wearing casual white cropped pants and a vivid floral print silk blouse. She took her seat in front of her camera and greeted her team scattered across the U.S. "Good morning everyone. Are the Chinese ready for launch?"

Declan Hagans answered from the nearby Raven Rock Mountain facility. "Yes ma'am. Their countdown shows four minutes till blast off."

"Excellent. If all goes as planned, we'll have all of our available defenses deployed. Then we wait and see if it's enough. I believe that we'll make it. I never had a doubt that this team could pull it off. I'm really proud of everyone."

While most of the team smiled and acknowledged the kind words, Trusond Patel wore a dour expression and sat silent. Abby noticed. "While we have a few moments, let's share some updates. How about we start with Homeland?"

Tru shifted in his seat, then began. "Ma'am, I'm really glad that we have all of our planet defenses deployed, because the rest of the country has basically stopped functioning. D.C., New York City and San Francisco are the only major cities still operating at full power, and that's hour by hour. Civil authority has almost completely broken down everywhere and with the lack of control, I can't even get an estimate of the number of casualties, but I assure you it's bad. For example, the last report I had from New Orleans was that half the city was in flames. I'm working to at least get some kind of top line report on other areas of the country, but I suggest we be prepared for the worst."

The depressing report wiped away all of the smiles that had graced the screens just moments ago. Abby sat taller, summoning her inner Winston Churchill. "As bad as it is, hope remains. Hope that our world will survive, and hope that we can rebuild an even more perfect union in the aftermath. Keep your chin up, Tru, I'll be counting on you and your team to lead that mission."

He allowed a weak smile. "Yes ma'am. Rebuilding will be much more gratifying than trying to stop this landslide. You can count on Homeland."

Looking now at Effie's image, she continued the briefing. "And what's happening in the rest of the world?"

Her smile belied the seriousness of her words. "Madam President, the most valuable item in the world right now is a gas-powered generator. Other than China and Israel most of the rest of the world is in the same condition as the United States, or worse. India and Pakistan are firing bullets at each other in Kashmir and they're one miscalculation away from going nuclear. It's like one of those dystopian movies coming to life, only scarier."

Abby turned the subject back to the nation in today's spotlight. "And when the dust clears, China will be the least scarred power on the planet, right?"

Effie nodded slowly. "Looks that way ma'am. They weren't torn by religious strife the way most of the rest of the world was and they already had strict controls on their society, so the idea of not going to work or lawlessness was tamped down. Now, they've had a few incidents, with Hong Kong and Tibet being prime examples, but overall, they're coming out of this in pretty good shape... that is if we make it."

Declan stepped back into the conversation. "Madam President, the Chinese are ready to launch."

"Thanks Declan, this is the real good news of the morning."

On cue a Chinese replay of the American launch two days earlier filled the screen. Even with the language difference, the same monotone cadence of control room voices narrated the blast off. Fifty missiles that once were targeted on American or Russian cities were soon blazing toward a new enemy, one that targeted everyone. As they exited the atmosphere the same cheers that had thrilled the American controllers now filled the control room of their Chinese counterparts.

Abby noted the similarities. "Despite all of our differences, we're all really the same. Maybe the world will finally understand that truth."

Chapter Fifty-Eight

Wednesday 1:00 P.M. Camp David / Four Days to Impact

Abby finished a workout in the Camp David gym, trying to burn off excess energy. With the shuttle having deployed all of its one-hundred nuclear devices successfully, as well as the faultless launches of both the American and Chinese ICBM's, her work load had dropped dramatically. Preliminary planning was underway to restart both the nation and the world should everyone survive, but with communications lines out and the thousands of personnel that would be involved in the effort focused on their own immediate problems, there was a limit to what could be done.

Bored, she picked up the secure phone and called the Acting Secretary of Defense. "Declan, how are you this afternoon?"

He was caught flat footed. "Fine, considering the circumstances, I guess. Is something happening that I need to know about?"

She mindlessly twirled her always present pen. "Nothing like that, Declan. I'm just feeling like a tiger in a zoo. I'm tired of my cage. I've got to get out of here for at least a couple of hours."

His internal alarm sounded. "Ma'am, your safety is our highest priority. I don't think it's a good idea to be going anywhere, especially with the state of our nation."

"Believe me, I understand your concern, but there has to be a few perks for a president, even in times like these. How about I do an aerial survey of the surrounding area, you know, like there had been a flood or some other natural disaster. I need a change of scenery."

His mind raced, wanting to please his commander in chief without putting her life at risk when inspiration hit. "Okay, okay. How about this? Take Marine One and come over here? A visit from the president would do wonders for moral in the complex and it's only a ten-mile flight. It will keep your exposure to a minimum and you'll be in an even more secure location. How does that sound?"

She smiled as she stopped spinning her pen. "It's not exactly a state visit to France, but at least it's a change. Thanks Declan, I'll see you within the hour."

Chapter Fifty-Nine

Wednesday 1:00 P.M. New York City / Four Days to Impact

Walker Ames sat in his basement flat in Brooklyn, an apartment specifically chosen because of the blazing fiber optic trunk line running under the sidewalk just outside his door. After years of hacking foreign financial institutions to fund his lifestyle and screwing with the U.S. military to feed his passion, he spent the past week coding new instructions into ICBM's to potentially save the planet. And to do that job at maximum capacity he had stopped taking his meds. Now his carefully calibrated equilibrium was off. He felt good about his contribution to mankind, but he now felt an overwhelming urge to make up for lost time delivering chaos to the rich and powerful in an egalitarian fashion. A secret message from his old army buddy had given him a super cosmic idea to regain his sanity.

While all of the hackers had been kicked out of the military computer systems following the launch of the missiles, he had covertly installed a hidden back door. With just a few key strokes he was once again happily changing code on a missile in Minot North Dakota, but this time it was out of sight of his handlers and would soon to be on a mission of his choice. Metal music blasted his ears through his wireless headphones as he loaded coordinates into a lone weapon of mass destruction.

Pausing only to fetch another energy drink, he finished the job in just over an hour. It was a breeze. He didn't have to crack their firewall and he had just spent a week learning the system. All the while he thought back over his path to this moment. *Fuckin' joined the army after nine-eleven, like a patriot... And decades later we're still their fighting with the Taliban... And how much money and blood have we invested in that place??? And how much profit has the military industrial complex made??? This is a fucked-up nation and whoever is at the top keeps sending our troops into harm's way... Like, why are we back in Lebanon again anyway??? Because the current asshole in charge decides that's what we need to do... It's time for a little payback.*

After he finished the coding, the hardest part was making sure that he had covered his tracks. It was one thing to hijack an ICBM, but something else entirely to get caught. *I want to be as famous as John Wilkes Booth or Lee Harvey Oswald, but not so much the dead part. No, that won't do at all.*

He sat, staring at the screen, obsessing not about the act of treason, but only about how to avoid jail or death. Then it came to him. *False flag! That's it! I'll run the command through China. That could fuck-up both evil empires.*

Satisfied with his plan he quickly bounced the launch order through as many still working relays as possible, eventually leading back to Pudong, Shanghai, home of the Peoples Liberation Army Unit 61398. *Can't be too easy. Needs to be hard to track, but not too hard. They need to feel like they worked for it. God, I'm good!*

He leaned back, proud of his work. Interlocking his fingers and popping his knuckles loudly, he was ready. *Time to make history!* He hit the enter key one last time and sat back, imagining the chaos his index finger had unleashed. First, terror in North Dakota as a missile launches seemingly on its own, toward an unknown target. A few minutes later, destruction would rain down. Shock as word filtered across this nation, then the world. Within hours the finger pointing and pandemonium would begin, taking who knew what direction. It all made him feel positively giddy.

Satisfied that balance was restored, and all was right with the world, he lit a blunt. A mellow buzz soon crept up his spine. *Saber Rattler strikes again.*

Chapter Sixty

Wednesday 1:30 P.M. Camp David & Raven Rock Complex / Four Days to Impact

The president's helicopter landed at the Raven Rock Complex, the facility designed with the capability to run the entire military in an emergency. The events of the past ten days had shown the wisdom of the multi-billion-dollar investment as the facility was running at full mission readiness for the first time since it's activation in the mid 1950's. It was probably the safest place on the planet. Soon after the president was ushered in, she met a receiving line of smiling career officers, most meeting a sitting president for the first time. Less than a minute in, alarms rang throughout the entire facility. Abby's eyes darted around, searching for Declan in the midst of personnel scrambling to their posts. When she spied him, she moved quickly. "What the hell is going on?"

He grabbed her upper arm firmly. "We'll find out as soon as we get you to a safer place." Turning, he yelled at Dallas, who had tagged along at the last minute. "Come with us!"

The alarms rang in Abby's ears as sets of huge blast doors closed behind them. They moved quickly, deeper into the granite mountain. Finally, they entered the communications hub operating at full battle mode.

"Declan, what's happening?" Abby demanded.

An officer Abby had never met rushed to meet them. "Sir, there's been an unauthorized launch from Global Strike Command. Trajectory has it inbound."

"English, Declan!" Abby said "What's he saying?"

The blood drained from the old soldier's face as he turned to face the Commander in Chief. For the first time since she met him ten years earlier, she detected a tremor in his voice. "Madam President, I regret to inform you that somehow a nuclear missile was launched from Minot Air Force Base... and it's headed this way."

He glanced back at the officer and demanded. "ETA?"

The officer turned toward a clock on a nearby wall and their eyes followed. "Countdown at four thirty-nine and running, sir."

Life and death routines that had been practiced tens of thousands of times played out with precision. Uniformed men and women sat at computer terminals that relayed information through key strokes and verbal commands. A large central screen featured a map of the United States with a growing green arc between North Dakota and their location near the Maryland and Pennsylvania border.

Declan gently cradled her elbow as he pointed toward a small group of officers. "That's Jim Alba, the base commander, and his team. Let's join them."

In the few steps over, Abby's spine stiffened and her eyes narrowed. Smart salutes greeted the duo's arrival. "As you were. Commander Alba, bring me up to speed.

While Declan and Commander Alba both stood about six feet tall, that's where their physical similarities ended. The older man was wiry and had probably been quick on his feet in his younger days. These days age had slowed him physically, but not mentally. Jim Alba on the other hand had had the thick build of a former football player who fought battles on the line of scrimmage. His broad shoulders ran square, like heavy lumber beams, giving him an outsized presence in the small group. His clear bass voice matched his body perfectly. "Ma'am, we don't have any answers yet on the who or how, but the rest is crystal clear. Someone hacked one of our ICBM's, changed the targeting and launched the thing before anyone even knew what was happening. We're not yet exactly sure if its heading here or to Camp David."

A new emotion, fear, now flooded Abby's brain. "Camp David? You think it might be heading there? Jill's there... and about a quarter of the cabinet. Are they safe in the bunker?"

The officer from earlier spoke aloud. "ETA three minutes and counting."

Jim was about to open his mouth in response when another voice came from the control area. "Confirmation. Camp David is the target. Repeat, Camp David is the target."

Abby grabbed Jim's muscular forearm, barely reaching halfway around. "Commander, shoot the damned thing down! That's an order!"

The big man looked down with dread in his eyes. "I'm sorry Madam President. There's no time. This thing isn't flying over from Russia or China. It's such a short flight from Minot that the anti-ballistic defenses didn't have time to take it down." He glanced up at the countdown clock. "It's going to be here in two minutes and thirty seconds and there's not a damned thing we can do about it."

Still holding onto his arm, she squeezed and pleaded. "Tell me they can survive in the bunker. Please, tell me they can survive."

He put his massive hand over hers, sandwiching it between his thick fingers on one side and his wide forearm on the other. "Ma'am, we just don't know, this has never been live tested. There is hope, but the odds of any bunker surviving a direct hit have gone down as our missiles have gotten ever more powerful."

Abby pulled her hand away and shouted. "Get my wife on the phone... now... no... damn it, get her on a video link! Do it now! Do you understand?"

Jim saluted. "Yes ma'am. We'll make it happen."

He strode away shouting orders and Declan moved closer. "Come with me, I'll get you set up on this end."

They hurried out of the communications room into a small booth as someone announced a new time over the intercom. "ETA, one minute."

Abby was set up and seconds later she saw Jill, tears running down her face. "Oh honey, I'm so sorry I'm not there to hold you."

Jill's tears turned to sobs as she shook her head in denial. "Abby, this can't be happening. This can't be real."

Abby leaned closer to the screen. "I love you so much, more than life itself." She paused, glancing up. "Oh God, if you're listening, I'm begging you, please save her, please save my wife! She doesn't deserve this. No one does! Please!"

Jill pleaded. "Can you get us out? Can you save us!"

Abby's breathing labored as her chest tightened. "Oh, Jill, I would do anything... give anything to sweep you out of harm's way, but there's no time. I think you'll be safe. I think the bunker will hold. We'll be together again soon. I love you so much!"

The tears flowed unabated as Jill replied. "I'm so lucky to have met you, my love. What a life we've lived... I just thought we had more time... at least until Sunday."

Jill's twisted humor caused Abby to snort as her own tears continued to flow. "Hey, I'm supposed to be the funny one, remember? That's the way we roll. Oh God, I want to hold you in my arms so bad."

Jill wrapped her own arms around herself. "I can feel your love, can you feel mine?"

Abby responded in kind, wrapping her arms around herself. "Just like you were right here, my love." She squeezed herself as hard as she could. "I love you so much."

Suddenly Jill's image vanished from the screen and the entire Raven Rock Complex shook from the enormous blast ten miles away. Dust fell from the overhead fixture, catching the fluorescent light like tiny stars blinking once, then fading to nothingness. Seeing her reflection in the darkened screen, Abby's voice lowered and a black coldness replaced her usual upbeat tone as she made a vow. "God help me, someone's going to pay for this."

Chapter Sixty-One

Thursday 7:00 A.M. Mecca, Saudi Arabia / Midnight New York / Three Days to Impact

The cloud moved from Rome overnight and descended on the Kaaba, the cube shaped building at the center of the Grand Mosque of Mecca. In its tightest configuration yet, the dark swirling cylinder covered just the stone structure, leaving the surrounding area open for the faithful to fill and swirl around in synchronized movement, just as in the yearly hajj. Salman bin Muhammad, the King of Saudi Arabia stood side by side with his younger brother, Prince Bandar bin Fahd, in an alcove of the Grand Mosque. Observing the massive swirling cloud, the king spoke. "Remember 2015, the deaths?"

"Two thousand crushed in a stampede of believers. Please, brother, must we speak of such things?"

"More than two million of the faithful attended last year, and now, with Allah proclaiming the end of times? How many will come? How many will want to fulfill their obligation while He is physically here, among us? Maybe a billion, or more? With five hundred million already camped outside, I tell you, the walls of this very mosque will not stand. It will be a blood bath, and I know of no way to stop it."

The prince stared, mesmerized by the swirling blackness. "We will use the army to restrict access, manage the flow. We are the custodians and can set any conditions that we deem necessary. They are in place as we speak."

The King spoke stoically. "And when the crush of humanity pushes, and it will push with intense devotion, do we order our forces to use all means necessary to resist? Do we gun down believers by the thousands outside the mosque to avoid the death of thousands inside? Death is coming and the House of Saud will be blamed either way. Then the mob may come for us."

The prince nervously stroked his beard. "Perhaps Allah will provide a miracle. like the Isra and Mi'ra Night Journey of the Prophet? Allah will protect us, if he is willing."

A single snort emitted from the king's nostrils. "Like he prevented the fall of the Russian president? Or the slaying of the Shiite Ayatollah? Or even the prevention of the death of the American president's wife, even if she was an abomination? No, my brother, Allah will save our souls, but seems to have no interest in saving our Earthly bodies."

The prince started, then stopped before starting again. "Brother...is it possible...never mind."

"This is no time to retreat into fear, Bandar, we are alone in the presence of Allah. Speak your mind."

With hesitancy the prince started a third time. "Brother... are you sure? I mean, these events are not in agreement with the Quran. Is it possible...?" His voice trailed off without finishing the sentence.

"Oh, dear brother. Hear with your ears! See with your eyes! Can you deny the holy words that you have heard? Can you deny the fearsome power that you see? Only Allah has the ability to create and to destroy. If this is not Allah, then who?"

A volley of gunfire rang from the soldiers temporarily holding back the mass of humanity now surging forward. The sound crystallized the prince's thought. "Then it's time for our exit. I'll alert the royal jet. Allahu Akbar!"

Chapter Sixty-Two

Thursday 8:00 A.M. Air Force One & Raven Rock Complex / Three Days to Impact

The repercussions of the attack on Camp David were mounting, starting with the ice-cold anger of President Abigail Banister. Now aboard Air Force One with no plans to land until either the destruction of the planet on Sunday or the restoration of order in the United States, should the earth survive the weekend. Tanker planes would refuel the jet as needed until one of those outcomes occurred. Until then, Abby would have only a few staff members and Dallas as physical company to go along with regular contact with her remaining cabinet members.

Her black mourning dress accentuated her coal black hair, now sprinkled with a little more gray, setting the tone for this morning's virtual meeting. "I want to thank each of you for your condolences following the tragic and senseless loss of my wife. My heart is broken and your thoughts and prayers are appreciated. In addition to the loss of my Jill, Dallas has suffered even more with the loss of his wife Maggie, and their children. In total, we lost over two hundred souls at Camp David, including a quarter of our cabinet."

Her usually sparkling eyes now glared as hard as violet veined granite. "I want to be very clear on three things. First, whoever did this must be found quickly and made to pay, even if it means starting World War Three. This kind of blatant attack on the United States, an attack on me, my administration, and my family, will not be tolerated. Understand?"

Subdued voices replied, "Yes, ma'am."

Her pen started tapping and her voice rose in volume as she continued. "The second thing is that I want a full report on who was responsible for putting me, my wife and all the others at Camp David in jeopardy. Why in the world were we placed in a location that was so vulnerable? Hundreds died, including the love of my life. How in the hell did that happen? I want answers and names, understand!"

Chastened, all replied in the affirmative.

She waited a few seconds before continuing, now allowing a bit of softness back into her words. "Lastly, I want everyone to know that I'm still counting on each of you. We've got a broken country to run for the next three days and I need each of you at your best. Hopefully, the planet won't be destroyed and we'll be blessed with the opportunity to mend our great nation. And while I want revenge on whoever did this and to hold those who placed us in this situation accountable, running our country must be our first priority. Is that clear?"

This question received a much more positive response.

"All right then, let's get started. Tru, you're up first. Where are we on finding out who did this?"

Safely broadcasting from the bunker at Mount Weather, Tru lowered his head and spoke softly. "Ma'am, once again, I am so very sorry for what happened, to Jill, and all the others. When considering who's at fault, my name must be put right at the top. I should have seen something like this coming. I should have taken the appropriate actions. Their deaths are on me, and I would like to tender my resignation today."

The pen tapping her pad was the only sound on the video conference as the president weighed her options. After leaving Tru in suspense she let him off the hook... kind of. "I appreciate you taking responsibility for this debacle and I have every right to fire you on the spot."

She drew in a slow breath, allowing her words to bite. "I will accept your resignation... but not until Monday... if we survive. The country is counting on us, and our best chance to hold this nation together is with you leading Homeland."

She then locked eyes with him onscreen in a cold stare before continuing. "Where are we in the search for the perpetrators?"

Tru was profuse in his gratitude. "Thank you, ma'am. I won't let you down again. I promise."

"I want revenge, Tru. That's what you need to deliver."

Her scorn burned cold and he launched into his briefing to ease the pain. "We've made some real progress, ma'am. We have three suspects and are bringing all of them in for questioning as we speak."

Her brow arched. "I thought the preliminary analysis was that the Chinese did this, that it was a slam dunk. What changed?"

"Well, ma'am, working with Declan and his cyber team the trail initially led straight to their digital spy hub. But the more we looked at the evidence, the more things seemed off. The Chinese have been so cooperative on everything up to this point, giving us unimaginable access to their defense systems. Because of that, we've been able to use that access to probe parts of their network from the inside and we didn't find anything linking them to this attack. They had to know that if they broke into our system and launched one of our own missiles against us, we had this capability. And if we did find anything, we could take down their entire digital network in minutes. Besides, if they wanted to send a missile, why not just send one of their own and claim they were hacked. That would have been a lot easier. It just didn't make sense."

"What does make sense?"

Tru rubbed his forehead as if trying to erase a stain. "Those hackers did an amazing job helping us get those missiles into space. I didn't want to invite them in, but we all agreed that we had to take the risk. And to be fair, because of them, we have a chance at survival, but we always knew we were making a deal with the devil. I think this attack is confirmation that we were right to worry."

Abby fell back in her chair. "Son of a bitch, one of our own did this! We better survive this asteroid so I can have the pleasure of seeing the bastard fry."

"Yes ma'am. I would like to be standing beside you when it happens."

"Alright, let me know as soon as we have the bastard." She waved her hand in a gesture to move on. "And how is the rest of the nation? I'm guessing it can't be good."

Tru tapped some keys on his computer and disturbing images joined him on all of their screens. "As you suggested, ma'am, things are pretty rough right now. First of all, the nuclear fallout from Camp David has drifted and contaminated parts of five states. Millions of people have been exposed in dozens of cities, including Boston and New York. It's made worse because we've had a hard time warning them due of the lack of power. There is not a single electrical generating plant operating in the country, not one. Most hospitals and many critical communications hubs have back up power, but even with that, they are facing severe staffing shortages and are barely operating. It's like the stone age... with modern weapons. This has been my nightmare from day one, and try as we might, it's happening, even after declaring martial law. And as bad as nuclear fallout is, that's not the worst of it."

"You know how I feel about bad news. Just put it out on the table for all to see."

His head bobbed once. "Yes. ma'am, so here it is. Religious conflicts have escalated in our country, just as they have in other hot spots around the globe. In Minneapolis, Muslim neighborhoods have erected barricades to fend off new attacks after hundreds were killed yesterday. Later in the day, five shooters blasted their way into a heavily defended synagogue in San Francisco shouting 'Death to the

Jesus Killers.' They killed forty. These are just two of the more egregious examples. There's not a faith group in the country that can feel safe and right now I'm at a loss on how to stop any of it before we find out what happens on Sunday. We're doing what we can."

Swinging between her natural optimism and deep despair, Abby's pen stopped tapping as she offered a weak smile. "Just think how much worse it could be without your efforts, Tru. There are people alive today because of what Homeland is doing. Just keep fighting the good fight for the next few days."

"Yes ma'am. We'll keep at it, and we already have the beginnings of a plan for first thing Monday morning. I have faith that we're going to save this world... or what's left of it."

Her weak smile strengthened a smidge. "Keep the faith, even in the darkest of hours."

Now she glanced at Declan's image on her screen and spoke weakly. "Is Defense in any better shape than Homeland?"

The circles under Declan's eyes were two shades darker this morning. "Once again, Madam President, I offer my deepest sympathies."

"Thank you, Declan."

Without hesitation he added, "Put my name right up there with Trusond's. I am even more culpable for the disaster that happened yesterday. Hundreds died because of my failure."

Abby's weak smile disappeared as she was immediately cast back into the depths of her grief. "Duly noted. Scholars will research this debacle for decades and I'm sure they will attach a full share of blame to your name." Her words were true and they tasted bitter in their delivery, but she felt they must be said aloud.

With all her might she fought the urge to cry, knowing that it would be her right, but also knowing that it wouldn't help. She sniffed, then wiped her nose with a tissue. "As with Tru, I'll deal with your situation if we make it to Monday. Until then, I'm counting on you at Defense."

Her harsh words seemed to wash over him as confirmation of the way he must have already felt. Accepting her scolding and temporary pardon, he began his briefing. "As Tru has summed up, we think we'll identify the domestic terrorist who did this in a few hours and we have a team of specialists working on ways to prevent anything like this from happening again. I know that's small consolation. We've learned a harsh lesson, one that must not be repeated, so that those who perished will not have died in vain."

Abby barely held back an emotional deluge. Her voice quivered, on the brink. "Yes. This can't be allowed to happen again. Please, continue."

Declan cleared his throat. He looked to be fighting a similar battle to control his own emotions. "Fortunately, there is good news to report. With Kalie's deployments and the ICBM's we've launched, it looks like we have our defense plan nearly in place. The latest from the team at Keck indicates that the asteroid will meet our most distant nukes early tomorrow morning. We'll know soon if any of this made a difference, may God help us all."

Abby reached her limit and lashed out. "May God help us all? As far as I can tell, God, if that's who this really is, hasn't lifted a damned finger to help us! He didn't save Ferron, nor Braxton. He didn't save any of the other millions of people who have died in the violence since his arrival, some in the shadow of his pretentious cloud. And he sure didn't save my Jill! So, just to be clear Declan, if we live to see Monday it will be in spite of God, not because of Him."

Chapter Sixty-Three

Friday 8:00 A.M. Space Shuttle Pinta / Air Force One & Raven Rock Complex /

2:00 A.M. Hawaii / Two Days to Impact

Kalie took a Valium to calm her nerves as she prepared to open the communication line back to Earth. In the solitude of the past two days she had reflected back on all of the decisions she had made in her life that put her here, alone, farther from Earth than any other person in history. Looking through the front windows of the shuttle, she could see the approaching chunk of rock that would end her life, and, perhaps that of every person on Earth. While she did not wish to die, she had come to the conclusion that she had been destined to sacrifice her life to give everyone else a chance for salvation.

She recalled the doors that had opened for her and not others, and all of the unexpected career twists and turns that equipped her to do this job. Was it God? Fate? Or just the randomness of the universe? She never fully settled that question in her mind but she was content, feeling in her bones that this was exactly how her live was meant to play out.

The extra time had also given her the opportunity to get her affairs in order, writing emails to her mother and father, to her friends at Space Rim, to mentors who inspired her, and even one to a special high school sweetheart. All that was left was a final communication to the president and the team back home, with a link to the guys at the Keck observatory. She settled into the pilot seat and glanced at the fuel gauge. "Just enough."

The countdown clock read five minutes. It was time. She flipped two switches and waited to hear familiar voices from Earth in her ear. "Hi Kalie, can you hear us?" The president sounded upbeat.

"Yes, loud and clear, Madam President. How about me, is the camera catching the view from the front?"

Abby wore a paste on smile, trying to mask her sadness at what was about to happen. "That's some view you've got there. It would be beautiful it wasn't so deadly. You guys at Keck getting this?"

Dr. Haskell glanced at Wade, then responded. "Yes, Madam President, loud and clear. This information could prove invaluable in the coming hours. Commander Robinson, we can't tell you how much we appreciate the sacrifice that you are making. On behalf of all of us here, we thank you for your service to our nation and our world. We'll go quiet now and collect as much data as we can.

Kalie replied to the guys at Keck. "Thanks. I'll keep an eye on the clock and check in one last time as the object approaches."

The president now directed a comment towards Hawaii. "Hey Keck team, the world also owes you guys a debt of gratitude. Without your discovery...." Her words trailed off. "Let's just say that we're glad that you gave us as much warning as you did."

Haskell was gracious to his young junior partner. "Thanks ma'am. Wade's here with me, and he deserves the lion's share of recognition. He's a talented young man with a bright future."

Now real happiness tinted Abby's recent melancholy affect. "And I hear there's a wedding tomorrow. Is that right?"

The warmth of Wade's blush seemed to travel through the distance. "Yes ma'am. I'm pretty excited."

"Just know that I'm coming to meet you and your new wife when things settle down here."

His cheeks reddened further, to a shade resembling a ripe Ambrosia apple. "Thanks ma'am. It will be an honor."

With the easy part of the call over, Abby turned her attention back to the hero of the hour. "Kalie, I'm so incredibly lucky to have met you... to have had the honor to work with you... and call you my friend. Your name will be remembered above all others forever. There is no way to really express how much the world owes to you."

Even with the Valium circulating in her system, Kalie's emotions surged. She bit the inside of her cheek, using pain as a way to redirect her mind. "Thank you, ma'am. It all worked out the way it's supposed to. I wouldn't trade places with anyone."

Abby noticed that her hand was trembling, and began tapping her pen as a way to calm her nerves. "Hey Kalie, the rest of the cabinet is also linked into the call. I've asked Trusond to say a few words on their behalf."

"Kalie." He stopped, trying to contain his emotions, before beginning again. "Kalie, on behalf of the entire team, we want you to know that we love you, and that you are, and will always be, an inspiration to us. You have set a new standard for service to the nation and it's been an honor to call you our friend. You'll be in our hearts forever."

Tears formed at the corners of her eyes and she wiped them one at a time with the backs of her hands. "I love you all, too."

She closed her eyes for a moment, then looked forward, toward the dappled gray asteroid, which had now grown much larger as the distance between had closed quickly. "Well, enough farewell talk, I've got one more mission to finish. Keck, you guys still have visual?"

"Yes, commander, we're tracking great."

Looking at the clock, she saw that it had wound down to one minute. "I'm going to be the first of what will be many man-made explosions trying to move this killer over a little at a time. Looks like there's a small indentation on the port side of the object. I think I'll aim for that unless you have a different idea."

Haskell's voice walked the tightrope between geeked out scientist thrilled at this up-close view of this historic event and the sincere sadness of knowing the human cost about to be paid. "You're sending great pictures, commander. This will really help us in the next few hours. We're good with that point of impact."

With the confirmation Kalie flipped the switches that would ignite the boasters of the shuttle, giving her every bit of speed possible to perhaps move the rock the first millimeter needed. With the extra push of the engines, the gap between the shuttle and the monster closed quickly. Eyes now locked onto target, Kalie's nerves settled. A new calm took over her body as she shifted back into mission mode and began speaking directly to the rock. "So, this is what a killer asteroid looks like. I thought that you would be... somehow bigger... uglier... but you're really just a plain Jane chunk of rock as dirty as a DC sidewalk... and dumb. Dumb as a rock."

She laughed softly at her last spontaneous joke. "Well, here's the thing, you big dumb rock, we can't let you kill us all, even if that's what God wants... at least not without a fight. So, I'm going to throw the first punch... and I know that you'll hit back... and win round one."

Valium, exhaustion, too much loss, and thousands of tears already spilled left her too spent to shed even a single additional drop. She continued her cold monologue. "Well, I've got news for you. You haven't met anyone like me, or any of the other people on Earth. And we've got a few surprises coming your way."

An alarm sounded as the warning system counted the final ten seconds aloud. As the screen now completely filled with the oncoming collision, Kalie's voice finally rose. She now shouted defiantly as she piloted the shuttle on its final approach to her selected point of impact. "We'll show you, you bastard! Earth can hit back!!! We ain't going down without a fighttttttttt!!!"

Chapter Sixty-Four

Friday Noon Air Force One & Raven Rock Complex / 6:00 A.M. Hawaii

Two Days to Impact

For the past four hours Abby has been mostly alone with her thoughts. Being confined to Air Force One traveling on randomized flight plans to avoid becoming a target of saboteurs from almost any conceivable religious sect, political fringe group or foreign adversary was good for her physical safety, but terrible for her mental state. Thinking of Jill, she had ordered the plane to make a detour over the blast site to see with her own eyes the huge crater that had taken out the bunker.

Her well of tears had run dry this morning following the kamikaze end that Kalie had chosen. She felt alone, more than at any time in her life. Sam, the Secret Service Agent and Dallas were the only familiar faces on the plane. For the moment, Dallas was mired in his own mourning. All of her other closest staff had been killed at Camp David or were in other shelters scattered across the country. In the noisy isolation she contemplated her decision to try and save the planet. Doubt crept in. Was she right to fight so hard to try and save the world, or should she have just accepted God's decision? Was this really God? Was it going to matter anyway? Should she have declared martial law sooner and perhaps stopped Carson Appleton? Would it have mattered? Puffy eyes and weariness kept her from reaching any conclusions on those weighty questions as she waited in her private hell until the noon briefing.

Lethargically, she kicked off the meeting at the appointed time. "Forty-eight hours until potential Armageddon. Words I never dreamed I would speak. I would like to start this meeting with a moment of silence in honor of our friend and colleague, National

Security Advisor and Shuttle Commander Kalie Robinson. She forfeited her life in valiant service this morning. Whether our efforts are successful or not, she gave her all so that we might still have a chance. Let's take a moment to remember her sacrifice."

The president let the moment extend, in part as a validation of the size of the loss and also to give herself an extra few minutes to get her head back into the game. There was too much at stake to wallow in self-pity, even though that's exactly what she wanted. *Come on Abby, these people... all people... are counting on you. There will be time enough for this shit when it's all over. Snap out of it and lead... or at least pretend.*

With a self-push she began again. "All right, we've got a world to save, so let's get this meeting started. Who's got the latest update on our monster rock?"

Dr. Haskell spoke excitedly. "We've been able to detect the first four nuclear explosions that Commander Robinson planted in the path of the asteroid. That's good news in that the weapons are functioning as hoped."

Abby pushed. "The real question is, have we moved it? Is the plan working?"

Haskell was a bit less animated in this response. "We're hopeful. The fact is this is going to be a long process. It might take fifty explosions to be able to detect enough movement to measure from this distance. I would like to be more definitive, but the distances are so great and the movement that we need is so small that we'll have to be a bit more patient to say for sure."

The pen tapping began. "You're new on these calls, Dr. Haskell, but you need to know that I'm not the most patient person, especially when the stakes are so high. I expect a more definitive answer next time. Understand?"

His answer was automatic. "Yes ma'am."

"All right, any other news about the rock before we move on?"

"In fact, there is, ma'am. We can confirm that the asteroid remains intact, and that's a good thing."

"I'm sure that I've been briefed on this, but remind me why we don't want to make little rocks out of the big rock. Wouldn't that be better?"

The corners of Haskell's mouth lifted a bit. "This does sound counter intuitive, but we want it to stay in one piece so each explosion pushes the entire object, ensuring that the whole thing misses Earth. If it starts breaking apart, we might get a situation where big chunks start coming toward us on different vectors. Our blasts then might be only moving some of the chunks as others fly toward us on their own unimpeded path. In that case, we might avoid the entire planet's destruction, but still suffer some really big impacts. What we're doing is using nuclear explosions to do some really delicate work."

Her humor resurfaced. "Kind of like using a hammer and set of pliers to do brain surgery?"

Everyone one the call smiled as Haskell laughed. "Exactly, Madam President. That's a great way to say it."

"All right then, I get it. Anything else we need to know before you log off and track that chunk of destruction while we try and keep everything else running here on our own rock?"

"No, ma'am. And I'll have more info the next time we speak, I promise."

"I'm glad that we have an understanding. And thanks again for all you guys are doing. You're our eyes and ears as this thing get closer. I know you won't let us down."

With that the astronomer logged out of the virtual meeting, leaving the usual participants. Abby wasted no time. "Tru, how's our country?"

From his bunker in Mount Weather, Tru started his update. "With the power out everywhere, it's getting harder to get a full read. Having said that, what we do know is that we're seeing more of the same. Religious groups did all they could to feed those without food, but all supplies ran out for everyone. We've now opened up all of the federal and state food emergency stores as well as distributing most of our supply of MRE's, and we're seeing less food violence. We'll have some tough days and weeks getting the supply chain up and running should we make it, but no one's starving through Sunday."

The pen rapped steadily. "That's good news, Tru. Well done. And everything else?"

He cast his eyes down. "Prison breaks are the newest fad, ma'am. Seems the guards are walking away in enough numbers that the inmates are gaining control in an increasing number of facilities. We've rushed troops to take up the slack, but we just don't have enough manpower since we're losing troop numbers as well. The biggest breakout was at the Louisiana State Prison with five thousand inmates released, and the worst in Florence, Colorado. Our Super-max facility there contained the nation's most notorious felons, who are now on the loose. Next week is going to be a bitch."

This bit of news seemed to stun everyone on the call, including the president. She forced herself to say something positive in spite of her black mood. "As bad as that is, I'll sign up for that future right now rather than go gently into eternal night. Anything worse than that happening?"

Tru held out his hands. "One positive from the shutdown of our power grid is that communication networks are down and that unrest is not rampantly spreading. A firefight between groups in Brooklyn doesn't necessarily mean trouble in Queens. I guess medieval living does have its perks."

She fought her depression. "That's the way to look at the bright side, Tru. Way to find some positives as our nation goes to Hell in a hand basket. Hopefully we start picking up the pieces on Monday."

He gave a half grin. "Yes ma'am. I'm counting on seeing Monday."

Turning now to State, she continued. "And Effie, how goes the rest of the world?"

The Secretary of State smiled broadly. "Madam President, right now there's China and Israel, oh, and I forgot to mention North Korea at the last briefing. They still have power as well. Then it's most everyone else. Two highly atheist nations with fairly self-contained power grids have fared well in a God fueled global collapse. On the other hand, Israel has lived in a near permanent war footing, so they were prepared like no other for this kind of existential threat. This is a new twist for them, but their systems were ready."

Effie filled out her report. "North Korea doesn't have much happening, but they do still have all of the generation capability that they had two weeks ago. And China, now that's a different story. All of their systems are humming along at near full strength. If they wanted, they could cause all kinds of trouble. The good news is that they haven't... yet. I'll leave it up to Defense to comment on our contingency plans."

"We'll get to Declan in a moment, but anything else I need to know about?"

Effie leaned on her cane for support. "Yes ma'am, there is. As you know, the cloud is in Mecca now and things have gone terribly wrong. I'll let Dallas cover that mess."

Abby glanced at Dallas whose eyes were bloodshot from grieving. He sniffed and in a near whisper began his report. "As you may know, every Muslim is required to perform a pilgrimage to Mecca in their lifetime, if they are physically able and can afford it. With the end of the world potentially approaching, a crush of millions has rushed to fulfill their obligation, and as an added bonus, perhaps get an early glimpse of Allah in the cloud. Reports are sketchy, but there may be as many as a hundred thousand people trampled in multiple stampedes. It's an unmitigated catastrophe."

Abby was aghast. "That's awful. How can tens of thousands be dead just for practicing their faith. And apparently God just watched it all happen, not lifting a finger to stop it? Jeez. So, what does the royal family have to say about all of this?"

Dallas shook his head. "Seems that when things began to get out of control, they washed their hands of it and got out of the country. They're reportedly on a small island in the Arabian Sea waiting it out, one way or another. And things may get worse tomorrow as the cloud moves to Jerusalem. That could make Mecca look like a warm up act. When you throw in the rioting after the pope was assassinated, the Russian coup, the Ayatollah's death, and our own sectarian massacres, organized religion isn't looking so good right now."

The assessment added to the president's gloom. "I wish I had a snappy comment to take the sting out of your assessment, but I agree. We have to find a better way to live with each other."

She took a deep breath, then forced herself to continue. "Anything else, Dallas, or are we good to move on to Defense?"

"Those are the big items, ma'am."

Abby turned to Declan. "All right, how bleak is the outlook from Defense?"

Declan stood board straight in his uniform. "Madam President, we live in interesting times."

His opening caught the president off guard. "I'll say, Declan. What's new?"

Without flinching he began his rough report. "I'm sorry to report that this is the weakest state of American armed forces in my lifetime. As Sunday approaches, we're seeing soldiers, sailors and airmen going AWOL in record numbers. Other than naval ships at sea, our preparedness in no better than fifty percent. The only good news is that except for China, all of our biggest threats are in the same, or worse shape. Russia is fighting a civil war in pre-electricity conditions. Thank God that China is our ally in this, or we could be in big trouble."

The president's earlier forced smile dissipated in the face of the blunt assessment. "And what happens if they decide to take advantage of the situation?"

"Well, ma'am, mutually assured destruction is still in play. While they can certainly mess with us in a variety of ways, we still have dozens of ICBM's fully functional and capable of wiping all of their major cities off the map, and they know it." He now continued without thinking about the ramifications of his next statement. "Nukes have their fair share of problems, but there has never been a better time to have them at our disposal."

The mention of nuclear problems pricked her heart as an image of Jill flashed in her mind and her darkness returned in full, without restraint. "Problems? You call what happened here a problem? A clogged pipe is a problem. A fender bender is a problem. But a domestic nuclear terrorist attack killing hundreds, including my wife? That, Declan, is more than just a problem. It's a catastrophe that is even now exposing millions of our citizens to radioactive fallout. So, I'd better not hear you or anyone else minimize what happen by calling it simply a problem, understand? It was a national disgrace, an abomination on our great land, and we had better not have any more disasters like it again!"

Chapter Sixty-Five

Saturday 7:00 A.M Jerusalem / Midnight Air Force One & Raven Rock Complex

One Day to Impact

Prime Minister Moshe Levi watched the arrival of the cloud to Jerusalem from a secure lookout a couple of hundred meters away. The city was perhaps the most divided on the planet with three major religions deeming it as among their most important locations. Its ownership, and battles for its control reached back to the very beginning of recorded history, and it was currently one of the most heavily armed places on the planet. Pulling his binoculars down Levi spoke wistfully with Asher Peres, his minister of defense. "Remember when all we had to worry about was a Palestinian uprising or a nuke from Iran?"

"Yeah, that's so two weeks ago. What's the worst that can happen now. The end of the world?"

His macabre rejoinder humored the prime minister, but now he spoke plainly. "Are we ready? Are all units in place, all reservists called up?"

"We're as ready as we can be. All forces are at full alert, and all checkpoints are manned. We've cut power to both the West Bank and to Gaza to lower their ability to cause problems, but who knows? Millions of Arabs have been moving to our borders in the past two weeks, but they've not yet tried to cross into our territory. At any moment, they could decide to descend on us like locusts, giving us no choice but to use all means necessary to defend ourselves. It's up to them on how they want to play this, but we will be ready... no matter the cost."

The prime minister raised his binoculars again, surveying the cloud as it swirled atop the Temple Mount, once the home of the both the first and second temples, each destroyed by foreign enemies. "Ash, do you think God will restore the temple? It has been promised."

Asher now raised his own binoculars to get a closer look at the phenomena. "Yes, that is our promise, but to do so would require God to destroy the al-Aqsa Mosque, the Dome of the Rock and the Dome of the Chain. That would show the Muslims once and for all that we are God's first and most favored people."

The president sighed. "Like you, I have prayed for the restoration of the temple since childhood. Every day I have prayed for this. And now, if God were to grant my prayer, I believe He would allow the Muslims to overwhelm our defenses and kill every Jew in the land." His voice now quivered. "I cannot pray for the third temple tonight."

Asher let his binoculars fall, pulling up when they reached the end of the strap around his neck. "Moshe! How can you say such a thing? Our God would never let that happen! We must all pray for the temple to be rebuilt, especially tonight!"

The grizzled statesman looked at him with sorrow. "Can you imagine the fury that we would face if that is what is revealed tomorrow? As strong as our defenses are, they would be submerged in a human tidal wave. Even the Americans do not have enough bullets or bombs to defend us should that occur."

"But our God would protect us! You must believe this!"

The older man put a firm hand on his fierce warrior. "Asher, you have seen what happened in Mecca and Najaf, and even Moscow. God let slaughters happen right at his feet, doing nothing to interfere with the affairs of mere men. How can you be so sure that he would treat us any differently?"

"Then we would use our nuclear weapons, which our God allowed us to develop. We must defend our land against the infidels."

"And kill more Arabs in one day than the number of Jews killed by Hitler in the entire holocaust? Do you believe that would be our God's will?"

He pushed the older man's hand away. "Moshe, listen to yourself! We are God's Chosen! It is written!"

Again, the Prime Minister raise his lenses to view the holy spectacle. "And so they each thought, my friend. And yet..." He left the rest unsaid before adding, "Please, I beg of you, pray carefully this evening."

Chapter Sixty-Six

Saturday 7:00 A.M. Air Force One & Raven Rock Complex / 1:00 A.M. Hawaii

One Day to Impact

While Abby had received regular updates throughout the past twenty-four hours on the ongoing attempts to alter the course of the asteroid, this was the first live update since yesterday. In the time between these virtual meetings she had taken her self-help inner dialog to new levels. *I must be strong for the nation and the world, they are depending on me. Put the needs of the team above my own. I can grieve when this is all over.* As hard as she tried, it wasn't working. Anger and grief burned in her soul, seeking revenge and solace. The best she could manage was to shove her hurt and malice down deep, vowing to push through these next hours with purpose and, if not with a smile, then not a frown either.

Working on her second espresso she spoke brightly, masking her true feelings. "Dr. Haskell, what's the latest? How is the asteroid tracking?"

His eyes lingered on a computer screen up until the final words of the president reached his ears. "This is fascinating, Madam President. I've spent most of my life working to see farther and farther away from Earth, looking at light that began its journey millions of years ago. Now I'm tracking an object just a few light minutes away. Incredible."

She chuckled, recalling how often Dallas had displayed the same academic joy in the past two weeks. "You're not the first on the team to geek out on this event, Dr. Haskell, just the latest. But right now, we need an update... hopefully a positive one."

His eyes cast down and a shy smile crept across his face. "Yes ma'am, I understand. Well, I come bearing both good and bad news. Which would you prefer to hear first?"

"We need all the positive vibes that we can get. Bring on the happy talk."

He rubbed his hands together briskly. "All right then. Good news first. I'm please to confirm that we have definitely made a difference in the trajectory of the asteroid. With one hundred and eighty of the two hundred and fifty nuclear devices detonated, we have made a measurable difference. Congratulations to all those who worked to bring this plan to life on such short notice."

Abby clapped her hands mustering every ounce of her small supply of enthusiasm. "That's fantastic, Dr. Haskell. So, this plan has a good chance to work, right?"

His shoulders tensed. "That's where things get dicey, ma'am."

He stopped, seeming to search for the right words, the best way to deliver the bad news. "Remember when we talked about some of the risks to this plan? That we hoped that the rock would stay intact, and not break into pieces as each of those nuclear devices detonated?"

"Yes, I remember. How bad is it?"

Dr. Haskell seemed relieved that she had taken this part of the news so well. "Well, right now it's broken into three roughly equal sized chunks, each of which could cause an extinction level catastrophe if they were to strike the planet. We have moved them all some, so we still have a chance. It's just that as each remaining nuke explodes in an attempt to nudge them all farther away, the odds have gone up that one or more of these still large pieces will break into even smaller bits. Remember, this thing started out over six miles wide and even a sliver the diameter of a basketball court could destroy a city the size of Chicago."

Abby's pen rapped steadily now as a dull pain began creeping up her spine. She lowered her voice. "Best guess, Dr. Haskell. How is this going to go down tomorrow?"

He ran his hands through his hair and sighed. "There's no way to predict what will happen with absolute certainty."

She snapped. "I get that! No one's going to blame you if things go better or worse than you expect. Just tell us, Dr. Haskell, what's your best guess given the data that you have now. What's the forecast for tomorrow?"

He looked straight into his camera and gave his blunt assessment. "Based on the way things are trending, here's what I think. I believe that we'll be able to shove most of the mass far enough away to prevent it from impacting Earth, and that would be a very good thing. However, I think it's likely that we're going to see more and more fragmentation until there are thousands of mini asteroids raining down on us, starting in just under twenty-nine hours. There's no way to predict the trajectory for each shard or the damage they will do. Some may land in cornfields, and do little initial damage, but a huge amount of material with be thrown into the atmosphere, causing years long climate changes. Other pieces will land in oceans, potentially causing tsunamis that could devastate cities around the globe. Any coastal city could be wiped out in just a few moments. So, while there is a possibility that humanity may survive, Sunday could see the largest single day of death since the dinosaurs were wiped out."

The virtual call went so quiet that a needle dropping to the floor from any site would have sounded like a clarion bell. After rubbing the back of her neck, the president spoke in measured tones. "This plan was a long shot from the very beginning, with many saying it was hopeless, but this team banded together and persevered through some dark days. We saw setbacks, like the explosion of the first shuttle. We endured personal loss, like with Braxton and Kalie... and even Jill."

She drew a deep breath, then continued, fighting to hide her growing physical discomfort and her own despair. "If you had told me two weeks ago that we would have to face all of that and still have a chance at an outcome, even as dire as this, it would have been painful, but I would have taken it. You've all done a hell of a job in the most difficult of circumstances."

While this was the number one topic for the call, there remained other items to discuss. "I'll expect hourly updates, Dr. Haskell. There may not be any actionable info, but we need to know what to expect and get the most up to date information out to the nation and the world as soon as possible. Even if we can do nothing more, the people deserve to know what's happening. Is there anything else we need to know before you log out and get back to your work?"

"No, ma'am. You've got the scoop for now. I'll send the next update in an hour."

"Thanks, and keep up the good work."

With a final, 'Yes ma'am' he exited the call.

Abby pivoted toward a domestic update and continued to deal with the pounding headache. She pointed a weak finger toward her Homeland Security Secretary. "Tru, what are the headlines from Homeland on this penultimate day?"

"Ma'am, it's kind of like driving around a city on Christmas Eve. All of the stores are closed and most everyone is gathered with family and friends, anticipating what they'll discover tomorrow morning. The level of all forms of violence has fallen to almost nil as the nation seems to be holding its collective breath. Some are praying to be taken into God's arms as others pray equally fervently for our success in saving the planet. It's like an eerie calm before the proverbial storm."

Speaking in a near whisper as much to herself as the team she replied. "As strange as it sounds, I can feel it at thirty-eight-thousand feet. With almost no lights burning last night, we navigated over deep darkness. It felt like a gnawing emptiness that yearned to be filled. I understand why people are gathering around candles or the rare portable generator to find comfort with one another. They are trying to push back against an unending night."

Tru's chin snapped up. "That brings me to a new topic, ma'am. We need to discuss where you'll be spending the upcoming evening. You're on Air Force One to minimize an attack on you, but starting at noon tomorrow, the main danger will be whatever chunks of that asteroid rain down on Earth. We made an error in your protection a few days ago, and I don't want a repeat."

Her pen tapped again. "Yes, no more mistakes." She held her tongue, resisting the urge to rage again at the personal cost of the last mistake. "Where would you recommend?"

Noticeably relieved, Tru explained. "I've talked with Declan and we're in agreement that the Raven Rock Complex is the best choice. All of these sites are better protected than Camp David, and with centralized military command there, it makes the most sense."

"Then Raven Rock it is. Any other highlights from Homeland before we move on?"

"That's the top of the pyramid, ma'am. We're continuing to work on plans for Monday, as best we can, but everything else falls several steps lower on the ladder."

She kept her comments brief, hoping to get through the update as quickly as possible. "Let's go to Defense next."

Declan seemed smaller today, as if the stress and strain of the past two weeks had worn him down. Regardless of the toll on his body, his voice remained strong. "Madam President, we look forward to your arrival later today. Seeing you here will definitely raise the spirits of everyone in the facility."

"Thanks, Declan. Please report."

"With the main mission of getting our ICBM's into space completed, we've been looking at the feasibility of being able to track and perhaps intercept some of the fragments of the asteroid that may threaten the U.S. We've never tested it, so there's no way to know for sure if we can do it, but we're going to try. It's not a full solution because we might only be able to break a mid-sized chunk into smaller pieces, which could still cause widespread damage, but perhaps avoid one huge blow. At this point we're throwing dice and hoping that we don't roll snake eyes."

The pounding of her head was now accompanied by even more intense light sensitivity, and her eyes felt as if an entire beach worth of sand was grinding with each blink. Her whisper was barely audible. "What's the best outcome?"

"We're going to prioritize some of our largest and most important cities for whatever protection we can offer. New York, Washington D.C., L.A., Chicago and Seattle top the list. If we make it to Monday, we would be in much better shape to start the recovery if these cities were spared the worst."

She limited her response. "Anything else?"

Declan's' eyes hardened. "Yes, ma'am. We've intercepted Chinese communications hinting they are running various scenarios on how to utilize their experimental space-based laser."

She could now muster only a one-word reply despite her growing anger. "Ominous."

His jaw set firm. "We've all experimented with space-based lasers to damage or destroy each other's satellites in the event of war. What we still haven't learned is if they plan to use it as a defensive weapon against incoming debris or as a weapon against our satellites or ground-based targets... like us. From what we can gather, they're having an internal argument over that as we speak."

The thin bandage over her fragile emotional state couldn't contain the rage and in spite of her full-blown migraine, she exploded.

"Damn it. Surely they're not going to be as petty as President Noskov. Don't they understand how short sighted that is? No wonder God, or whoever is in that cloud, isn't going to lift a finger to help us. We can be such a devious species."

"To be clear, ma'am, we just don't know. They could end up acting in good faith, but the fact is some of their upper leadership is pushing to establish a clear advantage in a post asteroid future."

Now her physical and emotional pain merged in fury. "Jesus fucking Christ! Get in touch with them and confront them with our concerns. Either we get a straight answer that assuages our suspicions or we go into emergency mode on how to take out that system. We need to be completely satisfied or we go on offense. Do you understand! We've done too much to save everyone from this object, and perhaps a deity, that I refuse to be taken down by a national foe."

He stood ramrod straight and replied crisply, shocked by her display. "Yes ma'am. I'll get the process started immediately."

His response briefly took the edge off her anger, but the residual emotional and physical pain colored her morose tone. She slumped back in her chair and covered her eyes. "How's the rest of the fucking world, Effie?"

Seeing the reception of Declan's news, Effie decided to pass and get the worst out of the way first. "The biggest story is Israel, so I'm handing off to Dallas."

Dallas looked even worse than yesterday, but he soldiered on. "The cloud has arrived in Israel. It's currently in the black stage settled over the Temple Mount area and the biggest question is whether we'll see the al-Aqsa Mosque, and the Dome of the Rock polished up like happened at the UN, or whether we'll see a new Jewish Temple standing in their place. If that were to happen the fear is that Arabs massed on the border would retaliate against Israel. It could result in the single biggest day of war casualties... ever. Millions could die if things went totally sideways."

Abby now slid her hands along the sides of her head, ending in a clasp in the back. She squeezed, trying to dull the throbbing. "Why can't we just be done fighting each other over a supposed God of love? How many more must die?"

Dallas shrugged. "I have the same questions, ma'am. I'll turn things back to Effie unless you have questions."

Getting no relief, she released her self-applied vice and glanced toward Effie's screen. "Continue."

Effie's voice softened to lessen the stress of the moment. "I've talked with Declan on our readiness and capabilities in the region to come up with options. The good news is that we have a carrier strike force in the Mediterranean at full strength but we agree that the challenge would be that however we responded, we would only be adding to the death toll. If those important Muslim shrines are gone tomorrow and in their place a temple is standing, there will be a bloodbath of biblical proportions."

Abby's inner darkness pressed even harder as she whispered her reply. "What are our options?"

Effie took a deep breath, then began delicately laying out alternative actions. "In talking with Declan, we came up with a couple of scenarios, both of which begin with a stern warning to each side that any attempts at genocide would be dealt with severely. And we quickly agreed that both sides would probably disregard this warning if conflict were to erupt. That would then leave us with two main options, both bad. The first is that we defend our ally, Israel, with all of our resources."

The president added the decidedly bloody conclusion. "And that would result in millions of dead Jews and Muslims."

"Yes, ma'am. That's the most likely outcome."

Abby closed her eyes again and her slender fingers rubbed her forehead hard. "And the other option?"

"We stand by and let them fight it out. Millions would still die, but there would be no blood on our hands."

Abby summoned all of her remaining strength and leaned in. "Effie, Declan, those are shitty options."

Declan re-entered the conversation. "Shitty options are what we've been dealing with for the past two weeks. Why should this be any different.?"

Effie added, "They've been spoiling for this kind of showdown for years. Maybe the best option is to let them and God settle it now, once and for all."

Abby fell back, shoulders sagging, completely spent, finally giving in to despair. "Make the warnings, then sit back and wait. If a new temple is revealed in the morning, stand down and let them fight it out. We'll leave it up to God to decide if He wants to stop a war that He starts."

Chapter Sixty-Seven

Saturday 5:00 P.M. Hawaii / 11:00 P.M. Raven Rock Complex / One Day to Impact

Wade stood barefoot at the end of a floral runner spread over the greenest grass on the island, just yards from the beach. In a surreal moment that he could have never imagined two weeks ago, Dr. Haskell stood beside him as his best man flanked by Jimmy Butler, his childhood friend who caught the last flight before the airlines shut down. All wore Hawaiian palm print shirts, with Wade in white linen trousers and the groomsmen in khakis. At the other end of the cloth aisle Qu stood in her off the shoulder, tea length white wedding gown, waiting for the processional music to begin.

Wade whispered to Haskell. "She's beautiful, isn't she?"

"She is. You're a lucky man."

Wade's grin, the soft breeze and gently rolling waves temporarily erased all concerns about what might happen tomorrow. While the impending events had accelerated the courtship, he looked down the blue-sky covered aisle. He was nervous to be sure, but happy. The music started and he whispered. "Here we go."

Hearing her original composition playing over the sound system, Qu took her first slow and measured step, not wanting to rush as she had seen so many other brides do in their excitement. Walking down the aisle, her balance was easy as both she and the bridal party went barefoot. The joy of the occasion overcame the nervousness of the day, except regarding the CBN crew filming for a network that had ceased to broadcast due to the nationwide power outage. She figured they were either recording it for broadcast at a later date, or were bored and wanted to go to the beach reception afterwards. Either way, she tried to give them at least a couple of direct camera smiles.

When she reached the end of the runner she turned and faced Wade, flanked by three bridesmaids dressed in matching fuchsia floral print sleeveless dresses. It all looked so normal that it was easy to forget the uncertainty of the entire world and just enjoy being enveloped in the happiness of the occasion.

Kenny Mohala, the owner of the *Riptide,* and also an ordained minister greeted the attendees. "We are invited together on this beautiful evening to share one of life's great moments: the joining of these two in marriage. We are invited here to recognize the worth and beauty of love and commitment in a world that could sure use a big dose of both. We come together not to mark the start of a relationship, but to recognize a bond that already exists and a new beginning of walking through life together, regardless of whether that walk is one day or a hundred years."

Standing under a yellow hibiscus covered archway, he finished with the general comments to the guests and now looked at the happy couple. "Wade and Quinn, you demonstrated to us all that no matter how dark the world around us may be, the love between two people can glow bright enough to push back the shadows. You have shown us that when many are paralyzed into inaction by fear, the love between two people can make the world a better place. And that while many turn inward, you have invited friends and relatives to a celebration of love. It is my hope that your decision to share this event with the world will serve as an example to choose planning a future instead of postponing living, to choose optimism over pessimism, to choose love over hate."

Motioning to the bride and groom, Kenny moved to the next phase of the ceremony. "Quinn and Wade, please join hands and pledge your commitment to each other."

Qu giggled and smiled radiantly as she and Wade clasped hands. Kenny continued. "Wade, do you here and now proclaim your love and devotion for Qu? Do you promise to affirm her choices, to trust her advice, to respect her career, and care for her during times of joy and hardship? Do you commit yourself to share your feelings of joy and grief? Do you pledge your faithfulness to her?"

With a slight nervous stutter Wade replied. "Y-yes. Always."

"And Qu, do you here and now proclaim your love and devotion for Wade? Do you promise to affirm his ambition, to trust his counsel, to respect his work, and care for him during times of joy and hardship? Do you commit yourself to share your feelings of happiness and grief? Do you pledge your faithfulness to him?"

Without hesitation, the beaming bride affirmed. "Yes. Always."

The bar owning minister now motioned Qu's young ring bearer forward. "Rings will now be exchanged as a symbol of the unending love that you have expressed for each other. May your lives together be like this unbroken, never ending symbol."

The more composed Qu easily slid Wade's ring on his hand. Wade nearly dropped hers in the grass. After completing his one job, the young ring bearer skipped back down the cloth runner to the delight of the attendees, many snapping pictures of the free-spirited youth on their phones.

With ring ceremony complete, Kenny transitioned to traditional pledges. "Wade, respond to these vows. I Wade take thee Quinn to be my wife. To have and to hold. In sickness and in health. For richer or for poorer. In joy and in sorrow. I promise my love and companionship to you forever."

Wade looked deeply into his bride's eyes. "I do. Forever."

Now the words were repeated for Qu. "Quinn, respond to these vows. I Quinn take thee Wade to be my husband. To have and to hold. In sickness and in health. For richer or for poorer. In joy and in sorrow. I promise my love and companionship to you forever."

Returning his loving gaze, she responded in kind. "I do. Forever."

Spreading his arms wide Kenny continued. "We are joining two families from different sides of the ocean. From these two families a new one is being created. Please lift your separate pitchers of ocean water representing your separate lives."

They each reached to the stand set to their side and hoisted a clear container of fresh Pacific Ocean water. Kenny waited as Dr. Haskell moved a small stand with a larger clear vase to the center of the ceremony. "Take your two pitchers symbolizing your past and pour them together representing your future together."

Kenny looked on as they blended their streams together in the unity vase. "Just as these streams of water can never be separated, so will your family now be forever as one."

The best man again stepped forward and moved the stand and unity vase to the side. Kenny proceeded, bringing the couple's hands together. "With the power vested in me by the state of Hawaii, I am honored to declare you as husband and wife."

He shot a smile at Wade. "You may kiss the bride."

A long kiss sealed the commitment and the smiling newlyweds turned toward their friends and family. Kenny pronounced, "Please welcome Wade and Quinn as Hawaii's newest husband and wife. May they have a long and happy life together."

Chapter Sixty-Eight

Sunday 6:01 A.M. Raven Rock Complex / 12:01 Hawaii / 1:01 P.M. Israel / Impact Day

Regular updates flowed into the Raven Rock Complex from observatories around the globe, detailing the progress as each nuclear device exploded in the desperate attempt to alter the course of the Jansky-Haskell asteroid. Dr. Haskell now logged into the call with the president and her cabinet. The surprise was that Wade and Qu sat beside him for the update. This briefly brightened Abby's dark mood. "I saw some beautiful photos from the ceremony. I wish that I could have been there to give my best wishes in person. Shouldn't you two be on your honeymoon?"

Wade blushed at the attention and answered as Quinn sat beside him, wide eyed and fixed as a post being on a video call with the president of the United States. "Yes ma'am, under normal circumstances. But this isn't exactly a normal day. I figured that since I was the first to spot this object, I wanted to see this through. Besides, we want to go to Italy for our honeymoon and all flights everywhere have been canceled. We're hoping to go later."

Abby smiled for the briefest moment. "Nothing would make any of us happier. With that goal in mind, how are things looking for the world this morning?"

Haskell took over from Wade at the Keck Observatory. "As we've been communicating in the past twenty-four hours the plan to divert the object has made a measurable difference. To clarify, the asteroid has split as a result of exposure to hundreds of nuclear explosions planted to change its course. One large piece has drifted far enough that we can say with certainty that it will miss Earth."

"That's good news for sure, right?"

The astronomer arched his eyebrows while twisting his neck. "Well, yes. It's better that it's going to miss us than hit us, but we're still far from clear. The remaining chunks in the zone of uncertainty could still wreak havoc here on the ground. We could be looking at millions dead in the next twenty-four hours... perhaps even worse. No matter what, it's not going to be pretty."

The first taps of the day of the pen on pad began. "Lay it out, what should we expect?"

Haskell looked straight into the remote camera. "Ma'am, there are still a few variables, but here are our best estimates. First of all, exactly at the time promised by the purported God being, the first showers of debris will start on the east coast of the United States at noon local time. As the earth spins, new parts of the globe will become exposed to the chunks of asteroid that were not pushed far enough away to escape the path of our planet. As I mentioned on an earlier call, as the pieces of the asteroid fall to Earth some places will be completely spared, others will see impacts in thinly populated areas. Direct hits on some major metro areas will almost surely happen. Chunks of this asteroid will be coming at us fast, and the results will be catastrophic. At this point it's all just random luck where they will strike."

Abby listened intently to the projected impact arrival with a stone-cold expression. "Sounds like we're in for a rough few hours, but thanks again for spotting this thing. Even with the short warning, you've given us our most precious weapon to save ourselves: time."

Haskell returned a half smile. "We only wish that we had spotted it sooner, ma'am."

Abby turned to Declan, standing beside her at the Raven Rock complex. "Update the others on the latest on plans to protect some of our major cities."

Declan looked into the camera. "As reported yesterday, we've mounted an all-out effort to fine tune our anti-missile defenses to shoot down the biggest hunks of the asteroid headed for five of our major cities. While we would like to be able to protect all our cities, we simply do not have the resources. In fact, we're not even sure that this will work for the places that have been prioritized, but we'll do our best to limit the destruction in D.C., New York, Chicago, Los Angeles and Seattle. We feel that our nation can bounce back fastest, starting Monday morning, if these vital locations are spared. Starting then, we'll be in full support mode working with Homeland."

With that as a segue, Abby looked at the camera at Tru, who actually seemed a bit more at ease than in the past few days. "Tru, you're up. Tell us about final planning from Homeland."

"Ma'am, I want to start by saying that I am personally glad that we're finally able to begin planning for what comes next. The promise that there will be a tomorrow has been like a weight lifted off of my shoulders."

Abby's brain knew that this was true, and she forced a positive response through the pall of her depression. "Good reminder, Tru. As grim as things might be, it still beats oblivion."

"Yes, ma'am, and Homeland is ready for today... and tomorrow. In the past twenty-four hours we've moved as many personnel and as much material as possible into protected structures. Sometimes it's cramming as much as we can into all kinds of underground formal facilities, like we're in. Sometimes it's making use of natural formations, like Mammoth Cave in Kentucky, Carlsbad Caverns in California and anyplace else that local commanders could find. We've also finalized rapid restart plans for key power plants near our largest cities. It's going to take some time and people need to return to work, but we at least have an outline in place for Monday morning."

"Good to hear. And you're right, it is refreshing to begin to talk about recovery instead of just survival."

Her forced lightened mood didn't last long. "Now, speaking of survival, is that bastard Carson Appleton still breathing?"

Tru looked down for a moment before returning her hard gaze. "Ma'am, I'd like nothing more than to be able to tell you that he had been captured or killed. Unfortunately, our efforts to find him have been greatly hampered by final staging for the asteroid arrival and the sheer low number of law enforcement officers still working. So many of our police and national guardsmen have simply gone home to be with their families. His apprehension will be one of our top priorities starting tomorrow, I promise."

She replied coldly as the threat of the migraine headache return gave way to the first throbs. "Head on a pole, or bound in chains. Either is acceptable, understand?"

"Yes ma'am. I understand."

Dismissing Tru and glancing to the next screen she now directed comments to Effie. "How did the world fare overnight. Is Jerusalem still standing?"

Effie leaned forward on her cane. "Yes ma'am, the city still stands. When dawn broke the al-Aqsa Mosque, the Dome of the Rock and the Dome of the Chain all remained, looking better than the day they were built. Muslims have flooded the city to behold the sight, and so far, Israeli soldiers have been in peace keeping mode rather than trying to stem the human tidal wave pouring into the old city. A blood bath has been avoided... at least for now."

Abby nodded slowly, not wanting to exacerbate the building pressure in her skull. "Seems cooler heads prevailed, that could be a good sign for the future."

"We'll see, ma'am. There have been a lot of false starts on the road to peace in the Middle East, but on Monday, this could give a new boost to the prospect."

"And China, what's the news there?"

Effie leaned in again. "We think they've decided to play defense with their laser system, like we are with our rigged up anti-missile defenses. Again, looks like cooler heads are making the decisions in favor of national defense instead of a riskier attack on us."

Her brooding mood and physical pain colored her response, matching her black eyeliner, mascara and eye shadow. "There should be no question that we'll fight World War Three if required, but I'm hopeful that it won't have to begin tomorrow. Anything else?"

Effie smiled. "Ma'am, to be blunt, the whole world is in the shitter. I could spend the next hour listing the problems, but almost all of them will be better if the sun comes up tomorrow and most of the planet is saved. I'll wait until then to see what really needs addressing."

The president sat erect, her make-up accentuated eyes capturing the florescent lighting of her underground bunker and looking more icy steel blue rather than the usual violet, her voice now barely audible. "It's been a challenging couple of weeks, for the world, for the nation, for this team... and for me personally. Looking back there are plenty of things that I wish I could have changed or done better, but as Effie once reminded us all, there are no do-overs in this world."

She paused, to catch her breath, stolen by the full onset of a cluster migraine headache. She winced, then fought the pain. "But through it all, I have never wavered in the belief that this is the best team ever assembled. To have gotten us to the point that we have a chance for the very survival of mankind has been a Herculean task. No matter what happens in the next few hours the world owes each of you a debt of gratitude that can never be repaid. Now we wait and see how the randomness of the universe plays out."

Chapter Sixty-Nine

Noon Raven Rock Complex / Impact Day

A thrown together collection of observers stationed around the nation and the globe were set to send reports into the Raven Rock Complex as the Jansky-Haskell asteroid arrival event unfolded. The ad-hoc team consisted mainly of active duty military, local reporters, merchant marine captains, assorted scientists, and even a few priests and ministers scattered around the world. The tension of waiting for the arrival had ratcheted up the already high stress. Some prayed for total destruction in order to be with their God while others with equal fervor hoped for a Monday sunrise. And with power out in most of the world, people were both figuratively and literally in the dark about which outcome was more likely.

The president and cabinet members all gathered around their screens in their secure locations. Declan glanced at the president and looked shocked. "Permission to speak frankly, ma'am."

Abby had entered the small room where Declan would receive some of the reports and pulled her seat back, toward a darkened corner. She rubbed her forehead, then put on the dark sunglasses she carried in her hand. "What's on your mind, Declan."

The old-fashioned gentleman soldier chose his words carefully. "Are you feeling okay, ma'am? You don't look so good."

She stared back blankly, glad to have the glasses for cover. After a sleepless night spent playing out how this day might go, her will to put a sunny spin on her reply was overpowered by exhaustion, depression and a pounding headache worse than any she had ever had. Sarcasm flowed freely. "I'm fine. In fact, I can't wait to hear first-hand how many Americans die today."

He offered an alternative. "You could rest in your quarters, if you like. Would that be better?"

She whispered. "We're making history today, Declan. As Commander in Chief there is nowhere else I can be, except right here at command central. You do your job and I'll do mine and let's hope that we don't screw things up even more in the next few hours. Am I clear?"

Doing what any good soldier would do, he gave a smart, "Yes ma'am," and turned back toward the screen where incoming reports would be filtered to him and others. Just then the first report was delivered from the Boston area. A satellite feed from the Coast Guard Cutter Alpha, floating about a mile off shore was routed to his screen. "Commander Shawna Jones reporting."

Declan responded crisply in a no-nonsense way as the president sat behind him in the shadows. "Commander, report."

"Yes sir, we're seeing mostly small objects appearing to burn up in the atmosphere, but a confirmed large piece of the asteroid has hit Brockton, just south of Boston. Reports are coming in of a massive number of casualties as hundreds... maybe thousands of structures were obliterated or set on fire. There are no fire suppression efforts underway at this time."

Declan glanced back at Abby, then replied as another report had been added to his cue. "Thank you, commander. Stay posted and report additional major updates."

A graphic on a separate screen estimated 25,000 casualties and before the commander could reply, another face filled the screen. "Good afternoon, this is Raleigh Edwards of WCBU-TV in Charleston South Carolina."

"Go ahead, Mr. Edwards. Please report."

"Pieces of debris are falling at a steady clip although we only have one report of a significantly large impact. A tobacco farm just north of the city was at the center of the strike that resulted in a crater over a half-mile wide. Estimates are that eighteen people have been killed with scores injured."

The estimated deaths were added to the running total as now reports began coming in too fast for one person to handle. Other officers began taking most of the calls as only the ones with the highest casualty counts were filtered to Declan and the president. By the time the next call came to them the casualty counter had reached thirty-five thousand.

"Lieutenant Miles Simpson reporting, sir."

"Report, lieutenant."

"Sir, a tsunami has inundated Wilmington North Carolina. It's estimated that a thirty-foot surge hit the city just after twelve hundred hours. Initial estimates are ten thousand dead."

The reports continued to come, one after the other, as the casualty counter reached one-hundred thousand before one o'clock. Abby began to feel numb, as if a sadistic dentist had overdosed her whole body with a massive injection of Novocain. One after another the calls continued, slowly marching their way west across the nation. She now only heard bits and pieces of the reports, as her consciousness seemed to leave her body. She desperately focused her remaining energy on the inexorable rise of the casualty counter, trying to stay connected to reality in this increasingly unreal ordeal.

Cities large and small were mentioned as Declan deftly fielded more reports. Bloomington... Jackson... Madison.... Dallas... Topeka. All echoed in her ears in psychedelic ways as one-hundred thousand became five-hundred thousand. It couldn't be real, yet nothing had ever seemed more concrete. Santa Fe... Boulder... Billings... Boise... Reno. One million became five million which then became twenty-five million.

Every time Declan asked how she was doing, she mechanically answered. "Fine. Keep going."

Confronted with overwhelming responsibility, that's exactly what the old soldier did, leaving her floating in her own dark world. Now Jill came and sat beside her and Abby spoke, but only in her mind. *"What are you doing here? You're supposed to be dead."*

The apparition answered in her usual sweet voice. *"Oh, I am dear. It just looked like you needed someone to talk to."*

Declan fielded a report from Phoenix. Abby heard the words 'direct hit' as the numbers continued to mount. Abby slipped back into... *"Jill, I miss you so much! I'm so sorry... it's all my fault."*

"Shhh. Shhh. Now, now, don't beat yourself up, sweetie. There is no way you could have known that would happen. I mean, no one had ever used a nuclear missile as a terrorist weapon. It's not your fault."

Thirty million appeared on the casualty board as she heard Reno... Provo... Salem... Sacramento... Oakland. *"How can you say that? Everything I did led to that moment. And now... and now more are dying... by the millions! We could have been together... to the end...if I hadn't pushed so hard! I caused this!"*

Declan cursed. "Son of a bitch! Another tsunami, this time it's Los Angeles! Did you hear that ma'am?"

Abby mumbled as clearly as she could. "Trragicc." Then she slipped away again. *See what I mean? Millions more have died while we've been talking. Your death, these deaths, they're all on me!"*

Jill slapped her, hard. *"Abby, did you make that asteroid? Did you send it on its path? Of course you didn't. If this is anyone's fault it's God's, or it's random chance. Either way, everything that you have done has been to save lives, not take them."*

Abby rubbed her cheek. *"Okay, you have my attention, and I get it, but still... look at that number. It might hit fifty million by the time this is over, and that's just in the U.S. Who knows world-wide? Has it been worth it?"*

"Abigail Banister, you know the answer. The numbers are big, but it looks like most of the world is going to survive because of you. And if you need more reassurance, ask that cute couple that just got married in Hawaii. I'm sure that they are thrilled to have a chance to live...and love, like we did. You know that's the truth."

In her haze she could picture Wade and Qu, standing on the beach, hand in hand, starting their new lives together. She smiled, then felt herself being drawn back into her body. She reached for Jill. *"Don't leave me! I love you! I need you!"*

Jill began to fade. *"Don't worry about me, I'll be waiting."*

Declan spoke and Abby rallied. "Looks like the worst has passed, ma'am. It's been a rough day, but we made it. We're going to be okay."

Abby pushed herself to her feet and stood, a bit wobbly at first, but steady in a few more seconds. She removed her sunglasses and her eyes now glistened, the hardness melted. "We did it, didn't we? All the sacrifice, all the loss, all the everything. It was all worth it... wasn't it?"

Chapter Seventy

Monday Noon Raven Rock Complex / One Day After Impact

Monday morning arrived and the sun rose over a human populated Earth. Two weeks ago, Kalie Robinson gave this outcome of partial success in deflecting the Jansky-Haskell asteroid less than a ten percent chance. After a full twenty-four hours of bombardment it was clear that, although the human race would survive, the death toll from the event was staggering.

After the dream visit from Jill, Abby slept a few hours and her headache from Hell abated. A rested President Banister called the virtual meeting to order. "Before we dive into dissecting what's happened in the past twenty-four hours and what we need to do get our nation back on its feet, I have a few thoughts that I would like to share. Two weeks ago, our world view was shaken by a world-wide transmission claiming that God was coming to Earth and we scrambled to determine whether it was a hoax or somehow real. Standing here today there is still debate on whether that being is God, or something else. But what is no longer in doubt is that mankind remains. We have proven that we can overcome external threats of gigantic proportions and work together as a species well enough to emerge triumphant."

She paused as she looked into each screen, into the eyes of her dedicated team of advisers, and saw joy and exhaustion combined in a look that victorious soldiers throughout history would recognize. "What we accomplished has not been without trials, tribulations and loss. We've had entire cities wiped from the face of the earth, millions killed on a single day. To be sure, the price paid in human lives lost and impacted is staggering, on a scale never seen before. Yet, we still stand. Yes, we're battered and bruised, but we're still here. It is with absolute certainty that I say that this outcome would not have been possible without the efforts, leadership and guidance from everyone on this team as well as from those we have lost on this journey. I am grateful to have has the opportunity to be part of this team. The world owes you a debt that can never be paid."

Spontaneous applause arose from each remote site as Abby clasped her hands together in a show of thankfulness. When the lengthy applause subsided, she got down to the business at hand. "Now, let's talk about where we stand and what we need to do to get us all back together in our nation's capital. Tru, what's the word from Homeland Security?"

Tru sprang to is feet with new energy. "Ma'am, it would take a full day to debrief on how our nation has been impacted, so for the sake of time, I'll only share the highest-level information. The headline is the death toll. Looks like we're going to be in the fifty to fifty-five million range which is roughly fifteen percent of the U.S. population."

He let that sink in for a moment, then continued. "While the debris hit all parts of the nation, there were a few really big impacts that significantly raised the numbers. Phoenix took a direct hit, and a tsunami slammed Los Angeles, resulting in millions of deaths from just those two events. There is also the issue of how this is going to impact our climate, but we won't even have models for that for a while. All in all, it was rough across our nation, but things are looking up already."

He flashed a slide up on the screens showing a crew working to string power lines outside of New York City. "We still have to worry about a threat from those hackers, but it seems now that the uncertainty is behind us people are taking first steps out of their cocoons, they are beginning to go back to work. The world didn't end and Americans are starting the process of picking up the pieces of lives that most had put on hold. I'm hopeful we'll be able to return to D.C. in less than a month. It won't be easy, but we have a path back to normalcy... or at least a new normalcy."

Abby's improved outlook was not yet fully assuaged. "Good news about getting back to the White House, but is there any word on Carson Appleton?"

Tru's eyes cast down. "No, ma'am. He's still in the wind, but rest assured, he's the most wanted man in the country. We'll get him."

Her left eye twitched. "Jill's death is on him... and I haven't forgotten your role in the lax security either. And I am still considering your offer of resignation. He's a dangerous man who needs to be brought to justice immediately. Are we clear?"

He lowered his gaze and spoke softly. "Yes ma'am."

With his reply she turned to Declan, standing beside her. "You've kept me up to speed throughout. How about a defense summary for the team?"

He cleared his throat and looked into the camera. "A lot of this information will compliment what Tru has just laid out. I'll add that our missile protection system for the five cities that we selected for protection worked well overall. We were able to intercept large chunks headed for both New York City and Seattle as well as a few smaller but still deadly slivers on paths to Chicago and D.C. There was damage, but it could have been much worse." He stopped for a moment before continuing. "Obviously, Los Angeles has been severely damaged, but that was not a failure of our system. A large piece of debris landed miles offshore causing the catastrophic wave that rolled through the city. It's a tragic loss of life and a hit to the vitality of our nation."

Abby glance up at him. "And the nation's defense capabilities? How vulnerable are we?"

Declan stood a bit taller. "I'm please to say that from an international standpoint we're in pretty good shape. While we did send a lot of our ICBM's into space to help shield the earth, we still have more on hand than any other nation. In addition, we got most of our ships out of harbor to diminish the risk of destruction from tsunamis, and that proved a wise move. We'll be back to virtually full strength as soon as some of our sailors who went AWOL return. The army did take a hit with several bases being either destroyed or degraded, but we can still field an effective fighting force on relatively short notice."

Pleased at his answer, Abby nodded approval without bringing up his offer of resignation. "Let's hope the world has learned a lesson from all of this and we don't need that capability."

"Yes ma'am, I share the same hope... but we'll be prepared to fight if they haven't."

The president now turned toward Effie. "That's the big picture in the U.S., How did the rest of the world fair?"

Effie's calm visage had remained throughout this ordeal. "Looks like no part of the planet was spared. The largest cities affected were Rio De Janeiro, Brazil, Melbourne, Australia, Tehran, Iran, Cape Town, South Africa, St. Petersburg, Russia, Warsaw, Poland and Shanghai, China."

Abby piped in. "I thought China had that fancy space laser to protect their biggest cities?"

She smiled wryly. "But they didn't have a system to protect the laser, did they? Seems it was knocked out by a fragment itself. A little bit of karma, maybe?"

The president laughed. "I know it's wrong, but I kind of feel that was some cosmic justice."

"Yes ma'am."

"And the overall mood of the planet?"

Effie glance toward Dallas before answering. "I'll let him cover the God angles but I can speak to the general state of affairs. It's much like here, which means a high number of casualties. We're working from an estimate of one point two billion killed." She took a breath before continuing. "That's a really big number and it will take time, but the planet will recover. Damage assessments are ongoing, and as Tru mentioned, we'll have to figure out the impact on climate change, but the world can now start turning back to normal routines."

Abby shook her head in disbelief. "One point two billion... It will be a long time before things feel normal, but I can relate to the pain and misery that so many people must be feeling today. Millions and millions of anguished survivors mourning their loss..."

She sat in silence for a moment reflecting on her own grief before turning back to the urgent business of restarting the nation and the world. "Speaking of normal, what's the latest on God and his cloud? Are they still hanging out in Israel, I think there has been some kind of statement on that?"

Dallas leaned forward. "Yes, the cloud is still in Israel... for now. A new Gabriel video has been sent to governments and the few remaining news networks still attempting to broadcast. He says that God will be making a statement later today on what's next. And, before you ask, I have no idea what he's going to say."

The president sighed. "Will it matter anyway? We know that the task of immediate disaster relief and rebuilding our nation has to be our first priority."

She sighed again. "I've got another question, and I know that any answer you give will be an educated guess at best, but humor me. How do you think religious communities are going to respond to what just happened? I mean, someone claiming to be God declared an end to mankind, but that didn't happen. Instead we're still standing, albeit on a severely damaged planet. How's that going to play?"

Dallas look down, seeming to bend to the weight of all that had transpired. Then he raised his head and spoke in a weary voice. "Ma'am, pardon my language, but who the hell knows? I can tell you it's going to be all over the board. Some will be angry...at us, at God, at both. Some will be happy... with us, with God, with both. Some will see that this is validation that God is alive, while others will see this as validation that this wasn't God at all. The only thing that I can tell you for sure is that religious leaders are going to take whatever meaning fits their agenda."

Abby spoke soberly. "You're right, I know it in my bones. Even after a supposed physical visit by God and miraculous stops around the globe, our religious institutions still can't agree."

Chapter Seventy-One

Monday 8:00 P.M. Jerusalem / 1:00 P.M. Raven Rock Complex / One Day After Impact

As the choir finished singing a song of praise, Gabriel strode to the center of the al-Aqsa Mosque. In the background a curtain was hung and a blueish-white glow filtered around and through the fabric. There were no privileged visitors inside as at the UN two weeks ago, only those watching on giant screens outside, and the lucky few around the world with functioning television or internet connections. Gabriel's crystal blue eyes twinkled as brightly as they had when he introduced himself on that first day. As in every appearance, his suit was impeccably fitted and regal. He smiled and seemed to radiate light as he delivered a short introduction. "Children of Earth. It has been an honor to spend time with you during this monumental moment of your history. Once again, it is my pleasure to present your Holy Father who wishes to speak directly to His creation once again."

He bowed, then stepped aside as the shining orb once again began to glow behind the curtain, just as it had when this Being addressed the world from the United Nations stage. When the light reached its brightest intensity, the same voice spoke. "Children of Earth, I am happy to greet you today. I came to you to offer assurance that no matter what happened, I would be here to receive you in my arms. And, while many have joined me in eternal bliss, many, many more remain on this beautiful world. I am pleased."

There was a pause as the glow seemed to pulse gently. "During the past two weeks your world has teetered on the edge between working together to save the planet and experiencing the end of this experiment, thus returning to my embrace. Throughout this time, I have been with you, always. I have traveled around the planet allowing My children to see firsthand that I am alive and caring of My creation. I have not forsaken you, nor will I ever."

The glow subtly changed to a brighter shade. "And now My creation will enter a new phase. You have shown both Me and yourself that as imperfect as you are, you can band together and do great things. As your Father, that makes me very proud."

The light glowed so bright that it shown through the stones. Instead of melting them, it illuminated the entire structure from the inside out. "Now, I will remove My physical presence from this corner of My creation once again, leaving you the task of choosing how you will live. You are My children and as any Father, I desire only the best. Please, My children, understand that love conquers all... and that I love each of you... in this moment... and for eternity."

The glow began to fade and Gabriel stepped forward once again. "His Holiness has expressed His love to all here and those viewing around the world. After one more hymn we shall leave your planet."

After the choir finished their final song, the golden net and all inside began to swirl and slowly rise. Those on the ground watched the gilded cloud lift. It rose majestically in a glowing golden spiral, rising higher and higher until the last glimpses crossed beyond the outer atmosphere. In a twinkle, everything was gone. Those who witnessed the departure in Jerusalem embraced each other, then milled about, unsure what to do next.

Chapter Seventy-Two

9:00 A.M. Washington D.C. / One Month After Impact

In the month after the events of Judgment Day Larry Knewell slowly transitioned back to his evening, opinion-oriented show focused on the politics of the day. Yesterday he grilled Homeland Security Secretary Trusond Patel on the size of his budget request to protect American computer networks from hackers. It was all very inside Washington politics, as usual. Today, however, he was back on morning TV interviewing two young people who had emerged from the Judgment Day event as the face of hope for a new start and a better future. Wade and Qu were scheduled to be in Washington later today as guests of President Banister for the New Earth Day ceremony which was also being celebrated in capitals around the world. Jared counted down. "In five-four-three-two-one."

Larry was relaxed and confident, reassured of his place in the business by scoring this exclusive interview with the new youth "it" couple. "Welcome to New York, I guess it's a huge understatement to say that a lot has changed for you two in the last month or so. What's it like to become overnight celebrities?"

Wade still blushed at the statement. He reached for Qu's hand as he answered. "It's taking some getting used to, but as long as we've got each other life's great."

Qu looked at Wade and smiled as she added her perspective. "It's exciting. We never expected our lives to take this kind of turn, so we're doing our best to live in the moment. Just take it all in and enjoy this wonderful world."

Their visibly strong connection seemed to truly warm Larry. "What's next for you two, now that the world is beginning to get back to normal?"

Qu almost glowed as she replied. "We're going on our honeymoon. We had mentioned in a local Honolulu interview that we wanted to go to Italy and it was picked up by the Vatican news service. We've been invited as special guests of the newly chosen Pope Urban the Tenth. Everything still seems unreal."

"And today, I understand that you're among the special guests of the president at the New Earth Day celebration in Washington. That must be exciting."

Wade's cheeks were still rosy, but not the cherry red from a moment ago. "She has been such an inspiration. Even after all that she's been through, she's checked in on us several times. She's such a genuine person and a truly great leader."

Larry shifted slightly in his seat. "There are a variety of opinions about her, but no one can argue with the fact that it's likely that none of us would be alive without her leadership... or without you spotting that asteroid in time."

His cheeks went full blown cherry red again. "That's been talked about enough. We're focused on our future now."

With that, Larry transitioned. "What are your plans, after the honeymoon?"

Wade glanced at Qu and she happily piped in. "I never dreamed that my career would take off like this. Wade's comments the day of the announcement of the asteroid discovery set off this crazy new path. I mean, who knew that even the CBN video of our wedding would become a global viral sensation?"

Larry interrupted. "That blending of the streams was about the most romantic thing I've ever seen."

Now it was Qu's turn to make Wade blush. "Yeah, that was Wade's idea. He's really that sweet."

Ken ordered camera two to cut to the now hopelessly blushing young man. Larry smiled and steered the conversation back to Qu, allowing Wade time to recover. "You were saying something about after the honeymoon?"

Qu squeezed Wade's hand and giggled just a bit as she continued. "I've signed a recording deal and will be going on a world tour starting next month. We'll record a live album along the way before going into studio with new material. I still can't believe it."

Larry smiled like a proud uncle. "Wade, what are your plans?"

Wade looked lovingly toward Qu. "I'm taking a year off to be by her side, celebrate her success. We didn't exactly have a traditional courtship, so we want to make up for some lost time together."

"And after that?"

The smitten young man now looked back at the host. "This whole thing kind of put my name in lights too. I've been offered a spot in Harvard's PhD program next fall. That should fit in perfectly with Qu's studio schedule. We want to make this two-career life work as best as possible."

Larry now looked square into camera one. "These two lovebirds have a flight to catch to get to the Washington New Earth Day celebration on time, so we need to wrap up our interview and send them on their way. It looks like they have a bright future together and I have a feeling we'll be seeing them here again soon on CBN."

Chapter Seventy-Three

Noon Washington D.C. / One Month After Impact

In the past month President Banister and Dallas Shendegar had become the most unlikely of pals. But with their shared ancient history, recent intense service and with both tending broken hearts from losing their families in the same violent attack, it made sense to them. And while the Herculean efforts to restart an entire nation consumed a lot of their time, there was still the emptiness of the evenings without their wives. On many nights Abby had invited him to share dinner and watch religious and secular leaders argue on CBN about what the past six weeks had meant, and what it could mean for the future.

Last night Abby had laughed while Pastor Shadwell continued to rail against some branches of Christianity that made gestures of reconciliation with Jewish groups. For him, the matter was black or white; it was either his Bible's way or it was apostasy. Meanwhile, Rabbi Feldman, Guru Mashni, and Dr. Kim announced that they were going on a cross-country speaking tour together reflecting on the words spoken by God, Vishnu, or the being posing as god, depending on which of them was speaking at any given moment. It all made for great television and in some ways had influenced what Abby would say to the nation and the world in her New Earth Day speech.

When China and the United States had agreed to name this day as the day that they would address their nations, most other countries jumped on the bandwagon as well. At noon local time around the globe leader after leader put their spin on what had happened and what they hoped that it would mean for the future. With the day beginning on that side of the globe, China was among the first to share their vision and Abby had listened to a recording of the message during breakfast. President Zhou's speech had focused on what a good decision it had been for China to restrict religion in their country as they were much farther ahead than most in the rebuilding process. While she wasn't sure how she felt about that, she liked that they he had kind words to say about the cooperation between his country and the USA. That was a good place to start in this phase of their ever-changing relationship.

On the other hand, Alexy III, Patriarch of the Russian Orthodox Church and now the figurehead president of Russia, used his speech to praise the God who he claimed had inspired the revolution in his country. Russia had declared itself an Orthodox Christian theocracy where religious power and state power would be one and the same. And in a sign of hope, Arab and Israeli leaders had offered kind words to each other in their speeches with similar sentiments, that if God had shown love for both Jew and Muslim, then there was hope that they could coexist.

Over a million people were filing into the National Mall to witness the event as Abby put the final touches on her address. Most, but not all agreed with the sentiment that she was in the company of Abraham Lincoln as one of the greatest presidents to have held the office. Soon she would stand on the steps of the Capitol Building where she had delivered her inauguration speech just two years prior. As historic as that had been, this one felt even more monumental.

At the same time, Carson Appleton was making his own preparations. For the past month he had been spirited from one safe house to another by his swiftly dwindling group of supporters, evading the tightening manhunt for the most wanted man in America. Now he squeezed through the ventilation system of a nondescript office building about a mile and a half away from the event. When he made it to the roof, he surveyed the scene and mumbled to himself. "It's not as far as the shot by that guy that took out the pope, but far enough."

He had the aptitude, but had washed out of Army Sniper School, deemed mentally unstable. "She idolizes Lincoln, so like him she must die in office. Lincoln denied the white man's natural superiority and this dyke denied God's will for this world. My God says the same sentence for both." He wanted to time his shot at an appropriate moment in her speech, so he settled in and put his ear buds in to listen.

After the perfunctory warm up speakers finished, the crowd was ready to hear from the president. She strode toward the lectern wearing a white skirted suit, and the people roared in support. She let the wave of approval wash over her, reveling in the acceptance and support of the decisions and sacrifices that she had made. It felt like a salve on healing wounds, for her and the nation. She waved triumphantly as her cabinet, plus Wade, Qu, Dr. Haskell, and Dallas, stood and joined in the applause at her request. "Thank you! Thank you, everyone!"

The adulation went on for a long time, and Abby did nothing to subdue the energy, knowing each person in the audience had their own story of loss or pain and needed this outlet. "Thank you all for being here today as we celebrate this first New Earth Day."

Once again, the assembled mass exploded in applause. She smiled as she turned to her team and now bade them stand again, to share in the adulation. Most enjoyed the public display of support, but Tru felt ill at ease. He had made it clear to the president that until he apprehended Carson Appleton he had not atoned for his role in the death of Jill, and he had also made clear that he disapproved of this venue for her speech.

As the crowd settled again, she laid out her thesis. "As an American I don't care whether you think God visited us, or an alien being visited us. Either way we learned valuable lessons from the experience. We learned that we are not alone in the universe. We learned that love for each other and for our fellow man seems to be a galactic principle. Most importantly, we learned that as a species we are at our best when we work together, that we can do incredible things. We learned that even problems that seem insurmountable can be overcome when we work as one global team."

The crowd cheered again and Carson cursed. "Mother-fucking slut. You think that everything is hunky dory? God offered us relief from this miserable world and you decided for all of us to turn Him down. God damn it, you are one arrogant bitch."

He rubbed his trigger finger with his thumb as Abby continued. "Many said that it couldn't be done, but our nation worked with others in ways that had never happened in the history of the world.

Technology and ideas were freely shared across national borders as we built an executed a plan to save the world. Sure, there were bumps along the way and many of us experienced heartache and loss."

She paused, smiling, thinking of Jill, then continued. "But, like you, I persevered... with hopes of a better future."

As the crowd roared again, Carson chambered his specially made explosive tipped round that should penetrate the bullet-proof glass surrounding the president. "All right, bitch, that's enough. No more talk about kumbaya or your homo wife. Time for you to die for your sins." He shifted the rifle slightly and put his finger on the trigger.

On the viewing stand Tru moved, unsure why. Without thinking, he stepped toward the president, startling her, causing her to trip and fall. In the next instant, the bullet exploded the glass, passed between Effie and Dallas, then splintered the platform rail before sending bits of granite from the underlying steps flying everywhere.

Secret Service Agents sprang into action, spiriting Abby into a limo, then heading to the nearest hospital, unsure if she had been hit. Screams filled the National Mall as realization of what had happened ignited a flight to safety, lest they become targets as well. Terror gripped everyone as they ran for their lives.

Chapter Seventy-Four

7:00 A.M. Washington D.C. / The Next Day

Abby walked slowly from the family quarters to the briefing in the Situation Room, nursing sore ribs. She had put makeup over the bruise on her forehead sustained in her fall, but it remained visible, like a shadowy ledge under the surface of a lake. She entered to a round of applause from everyone. Blushing, she gingerly made her way to the head of the table shaking hands along the way. "Thank you, everyone. Thank you. Now please, be seated."

As everyone complied, she lay her pen down, determined that there would be no tapping today. Despite her bumps and bruises, this day felt new and fresh, like sunrise after a night of tornadoes. There was much damaged to be repaired, but the threat had passed. She smiled at Tru. "Let's hear it for our very own Trusond Patel, the hero of the hour. Without his action I wouldn't be here today and I can't begin to thank him enough for what he did."

The applause continued until the blushing Secretary of Homeland Security stood, acknowledging the recognition. Despite the stitches on his cheek and his arm in a sling, he too had emerged from the assassination attempt with only minor injuries. "Thanks everyone. I'm just relieved that our president is safe."

He sat, cheeks still crimson red from the praise.

Abby maintained her appreciative gaze toward him. "Tell us, Tru, how did you spot Carson Appleton so far away? I mean, it was over a mile."

Tru looked a bit bewildered. "Ma'am, to be honest, I'm still not sure. We had intercepted chatter of his intention to do something, but had no actionable intel. I just know that I felt hyper aware, my senses in overdrive. I guess I saw what must have been a flash of sunlight reflected from his rifle scope, and I acted, almost on autopilot. I can't explain it, it just happened. Maybe it was a God thing, I don't know. I'm just so relieved. I couldn't stand to be responsible for anything happening to you, especially after..." He choked up, tears spilling, unable to finish the sentence.

Even the thought of what happened to Jill couldn't ruin Abby's good mood today. "Let me be clear, Tru. You've more than redeemed yourself. I owe my life to you."

He blushed again, more comfortable as able administrator than hero. "Thank you."

With recognition completed there were a few more things she wanted to know as the day started. "What's the latest with public enemy number one? Are we going to see his execution anytime soon?"

Back in his comfort zone and with tears wiped away, Tru rattled through the latest. "He's in federal custody and a psych eval is scheduled. He's claiming that God ordered everything he did. It's going to take some time, but the two possible paths for him are execution or life in prison. I'm fine either way."

"Hmm. I can live with either as well, but to tell the truth, I do prefer one outcome over the other."

She next turned to her soon to be confirmed permanent Secretary of Defense. "Declan, sounds like progress is happening on our new post-event mutual security pact. What's the latest?"

Declan seemed rejuvenated after a few weeks without worry of a planet ending incident. "Yes ma'am. Having confirmation that we're not alone in the universe and then a close encounter with planetary destruction, we're finally making real progress on a true global defense structure. Of course, we're still working through national rivalries and old grudges, but we're actually making good progress. With us and China working together, there's a lot of momentum. This was a wake-up call no one can ignore."

"Too bad it took facing extinction to get us to see our true common interests, but it's a real first step. Speaking of first steps, Effie, I hear we're making progress in the Middle East?"

The smooth as molasses tones of her voice warmed the room. "Yes ma'am. With most Muslims and Jews believing that God had visited without choosing a side, there is talk of mutual recognition. There are a lot more steps to achieve lasting peace, but that's a major improvement."

"Anytime we move toward peace and away from war is a good day. And speaking of God, what's up in the world of religion? I'm guessing that these events have shaken some faiths to their cores.

Dallas, too, looked reinvigorated. "Well yes, and no. Fundamentalists of all faiths who rejected the idea that this being was God have not changed at all. In fact, that guy on CBN, Pastor Shadwell, he's seen his congregation more than double. Then there are those who believe that we erred in saving the world, that we would all be in a better place if we had only accepted God's offer of immediate eternal life. They are trying to figure out their next steps. They didn't get the outcome that they wanted, but God is gone... again. How should they move on?"

He shifted in his seat and continued. "On the other end of the spectrum, many other faiths groups are talking of merging, based on their belief that this was God, and that his messages of love and directive to care for the poor supersedes all other revelations. It's refreshing to see different faith groups building coordinated massive public outreach activities to help those least able to help themselves. They are going to do a lot of good."

"Interesting, and the atheists, what do they say?"

Dallas grinned. "It's been a real time of reflection for many. Some believed that there was no God because there was no direct evidence of his existence, but after all that has happened, that view became harder to maintain. As a result, many have become believers. Others claim that this wasn't god, but instead a first encounter with an alien civilization, but they struggle with why aliens would come here claiming to be our world's God. And they still haven't come up with a good answer. Many bring up the point that this so-called god was willing to sit idly by while his creation was destroyed. They ask, 'If this is God, is he worthy of worship?'"

He brought his hands together. "But mostly, they all agree that whoever this being is, he had a message directing us to take care of the weak and the poor, and to stop fighting in his name and care for our planet. They say that's a message that they have always embraced. Like I said, a lot has changed, but a lot hasn't."

After her key advisers had spoken, Abby stood to address her team. "I've said many times in public and in private that this is a truly great team. I say with full confidence that this world would not be habitable today without efforts and contributions from each of you. You are owed a debt that can never be paid. We also owe a debt to members of our team that didn't make it. Ferron George, Braxton Phillips and Kalie Robinson paid the ultimate price to secure our safety."

Her voice quivered as she continued. "As for me, I feel the pride of what we've accomplished as well as the sting of what we have lost, individually and as a global community. Dallas and I both lost our families in a nuclear terrorist attack, and one point two billion other lives were lost to the asteroid. The cost of survival was high, but worth it. Our species did not go quietly into that good night."

She paused again, determined to finish without shedding more tears, feeling enough had already fallen in the past few weeks. "Personally, I'm still trying to sort out my beliefs. What we saw was real, tangible and profound. But was it God? And if it was, or wasn't, does it matter? I'm still working through these and other personal issues."

Her spine stiffened and she stood straighter. "What I do know is that our Constitution guarantees freedom of religion, to believe or not believe as each chooses. What I also know is that we have lives to rebuild, cities and neighborhoods to rebuild, and nations to rebuild. We will do this with the possibility of global cooperation that could have scarcely been dreamed of a couple of months ago. What I also know is this was the best team to save the world, and with that job complete, this is the best team to build our new world. This planet is a better place because of you. Now, let's go do something great... again!"